WILFRED
and the
HALF-PINTLE

WILFRED
and the
HALF-PINTLE

PETER STRIDE

ISBN: Softcover   978-1-7960-0721-3
             eBook   978-1-7960-0720-6

Print information available on the last page.

Rev. date: 10/07/2019

To order additional copies of this book, contact:
Xlibris
1-800-455-039
www.Xlibris.com.au
Orders@Xlibris.com.au
803953

ABOUT THE AUTHOR

P eter Stride is a recently retired consultant physician living in Brisbane. He graduated MB BS from the Middlesex Hospital, London in 1970 and migrated to Australia in 1975. He is a Fellow of the Royal Colleges of Physicians of Australia, Edinburgh and London, and has a higher medical doctorate, D.Med, from the University of Queensland.

History has been a passion since primary school days in the birthplace of Sir Francis Drake and attending the same public school as King Alfred, though some years later. Growing up in England and overseas as a child of a physician in the Royal Navy one is surrounded by living and ancient history on land and at sea.

Peter has some sixty publications in the medical press, some relating to aspects of the medicine of history, and currently publishes political satire in the Australian Bridge Magazine.

After thirty-seven years working for Queensland Health and the University of Queensland, he resigned to spend the last five years working as a peripatetic locum physician in every Australian state becoming familiar with the 'outback'.

Peter has been married to Rosemary, a former nurse and English teacher, for forty-eight years and enjoys the company of his three children and eight grandchildren who all live nearby. He has published one previous historical fictional novel, 'William Hobbys, the promiscuous king's promiscuous doctor', about a doctor during the Wars of the Roses and appreciates travel, friends, wine and duplicate bridge.

PREFACE

This novel is the consequence of several passions and motives. Firstly, a conviction in evidence-based medicine. Modern physicians are not opposed to natural based therapies. The origin of a medication is much less important than the evidence supporting its efficacy. A third of commonly prescribed medications are derived from nature. Penicillins are derived from a species of fungus, as are the cholesterol-lowering group of drugs known as statins. ACE inhibitors for blood pressure and heart disease are derived from the venom of the South American pit viper. While virtually all commonly prescribed standard medications have side-effects, they are known, documented and hopefully carefully excluded with each individual's prescription

Physicians are opposed to fraudulent peddling of often expensive pseudo-medications for which there is no evidence of benefit and often clear evidence of harm. All pharmacies display such therapies and their outrageous claims at the shop front. Pharmacists with scientific degrees from reputable universities join those seduced by the dollar. 'Natural remedies' without supporting evidence are sold to a gullible populace for great profits. Why would such a company making hundreds of thousands of dollars yearly waste profits evaluating their products when the purchasers appear to oppose or ignore established systematic trials and facts in the current post-scientific era.

Secondly, and allied to this is the unfortunate virtual absence of accurate research into the benefits of plants derived compounds. Yet, continuing this theme, the 'Big Pharma', the Great Satan intent on making money from misfortune in the eyes of many, rarely evaluates natural possible therapies as neither a plant, nor its contents can be patented. Some evidence is emerging that the nine herbs of the Anglo-Saxon therapeutic armamentarium have a role in curing cancers, but little research funding is spent in this area.

A copy of the author's publication outlining the latest research into the antimicrobial and anti-malignant properties of the nine Anglo-Saxon herbs or charms is added as an addendum to the novel. Six show promising benefits.

Thirdly, having an attachment to the poignancy of lost causes, I find it hard to accept the prevailing paradigm that the Norman victory at Hastings ended the 'Dark Ages', and brought civilisation and culture to England. In truth, the Norman occupation brought brutal subjugation to most of the island's people. The 'Dark Ages' in many ways were a period on enlightenment and learning for all. Anglo-Saxons were used to common rights for all under the laws developed by King Alfred. Women had individual rights as landowners and a position on the councils before William the Bastard's fortuitous ascent to the throne on that fateful October 14th, 1066. Women may have been placed on a Norman pedestal of chivalry, but it was a pedestal of disempowerment for women used as brood mares.

Fourthly, the favourite quotation "miseris succurrere disco" from one of Virgil's poems, chosen by Wilfred in the text was of course, the motto of the late lamented Middlesex Hospital, the author's medical school in London.

Fifthly, there is evidence that Alfred suffered from some form of gastro-intestinal disease. One suggested possibility is that he had Crohn's disease.

Finally, the author spent some years in Sherborne, and, on infrequent visits from Australia, still finds it a place of traditional tranquillity, where the virtues of 'Old Englande' have not been destroyed by the 'new think' brigade intent on the mindless destruction of all ancient mores, even those of proven benefit, where the old Abbey with its wonderful fan-vaulting is a site of peaceful meditation for the cultural Christian, and where the bones of Æthelbald and Æthelberht, two Saxon kings are on show.

CHARACTERS

1 Historical characters

<u>The House of Wessex</u>

Alfred the Great 849-899 King of Wessex 871-899
King Æthelwulf, King of Wessex 839-858 – Alfred's father
Queen Osburh 810-855 – Alfred's mother
Æthelstan (1), died 852 – Alfred's eldest brother
Æthelbald, King of Wessex 858-860 – Alfred's second brother
Judith – 843 – 870 Æthelwulf's second wife, Æthelbald's wife
Æthelberht, King of Kent and Wessex 860-865 – Alfred's third brother
Æthelred, King of Wessex 865-871 – Alfred's fourth brother
Æthelhelm, Æthelred's eldest son
Æthelwold Æthelred's second son
Æthelswith, 838-888 – Alfred's sister and wife of King Burgred of Mercia
Ealhswith, died 902 - Alfred's wife
Æthelflæd, 870-918, The Lady of Mercia - Alfred's 1st child
Edward the Elder, 874-924, King of the Anglo-Saxons 899-924 – Alfred's 1st son
Æthelgifu, 875-896, Abbess of Shaftesbury– Alfred's 2nd daughter
Ælfthryth 877-929, Alfred's 3rd daughter
Æthelweard 880-922, Alfred's 2nd son
Æthelstan (2), 894-939, King of the Anglo-Saxons 924- 927, King of the English 927-939 – son of Edward the Elder

Rulers of Mercia

Burgred, King of Mercia 852-874 – husband of Æthelswith
Ceolwulf II King of Mercia 874 – 883
Æthelred II 881 – 911 – husband of Æthelflæd

<u>Bishops of Sherborne</u>

St Aldhelm – Bishop of Sherborne 705-709
Ealhstan - Bishop of Sherborne 820-867
Heahmund - Bishop of Sherborne 868-871
Athelheah - Bishop of Sherborne 874-884
Wulfsige I – Bishop of Sherborne 884-896
Asser – Bishop of Sherborne 896-909 (Welsh monk from St David's)

<u>Welsh and Norse Gods and Goddesses</u>

Bloddwyn
Nelferch
Brighid
Ceridwyn
Odin
Thor

<u>Danes and Vikings</u>

Ragnar Lodbrok
Ivar the Boneless
Halfdan Ragnarsson
Sigurd Snake-in-the-Eye
Guthrum

<u>Ancient Britons</u>

Taliesin
Boudica
King Arthur

Merlin
Vortigern

2 Fictional characters

Wilfred
Gwendolyn - Wilfred's mother
Rowena – Wilfred's sister
Finnian – Wilfred's father
Cerdic – Wilfred's friend
Elvina
Kendra – Elvina's mother
Mona – Elvina's sister
Synnove – Elvina's friend
Orva – Elvina's friend
Ceridwyn – Wilfred's daughter
Ceridwyn – Welsh priestess

Brother Samuel *
Brother Peter *
Brother Parsifal *
Brother David
Brother Osric – prior of Sherborne Abbey
Ragnar Fourfingers – Danish warlord
Hakon Halfnose
Hjalmar
Brynjar
Jarl David *
Abdul
Godwine
(identifiable contemporaries*)
Merchants and patients

Sherborne and area citizens - John, Wulfstan, Durwyn, Meghan, Ellsworth, Betlic, Cwene, Woodrow, Hollis, Acwel, Eagdyth, Alodia, Norvel, Gifre, Nelda

Place names

Braescfeld – Braishfield

Camboritum Grantebrigge – old Roman and Anglo-Saxon places near the current city of Cambridge

Oxenaforda - Oxford

Stanheng - Stonehenge

Winton-ceastre - Winchester

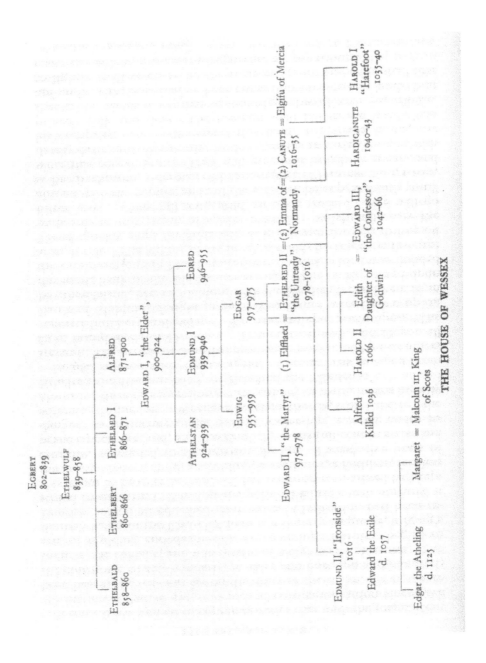

THE HOUSE OF WESSEX

WILFRED AND THE HALF-PINTLE

'In this year, dire portents appeared over Northumbria.
They consisted of immense whirlwinds and flashes of lightening,
And fiery dragons were seen flying in the air.
A great famine followed, and a little after that, on 8 June,
The ravages of heathen men miserably destroyed God's church on Lindisfarne.'

Anglo-Saxon Chronicle 793

It was the worst of years, a catastrophic transformation after two centuries of relative peace and tranquillity. Some days the landscape appeared on fire from horizon to horizon. Unearthly infernos illuminated the night sky, the burning stubble of ripened but unharvested crops threatened starvation in the forth-coming winter. The blue skies and green vegetation of this earthly paradise were replaced by the red and black of the abyss. The burnt-out shells of previously safe homes, interspersed with rotting mutilated corpses, littered the countryside.

Bearded warriors of a brutal primitive religion from the east were unyielding in their attempted annihilation of Christian civilization. A sophisticated kinder Saxon culture, so recently developed, threatened to drown disastrously in a sea of its own blood. Swords were these barbarians' visiting cards: they killed men and women, young and old, indiscriminately, mercilessly.

Christian churches were one of their favourite targets. Holy men were beheaded and holy women were raped first. Anything of value was looted. Holy books of indescribable beauty and meaning were burnt in abysmal ignorance. Women desires and emotions were of no consequence to the invaders: they were of little value like cattle or dogs, to be used, abused, then discarded.

And a young small boy vowed improbably to defeat the brutish invaders, save the incinerating environment and to follow faithfully in his father's footsteps as a dedicated healer, although he was only eight. Big vows for a very slight youth. Wilfred was his name.

It was just past the middle of the ninth century in England, 859AD by the Christian calendar in a small community known as Braescfeld. People had lived there securely since time began. The ground was full of flintstones making useful tools long before metal working was discovered. The Romans had built a patrician's villa here though it was now a ruin largely disappeared under ivy. Many of its stones had been removed for other less elite dwellings.

The flints made it difficult to till the soil, but it had a homely feeling as though people belonged there, to use the land fruitfully and watch their families grow in peace. Their ancestors, the old ways and the old gods watched anxiously, lovingly over the families ensuring the fertility of the land and their safety.

However, the final eclipse of Anglo-Saxon Christendom and their social culture was approaching their green haven of previous security. The pagan hoards from Demark and other Scandinavian nations threatened to overwhelm the last brave stand in Wessex. They followed the fierce Norse Gods and the inspirational raven banner into battle and cared little for neither the old Druid ways nor the newer Christian God. Glorious death with a bloodied sword in hand was their long-term ambition, guaranteeing entry to Valhalla.

The Anglo-Saxons claimed a higher morality, but in reality, they knew the Danes occupied the shadowy space of gratuitous violence they had only just renounced a century or two ago. The Danes were a dark mirror through which the Saxons saw their past, a past of evil barbarism and pagan beliefs they preferred to forget. Christianity was their new conceit, their proclaimed higher integrity.

Armageddon however, had finally reached Braescfeld.

In the middle of their once serene village a small group of men lay butchered, beheaded, gutted. One mutilated corpse, tied helplessly to the Braescfeld preaching cross, was the ill-fated victim of the Viking blood red eagle. An agonising death in which the posterior ends of his ribs were chopped from the spine with a sword or axe, then while still just alive, his chest wall torn open from the back and spread to resemble eagle's wings, such that his lungs could then be ripped out, finally, thankfully, terminating life and unimaginable pain.

Their pathetic attempt at a defensive shield-wall had been no match for hardened warrior Norsemen. Danish axes and swords rose and fell unmercifully, slicing through flesh and bone. For most villagers death was relatively swift. Spurts of Saxon blood covered their foes and the ground. The older ladies' bloodied corpses lay scattered around having been raped and then their throats cut.

A captive file of seven young women, naked, beautiful, terrified but singing defiantly, linked by chains through their iron neck collars, was being marched slowly reluctantly eastwards. Their most optimistic future appeared to be following regular pack rape. Their captors, a blood-bespattered Danish war band, strolled nonchalantly around them, laughing, joking, and thanking Odin for their spoils. They were quite oblivious to the barbaric destruction they had just wrought on a frontier Anglo-Saxon village, just a little disappointed to find the village was too small to possess a church full of possible gold icons, jewels and other booty. Neither the opposition nor the spoils had been as exciting as hoped. None had even the slightest injury.

Their leader rode the only horse previously owned by the villagers at the head of his men, their captives and the four scrawny cows that had once been the life blood of the village.

His grim helm had been scarcely needed for protection of his head in the one-sided battle. They called him Ragnar Fourfingers. Wilfred had heard of him. The story was that he had been captured as a boy in Northumbria by a marauding band of Scots. They sent his little fingers with a ransom note to Ragnar's father, a Viking jarl proclaiming that the Scots did not have a sense of humour. They did not have heads either once the jarl caught up with them to free young Ragnar. The jarl likewise had no sense of humour.

Ragnar looked at his fellow warriors and his female captives: 'Sorry men, that was not much exercise for the morning, and not much treasure.' A renowned war lord should fill his warriors' hands with their enemies' blood and captured booty. He should provide arm bands, preferably of gold or silver, engraved with Viking runes to commemorate their gods and their victories. He should provide pleasing young women for his victorious fighters. Their acquiescence was unimportant to Vikings, most preferred the sexual conquest of the unwilling.

Ragnar looked at his sword, Soul-slayer, an ironic reference to his penchant for killing Christians. 'Not much work for you either,' he said as he wiped the blood off his blade. 'Never mind, perhaps the ladies will provide a bit more sport when we return to camp. I think they are singing a love song to us!' Some rather insecure laughter emerged from the group. Truth to be told, the determined chanting made them feel edgy, though none would admit that to the others, how could females singing make a true, bold Viking warrior nervous?

The only life left behind was a small group of traumatised children hiding behind their homes, cowering in disbelief, sobbing, shocked, suddenly, brutally orphaned. Wilfred, self-possessed for only eight years old, watched cautiously, anxiously from behind his home, a smouldering bark hut, as his mother Gwendolyn, a high priestess, and his older sister Rowena, a virgin acolyte, disappeared. The bereaved young man thought he would never ever see them alive again.

Wilfred's father had schooled him from an early age to be aware of the beauties and benefits of nature. The majestic trees and the docile animals of the forest were his friends, manna for his soul. Wilfred loved and feared the ferocious nature of the predatory carnivores of the forest, since they perused him as a potential food source. He knew they killed only to eat, unlike these barbarous human invaders who had just killed for pleasure.

Till now Wilfred had been thankful for his father's reassuring presence when they confronted the wolf pack. Now a fatherless boy would need to stand up for himself.

Cerdic, two years older than Wilfred, stood fiercely brandishing a short sword, threatening dire revenge, once the war party was safely beyond sight and sound. 'Come back you cowards, you Danish scum, come back here and fight like a man. I'll kill you all,' he yelled menacingly. Fortunately for Cerdic, Ragnar and his men failed to hear his high-pitched squeaking or chose to ignore it.

A sound wafted to Wilfred on the summer breeze. The captive women were humming and chanting, humming and chanting, as they disappeared from view. He had heard that once before. The village women had sung a serial rapist to death after a court with twelve men, the thegns of the wapentake, sitting in judgement had found him not guilty yet again. He had been having a celebratory ale with some equally undesirable male friends after the dubious verdict. Suddenly as the chant climaxed and ceased to an eerie silence, the acquitted malefactor appeared to choke on his drink, then be seized around the throat by some invisible force. A moment later he fell to the ground stone dead. His fellow drinkers dropped their ales and fled for their lives. They recognised the awesome power of the old ways and the high priestesses.

The sound sent shivers down Wilfred's spine, knowing they were laying ancient but merited curses on the captors. In some unworldly way it frightened him more than the Viking axes.

His father, Finnian, one of the few Druid priests still found in England lay dead on the ground, his bloodied disembowelled weaponless body already cooling amongst the corpses. Wilfred's hands were slightly burnt from dashing into his family hut, which the Danes had torched, to grab his father's magic sword and an old oak box. The sword was ironically named Peacemaker. The smell of burning flesh pervaded the village as three piglets squealed in terminal agony in the fiercely burning pig house.

Unfortunately, Finnian did not have time to seize his blade as the Danes attacked simultaneously from two sides, undetected till they charged. The sword had previously worked well as a peacemaker, for very very few would challenge the mystical pattern-welded blade with spiritual Celtic engravings in the hands of its legendary master swordsman. Those that did usually regretted it; though disarming an opponent was generally adequate for Finnian. The Druid rarely was forced to draw much blood.

The box contained his father's treasured manuscripts of Druid culture and herbal healing, and a leather bag containing carved pieces of the strategic board game, hnefatafl. Wilfred's father told him that they came from Merlin and that the set was a talisman to be treasured. He pulled the ageing parchments and the leather bag out and placed them inside a satchel he had around his neck, throwing the box back into the furnace. Wilfred strapped the heavy sword to his back. It was nearly his height, but Wilfred knew he would grow into it. The Saxon boy-warrior would need it to defend those dear to him, and one day to have his revenge against Ragnar.

The health-giving secrets he needed to uncover were somewhere in the written documents of the Anglo-Saxon nine herbs charm. Wilfred could recite their names in his sleep. They were Betony, Chervil, Crab-apple, Fennel, Mayweed, Mugwort, Nettle, Plantain and Watercress. He had already been schooled in the ancient wisdom of the Druids to heal the sick and care for the land. He knew about the star signs in the night sky and the Druid divinities of mother earth. Knowledgeable for his years, he knew he still had much to learn.

Cerdic anxiously surveyed the group of ten traumatised children, aged from two up to near his age. Some were stunned to silence, some weeping at the sight of their dead fathers' bodies and at the terrifying loss of their mothers and big sisters. Weeping at the sight of the brutal slayings they had unwillingly witnessed. Weeping at the loss of their family, their childhood innocence and their cherished homes.

Cerdic felt the weight of leadership, as the oldest boy in the surviving group of children. He and Wilfred often fought, Saxon against Dane, wooden sword against wooden sword in the carefree meadows of youthful exuberance. The girls were permitted only to crown the glorious victor and feed the young warriors with home-made cakes. Now their very continued existence was threatened, it was no longer children's games.

'We must go west, to Sherborne, the capital of Wessex, it will take about seven days to walk there', Cerdic ordered. 'We must find Æthelbald, the Anglo-Saxon king with his war lords and their army. I will join their shield wall. I shall return with the Anglo-Saxon army, and kill those Danish scum who attacked us. I will challenge that Ragnar fellow to a duel, man to man, iron against iron, and spill his guts on the land.'

Cerdic, although prone to unrealistic boasting, knew where to find help, and knew he now had an adult's responsibility for the smaller children.

'Wilfred, you and I must carry the two toddlers most of the time. We must avoid other people as much as possible in case they are Danes, or in case that war party attacks other villages and we end up in the middle of another massacre. We will keep to the fields and forests as much as we can,' commanded Cerdic.

One of the girls at the back of the group said quietly but authoritatively, 'It is approaching high summer fortunately. We can eat the blackberries and blackcurrants growing in profusion in the hedgerows, they have fruited early this year.'

'Yes, yes,' said Cerdic importantly, reluctant to take advice from a mere girl, 'I will collect apples and pears from orchards if nobody is watching.

Wilfred and I can lift eggs from chicken coops when it is getting dark if there are no farm dogs barking at us. I will make sure we all have enough to eat till we reach Sherborne. We will not be able to have a fire in case Danes see our smoke.'

Wilfred added, 'we must not sleep under an apple tree, or the fairies will carry away the little children.'

'Rubbish!' responded Cerdic.

As they progressed slowly through the countryside, the weather and colourful scenery contrasted starkly, ignorantly with their blackened homes and their dark feelings. The sun shone out of deep blue cloudless skies. The aroma of late honeysuckles and dog roses in the hedgerows replaced the sorrowfully memorised stench of burning homes and animals. Buttercups and cowslips coloured the fields, foxglove and columbine flanked the woodlands. Nature's vivid beauty did little to raise their dark moods. It was scarcely noticed as they put one foot in front of another monotonously, silently for league upon league.

At dusk, on the seventh night, Cerdic and Wilfred crept silently into the back of a farm and looked around. 'Shush,' whispered Cerdic, 'there doesn't seem to be anyone still working outside. See, all the lamps are alight in the farm house. I can't see or hear any dogs. I am hungry. We still have a day or two walking to reach sanctuary in Sherborne. As the leader of this group, I need a man's meal, I need some meat. You will understand one-day Wilfred, but you are still a boy. If we are attacked by more Danes, it will be my job to fight them off! See that chicken house, we are going in there to collect eggs. I am starving for a decent meal. I am going to capture a chicken and eat it!'

Cerdic crept in and stroked one of the chickens gently without disturbing it for a moment. He slowly edged his finger up around its neck and then suddenly closed them before it could squawk. He wrung its neck and then took several bites of raw flesh, while Wilfred collected half a dozen eggs, before they crept out and back to the waiting group.

The girl at the back, a redhead, watched Cerdic biting the raw flesh. She declared disapprovingly, 'the bible says, "do not eat the meat raw", Cerdic. In Exodus. Even the Druids believe raw chicken will take you down the wrong path in the dance of life and death. My mother said you should never eat uncooked meat, especially chicken and pork. If we can't have a fire, the rest of us will eat the eggs raw and the fruit you have collected.'

'Bah said Cerdic dismissively, 'I need some meat. I am the man in charge of this group.' Girls' advice was beneath Cerdic.

On the morning of the eighth day, they passed the ruins of an old village. Stones were scattered around a large area, apparently the abandoned remnants of a large and ancient community. An eerie feeling of past disaster pervaded the long deserted and now silent brooding habitation. A large midden lay close to the group's path.

'Look at all those piglets' bones in the midden,' said Wilfred, 'they all look about a year old or less. Their skulls are dissimilar, so they are not all the same breed. Those pigs would have been collected from all over the country and slaughtered for a feast at the end of the year. It would probably have been for the festival of Alban Arthan, the longest night, after which the sun returns to warm the land and grow the crops.'

'My father once told me about this place,' continued Wilfred, 'I think he called it Durborough Walls where the Durotriges people lived before the Romans killed most of them. Spirits still haunt this place awaiting revenge that will never come, for the Romans have departed. Durotriges were the builders of the amazing great stone monument at Stanheng. They were inspired by the gods to feats of superhuman strength raising huge monoliths of rock.'

'Over there you can see some old wooden posts in a circle with an opening facing the midwinter sunrise. Across the other way is a pathway facing the mid-summer sunset which will take us down to the river where we can fill our water bags.'

'Wilfred, will you fill my water bag for me?' whispered Cerdic weakly, 'I am tired with all this walking carrying this little one. I shall sit down for a short while.'

After collecting water, the band of children set off again, but their progress seemed slower, Cerdic really was looking pale and tired, so Wilfred carried little Synnove for several hours. She wrapped her arms tightly around his neck and between sobs asked, 'Wilfred, if those nasty Danes killed the faery-folk, who will protect us from the wolves and hobgoblins in the forest?'

'Don't worry, Synnove, only people who believe in the fairy's and elves and love them as our protectors can ever see them. The Danes would not have seen them or been able to hurt them. The nice elves will shield us from the bad gremlins.'

As their eighth day walking on the trail was nearly ended close to dusk, they could see some grey upright stones across the plain on the horizon. Recognition came to Wilfred again. He turned to Cerdic, 'Those are the ring stones of Stanheng, my father said he would take me there in my tenth summer for the festival of Alban Hefin. They are the source of the Druid priests' power. I told you about the Durotriges who lived in the ruins an hour back. They were the builders of this place about three thousand years ago. Someday I must go there.'

They continued for another hour before Cerdic sat down looking unwell. The heat and humidity of the day had not helped him. It was the start of the dog days, the hottest time of the year, when the Dog Star shone brightly in the night sky. Wilfred paused, 'You are looking pale Cerdic, are you alright?' Cerdic nodded unconvincingly, but said, 'we will stop for the night here.'

By the morning of the ninth day, Cerdic was wracked with stomach pain, spewing and the bloody flux. Cerdic and all the children looked hopefully, but forlornly at Wilfred.

'Your father could have healed me; please, can you help me?' croaked Cerdic hoarsely, pleading despairingly.

Wilfred pulled his father's manuscripts out of the leather satchel. He found a page headed dysentery. It recommended giving a mixture of pottage and water and then observing the result. Wilfred had collected some ground wheat in the last farmyard.

'Here, Cerdic, here is a mixture of grain and water advised by my father's papers, see if it helps,' suggested the youthful and optimistic healer.

Within a short time, the mixture flowed profusely out of Cerdic's bowel. Wilfred read on, the manuscript said if the pottage is retained a cure is likely, but if it flows out, it is best not to treat the sufferer as death is most likely.

Wilfred sadly gathered the papers together and replaced them in the satchel, noticing at the foot of the first page, a comment in his father's writing, "Which herbs will cure cancer? watercress seems the best."

Wilfred did not really understand the meaning of the question, what is cancer he wondered, but vowed silently that he would find out to honour his father's legacy and finish his life's work. Vital work that had so tragically terminated by ignorant brutality. Wilfred also promised himself that one day when he was a grown man, he would find Ragnar Fourfingers again. He would change his name to Ragnar Halfpintle, then Ragnar Nohead with the aid of Peacemaker. He would make pieces of Ragnar.

The party rested perforce in a deserted copse of oak trees while Cerdic grew weaker by the hour, his skin was ragingly hot to touch, his eyes became dark and sunken, he shivered uncontrollably, he vomited all fluids offered to him. Cerdic's bloody flux became more severe and uncontrollable. The ancient healing powers found in oak circles seemed absent. The other children looked desperately at Wilfred, but he did not know how to help. Wilfred hated his ignorance and inability to help. He resolved to become a more effective healer as he grew up.

Cerdic became delirious, hallucinating, 'I can see a war party of Danes approaching, get me that big sword of your father's and I'll chop them into little pieces,' he gasped.

'Don't worry,' advised Wilfred, 'they are going away,' noting the mass of foxgloves Cerdic mistook for a war-party of Danes in his confused state. Wilfred gave Cerdic sips of water as one of the girls, the red-head cradled his head.

However, Cerdic's skin became cold and blotchy, his forehead covered in a cold sweat and his breathing became laboured and rattly.

He looked for Wilfred and called him, grasping wrists, 'My brother Anglo-Saxon, my time is sadly approaching. The dance of death calls me. You must lead the children to Sherborne, it is only just over a day's walk from here. By then I shall be with the Lord keeping the Danes out at the gates of heaven; good luck and may God go with you.' Cerdic fell back and took his last breath.

Elvina, the fiery redhead, the voice of common sense from the back of the group, was the oldest girl. At eight she was the same age as Wilfred. However, she was much shorter, elfin like her name. She had been saying prayers quietly beside Cerdic as he deteriorated. Elvina's father had been killed with the other men, and both her mother, Kendra and her elder sister, Mona had also been abducted by the Danish war party.

Showing maturity beyond her stature and age as so many girls do, she stood and grasped Wilfred by the shoulders and looked up into his eyes. 'Wilfred, we must bury Cerdic, and then you and I must complete this tryst for our parents, for Cerdic and for these little children. Little Synnove here is only two, you and I must carry her most of the way. We must ensure she has adequate food and water.'

Elvina displayed the centuries-old wisdom of motherhood, practical knowledge passed down from shrewd mother to young eager daughter since the dawn of time. She also had a steadfast belief in the Christian God and the life everlasting. Cerdic had sadly, arrogantly, thinking men knew best, ignored her opinions coming from the back of the group to his cost, his life.

The two of them dug a shallow grave in the moist soil and reverently covered Cerdic with earth and rocks. Elvina said a few Christian prayers and Wilfred recited some of Finnian's invocations to the earth mother. Elvina fashioned a cross from two branches, then they stood back looking at the grave with tears running down their cheeks. Overwhelming childhood emotion outweighed the lack of ceremony of a traditional church funeral and a Latin mass. Death, with its insatiable appetite had followed them from their childhood home. It would follow them like a pack of slavering wolves following an innocent newborn lamb till they reached the safety of the monastic town.

Elvina took some deep breaths to compose herself. At that moment she hugged Wilfred tightly but briefly, giving each other strength. Elvina not only had fire in her hair, she had fire in her green eyes and fire in her soul. Wilfred felt supported, loved, confused and overwhelmed at the same time. How could she show such mature resolve? How did this little girl make him feel so strange?

Wilfred thought his future if he survived would also include his father's legacy of treasuring the wild forests and murmuring rivers of Wessex. It would include his father's legacy of healing with wild herbs. He would have to learn how to treat the flux so people as sick as Cerdic might not die under his care. It would be curing this cancer mentioned by his father, whatever that is. It would include preserving the old ways of his father's fathers.

Repelling the Danes' rapacious destruction of his homeland would be important. Wilfred realised he would need to become a skilled swordsman like his father, but the sword, Finnian's Peacemaker, would only be used in the last resort. He would need to build up his strength, so he could handle Peacemaker. He would also need to be able to outrun any Danish warrior till he became a man. Sometime he would find Ragnar Fourfingers and make him deeply regret his evil deeds.

His father had told Wilfred that if the Danes could understand the old ways, old in Britain long before the Romans came; perhaps they could see there was plenty in this bountiful country. More than enough for all to live in harmony with the land. The green forests, the flowing rivers, the plentiful fields, the bountiful seas and the snow-clad mountains in winter could be shared by all.

Somehow, he felt Elvina would be involved in his future. For a girl, she had so much hidden strength, and an inner peace, in-spite of the massacre at Braescfeld, in-spite of losing her parents and big sister. She was as brave as any man. Braver. Provision of good food for young and old had been learnt on her mother's knee. Caring for younger children appeared to come intuitively. Solutions to their current precarious position seemed fathomable with her responsible instinct and un-child-like perspective.

Every time he thought about her, he felt even more confused. Every time he admired her all-round competence, he felt more stupid and juvenile.

SHERBORNE

B y the following evening, tired, bedraggled, foot-sore and hungry, they banged on the huge oak doors of the Anglo-Saxon monastery founded over a century ago by St Aldhelm when he was Bishop Aldhelm of Sherborne. A sanctuary at last. The door creaked open. A young monk in a brown robe confronted them. His face took on a look of consternation at seeing the collection of unkempt, exhausted children. Synnove was asleep in Wilfred's arms. Elvina spoke before Wilfred had collected his thoughts.

'Thank you, father, we seek sanctuary. We lived in Braescfeld, a little village ten day's walk east of here, but the Danes attacked us. They killed our fathers and the old women, abducted our mothers and our big sisters, then burnt our village. We have walked for ten days carrying the little ones with little food. We are exhausted and beg as Christians for your help.'

Wilfred thought how well Elvina had spoken, he would not have thought of saying they were Christians.

'A furore Normannorum libera nos, Domine!' said the young monk.

Elvina looked at Wilfred, 'that means deliver us from the Northmen's fury, oh Lord.'

15

Wilfred scowled at having his ignorance of Latin, the classic language of educated and religious Anglo-Saxons, exposed.

They were welcomed in, in the name of Bishop Ealhstan of Sherborne. The thick doors closed securely behind them relieving the threat of hunger and death for the first time in over a week. Monks were summoned and fussed around the children. The kitchen was reopened. They were provided bread and soup, then mattresses in the dormitory. Fatigue and relief soon overwhelmed them all.

Within minutes nearly all were asleep, though not before Elvina gave Wilfred a kiss on his cheek and another hug both to his embarrassment, and to some strange pleasure. She whispered gratefully into his ear, 'Well done strong friend, Wilfred, you have become a man in the last week, we would not be here without you, the future has some important jobs for you. May the Good Lord walk with you and give you guidance always.'

Wilfred felt a certain pleasurable frisson of something he could not understand but was lost for words to reply. They would not have succeeded without Elvina either. He lay awake long after the others had succumbed to exhaustion. Fearsome dreams of Elvina being captured by the Danes mangled his sleep.

Early the next morning just after sunrise, Wilfred slipped out before the others stirred. Bright warm fingers of sunlight flickered through the trees. Blue smokeless sky heralded another balmy and peaceful summer day. He found a boy a little older than himself, bashing a bag of sand hanging from a quintain with a wooded sword, muttering to himself, 'die Dane, die Viking, the Anglo-Saxons will take this land back and throw you into the sea from whence you came. Die bastards! Die!' He bashed the bag as though his life depended upon it.

When he spotted Wilfred, he stopped and surveyed the boy, 'Hey you, halfpintle, can you fight, come here, I'm Alfred' he said. 'Here is my other sword, you will be the Dane and fight me.' Wilfred took the other wooden sword, raised the hilt to his lips to salute his opponent, and said, 'I'm Wilfred and I hate Danes more than you. My ancestors were ancient

Britons, prosperous landowners long before you Saxons or the Romans arrived. Protect your-self!'

Wilfred's father had taught him how to handle a wooden sword. For his age, he was fast and agile. He had been much better than Cerdic.

The wooden swords clashed vigorously for a short period and both stopped to regain their wind. Alfred looked at Wilfred with surprise and new-found respect. Alfred usually had little difficulty defeating boys his own age or even bigger. On the third prolonged clash of weapons, Alfred's two-year age advantage told. The bigger, stronger and even faster boy beat Wilfred to the ground and held his blunted sword point to Wilfred's throat before lowering his blade and extending a welcoming arm to pull Wilfred up. 'Wow, well done little brother, you fight really well. Wilfred, you will be my liegeman if I am king; you will be my right-hand man in the shield wall.'

Wilfred clasped wrist to wrist and gasped, 'Alfred, I am your liegeman in the fight against the Danes, I will be your healer, your seer or your priest of the old faith, I am always your brother, but I will not fight unless I have no option.'

Alfred looked surprised but continued, 'I am the fifth son of King Æthelwulf and Queen Osburh, though since my father died last year my second brother Æthelbald is now king in Wessex. Did you know Æthelwulf and Æthelbald slaughtered thousands of Danes as the Battle of Aclea only eight years ago, when I was only two. We will go on killing them every time they return.' Alfred boasted with youthful bravado, then continued, 'My first-born brother Athelstan sadly died also when I was only two; he was killed fighting the Danes at sea near Sandwich. God took him before my father, so he never became king.'

Alfred resembled Cerdic, but with responsible realism tempering youthful arrogance and audacity, Wilfred judged.

Wilfred gasped, 'You are a royal prince of the House of Wessex. We have come seeking your help and shelter. I could have hurt you fighting! Then I would have been in trouble!'

Alfred replied scornfully, 'You are not big enough to hurt me; mind you, you are quite good with a sword for a half-pintle.'

Alfred paused, and then continued confidentially, 'Did you know Æthelbald married my father's second wife Judith, the daughter of the Carolingian King Charles? That is the most noble blood line of kings, even more noble than the House of Wessex. But Wilfred, some people say it is wrong to marry your widowed stepmother, they call it incest. Do you know what incest is? My priest says it is from the Latin incestus meaning dirty, but Judith is always bathing.'

Wilfred shrugged his shoulders uncomfortably; he had never heard the term before. He realised that his very limited knowledge of Latin made him look foolish. Elvina seemed to know about marriage things, he might ask her, if she would talk to him, but for some strange reason he did not want her to become a friend of Alfred.

Alfred surveyed his new friend curiously, 'Whence have you come?'

Wilfred had regained his composure. 'I lived in Braescfeld, a village east of here, but nearly two weeks ago Danes attacked our village without warning. They killed all the men including my father, and the old women, then bound the younger women in chairs, including my mother and big sister and led them away, and finally stole all our livestock. The younger children escaped, and we walked for ten days to reach here and find help.'

Alfred looked at Wilfred thoughtfully, respectfully. 'That was a mighty feat with little children and having to find food and water. You are welcome here. I'm sorry to hear about your family. I was only five when my mother died, though I remember her reading to me. My father died last year when I was nine, so we are both orphans.'

Alfred pronounced knowledgeably, 'you appreciate that the monastery where you are staying was originally founded by St Aldhelm when he was bishop of Sherborne. You know Aldhelm was a great writer. He translated holy books and poems from the Latin for our Anglo-Saxon people, becoming the first great man of letters in Wessex. I want to become like him and write books, when the fighting is over. I must show you some of my copies of his stories and the morals behind them.'

The young prince continued reassuringly, 'Don't worry about the Danes coming into Wessex. They have been trying to take Wessex by force since the time of King Beorhtic more than fifty years ago. Long before him King Ine said strangers should be slain and that is what we will do. Slay them all. That is why we are doing our weapons training so diligently. My brother, the king, will ensure that we are all completely safe here for the Saxon fighting man is much mightier than the Dane. Saxon armies took this land four centuries ago from the Romans. Before us the Romans had the greatest army ever, but we beat them, we defeated their last legion here. The Anglo-Saxons are the greatest fighters ever!'

Wilfred thought Alfred sounded even more like Cerdic. He silently wished Alfred greater success than his unfortunate boastful friend.

Alfred continued, 'Nennius says Vortigern was the last king of the Roman-Britons. He asked us Saxons to fight for him against the Picts, then turned against us. God killed him for treachery, and for doing something naughty with his daughter, with fire from heaven. It was a divine prediction to the Saxons that our God would care for us if we followed his holy scriptures and teaching. We will finally and totally defeat the Danes one day. We will not lose Wessex, never ever.'

Wilfred recalled his father had told him that Vortigern was a failure, and that Merlin had held off the Saxons for years with old Druid spells. History apparently could be seen in different ways.

Alfred paused thoughtfully, 'By the way, is that redhead part of your group? I saw you all arrive last evening. She's really pretty. What is her name?'

Wilfred was reluctant to even discuss Elvina with the larger boy though he knew not why. He just shrugged his shoulders again in feigned ignorance.

Wilfred looked at Alfred thoughtfully. 'You beat me at swords, now I will beat you at hnefatafl,' he challenged.

'Hnefatafl, what is that, a pagan game?' replied Alfred dismissively.

It was Wilfred's turn to sound clever. 'Nay my prince, it is a strategic game for kings, for clever people. You will learn careful analysis of positions to protect your kingdom from the pagans as you call them.'

Wilfred collected the bag of pieces and a hnefatafl board written on the back of one of his father's manuscripts. He set out the black and white pieces. They were little carved effigies of warriors from the waist up. Fierce helmeted figures carrying a sword and shield. The white pieces had a cross engraved on their shields, while the black ones bore the hammer of Thor on their shields. Two of the white pieces were slightly larger; one wore a crown on its head and a cross on its shield. The other had an eagle carved on its shield.

'See these black ones; you can see them as Danes. They will try to destroy the white king,' explained Wilfred. He choked back a tear recalling that these black barbarians had recently murdered his father, the king-like loveable mentor of his childhood.

Alfred looked in astonishment at them. 'What are these and of what are they made?'

Wilfred explained, 'The game is the product of a clash of cultures. The game hnefatafl comes through the Celts originally from Germania. It has been a trial of battle-hardened intellects from pre-Roman times. The black pieces are made of ebony wood and the white ones of ivory elephant tusks both from distant places in the old Roman Empire. My father said they were carved in Mercia at the end of the Roman occupation. See this piece has the Roman Eagle carved on its shield. The legions would fight to the death to prevent it being captured.'

'He said these were once owned by King Arthur in Camelot. Arthur had a new piece added with a crown and cross carved on it to represent the king, a Christian king. However, that one is carved in walrus ivory and therefore less rare and valuable. He gave them to Merlin, and they have been handed down since over several hundred years to the head Druid priest in Britain. My father had that role before he was murdered. They are a powerful good luck charm that will bring good fortune to those who respect the beliefs they represent. You can have the white pieces with the king.'

'Bah! What nonsense. Sadly, it did not bring good luck to your father from what you say. It looks easy, like a child's game. I expect I will win quite quickly,' claimed Alfred immodestly, 'I usually win most games.'

However; after being told the rules of the game, he found his king encircled and captured in a surprisingly short space of time.

Wilfred smiled at him but did not need to say anything.

Alfred was not used to being out-thought by anyone his age, let alone one younger. 'Hmm,' he grumped, 'this game is more complex than it seemed at first sight, we will play again after I have thought about the tactics. You will never catch my king again!'

'We will see.' smiled Wilfred.

DECEMBER 860

A year went by. Bishop Ealhstan approached Elvina, perceiving her as the obvious natural leader of the group of both boys and girls. 'Elvina, the monks and I think your group of children are growing steadily and now need to be separated into a boys' and a girls' dormitory. The girls will move to the room upstairs and the boys stay here downstairs.'

'Thank you, your worship,' Elvina bowed gratefully, 'I will get it arranged immediately. One day we would hope to repay your Christian charity.'

Wilfred returned from one of his long walks to find Elvina had disappeared from their dormitory. She was not to be found at first in the monastery. He thought she might be avoiding him. His loneliness became worse over the next few months. Wilfred had studied his father's documents carefully, but often struggled to understand the inner meaning of the old language.

Elvina appeared totally absorbed in her group of new female friends in the town and in helping the little children of the community. She rarely even noticed Wilfred. Elvina was so, so self-assured, so confident and happy. Although her father had also been brutally butchered before her eyes and her mother and sister enslaved in chains too like Wilfred's, she never seemed to have black days as he did.

Some days or even some nights, Wilfred would sit alone in the big forests up the hill to the south of the town. The big blue sky was his ceiling, but it did not lighten his moods. The bare branches and paucity of life in bitter winter mirrored Wilfred's bleak feelings. Some days the icy rain mingled with tears running down his cheeks. He recalled his mother saying he wept only tears, not blood, and that unhappiness would soon pass. It seemed a long time passing.

Although the days would soon start to lengthen in the new year, so the weather would initially grow colder. The winter aconite yellow flowers did not colour his humour, though he registered they were too poisonous to use as medicine. Light snow falls left his body as chilled as his feelings.

The forest endeavoured to sing to him. A few birds chirped in the trees, the streams murmured softly as they flowed downhill to the distant south coast. The cattle lowed in the faraway fields. The occasional owl hooted, and the wolves howled to Wilfred at night. The full moon, the silver eye of Ceridwyn, the moon goddess, looked down from the night sky, sympathetically, unavailingly. None raised his spirits.

He could not forget the family he had lost. Rowena, his big sister had been a second mother. Cerdic had been his friend, a big bossy brother. Elvina was nowhere to be seen most of the time. They had played together all the time as little children. When boys and girls were innocent friends. Co-conspirators in the undisturbed green pastures of childhood. Their mothers had been best of friends. Before, before….before something unexpected, inexplicable, complicated his private perceptions of girls, especially the redheaded one.

Alfred was his new friend, but some days he was involved with affairs of greater importance than Wilfred. Alfred was an ætheling, a prince of the blood royal, Wilfred was, well little better than a slave or a worm. Alfred was destined for an important role in the future of Wessex, much more important than anything Wilfred saw for himself.

Some days only the creatures of the forest were his friends. He could not see the elves, nor the faeries, but he could feel their presence watching over him. As long as he cared for them, they would care for him and enhance his healing powers. In the midst of the forest was a grassy knoll, where Wilfred was sure the elves dwelt. As recommended in his father's papers, he sprinkled the blood of an ox on the surface, and left them a little meat, carefully and secretly preserved from his platter in the monastery to ensure their support.

The deer and the rabbits, the voles and the weasels became accustomed to his presence. A doe watched him carefully over several visits to the forest. Wilfred would talk to her about his life and his losses. He offered her apples which she would finally accept from his hand. She did not respond but her big brown eyes appeared sympathetic to his plight.

Some nights he saw the badger appear cautiously from its set. Wilfred felt some unfortunate unwanted emotional affinity, an affinity of depression, with the badger, or brocc as the Celtic people called it in the elder days. Like the burrowing creature, his mind dwelt much of the time in darks holes under the ground. His feelings, like the badger's fur were mostly dark black, with occasional flashes of white like the animal's snout. Flashes of light when he saw Elvina, flashes of white when he thought he could maybe become a great healer.

Most days were black badger days when, like the animal he could eat worms, and none would care. One night a badger emerged from its burrow, a burrow perhaps a hundred years old used by the animal's ancestors. It padded on its five toes contemptuously toward Wilfred, then turned its back, ejecting some foul-smelling liquid from its anal gland on to his shoe. Fluid to claim ownership of the area. Fluid to attract a mate. Fluid to express scorn to Wilfred's presence and his aspirations.

The badger then returned to its feast of an unfortunate hedgehog whose defence had been unravelled. Clearly the badger dealt with nature's barbs more competently than Wilfred.

Some days Wilfred remembered his father's fervent passion for the countryside and his desire to maintain the forests. Wilfred nearly always collected acorns to carry with him, however sometimes the pigs had eaten all the acorns first. The system of pannage allowed pigs to graze in the forest in autumn, in return for the owner of the pigs giving one of his herd to the land owner. Not only did this fatten pigs before slaughtering, but it removed the acorns which were poisonous for calves and ponies. Expectant sows were also allowed to forage during the daytime while breeding but had to be penned by their owner at night.

Apart from collecting acorns when possible, Wilfred often carried seeds for other trees, the ash, the beech and the chestnut as his father had taught him. Finnian's manuscripts said the ash tree was important for making spears from its long straight shoots. It also said that if a wart was pricked with a nail and the nail then driven into an ash tree, that the wart would be cured. The Norsemen believed that their gods fashioned the very first man from an ash, not that Wilfred gave much credence to the Norse mores.

The beech was important to produce writing tablets from the bark, and important to protect travellers who sheltered under one at night from snake-bites while they slept. Some of his father's manuscripts were written on beech bark.

Wilfred planted circles of acorns on remote barren hill tops, hoping to recall the time-worn beliefs with oak circles of age-old powers. The Druids saw the oak as their most sacred tree, it was sacred to the thunder god who then favoured it with mistletoe. Mistletoe was an emblem of continued and coming life though the long winter months. The white Mistletoe berries represented the life force and men's seed.

If there was less need of Anglo-Saxon warships and longboats to fight the Danes, there would be more oaks in the forest. He planted other seeds at the far edge of the forest in the hope they would grow faster than the foresters chopped down the trees near town.

Wilfred always kept himself supremely fit, ready for when the Danes came again. Many days he would run up the slope south of the town into the woods, then several leagues to the edge of the forest and back. Other days he would climb the tallest oaks strengthening his arms. He could hang from branches with one arm with ease.

Sometimes he thought about falling from the tallest branch. Just letting go. That would put an end to all his loneliness. He would join his father and Cerdic in the otherworld. Perhaps he would find his mother and his sister. There would be more friendship and company than he had in Sherborne. Wilfred wondered if anyone would actually notice if he had been killed by the fall.

He though Elvina would probably not notice his absence. The badger would probably eject that revolting fluid on to his corpse. The wolves and the crows and the pigs would completely remove any trace of his mortal remains before anyone noticed. His disappearance would be a mystery of only transient concern in town.

However, he banished such melancholy thoughts from his mind. He must honour his father's name, he must complete his oaths before death took him to the otherworld. There were diseases to cure, and forests to restore.

He continued to anticipate that his very survival would depend on his fitness and strength in the foreseeable future, so he continued his punishing schedule of running and climbing. His slender build concealed considerable power.

Sometimes Wilfred liked to look inside the abbey church at dusk. The cool tranquillity of the soaring sandstone columns reminded him of the forest as night fell and the creatures of the day sought their rest. The chanting of the monks had a timeless quality that reminded him of the choir of his father and other Druids. However, the Abbey did not have the creatures of the night awaking and commencing their secret snuffling in the undergrowth, intertwined with occasional death squeals as the owl or the weasel struck. The spirits in the church were only those of the dead not the living, though he felt the spirits of the dead also inhabited the forest through the dark hours.

Yet on one occasion he could hear some quiet snuffling inside the church. Peering inside in the gathering gloom, he saw Alfred in the front pew sobbing quietly to himself. 'Why, my prince, what ails thee? I thought you would be always happy. You are a royal prince, you live in a royal palace, you have the best of food and clothes, your brothers are royal princes, and you seem surrounded all the time by pretty girls who actually notice you.'

Wilfred put an arm round Alfred's shoulder. 'This is a special time of year for us all, it is nearly the winter solstice, for me the Yule festival of Dagda and Brighid. For you, Alfred, is it not your Christ's Mass, yet you are unhappy?'

Alfred wiped his eyes and blew his nose on his sleeve. 'My brother, King Æthelbald died here this morning. He was not my oldest brother, I told you Athelstan died when I was only two, I do not remember him. Æthelbald will have a memorial service in two days and be buried here in Sherborne Abbey church. We will need extra prayers for him because he married his father's widow. Some people say that is a mortal sin. My third brother Æthelberht, King of Kent, will become King of Wessex, as Æthelbald had no children. Perhaps he was condemned to be childless by God for marrying Judith!'

Alfred continued, 'After the funeral, I shall be going to Kingston upon Thames to witness my brother's coronation. Æthelberht will unite Kent and Wessex becoming king of both. Long may he reign, please God. May our armies of Anglo-Saxon warriors smash the Danes. Jeremiah was right, in the bible, chapter one, verse fifteen, it says, "Then the Lord said unto me, out of the north an evil shall break forth upon all the inhabitants of the land." With the Lord's help we will throw them back into the sea.'

Alfred's royal duties prevented the two friends spending much time together. Wilfred returned to wandering in the forest. However, the advent of spring with the joyous frolics of new-born young animals and the purple carpet of bluebells on the forest floor did little to alleviate his misery. Wilfred endeavoured to identify beneficial plants and flowers mentioned in his father's paper as they sprang into life. He memorised their location for when he would start to assemble a collection of healing herbs.

Months passed, the seasons rotated. Little happiness came into Wilfred's life. Æthelberht's five-year reign was mostly peaceful, though one band of marauding Vikings launched an attack on both Wintan-ceastre near the coast, and Kent before being repulsed. Wilfred continued his meticulous reading of his father's manuscripts, but he found great passages difficult to understand. Somehow, somewhere, in this very Christian town he would have to find someone knowledgeable in the old ways and language to explain the occult meanings.

Alfred and Wilfred grew to be tall young men, though both retained their slender build. They were both known for being thoughtful and quiet. While Wilfred spent most of his time outside in the woods and forests, Alfred became increasingly skilful in the use of all weapons. Wilfred watched from a distance and secretly absorbed the advice given to Alfred by his warrior tutors. Many of the town-folk who knew him thought Wilfred was a coward for eschewing the swords of iron.

One Friday afternoon, Alfred sought out Wilfred. 'Come with me Wilfred. Cheer up, we are going to try something new, we are going to have some fun. The publican at the Plume and Feathers tavern has been granted more land by my brother at my suggestion and he wants to return the favour. He has some special new ale for us to try. I have managed to evade my minders and my brothers. Sunniva and Alodia here are coming with us to enjoy the entertainment. Do you know them, they are really pretty and friendly?'

The two blonde girls had their arms through Alfred's. They giggled and stuck out their chests to demonstrate their developing womanhood. Alodia looked at Wilfred from under her eyelashes. 'Wilfred, you are nearly as tall as Alfred, and nearly as good looking!'

Both girls laughed and Alodia took Wilfred's arm to his intense embarrassment. He looked around to be sure Elvina had not seen this encounter.

'Come on then, off we go!' called Alfred.

At the back of the Plume of Feathers, Renweard, the hotelier knuckled his forehead to Alfred. 'Sit down young masters and mistresses, this table is only for you. This firkin is my newest brew and I would love you to try it. Here is a pottle for the boys and a gill for the girls.'

Renweard filled their drinks to the brim and departed. Alfred raised his pottle, 'waes hael to us,' he announced touching vessels with the others and downed his pottle in one huge continuous swallow.

Sunniva and Alodia raised their gills, agreed. 'waes hael!' and emptied their vessels. Wilfred raised his, took a large gulp and nearly choked on the bitter fluid.

Sunniva laughed and came to sit uninvited on Wilfred's lap. 'I'll help you,' she offered, holding Wilfred's pottle to his lips. Alfred pottle was refilled by Renweard. Alodia sat herself on Alfred's lap and rested his pottle on her pubertal breasts which were now half-exposed.

Half an hour later the firkin was nearly empty, Wilfred was struggling to remain awake and not vomit, while Sunniva was becoming increasing familiar and uninhibited with his body. 'You have such strong arms and beautiful hair,' she whispered in his ear, 'are you as strong all over?'

The last thing Wilfred could recall was seeing Alodia still sitting on Alfred's lap, now with her underdress rolled down to her waist, and his head resting on her naked ripening breasts.

The next morning Wilfred awoke in his bed, stripped and nursing a pounding headache, a new experience for him. Brokkr, the Norse blacksmith had found an anvil in the middle of Wilfred's forehead, and was pounding it with enthusiasm. He dressed unsteadily and left the monastery. Blinking painfully in the bright morning light, he sought out Alfred. 'what happened last night, how did I end up naked in my bed in the dormitory and did I do anything wrong, or make a fool of myself?'

Alfred smiled and called, 'Alodia, Sunniva, Wilfred is here. He is worried he may have done something wrong last night and wishes to apologise.'

The two girls entered and collapsed in giggles, Alodia said, 'No Wilfred, you were a perfect gentleman last night, you were too drunk to misbehave. Sunniva and I crept into the boys' dormitory and put you to bed. You are getting to be a big boy, aren't you, or you could be.' Sunniva tittered. 'But anytime you would like to misbehave in future, please come for us.'

Wilfred was mortified that they had undressed him and seen him naked. Girls! He thought those two very beautiful and friendly young ladies might entertain Alfred. Together they may discover the secrets of making babies. Wilfred had seen cattle and rabbits mating and presumed it would be similar for men and women. It all looked rather embarrassing and messy, but Alodia and Sunniva seemed keen on the idea. Wilfred thought they were unlikely to end up as his wife, whatever Alfred was doing with them now. An ætheling would seek a lady of royal blood and less promiscuity. One as pure as the babbling brook in the forest.

He hoped Elvina did not hear about the embarrassing event and vowed to drink ale at a much slower pace in future.

Alfred having distained the wooden sword, became increasingly adept with a steel blade. Training was with helmets and to first blood only. His tutors had the challenging task of honing his skill without wounding an ætheling, a prince of the royal blood of Wessex. Alfred's practice sword had a sharpened tip, while his instructors used swords with a blunted tip. There was always a possibility, nay a probability, a dark cloud on the horizon, that he may risk his life in future in the pitiless front of a shield wall to defend Wessex, to protect his land and his people from the marauding Danes.

Wilfred was relegated to teaching the younger boys with wooden swords as he refused to use his father's blade till essential, till a life-threatening occasion confronted him. Most saw avoidance of violence as weird, cowardly.

Before falling asleep with exhaustion each night, Wilfred studied his father's old documents. Father was able to impart wisdom to son, even though he was no longer physically present. Sometimes in candle-light rooms, Wilfred felt his father's shade looking over his shoulder. Wilfred hoped it was with approval.

The writing was in old Celtic, some in obscure verse with some words Wilfred could not translate. Hopefully he would encounter someone with the old knowledge down life's road, but so far without success. Some of the treatments suggested different cures for the same complaint.

The papers suggested treating headache with powdered hammerwort lather rubbed into the scalp, or steam a mixture of hindhealth, groundsel and fencress into the eyes, or even put beetroot and honey up the nose. Some of the ingredients would be hard to obtain. Some of the plants he had never even heard of.

Remedies for eye disease included raven and salmon gall, fox grease and roe deer's marrow. There were so many choices. Wilfred thought he would need to keep notes of what he had tried and to what effect. Finnian had written on the bottom of the page about fennel, "may be good for cancer." Wilfred would remember watercress and fennel should he encounter someone suffering from a cancer.

Wilfred could see that to become a skilled healer he would also need to read the original medical Greek and Latin texts. He would need to be at least as good a Latin scholar as Elvina, hopefully that could be something he could do that would impress her. The sole druid follower joined Alfred and the monks to study, particularly Latin and Greek. One of the brothers, Brother Samuel, was a fluent Latin scholar. As a young man he had studied in the monks' school between Camboritum and Grantebrigge, the leading seat of classical learning in East Anglia before its destruction with the arrival of Guthrum's raiding parties.

Sam, as he was known behind his back, or sometimes Sam Hey, for his propensity for shouting, 'hey you come here!' to any classroom malefactor, had been teaching Latin and Greek to his fellow brother monks for years. Sam was more than happy to commence a Latin class for the boys of the town. Although a monk and now predominantly a peaceful man, Brother Samuel was also known as a competent sword fighter when necessary. He preferred to arrange the rear-guard fighting retreat if defeat was looming to hold together the king's warrior guard and help him safely from the field. Uninjured, free to fight another day.

He trained a small special force of some forty men to surround the king and fight ferociously while slowly walking backwards with never a gap between their shields, and never a fallen sword.

Sam was also a stern man who expected high standards in everything. Success and classical learning were more important for him than esteem. Students not paying adequate attention or keeping up with the required work would often be caned. Brother Samuel has two rods, one birch, and the other hazel. When a beating was required, on each occasion he though briefly, humming to himself before making his selection. How he decided on the most appropriate shaft for that day remained a mystery to his boys, he seemed to have some obscure method to fit the offence to the rod. From the boys' perspective, the two produced a remarkably similar sensation.

Wilfred's manuscripts wrote of the hazel tree adding knowledge and wisdom, but this related to the consumption of hazelnuts, not a thrashing on the behind to aid knowledge and wisdom. It seemed however to achieve the same desirable end-result. Wilfred decided against offering this information to Brother Samuel. It remained an alternative, but perhaps preferable form of trauma to what the young boy's posteriors received from a few of the monks, especially the senior fat one.

Wilfred's father had also written about the birch. It was said to relieve muscular pain, well clearly not in Samuel's hands. It was used for the Beltane Festival fires. Wilfred was not going to tell a devout Christian about that. Branches of birch twigs were used to drive out evil spirits, perhaps that was what Brother Samuel thought he was doing with the birch cane, mused Wilfred.

Alfred had a gift for languages; he only had to hear something, anything, once to remember it clearly. A royal prince was not necessarily above being caned in Brother Samuel's opinion, but Alfred's studies were always well done. He loved learning much more than weapons training.

He told Wilfred, 'one day I hope the quill will be mightier than the sword. When disputes are solved in courts under the Anglo-Saxon Law, not by the better swordsman or bigger bully regardless of the rights of the matter. When verdicts are reached by juries of twelve true men and women of Wessex. When evil-doers are punished appropriately by the law.'

Alfred usually avoided the birch and the hazel.

Wilfred progressed well becoming the second-best student amongst all the boys and young men of the town; he was a rare recipient of the cane. Strangely Brother Sam always chose the birch for Wilfred on the rare occasions it was considered necessary. His posterior then felt as though the Beltane fires had lodged there.

Both young men became adept in the translation of the Gallic Wars by Julius Caesar, the brother's favourite Latin text. Alfred committed Caesar's battlefield tactics to memory for future use. Caesar had been such a successful general, surely his strategies could be used by the Saxons to destroy the Danes.

Wilfred's favourite quotation was from one of Virgil's poems, "miseris succurrere disco", I learn to succour the sick. That would be his life's ambition.

Alfred persuaded another of the monks, Brother Peter, to teach religion and history. He had apparently been born in Scotia, but his mother brought him south as an infant to avoid their wild pagan ways. He had studied history and religion with the monks in Oxenaforda before coming to Sherborne. Brother Peter was also become the local curate in some nearby villages; hence he became Peter the Curate to the boys, but not to his face. He was a gentler monk that Brother Sam and rarely used to beat the boys.

Alfred and Brother Peter's favourite text was Bede's Historia Ecclesiastica Gentis Anglorum, a history from the invasion of Britain by Julius Caesar up to a century and a half ago. Alfred was particularly fond of this book as Bede described the conversion of King Edwin to Christianity by Bishop Paulinus a hundred and eighty years after the arrival of the Anglo-Saxons in England and six hundred and twenty-seven years after the birth of Jesus. Edwin and Paulinus had then supervised the construction in stone of the first large Christian church in York.

The Vikings had captured York and renamed it Jorvik. One of Alfred's ambitions was to recapture that city and dedicate it again to the glory of God. Paulinus's church would be reconsecrated in the Christian faith after it had been desecrated by pagan practices. Apparently, the Danes stabled their horses next to the high altar. Alfred was deeply disgusted.

Wilfred attended these religious sessions politely but without great motivation. He found some of the history interesting, though Brother Peter seemed only interested in the period since Julius Caesar first invaded Britain.

Wilfred's father had spoken of Caesar's landing as invasion day. That was July 6th, fifty-four years before the birth of Christ in the now dominant Christian calendar. Invasion day was the day his family lost their huge land holdings along the south coast for ever to the legions of Rome. Alfred, for all his knowledge of history appeared quite unaware of this. However, the land retained its memories. An awareness of the past and the old ways was imbedded in the soil. It could not be seen or heard, but it could be sensed. The hills and trees, the forests and rivers recognised Wilfred as a bearer of significant rank.

Wilfred was aware that his family never regained their status or wealth again, not from the Romans, or the Britons or the Anglo-Saxons. The chance of ever gaining title to his native family lands in the future seemed absolutely minimal.

Brother Peter said nothing about the ancient Celtic culture or the Druids, apart from the brutal murder of all the unarmed Druid priests and priestesses at the invasion of Mona. The first attempt to capture Mona had been repulsed by the Druid high priest summoning up a mighty wave to flood the channel and causeway to the island, Wilfred's father had told him. Several Roman legionaries were washed away.

The second time, the Romans came with a series of pontoons across which a whole legion accessed the land and casually, pitilessly slew all the island's inhabitants, including defenceless women and children. Brother Peter apparently thought that the eclipse of the ancient culture by one he saw as superior was a good thing.

At the end of one session Wilfred turned to Alfred and asked, 'I think you know more history than Brother Peter, why do you find the history of Mercia and Northumberland so long ago so interesting?'

Alfred responded thoughtfully, 'my dear friend there are three reasons, firstly the Anglo-Saxons will take the north back from the Danes one day, I want to know about the place where they live. I want to know all about the battlegrounds of tomorrow before I stand there in my shield wall. I need to know every contour, every hill and river to select places of safety and places for battle. I need to know the right battle tactics for each of those places.'

'Secondly, only those wise kings who converted to Christianity achieved much success on this island in their lifetimes and should deservedly go to heaven. Thirdly and most importantly, history is littered with disastrous mistakes made by kings and emperors, if I do not learn from them; I am doomed to make the same mistakes. One mistake may lose my life and my kingdom. I also think teaching children about myths and legends as well as history helps their spiritual growth. It gives them a better understanding of good and evil, it helps them distinguish heroes and villains.'

Wilfred preferred to observe the monks who treated the sick people of the monastery and the town in the infirmaria, one of the rooms at the back of the monastery. He observed carefully their techniques for amputating limbs and other surgeries. One of the monks, Brother David, noting his enthusiasm, allowed him to assist, though the other brothers usually tossed him out. After a while, Wilfred and Brother David began to discuss herbal remedies. David had an open mind for a monk and thought deeply about Wilfred's ideas. Interesting discussions followed when none of the other monks were within earshot. David used the nine herbs of pagan Anglo-Saxon origin without a qualm but believed they would only work through

WILFRED AND THE HALF-PINTLE

the hands of his Lord if he recited the paternoster or Lord's Prayer when prescribing.

David told him Osric once said covetously, 'mass priests can perform the leechdom if a man hath enough means to pay for treatment, and both pray to the Lord for healing.' David, unlike the greedy Osric, but like Wilfred, never extracted any fees, but accepted offerings of gratitude.

865 MAY

One warm early summer day when Wilfred was fourteen, Alfred called his friend to join him, 'You have heard that my third brother, King Æthelberht died. He was only twenty-nine. Wessex greatly needed him for much longer, but it seems God had an even greater need for him. Æthelberht said it seems kings are made for honour, not for long life! He will be buried here in Sherborne Abbey beside Æthelbald. My fourth brother, Æthelred will become king. He is only eighteen and not yet married with children. Wilfred, I am now next heir to the throne though I am only sixteen. I am the only Ætheling, as you probably know, an Anglo-Saxon term for a prince of the royal blood entitled to the throne. Secundarius is my title according to the bishop. Normally that would be a great honour, I should feel a mixture of pleasure, excitement, fear and responsibility.'

Alfred paused, swallowed and sighed, before continuing quietly, 'unfortunately, it is rumoured a mighty Viking army is on the way to Mercia. May Æthelred have a long successful reign and repel them. I will fight beside him in his shield wall. Wilfred, but I am afraid he may be killed. My proverbs say that every day you are afraid, you ought to thank God for your life, but I may be known forever after as the king to lose Wessex to the Danes, my kingdom and my life, perhaps to the blood red eagle. The pages of history will record me as a weak king, a loser, not a conqueror like Caesar. A lamb before the wolf. Wilfred, I am not ready for that. I am not old enough, or strong enough. You must stand beside me.'

Wilfred replied half encouragingly, 'I will stand by you always, though I do not want to fight beside you.'

Alfred continued knowledgeably, trying to cheer himself up, 'Gildas the Wise, the historian of the Britons after the Romans, reminded us of the prophet Malachi, stating that the day of the Lord would come and that the evil-doers will be burnt as stubble. Hopefully that will come under Æthelred. I think I told you, when I was four and again when I was six, I was sent to Rome and Pope Leo IV consecrated me as a future king, even though I was the fifth son and do not wish to be king. Perhaps the Lord had told him of my future. Rome is a grand city, it is the spiritual home of Christianity. Leo was a great Pope; his forces defeated the Saracens at the Battle of Ostia in the year of my birth. He also stood sponsor for me on my confirmation, as my father King Æthelwulf requested.'

Alfred frowned and resumed, 'my father took Judith, the daughter of King Charles the Bald the Frankish King, to be his second wife on that trip. My mother Queen Osburh had died the year before, just before my fifth birthday. Judith was only twelve or thirteen then, only a little older than me, though she became my step-mother. She was then a little younger than your friend Elvina. Do you think Elvina is old enough to be a wife?'

Wilfred hated Alfred talking about Elvina especially when it came to topics like marriage. Surely the prince did not covet Elvina as he did, silently hopelessly. He just shrugged his shoulders feigning disinterest and ignorance as usual.

Wilfred thought for a while about Alfred's description of Rome, then responded. 'Yet Alfred, your Roman god, your one mighty god, your Christ, could not prevent the barbarians sacking Rome. I have heard about Rome, some of the Christian brothers from the monastery have also been there. Your Vatican City is falling apart, the Coliseum is no longer in use for murderous games, nor is the Forum or the Circus Maximus. The stones are removed to make lesser buildings. Your religion can not renew itself like mine.'

'My forests of oak will last forever; old trees die, and new ones grow from little acorns. But first my god generously grants the great oak a life of a thousand years to live in harmony with the forests and to lovingly shelter the living creatures who share the forest. Your god wisely grants man, the universal destroyer, even your Roman Christian men, a mere fifty years at the most.

You may believe our ways belong in the past, but memories of the old Druid ways are imprinted today everywhere, in all the rivers and hills, in all the woods and ringstones. We see a spiritual dimension in all forms of life, we may worship one Great Spirit, a god or goddess, or both, or many more.'

'For us the Great Spirit exists in all living things, we are bound together by love of nature and tolerance of all beliefs. This land is guarded by the shadow creatures. They live in a space between this world and the other world, in the space between day and night, between the seen and the unseen. They help only those aware of their presence. One day they will help you.'

Wilfred was now in full flood on his beliefs. 'We are not bound by your commandments, your rigid rules of life that engender fear. You Christians claim you do not recognise or fear the old gods, yet neither a Christian nor pagan Roman Legion would never pass through a misty forest in the night.'

'They claimed to worship Mars, their god of war. They claimed to be fearless martial warriors; yet they were frightened of the old forest guardian spirits even in the daytime. They avoided the evil eye of the woodlands at night after a legion once completely disappeared in a dark northern forest between sunset and sunrise. You say your Christ is a Lord of peace, yet Christians are always fighting, not just against other beliefs, but even amongst themselves, from Rome to England, they are forever at war.'

'Your Gildas goes on all the time about judgement and punishment for any evil. The only good he seems to find is in the beauty of our earth. He says the many coloured flowers are like a bride decked with jewels, that the murmurs of brooks lull us to sleep, and the lakes pour forth refreshing water. Yes Alfred, I read too and agree with Gildas. There is more beauty in the land than in man.'

'We Druids prefer to sit down in harmony to solve our problems. We are the current caretakers of Mother Earth, the spiritual guardians of our people. We encourage everyone to live a peaceful healthy holistic life and to care for our homeland.'

'Yes Alfred, I will be your liegeman, but I will not fight in your shield wall, I will not take blood from another man. I will be your seer and your healer. When you have plans for the future, I can tell you if you will be blessed with good fortune or not. Should you be sick or wounded, I will make you better if I possibly can. I will care for your warriors on the field of battle.'

'You don't believe you can see the future, do you?' Alfred said scornfully, 'that's all rubbish! My book of proverbs says, do not try to find out what is going to happen to you by casting lots, but do the best you can; God will easily decide his will respecting you and your need, although he doesn't tell it to you beforehand' Alfred, however, found it hard to disagree with anything else Wilfred had said, though he did not admit that.

'My Prince Alfred,' responded Wilfred, confident in his beliefs, 'what a good job we shall not be casting lots then. There are more accurate ways of seeing the future. Three days before the Danes came to our village, my father examined the entrails, the sheep's liver was full of blood red spots, and many yellow horizontal lines, this foretold of blood and dead bodies, how can you doubt it?'

'Well do one for me,' said Alfred doubtingly, 'those sheep in the pen over there are to be slaughtered for tonight's feast. We commemorate the life of poor Æthelberht and celebrate the accession of my fourth brother, Æthelred. You can't have your ritual Druid procession, Bigang is that what you call it, with a sacrifice to your false gods. Show me later what you can foretell for me, not that I will believe any of it. Not one word!'

Alfred changed the topic of conversation, 'Come, I have something else to show you.' In the royal pavilion, Alfred picked up a bag of purple velvet. 'Feel this fabric, some Arab traders sold it to us, it is called velvet.'

Wilfred felt the soft regal fabric; it certainly had a warm special feeling. Alfred tipped out the contents. It was a hnefatafl set! Alfred's hnefatafl set! The warrior pieces were made from dark oak and pale pine. The shields of the dark oak pieces were engraved with the hammer of Thor and a raven, and the pine shields were engraved with the wyvern of Wessex and a dove. The Viking warrior pieces were all biting the top of their shields, a depiction of their insanely fierce warriors, the berserkers. One larger one, the king also wore the crown on its head. 'See the symbols of war and peace, but don't think doves can't fight when essential!'

Alfred had also a board made of oak with the squares carefully marked. Wilfred declined Alfred's not-so-subtle offer of a large goblet of mead before starting the game. A game followed. Move preceded counter move as two intelligent strategists strove for the upper hand. Alfred had been sitting privately studying the game to understand its strategies. The bells of Sherborne Abbey struck the quarter hour, then another and another. Alfred finally broke out of Wilfred's circling black pieces with his king and captured one of the Viking bases, a corner square bringing the game to a conclusion. He gave a satisfied sigh. Their score was now one-all. The two teenagers looked into each other's eyes seeing friendly rivalry with sincere respect and comradeship. They laughed and clasped forearms. Wilfred now gratefully accepted the goblet of honeyed wine.

'I will tell you what the future holds for you tonight. I expect to inform you that you will lose the next game!' Wilfred said. The friends laughed, touched goblets and downed the rich royal mead.

Dusk developed, the area outside the Abbey was lit by the flickering light of multiple flares. Crowds gathered noisily in the still warm evening, mostly in a good humour with food and wine to enjoy, and memories of King Æthelberht to share. Dark corners seemed free of malign spirits, rather they seemed to partially conceal unbetrothed couples or married men and women with another's spouse, engaged in mutual though illicit entertainment and pleasurable exploration.

Prospects of the imminent Danish invasion were happily forgotten for the night. Cooking fires were alight ready to roast the sheep on a spit. Cauldrons full of chickens and fish and vegetables bubbled merrily. Goblets of wine and ale were drained and refilled. Alfred led one of the sheep behind the houses to where Wilfred awaited.

Wilfred muttered to himself in some unintelligible Gaelic tongue for a while, and then expertly cut the throat of a sheep. Death was almost instantaneous with minimal distress. When the blood flow abated, he rolled the carcass onto it back and then sliced opened its abdomen, the intestines steamed in the cooling air, as he peered into the abdominal cavity. His deft hand pushed the intestines aside to give a clear view of the liver.

'This is good, very good,' said Wilfred. 'there is only one large red mark on the liver. You will have one black time, only one period of major problems in your life, but not beyond your ability to overcome them.'

'The divisions in the liver are narrow and shallow; you will work with a united people, though first you must work with your brother. My father looked into the future many times, he saw the line of Saxon kings will end when brother fights brother, to be replaced by a barbaric tyrant from over the water who will destroy this country and the Saxon people. It was such a common finding for him that he thought brother fighting brother may even happen twice or thrice in the future.'

'The spleen edges are unusually sharp; you will be a successful warrior, a great fighter. The appendix is in front of the bowel, as you will be in front of your people. You will be a leader of men. I have seen several of these performed by my father, but this is the best I have seen. This foretells a great future. This foretells an ability to overcome all challenges. My Prince

Alfred, you will be remembered as a great man,' said Wilfred looking up and smiling at his friend.

'Bah, rubbish, absolute rubbish,' scowled Alfred, with a private smile to himself, in these troubled times a man needed all the good auguries he could get. 'Get that carcass over the fire. I will enjoy the meat even if not your flattery.'

Two days later Alfred sought Wilfred discretely. 'You say you can heal people with some ancient herbal law?' he asked quietly.

'Sometimes,' replied Wilfred noncommittally.

'Well,' Alfred said very softly while looking around to ensure he was not overheard, 'I have a problem the royal physicians can't solve. I have bouts of tummy pain, sometimes I have the bloody flux and my arse gets very sore. I spend stounds in the dunnykins. My physicians think the monks are sticking their pintles up there, but that has never happened. I gave one a wack in the balls with my wooded sword a few years ago when he threatened me, and they have left me alone since. They say prayers will solve it but so far I have also got sore knees to add to my sore arse!'

'Elias, the Patriarch of Jerusalem sent me some medical remedies for the alleviation of constipation, diarrhoea, pain in the spleen and internal tenderness. If I remember correctly they were scammony, ammoniacum, traganth, galbanum, balsam and petroleum. My priest-healers did not seem to know how to use them. Perhaps it was no surprise when those did not work.'

Wilfred drawing on his experience with Cerdic asked Alfred, 'Have you eaten raw chicken, or even chicken that is still pink?'

'No,' said Alfred, 'the royal kitchens are very careful to cook pork and chicken well.'

'Come with me, I have some important food to trial on you,' requested Wilfred. He went back to the monk's kitchen with Alfred and made some pottage. 'Drink this and tell me if it gives you the flux overnight.'

The next morning Wilfred sought Alfred. 'No problem, no flux, what was it, what did it tell you? said Alfred curiously.

Wilfred was pleased to hear this. Alfred would be a survivor. 'It tells me you are not about to die, and that I may be able to cure you!' replied Wilfred. Alfred failed to look impressed at this reassurance. The next question for him was the cause of Alfred's complaint.

'I need to look at you,' said Wilfred. He peered carefully into Alfred's mouth noting a couple of little ulcers. He felt Alfred's tummy gently. It was a bit tender all over, but there were no hard lumps to indicate a cancer. The abdomen was not rigid which would have indicated a perforation or some other severe problem. He placed his ear on the royal abdomen hearing fairly normal but very active gurgles from the royal intestines. Then the two of them looked around to ensure they were not observed.

Alfred dropped his britches and bent over while Wilfred peered respectfully at the royal anus. It was all red and inflamed with some little tags of skin protruding. Alfred covered his modesty and Wilfred said, 'I have read of this into my father's texts. There is some internal infection and inflammation which comes and goes.'

'You must take a tea. I will prepare a mixture of chamomile, onions, garlic and peppermint to drink twice daily and some butter mixed with honey pasted onto the sore bits around your arse. I will go now and make both remedies. You can drink the tea and you can apply butter and honey mixture yourself.'

Once they parted, Wilfred made a little effigy of Alfred from beech wood, stuck on a wreath of oak leaves as a crown, and placed it in an oak tree on the edge of the forest. His father had said this would help healing. Well Alfred was such an important person, Wilfred thought he would try everything. A few days later, on the seventeenth night of the new moon, after sunset, but before moonrise, Wilfred picked an unripe white mulberry. He plucked it as recommended between the thumb and ring finger of his left hand. He crushed it and added a little hot water, then took it to Alfred.

'How are you today my prince?' asked Wilfred hopefully.

'Improved,' said Alfred, both grateful and surprised, 'my arse is less painful, and the flux has stopped.'

'Here,' said Wilfred, 'this is mistletoe tea, it is very bitter, but it is only one berry and is very good for internal infections and bleeding. Drink it down in one big swallow as though you were drinking ale.'

Alfred laughed recalling Wilfred's first attempt at drinking ale, then swallowed it quickly, screwing up his face at the bitter taste.

'Yuk, that better be good for me, it tastes awful!'

Two weeks later Alfred approached Wilfred and clasped his wrist. Alfred looked into his younger friend's eyes with a mixture of bewilderment, gratitude and respect. 'God moves in mysterious ways, very mysterious ways; a young pagan has cured my pains and soreness, and the bloody flux when my experienced royal Christian physicians with God's help could not do so. Wilfred, do you know of St Wilfred. He had the same name as you. He was a Northumbrian noble who travelled to Rome and then became a bishop. He converted many in Northumbria to Christianity and played a large part in establishing the church there. Water in which he had washed could work miracles and on the service for the first anniversary of his death, a large pure white arc was seen in the sky arising from the basilica where he is buried. Are you sure you are not descended from him, you have worked a miracle for me?'

Wilfred smiled and shook his head. 'I have been told about that Wilfred by the brothers. I understand that he died a very wealthy man. I asked the brothers how he could enter the kingdom of heaven as they said it was easier for a camel to pass through the eye of a needle than for a rich man to enter heaven. They beat me with the cane, told me I had no faith and ignored my question.'

Alfred responded again, 'God moves in mysterious ways, as do the monks. Serves you right for asking questions the wisest man cannot answer!' and then continued after a thoughtful pause, 'stay around Sherborne, I shall have need for your skills.'

Alfred thought again briefly and added, 'Wilfred, you need somewhere to practice your skills and prepare your herbal remedies. I have a small house in Cheap Street. You shall have it as long as you like as a small token of appreciation for what you have done for me.'

Wilfred was most grateful. He thanked the monks for their kindness and hospitality, packed his satchel with his few possessions and left the monastery. Brother David shook his hand discretely and asked Wilfred to keep in touch. They others all seemed happy to see him gone for they thought he was a bit strange. He established his new home amongst the merchants of Cheap Street.

Wilfred had been in his little house for a week. There was a little loft at one end where he could sleep, and a central hearth where he could prepare herbal teas. He had been out gathering some herbs in the forest and now had a row of pots of medicinal herbs on a shelf. He had planted a few herbs in his garden, his own wyrt tun.

There was a knock on his door. The carpenter from two doors up the hill was there with a sulky looking pale youth, perhaps a little older than Wilfred. 'Are you Wilfred, the prince's healer? You look very young. Did you really fix Prince Alfred?'

Wilfred nodded cautiously, that was a promising description of him to start his career. Alfred must have sung his praises as Wilfred had told nobody of his success. He was not close enough to anyone to relate that story, and anyway it would be inappropriate to tell anyone of Alfred's ailment.

'I'm John the carpenter from up the hill, this is Wulfstan my apprentice. He has a sore leg. He cut it while sawing a piece of timber nearly three weeks ago. We have been to the monastery daily for two weeks to see their priest who sees sick people, but without improvement. Wulfstan must spend half an hour praying, and then has paste of parsley and sage applied. We have to put money in the collection bowl or the treatment does not work. When he doesn't get better, he is told it is because he is sinful, and he is told to put in more money. Wulfstan has no more money and he doesn't have time for sin. I work him too hard! And he is too young for mortal sins.

John peered at Wilfred again, 'you look very young to be a healer; can you fix it?'

'Maybe I will be able to fix it, I need to have a careful look at the wound. 'Wilfred replied warily and then put Wulfstan gently on his bench. He had a large red oozing festering stinking sore on the front of his thigh. Parsley did little for infected wounds and sage was good for intestinal or brain ailments. Wilfred explored the wound gently with a long fine metal probe finding a large splinter of wood. He pulled this out with some fine pliers and a mass of foul-smelling pus poured out.

Wulfstan gave a sigh of relief, 'wow, God, that feels better, that has taken most of the pain away! Why couldn't the brothers do that?'

Wilfred applied a mixture of ox gall, onion, wine, leek and garlic into the wound. He had prepared this over a week ago leaving it in a sealed brass vessel according to his father's instructions. Finnian said it was advisable to keep some prepared at all times as it was often required. Wilfred found the mixture to be a smelly slime as expected but it was documented as being the best for nasty skin infections.

He then placed a clean dressing over the lesion pulling the edges close and bound it. It was too infected and old to suture. Wilfred refused John's offer of money and ushered them out.

Ten days later Wulfstan knocked on his door. The unhappy, sulky expression was gone. He beamed at Wilfred and clasped his wrist with surprising vigour, then hugged him. His leg was healed with a small ragged scar.

He presented Wilfred with a little wooden box with a slot on the top, a key and a lock. He said, 'you are the best Wilfred; I shall not be going back to the priest ever again when I am sick. He even suggested I should drop my breeches and bend over for him to help my leg get better, dirty bastard! I made this box specially for you Wilfred out of Wessex oak. John put a silver penny in here for you. I am sure you will make many more.' They clasped arms again, then Wulfstan gave him another bear hug and departed.

A silver penny was the standard pay for a day's work. Wilfred was pleased and grateful. His cure had enable Wulfstan to return to work quite soon to John's financial gain. His father's mixture has worked surprisingly well.

Knowledge of Wilfred's healing skills spread rapidly up and down the commercial hub of Sherborne by word of mouth from John and Wulfstan. The busy thoroughfare of Cheap Street included a butcher, a tanner, a carpenter, a baker, a metal craftsman, a blacksmith, a pottery and some weavers. The last produced tough fabrics from nettles and flax, and warm garments from the wool fleeces. Fire was always a hazard here from the blacksmith and the metal worker's forges and the potter's kiln. Buckets of water were kept on hand in all the shops.

Before long, many other merchants had seen him with their ailments and the system of barter there expanded to include Wilfred. Often silver pennies were left in Wilfred's box. Other left meat or vegetables, clothing or bread, pottery or jewels. The metal worker who left the jewels said, 'this is for your young lady, I know the quiet fellows are the ones to watch.'

Wilfred thought sadly to himself, 'I have no young lady, I see Elvina almost daily, but she never sees me.'

An unwanted guest crept into his mind's eye. That uninvited icon of Wilfred's emotional well-being, or unwell-being, the badger, carried Wilfred down into a dark friendless space where his future diet would consist only of worms, while Elvina laughed and flirted with all the other young men of the town.

Wilfred dragged himself back to the other problems of the day. While the butcher was in Cheap Street, the wholesale slaughtering of animals was not permitted in the middle of a commercial centre. The abattoir was therefore on the edge of town on the River Yeo. The source of water for the townsfolk was safely well upstream from the abattoir.

Little was wasted there; hearts, kidneys and livers were seen by most as a delicacy. Intestines were used to make saussiche with blood and meat scraps. Lungs were a grim reminder of the Viking blood red eagle and were shunned. Only a little unused offal was tossed in the river, but it would not benefit Yeovil, the next village downstream, and their water supply. Strangely this town used to be called Scir Burne, meaning clear stream. That Anglo-Saxon name had been transmuted into Sherborne less than a century ago. It was certainly no longer clear downstream from the abattoir.

Wilfred resolved to try to prevent this once he had acquired a worthy reputation in town, once his opinion was widely respected. The tanner ensured his hides were scraped in the abattoir, though his property in town still reeked of the urine used to soak the hides.

A few days later Durwyn, the proprietor of the tavern at the bottom of the hill, the Half Moon Inn, arrived at Wilfred's door carrying his semi-conscious little three-year-old daughter Meghan. 'Wilfred, Meghan has just been bitten by a snake; I think it was a poisonous adder. I think she might die soon, please please can you help?'

Wilfred laid the little girl on his bench. She was pale and sweating, crying and moaning. Her heart rate and breathing were very rapid. Her right ankle was very red and swollen. Fang marks were visible just above her ankle bone. Meghan's mother stood weeping silently in the door way holding the dead snake by the tail. It was indeed an adder.

Wilfred calmly asked Durwyn, 'will you skin the snake and place the snake fat on a pan over the fire, please.' Inside he felt anything but calm.

More like the raging sea, as his reputation around town would depend upon his first few patrons. However, he already understood the healing effect on the sick and their dear but very anxious relatives, of an external appearance of quiet confidence.

Wilfred rapidly made a poultice of crushed dandelion and flour, applying that firmly to her bite just above the right ankle. Then he picked up the bottle of powdered purple dragonwort and catmint from his shelf and dissolved a spoonful in hot water. He persuaded Meghan to sip slowly on a goblet of this preparation. Shortly after she fell painlessly asleep. Finally, Wilfred rubbed a solution of henbane root powder and warm melted snake fat around her swollen ankle. As the next hour passed while healer and parents watched uneasily, Meghan's colour improved and her heart and breathing rates settled. The swelling and redness around her ankle slowly diminished.

Soon she awoke, smiled at her father and mother, and said, 'where are we, this isn't home? What are we doing here? Is it time for lunch Papa, I'm hungry?'

Durwyn hugged Wilfred, thrust his arm up and down as though filling his bucket from the parish water pump, and then said, 'you are a miracle worker Wilfred, I'm not sure what power works though you, but there will always be a welcome for you in the Half Moon.' His wife gave him a motherly hug and planted sloppy kisses on both his cheeks before Wilfred could evade her. Her joyful, grateful tears ran down Wilfred's cheek.

'A free meal and a cup of ale will always be available for you in the Half Moon, Wilfred, whenever you desire from this day onwards,' she promised

Wilfred now had a personal space to spread his manuscripts, and a room to collect and store herbs from the forest. He watered his new herb collection in his back garden regularly if there had not been rain, though that was not often. It always seemed to rain in Sherborne. The plants were growing steadily.

Arms full of herbs from the forest were collected, dried on racks and ground into powder to store in large jars on his shelves.

After a couple of months John, the carpenter, was back accompanied by a lady. 'This is my wife, Ellsworth. She has a breast lump. The monastery has prayed over it and rubbed parsley ointment into her breasts, both sides with rather too much enthusiasm for my liking. Osric says it is to stop it spreading to the other side. But the lump is getting bigger. Osric, greasy greedy Osric with his little piggy eyes, says paying more money will always enlist God's help.' John announced irreverently, accurately. 'They say it is because she is too sinful. I told the prior that Ellsworth has always been faithful. If anyone should be sick for being sinful it should be me, but that is another story. Can you help please?'

Wilfred sat her down in a chair and gently, discreetly, peeled down her tunic. Indeed, in the left breast there was a hard lump. It would not move over the chest wall, it appeared fixed to the chest wall. The skin over the lump looked like orange peel. It was fixed to the skin. Under her left arm, Wilfred could feel more little lumps. He felt her abdomen; the liver was not enlarged. He tapped her bones. He found a painful spot in her upper spine. Ellsworth clearly had breast cancer.

Wilfred had read about cankers and tumour in various books and manuscripts. His father's manuscripts mentioned the obvious features of breast cancer. This was clearly typical of a breast cancer. The appearance unfortunately was like descriptions of quite advanced breast cancer that had spread into her glands and bones.

Wilfred wondered what treatment he should give. However, his father's manuscripts did not have a definite recommendation on specific treatment. Finnian wrote that cancerous lumps could not be cut out. That would cause unbearable pain followed by inevitable recurrence of the cancer. It did say nettle tea or poultices with red clover were good for some hard lumps. It did say watercress and fennel were good for cancers.

'My dear John and Ellsworth, I am sorry to say this is a serious tumour, Ellsworth, you should prepare yourself and your family for the worst, but

I will do my best. This is nettle and watercress tea, dissolve one teaspoon in hot water three times daily and drink that. This is essence of fennel and mistletoe, have one drop at bedtime.'

Wilfred then made a poultice of powdered red clover mixed with bran. 'Apply one of these each night to your left breast.'

Three months later, Ellsworth returned, she was feeling better and the lump was smaller and less painful. It was still fixed to the chest wall but not to the skin. The skin over the lump was now normally smooth, not like orange peel. The glands under her arm had disappeared and her spine no longer had a tender vertebra. They both thanked Wilfred effusively and clapped him on his back.

John said, 'your treatment is much more effective than the monks, here is a silver penny for your box.' As they departed happily arm in arm down the thoroughfare, Wilfred had a momentary distressing picture in his mind of Ellsworth in her winding sheet.

Another six months later, Wilfred attended Ellsworth's funeral.

John, between tears said, 'thanks Wilfred, you gave us more time together and we prepared our children for life without a mother. Ellsworth had much less back pain for a few months, your treatment was far better than the monks' rubbish.'

Wilfred felt frustration, he was still a failure. The badger was back. Wilfred felt plunged again into the dark spaces in the animal's set. He walked out of the graveyard and sat alone. A few tears ran miserably down his face.

This therapy had some success, but only for a while, then ultimately failed. How could he do better? Nettles and mistletoe, watercress and fennel only provided short term benefit for breast lumps.

A test for Wilfred arrived the very next morning. There was a sharp knock on his front door soon after sunrise. Wilfred sleepily opened the door to find Elvina, his heart skipped a beat, had she come especially to see him!

She was becoming a most beautiful young lady. She had a smile to die for, but it never seemed to be aimed at him. She was developing a most attractive figure, but it seemed to be on display for all the other young men.

'Elvina, how gggood to see you, ppplease come in.' he stuttered in surprise and delight.

However; Elvina was not alone, she was accompanied by a group of small children and another young lady.

'Hello Wilfred, this is my friend Orva, and these are our little charges. They either have parents at work in the fields or sadly some are orphans. They all have something wrong with them, will you see them please?'

'Please,' said Wilfred, 'come in Elvina, it is good to see you, bring them all in.'

Elvina said, 'thank you, Orva will stay with you, I have other things to do.'

Then with a swirl of her red hair and a flounce of her hips she was gone. Wilfred followed her down the street with his eyes, disappointed again. She seemed to be avoiding him. Perhaps she hated his Druid philosophy; perhaps she had another male friend. Wilfred felt really upset at that prospect. Jealousy nearly made him forget why Elvina came in the first place. The troubled youth felt surrendering Elvina to another man could make him loose his mind in unfathomable pain. With an effort he regained his composure. Sadly she was not really his.

Wilfred set to work gently with the sick little children. The first two had burns, one from a fire for which he applied a mixture of woodruff, lily and brooklime after heating the mixture in butter, and waiting briefly till it cooled. The second burn was from boiling water for which he took a bottle of elm rind and lily roots previously boiled in milk. He applied some to the burn and covered it with a clean linen patch. Then he gave the remaining mixture to Orva to be applied three times a day for three days.

The next child had been coughing for a week. Wilfred gave Orva some Marubie powder. 'Here this is white horehound. Mix one spoonful of it with two spoonsful of this one, it is red clover powder. Dissolve it in hot water, mix it with honey and take a spoonful three times daily till she is better.'

The fourth child had a sore ear. Wilfred found his jar of betonice powder and another of rose oil. 'Here this is wood betony; dissolve it in this rose oil and some warm water, then put a few drops into the ear three times a day for three days.'

The fifth child had toothache. Wilfred could see one black tooth with surrounding redness and inflammation of the gum. He pulled out the tooth releasing some smelly yellow pus and a shriek of transient pain, then found some black pepper powder, and seeds of mustard and cress. He ground them up and dissolved them in vinegar and honey.' Use this as a mouth wash twice a day after food for three days. Hold the liquid in the mouth for a count of a hundred, and then spit it out.'

The final child had some very itchy spots from the burrowing worm. Wilfred provided a salve of powdered holly leaves. He had depleted his medical supplies drastically and would need a trip to the woods tomorrow for replacements. Fortunately, his father's papers accurately detailed each of the conditions from which the children suffered and what specific therapy to prescribe.

Orva watched in awe as he solved one problem after another with tenderness to the children and extreme competence, he always seemed to know exactly what was wrong and what to do. She gave him a big hug, then a kiss on each cheek, saying, 'one from me and one from Elvina!'

Wilfred started ruefully, 'I don't suppose she would, would like to.....oh never mind it doesn't matter.'

The next morning there was another knock on his door and a young woman's voice called out, 'Wilfred are you in?'

Wilfred rushed optimistically to open the door, it sounded a bit like Elvina's entrancing voice, but it was only Orva.

'Hello Wilfred, thank you for seeing our children yesterday. I told Elvina how clever you are. How you knew exactly what treatment to give for all those problems. The children all seemed to be much better by this morning, Elvina said to say thank you.'

Wilfred hoped that one day, Elvina might come in person to thank him.

Orva paused, looked at the ground and fiddled with her hair for a short while. Then she looked up at Wilfred and said, 'do you want an apprentice, I would love to be able to do a tiny bit of what you do for children's health, can I be your assistant please, can I collect herbs and grind them into powder for you? Can I learn what herb is used for what disease? I will do anything you want. Please.'

Wilfred was surprised but thought a second pair of hands to collect herbs, dry them and grind them into powder would be so useful. His supply of therapies could be doubled.

'Why yes, that would be ever so helpful, can you start now?' responded Wilfred gratefully.

Orva entered the house with a winning smile and said, 'tell me what to do and I will work for you from sunrise to sunset.' She paused and looked up at Wilfred from under her long dark eyelashes, then added in a confidential whisper, 'If you would like a companion upstairs as well, I am all yours anytime you like, if you know what I mean.'

Wilfred thought he knew exactly what she meant and was overcome with acute embarrassment. The bigger boys in town seemed to think of nothing else. Wilfred understood from them that people seemed to get even more pleasure than the animals mating in the fields. The animals seemed to spend a long time in pursuit and noisome mounting for a transient intimacy of dubious pleasure.

However, neither of them was quite yet fifteen and he would rather be with Elvina, 'er, no, er I mean yes, um, it is said that kissing is out of season when the gorse is out of bloom, so no, but your help downstairs with my herbs would be invaluable. I don't have time to grind all the herbs to powder that I need, so come with me and let's get started.'

867 JANUARY

O ver the next two years Wilfred, with Orva's help, developed his therapeutic armamentarium. Not only did he have a plentiful supply of the nine herbs of the Anglo-Saxon charms, but many others in addition. Parsley, sage, rosemary and thyme, mint, hyssop and chervil grew well in his garden. The grocer allowed him to pick fruit as needed from his orchard.

His shelves were laden with many other oils and powders collected from forest plants. He had more weapons to heal than the Saxon army did to harm. The butcher, who liked herbs to dress his meat allowed Wilfred space in his garden to grow basil, betony, camomile, chives, dill and fennel. Wilfred and Orva spent many constructive hours with his pestle and mortar making powers from all this natural produce.

He continued his diligent but difficult study of the archaic manuscripts, rewriting copies in Saxon on fresh vellum as many of the old texts were crumbling with age. Wilfred found another recommendation for diarrhoea, perhaps he could try this on Alfred if he had a relapse. The paper advised laying a hen's egg in vinegar for two or three nights, then beat it with butter and oil and drink it warm.

Orva worked industriously beside Wilfred making a second copy of all Finnian's manuscripts which John kept for him in a box in the attic of the Half Moon in case either property was damaged by fire. Orva never suggested again that they should sleep together but her frequent longing gazes into his eyes implied the offer of intimacy was always on the table.

Most importantly, growing numbers of the town folks came to see Wilfred with their ailments increasing not only his reputation, but also the silver pennies in his oak casket, and most importantly his knowledge and experience. Wilfred kept notes of his experience with various herbal options for diseases. The barter system worked well in Cheap Street. Wilfred was never short of the butcher's best cuts and the freshest fruit and vegetables.

When Wilfred was sixteen a rumour went around Sherborne that Bishop Ealhstan was seriously ill. Wilfred was sorry to hear this as Ealhstan had welcomed Wilfred and his group of children with open arms to the Abbey after the tragic massacre of their families. He had allowed them to stay indefinitely till alternative families could be found to foster the children. The Abbey kitchen was always open for hungry young mouths. Wilfred only became aware later that some of the monks unselfishly gave their meagre rations to the growing children. All except Osric, the fat one.

Ealhstan never criticised Wilfred for his beliefs. In fact, he never seemed to find fault in anyone, he could only see virtues in everyone. Regardless, he would help them all to live a better life with his God's guidance. Ealhstan indeed had a most kind heart, unlike some of the other priests who were avoided by all the little boys.

Wilfred heard that the bishop had a large infected lump on his thigh, that he was pale and delirious. Wilfred was told that the monks were praying for his soul and that he was being bled. Wilfred was appalled. There were times when blood-letting was dangerous. Blood should not be let on the six 'fives' of each month. The five-night, ten-night, fifteen-night, twenty-night, twenty-five night and thirty-night were contra-indicated. The moon was currently waning; surely all knew that this was also the wrong time for bleeding. It was early spring which would normally be the best time to bleed out the evil humours that had been imbibed during winter, but the correct moon-time was essential.

An abscess needed draining and the standard application of a salve of garlic, leak, wine and ox gall. Possibly he was anaemic and would respond to some red wine warmed by a red-hot poker. Wilfred knocked hesitantly on the large oak door of the Bishop's house to ask if he could help.

Osric, the fat prior angrily opened the door. 'Yes, what do you want, are you Wilfred, the weird pagan boy who used to stay here?'

'Father,' said a nervous Wilfred, 'I have heard that Bishop Ealhstan is sick. He has always been kind to us since we arrived here. I wanted to see him to see if I can help in any way to make him better.'

However; Osric, the prior, an obese patronising man, laughed mockingly. 'You, you little Druid runt, you of the antichrist. We should burn you at the stake. You are an arrogant brat if you think for one moment that you could help when God's ordained priests cannot, piss off. Just piss off.'

Osric slammed the door shut rudely in his face. Wilfred felt totally crushed. There was only one important person in any of Osric's conversations. There was only one worthwhile opinion in the whole of Sherborne in Osric's view. It certainly wasn't Wilfred. It never would be Wilfred.

Wilfred hated the prior, he had an unpleasant reputation that lead all the small boys to avoid being alone especially with him. He had an unpleasant smell. He rarely was seen at the monk's washing conduit. Osric was supposed to mean divine ruler. There was not much divine about this Osric.

Three days later Ealhstan died. A long memorial service was held for him following which he was buried in the Abbey. Osric took the service. His eulogy to Ealhstan actually gave the credit for the bishop's good deeds largely to himself. He said Ealhstan had received the best treatment from the monks, but that God clearly has a greater need for him.

Osric also announced that he would be taking the Abbey services from now on till the new bishop was appointed. He asked the congregation to join him in prayer to ensure that God's preferred servant was chosen. Osric obviously thought he was by far the best man for the job.

Alfred, somewhat unhappy with Osric's self-praising eulogy stood up authoritatively in the front pew. 'My lord prior, may I also add a few words?' Alfred continued, he did not need Osric's approval. 'We should remember Ealhstan was a formidable warrior for Christ, not only did he show all the Christian virtues of poverty, humility and chastity in caring for his flock, he was also a warrior on the battlefield.'

'In the year of our lord 848, only nineteen years ago, he lead a Saxon army to victory against the Danes at the River Parrett. The ealdormen of Dorset and Somerset, Osric and Eanwulf supported Eahlstan with their fyrds and great courage. We should remember those three men as brave generous leaders, an example to us all.'

The congregation shuffled and murmured quietly in approval. They all knew that the Osric in the pulpit lacked those virtues, which was exactly what Alfred had meant them to see. Osric scowled, muttered thanks briefly and concluded the service.

Wilfred in the meantime was totally frustrated. He could hear the badger laughing at him from deep under the ground. It looked possible that the egregious Osric would be the bishop and totally exclude Wilfred from the infirmaria. Nobody in the Abbey believed Wilfred had anything to offer. Nobody supposed that such a young man rumoured to believe in the old spirits would have any relevant knowledge of healing, except old Brother David. Wilfred was sure he could have done something for the unfortunate bishop.

Wilfred resolved he would need to have greater knowledge of his father's treatments, and all other classic medical texts that he had not read yet. He would try to build up his reputation in the town.

He would need to understand the parts of the manuscripts that were obscure. Some of the remedies were things he had never heard of, like white moring, pellitory, and wolf's tail, was that a plant or part of a wolf's tail? Elencampne was something he did not know as was costmary. Wilfred was not sure he had the spelling correct as his father's hand was not always legible, and some of the pages had been scribbled by someone else. He would need to show his treatments could work. The young Druid aspiring healer would need to find somebody with knowledge of the old language and the old healing. He would not be mocked ever again by an ignorant smelly man even if he was considered eminent in the church hierarchy.

Shortly a pleasing rumour went around Sherborne that a better man would be the next bishop. All the citizens, except Osric were delighted to hear that Heahmund was appointed to be the next Bishop of Sherborne. He was currently rumoured to be in a retreat praying for strength to manage the onerous position. Osric was still acting bishop. Osric appeared very impressed with his importance, though was most surprised not to get the top job himself. Ambition and greed were much greater virtues than humility or poverty in Osric's world.

Wilfred thought Heahmund would need all that praying and strength to deal with Osric.

FEBRUARY 868

A messenger arrived from Alfred at Wilfred's room. He bowed to Wilfred for while his allegiance was mostly to the Christian god, some parts of his philosophy still inhabited the old Druid oak groves. 'Greetings Lord Wilfred, Prince Alfred would love to see you and tell you some good news.'

Wilfred headed to the royal hall to find Alfred sitting mesmerised on a strange pair of chairs with an exquisite young lady. One chair pointed forwards, and it was fixed to another chair pointing backwards so the couple could stare intimately, longingly into each other's eyes, as indeed this couple was. She had gorgeous long blonde hair down to her waist. After a few moments, Wilfred coughed politely.

Alfred dragged his gaze reluctantly from the eye-catching young lady to look at Wilfred. 'Ah, my personal healer and good friend, welcome, Wilfred this is Ealhswith, daughter of Æthelred Mucil, Ealdorman of the Gaini, one of Mercia's noble tribes, and of Eadburh of the Mercian royal family. Eadburh is a descendant of King Coenwulf of Mercia. So, you see Wilfred, when Ealhswith happily consented to become my wife I was deeply honoured. My Royal line does not go back quite as far in history.'

Wilfred thought that they were like a pair of elegant pure white swans pair-bonding for life. Alfred's transient dalliances with the odd goose or turkey were in the past. Sunniva and Alodia had been a pair of tasty turkeys.

Wilfred grasped Alfred's arm, 'My most sincere congratulations, my royal prince.' He turned to Ealhswith, bent down humbly on one knee and raised her dainty hand delicately to his lips, 'My lady Ealhswith, you are marrying the finest man I know, congratulations, may I be your liegeman in life and limb and earthly worship as well?'

Alfred smiled warmly, 'We need your more practical support, ensure we are both healthy for our wedding in April, though I have remained really well on your treatment.'

Wilfred responded, 'Mugwort tea is very good in maintaining a woman's wellbeing, and my dear prince, you should continue regular mint and ginger tea.'

APRIL 868

Alfred remained in blooming good health for the months leading up to his wedding day. He and Ealhswith married on a beautiful spring day. The sun shone from a cloudless sky. Newborn lambs and calves frolicked in the fields. Bees hummed around the colourful blossom. Sherborne Abbey was strewn with golden daffodils and white and yellow tulips. The altar was draped with a Wessex Wyvern banner. Bishop Heahmund took the service. He spoke sincerely from his heart to unite Alfred and Ealhswith's. The bishop radiated grace and humility. He was everything Osric was not. He was also brief and to the point, being well aware the people were looking forward impatiently to the wedding feast.

The choir boys sang like angels and every spare seat in the abbey was occupied. Even Wilfred was moved by the occasion. It must be like Alfred's heaven, but with love and beauty, not rules and threats. Elvina sat across the aisle from him happy with her bunch of young female friends. She never looked at Wilfred, not once. Alfred was right, she was pretty, very very pretty. At least there were no boys with her.

Afterwards at the wedding breakfast, sheep and cattle, chickens and ducks roasted over open bonfires outside. Cauldrons full of potatoes, carrots, onions and cabbage boiled over roaring log fires. Even the fat carcase of a roast pig was rotating slowly over a fire, a much-enjoyed rare delicacy in these parts. A roast boar's head decorated the bride and groom's table in the monastery dining hall, stuffed apples vanished down young throats and copious quantities of ale and mead disappeared down older throats.

King Æthelred rose and silence fell respectfully over the room.

'Men and women of Wessex,' he announced, 'Today is a wonderful day, a special day, one to cherish and remember amongst the dark days in the past, and unfortunately perhaps in the ones to come. God has blessed this day with blue skies, sunshine and magnificent flowers. Today we join my own dearly beloved brother and his most beautiful bride to celebrate their wedding day.'

'They are a special couple deserving each other. My brother has always given me full loyalty, he is my partner in the shield wall of life. The Danes will rue the day if they return. They will meet the best swordsman in Wessex. Alfred lives a true Christian life of honour and peace, of study and knowledge. He corrects my Latin and despairs of my Greek. Sadly, his friends say he is better looking than his king.'

'Today he pledges life-long fidelity to the only lady worthy of him. In her bridal gown bestrewn with flowers she is as beautiful as the day. Her blood line is the greatest in the kingdom. Her father, Æthelred Mucil, Ealdorman of the Gaini, is descended from one of Mercia's noble tribes. Her mother is Eadburh of the Mercian royal family, and therefore a descendant of the great King Coenwulf of Mercia.'

'I predict a great future for them and for their children. I am sure they will manage to produce sons and heirs more effectively than their current king, or my brothers who predeceased me! Please all join me in standing, raise your goblets and toast Alfred and Ealhswith!'

A thunderous roar echoed around the room as all rose, shouted 'Alfred and Ealhswith' downed their honey mead, and pounded the tables with fists, knives, goblets or anything to register the universal acclamation.

Numerous other toasts were vigorously celebrated. Many of the party moved back outside. The early summer sun still shone brightly. Couples danced energetically around a maypole erected a little prematurely in the year to celebrate the nuptials while the royal band played. Food and drink was consumed in prodigious quantities. The town had rarely had a better day.

When the sun set the couple were encouraged into their matrimonial bed, with ribald jests from the younger men and some grooming from the bridesmaids. Both Alfred and Ealhswith appeared deliriously happy, oblivious of the many well-wishers surrounding them. Elvina then took charge as she was often inclined to do even though only seventeen, and escorted family and friends out of the door for the bridal couple to spend their first night together undisturbed. She smacked Wilfred firmly on his posterior to hasten him out, a gesture which left him totally bewildered, was that because she liked him or because she didn't like him?

The guests then returned to the tables to endeavour unsuccessfully to drink all the residual ale and mead. Much later Wilfred was deeply asleep, and the full moon was high when a thunderous knocking on his door returned him unwillingly to a semi-conscious state. A royal page stood anxiously at his door. 'Come quickly please Wilfred, Prince Alfred is in severe pain.'

Wilfred grabbed a bag of medical equipment and ran anxiously to the royal hall. What could have happened? Perhaps Alfred had a pintle problem, perhaps with his foreskin. Maybe it could not be retracted or perhaps could not be pulled forward. Surely Alfred would have been circumcised as was the Christian tradition. Indeed, he had definitely been circumcised as Wilfred recalled from when he examined the royal personage's nether quarters.

Rumour had it that more than one woman had been seduced by Alfred's charm and good looks. Sunniva and Alodia implied they had both been intimately acquainted with the royal pintle on more than one occasion, but Wilfred was never sure if he believed their shameless boasting. That was one aspect of Alfred's life they never discussed. Presumably Alfred knew how to perform his husbandly duties. Had Ealhswith resisted his marital advances forcibly?

He entered the royal bedroom hurriedly to find Alfred lying on the bed looking pale and holding his abdomen in distressing pain. He was obviously having an acute flare up of his bowel inflammation. Ealhswith was looking very concerned.

'Dear Wilfred, thank you for coming so soon. I haven't done this before, you know er this,' she waved at the royal bed, 'did I do something awfully wrong? Does it hurt men so much to give women their seed? My mother said men obtained unbelievable pleasure, but women only suffered pain and embarrassment, I think she had it the wrong way around, I have never experienced anything as good, it was a fantastic sensation, but Alfred is in terrible pain! He has had the flux. It all happened suddenly after he.... after he... well you know. This must be entirely my fault!"

'My lady Ealhswith, I cannot think you would ever do anything wrong, tonight or at other times. It is a health problem poor Alfred has from time to time. I can probably fix it.'

Wilfred ran back to his room to collect some medication and his treatment horn, then returned hastily. First, he gave Alfred some henbane in mead, then more peppermint and ginger tea, half a cupful to drink.

Then he ordered Alfred to lie on his side and said, 'My lady Ealhswith, please close your eyes. Alfred, I am going to give you the other half cup full.'

Alfred went paler, 'How?' he asked anxiously, looking fearfully at Wilfred's horn.

Wilfred pulled up Alfred's nightgown, thus answering Alfred's question, inserted the end of a horn, open at both ends, into the royal anus and ran the other half cupful into the horn. Within five minutes Alfred was sleeping peacefully from the effect of mead and henbane.

At first light Wilfred was again reluctantly awoken by thunderous knocking on his door. Surprisingly, Alfred and Ealhswith stood there, Alfred's pain and pallor resolved, his zest for life obviously returned and the reins of three saddled horses in his hand. He grinned sheepishly, then grasped Wilfred's forearm firmly and said, 'Thanks little brother, I feel terrific, all the pain has gone. You will be pleased to know our marriage has been consummated again this morning. Fancy a horse ride before breakfast? Bring your hunting horn and give it a blast to frighten the foxes, or even the elves you believe in! It frightened the hell out of me!'

Wilfred returned the grasp, blinked uncomfortably at the bright sun, said 'No thanks, come back at lunch time. Those elves and faeries are descended from your Eve in your Bible. After her fall, she had many men intimately and then many children. She was ashamed to let God see them all and your God said, 'let those who were hidden from me be hidden from all mankind!' So, they remain invisible to this day. And by the way, that was not my hunting horn, my hunting horn is much bigger. You were very lucky I brought the right one!'

He closed the door in the hope that a little more sleep would cure his headache.

MAY 1ST 868

The sermon six days ago, may have been counterproductive. Osric had lectured, or rather hectored the congregation on the evils of the old religion in general. It was one of his favourite topics. He usually stared accusingly at Wilfred whenever he railed against the old ways. This time Osric singled out the appalling concept of the coming ancient Druid festival of Beltane. Appalling to Osric.

In Beltane, unmarried couples, even those married to someone else, copulated together enthusiastically on the land during the hours of darkness on May Day in the stupid belief, stupid in Osric's opinion, that spilling seed on the ground would improve its fertility. The Druids believed that the more partners on the one night, the more spilt seed, the better for the soil's fruitfulness. Marital status was not considered relevant just for that night, Unmarried partners, one's own spouse or as many of others' spouses as possible was the rule. The Druids thought fidelity was required for three hundred and sixty-four days a year.

Unfortunately, most of the congregation had not heard of this curious event, thus the concept generated significant interest amongst most of the males and amongst some of the younger females, not a few of whom were married to underperforming husbands. Many were not as shocked as Osric claimed to be. A religion that promoted adultery for one night a year might gain some converts! And Osric thought the congregation were paying close attention because they were sickened by the old faith!

Wilfred thought Osric must have been moon-struck to inform the congregation about Beltane. Wilfred would have loved to treat that for him! The recommended therapy was to fashion a whip from dolphin skin and flog the afflicted buffoon!

Following the sermon, Wilfred had obtained one of his blank pieces of parchment and written *Wilfred* and *Elvina* on it. He then touched the document to his forehead, his lips and his heart, and hid it in a hole in an oak tree deep in the forest. It was an old Druid spell to catch a girl-friend that his mother had told him about. He was sure this was wishful thinking. He was sure Elvina cared nothing for him. Beltane would just be another lonely day. A day for Wilfred to share tearfully with the demoralising badger.

Certainly, as sunset approached on Saturday May 1st, 868, there was a quiver of excitement in the air. The clouds in the sky were speckled with the rays of the setting sun like the scales of a fish. Wilfred recognised a mackerel sky. It portended a change. Perhaps in the weather when it would never be either wet nor dry for long periods the following day. Perhaps it portended a change in his life. His mother always said to beware of the mackerel sky for something major was about to happen. He did not really expect his life to improve. Something bad seemed a more likely event.

Wilfred was chatting amiably to some male not very close friends when Elvina called to him. He did not really have any close friends. Elvina had appeared to ignore him since they arrived in Sherborne nine years previously. However; he had observed discreetly that she had grown into a gorgeous striking woman, trim but shapely, with a pretty face peppered with freckles, and long red hair covering her beautiful breasts. She had established a reputation in town not only for her beauty, but her vivacious character and her loving nurturing of little children.

Older women sought her as a perfect marriage partner for their sons. Many of the young men had looked at her with lustful intent, some requested her company, only for all to be rejected politely but immediately.

Elvina had discretely been observing Wilfred develop into a tall young man, comely and surprisingly wise beyond his years in council, and very competent with wooden swords, though he repeatedly refused training with steel swords for fear of hurting someone. She heard about his medical skills from Orva. He often disappeared into the nearby forests for hours collecting medicinal plants for those prepared to try the healing skills of one so young.

Elva had heard that he ran many leagues through the forest every week. He certainly looked very fit.

While he socialised with the other young men, he preferred his own company. Elvina excited him, he could not explain how. He felt too insecure to approach her, though he desperately wanted her friendship.

Other girls sought his company. Sunniva and Alodia made it clear their bodies were available any time, any place with Wilfred, but they made it equally clear they were available for anything with just about any man any time. Wilfred found their lusty confidence intimidating. Wilfred did not especially like either of them or any of the other girls. He kept the beautiful Orva at arms-length, it was a very productive working relationship only. Mostly he preferred his own company and the solitary peace with the wild animals in the wood lands. Except the badger.

He strolled nervously over to Elvina and smiled hopefully. She put her hands up on his shoulders and looked searchingly into his eyes for a few moments without speaking. Wilfred recalled that fateful day nine years ago when she had addressed him in the same half-intimidating, half-affectionate fashion. But now he was expecting perhaps a reprimand for his adherence to the old Druid faith while she was becoming a more devout Christian. Perhaps she would support Osric's judgemental sermon about Beltane, though to date Wilfred had been too shy, too embarrassed, too young to enjoy the pleasures of that night.

'Wilfred,' she asked, 'How well do you know my friend Orva, she boasts she knows you well, even intimately?'

Wilfred blushed and stammered, 'er... not closely, not er intimately, she helps me collect herbs in the woods and prepare powders for treatments. She sits in my rooms when I am seeing sick people and I teach her the little I know about healing. We are helpful colleagues at work only. She...she has never...er.. never been in my loft bedroom or anything... like...like that. In fact, nobody else has ever been there, er.. with me'

Elvina looked thoughtfully into his eyes seeing only honesty. 'Wilfred, I have watched you grow into a handsome young man. I have watched you develop amazing skills as a healer. I have watched you absorb knowledge enthusiastically from anyone who will teach you. I see your passion to learn more and help others. You have not noticed my smiles. You have not noticed how much I think of you. I hope you will not reject my next request.'

Elvina paused, swallowed hard and continued, 'I could have participated in Beltane last year, I was old enough, but I was not ready. I am still a virgin. This year I am ready, but it will be only with you, only if I am your solitary lover for tonight, and after that I will never lie with you again unless we are married. What do you say to that? I hope you do not despise me for being too bold and uninhibited.'

Wilfred was totally stunned for a few moments; his improbable erotic fantasies and dreams were suddenly most unexpectedly translated into an immediate gorgeous reality. It was almost unbelievable. His missive to the oak tree, an old Druid spell had perhaps worked! He thought Elvina had been ignoring him for years. He thought she considered him to be worthless.

He placed his hands on Elvina's shoulders, and looked down incredulously into her beguiling green eyes. He could see passionate desire for him, much to his surprise. He responded in amazement, 'Do you really want me Elvina? I thought you did not think much of me.'

Elvina blushed in the fire light and looked up at him, 'I have always thought the world of you Wilfred since that tragic day nine years ago when our fates were thrown together forever. You fought for Cerdic's life. You led us all to safety. The very little ones would have died if you had not borne them on your back and kept them fed. Now the whole town talks of your healing skills and your modesty. All the little children tell me they will only see Wilfred if they are sick, because you are so gentle. I hear of your ambition and passion to improve your skills till you can cure cankers. Wilfred, I am all yours should you want me, now or preferably for ever.'

Wilfred with his face away from the firelight blushed invisibly in the dusk, swallowed hard and said, 'Oh yes, yes Elvina. I too thought the world of you since that day. I still cherish the memory of you giving me a kiss and a hug. Not once but twice. I have felt unloved from that moment to this.'

'I too have not done... er... this before either, but I have read the manuscripts of what I must do. I have seen many animals doing... doing it. I think I know what to do. Oh yes, I will see you under the oak on the sloping field in quarter of an hour. It will be a treasured experience to be with you, our first time will be with each other, and your wish for our future together is a totally wonderful prospect for me too. So, yes, yes my most treasured Elvina, I would love you to be my wife for ever and ever!'

Wilfred was in a turmoil of excitement and of nervousness. He hoped that he would be able to manage without making a fool of himself like his first time with ale. Sunniva and Alodia had heard what was happening and cheered, 'go Wilfred, go Elvina!' Both young lovers were embarrassed by this public acclaim and awareness.

Three hours later, Wilfred and Elvina ambled sleepily back into town, arms linked adoringly in postcoital bliss, their passion and respect for each other and their gentle natures had overcome her initial minimal discomfort and their awkward inexperienced fumbles in the dark. They had well and truly fulfilled their obligations to the Beltane festival and the fertility of the land. And to each other.

Suddenly a large male loomed up threateningly in front of them in the firelight. It was Hakon Halfnose, a part Saxon, part Dane bully, so called after losing half his nose in mortal combat in a shield-wall according to him. Other rumours suggested it was a feisty woman he underestimated in a rape attempt when he was drunk. Not all believed his conceited stories of triumphant shield walls. Orva was on his arm, but he pushed her callously away.

He leered drunkenly at Edwina, 'so Wilfred, it's my turn with Edwina now, my turn to spread a little seed on the land with her, get lost you pathetic little man. I'll show her how a real man, a man of experience with women does it. I'll give her more pleasure in one hour than you ever could.'

Wilfred stood resolutely, fearlessly in front of a trembling Edwina, 'if you touch one hair of her head Hakon it will be the blood red eagle for you, you, drunken half-cast, 'replied Wilfred. Hakon snatched Elvina's arm as she screamed, and Wilfred punched his residual nose. Hakon grabbed Wilfred's arm, 'meet me now with swords and I'll teach you a lesson you young weakling, and real steel, man to man, none of your children's pitiful wooden swords.'

Wilfred said angrily, 'I will be right back to accept your contemptible challenge. I will face you shortly with swords, steel to steel, man to man, and don't you dare touch Elvina ever again, or your guts will be spread on the land.' Hakon just laughed derisively.

Word went around the festive gathering quickly that bad blood would be spilt on the land as well as seed. A large animated crowd bearing flaming torches developed rapidly waiting impatiently in a large circle. While few liked Hakon, they recognised his apparent brute strength and his claim of experience fighting in more than one shield wall. Betting placed Wilfred at a four to once against any chance of winning, as money exchanged hands among excited crowd. Wilfred returned in a few moments with a large sword inscribed with obscure ancient engraving that had been his father's. None knew he often took the sword into the forest to practice with it, to gain the strength in his wrist and forearm to wield it dextrously. None knew he had become extremely adept with the ancient weapon.

'First blood?' he enquired of Hakon.

'First blood is for cowards, get on with this you puny weakling, no quarter neither asked nor given. You are a dead man walking. Winner takes Elvina. Indeed, I will take her with great pleasure whether she likes it or not beside your corpse, or perhaps as you breath your last watching us!'

He rushed at Wilfred who confidently sidestepped his first inebriated swing and ducked easily under the second. Hakon tried to focus, his next few thrusts were more calculated, but Wilfred effortlessly evaded his clumsy efforts by turning Hakon's blade aside each thrust with Peacemaker. Wilfred's few backers gained hope. Wilfred was quick on his feet and was surprisingly skilled with his heavy blade. He did not appear the least bit frightened.

Hakon stepped back, regained his breath, focussed his bloodshot eyes, raised his sword above his head and rushed at Wilfred swinging his sword downwards with a blow such as, so he claimed, had cleaved a man from skull to abdomen more than once previously. Wilfred took the full force of the blow above his head with his blade of steel held by a wrist of iron, a wrist also tempered by hours climbing the tallest oaks, tempered by swinging from one hand for increasing lengths of time. Times when letting go had seemed a good idea. Not now with the love of his life watching in terror.

He displayed unsuspected strength, with Peacemaker held aloft above his head meeting Hakon's blade with a mighty clash of steel. Sparks flew off into the darkness. Wilfred's arm remained unmoved above his head. Wilfred's sword, a pattern-welded sword crafted with the best European technology and imbued with Celtic mythological engraving and powers was unmarked, but Hakon's shattered into several pieces. Hakon stumbled, and aided by Wilfred's ankle and a shoulder charge, sprawled on the ground. In a flash, Wilfred's blade pricked his neck. Hakon pleaded pathetically for mercy.

Wilfred's blade travelled down his chest and abdomen. With a quick flick, he sliced through Hakon's breeches, revealing a shrunken manhood to the crowd, amid jeers of his proclaimed ability to perform much on this Beltane night.

'So Hakon,' said Wilfred contemptuously, 'your pintle is even smaller than your elf-shot nose. From now you will be known as Hakon-halfpintle, or perhaps Hakon noballs. It is said that you were born on a black moon Hakon. The size of your manhood confirms the old saying, no moon, no man. Your miserable pintle will never please a woman, nor father a child. Not even an incuba would bother to seduce you! Your presence at a Beltane festival is a mere delusion on your part.' The spectators roared with laughter; they were having more fun than even Osric predicted. Hakon whimpered pathetically, 'don't hurt me, Wilfred my good friend, I was only joking. I would not have hurt you.'

'Roll over and shut up,' ordered Wilfred.

Hakon rolled over pleased to conceal his threatened virility, only to feel the end of Wilfred's blade prick his spine where his second rib joined the spine, the start of the blood red eagle. Hakon rolled into the foetal position and sobbed, 'Mamma, Mamma!' Hakon saw his life suddenly ending, but slowly with the unspeakable agony of having his ribs spread open and his lungs ripped out. He saw his wide-spread reputation as a fierce warrior, one he had carefully unpleasantly cultivated for a year or two, rapidly disappearing.

The surprised crowd jeered in total disgust. Wilfred withdrew his sword and said, 'take your miserable body away, away from this town, should you threaten my family again, I will rip your lungs out, and don't think the valkyries would even contemplate taking a worthless grub like you to Valhalla, be gone!'

Hakon climbed to his feet shamefaced and pulling his breeches around him in embarrassment he stammered at Wilfred, 'next time we meet in the shield wall Saxon, and I have Head-Chopper in my hand it will be different. You will get the eagle then.'

Hakon slunk off followed by derisory laughter and was never seen in the town again. The crowd cheered and cheered in amazement and joy. They slapped Wilfred on the back and pumped his arms. Goblets full of ale were placed in his hands. The few who saw more in Wilfred than meets the eye were especially delighted with their winnings. They thought Wilfred was a strange fellow with miraculous healing powers. Most never saw him as an accomplished swordsman or a courageous warrior.

Elvina threw herself into Wilfred's arms, crying tears of relief, 'Wilfred, you complete idiot, you could have been killed, I have just found the love of my life and I thought I would lose you, Hakon is such a big heartless brute! You have saved me from being hideously raped. I did not know you could use that sword!'

'Nor did I really,' smiled Wilfred modestly, 'but I hoped the technique would be just the same as a wooden one, and this sword has ancient powers unknown to your Christ Lord or to the Danes and their Norse Gods! The truth of a man's courage is not in the size of his body or the extent of his boasting. I did not fear Hakon. I would not allow him or anyone to ever harm a hair of your head!'

Alfred and his new wife, Ealhswith emerged from the crowd thrusting a priest before them as Elvina hung on to Wilfred as though she would never ever let go. It was Osric. While the entire crowd were clearly enjoying all the night's entertainment, he was scowling unhappily. The stupid townsfolk had clearly misunderstood the dire message of his last sermon, a message from God about venal sin. He had been walking grumpily around the fields in the dark threatening hellfire at all the moving shadows. However; it was rumoured that he had disappeared in the dark briefly with an unwilling choir boy. It was not a process believed in the old philosophy to enhance the yield of the crops. It was also not something he had never done before according to the town rumours.

Alfred said joyfully, 'Wow Wilfred, you have become a great fighter, better than when you were eight. That was amazing, brilliant, courageous. Wilfred and Elvina, I overheard your earlier conversation. As you are aware Ealhswith and I can strongly recommend the pleasures of matrimony. Osric, you should finish the job, marry this pair now, and they will avoid your eternal damnation.'

The prior appeared hesitant. 'He,' Osric said scornfully pointing at Wilfred, 'is not a baptised Christian, and the bans have not been read in the church on three consecutive Sundays. It can't be done!'

Alfred replied, 'here are three gold coins, one for each ban, will that ease your spiritual anxieties?'

'And one more for the ceremony,' whined Osric. Alfred handed over one more coin. 'I will do it to save these unbelievers from hellfire,' grumbled Osric, greedily pocketing the money.

Osric continued, 'So, Wilfred and Elvina, I can reassure you that marriage is a great institution blessed by the Lord, are you both ready for this? The church will not approve of any more Beltane festivals for you both.'

Elvina again looked quizzically up into Wilfred's eyes facing him again with her hands on his shoulders. 'Last night Wilfred, I peeled an onion, wrapped it in a cloth and placed it under my pillow, then I prayed to St Thomas, let my truelove come tonight that I may behold his face and him in my kind arms embrace. I dreamt of you Wilfred!'

'Oh yes, I dream of you most nights Elvina,' he smiled, 'oh yes, let us be married and you can move into my house and we can return to the field every night!'

Thus in a few surprising hours, Wilfred and Elvina lost their virginity and gained a spouse, while Wilfred gained an unsought but deserved reputation as a very capable fearless swordsman with a magic blade.

Hakon was exposed unexpectedly as a blustering bully and a coward.

And Alfred moved the pair into a larger house in Cheap Street, where Wilfred planted a good-luck holly tree to continue his change of fortune.

Wilfred also transplanted his wyrt tun, he even had enough space in the bigger garden to grow some white poppies to add to his collection of pain relieving herbs.

AUGUST 868

T hree months went by. Wilfred and Elvina spent a lot of time together indoors or outside lost in the forest. Neither seemed able to believe their luck. Both had been disappointed to think erroneously that the other had no interest in them for years. They had some catching-up to do. Sunny summer afternoons spent together in the depths of the forest flew by as they discovered surprising but intimate delights about their own and the other's body. Elvina's new-found erotic skills with her lips and her fingers at times gave Wilfred the sensation of being speechless and completely paralysed from exquisite pleasure.

Wilfred was aware of the order of importance of the senses from old King Æthelberht of Kent's laws of compensation for damage to the senses. These in turn were based on the old Roman laws. They listed the eye and vision first, followed by hearing, then smell and taste before touch coming surprisingly last. Wilfred however could not remember being quite so overwhelmed by anything he had seen or heard.

Once Elvina looked at his glazed expression, 'Saint Augustine thought sensory experiences were taken from the outside to the inner soul, I don't think he meant this, but he may never have experienced this!'

'His loss, my gain,' whispered Wilfred.

Unlike their perilous journey of nine years ago, they both appreciated the beauty of the country. The bright colours of early summer enhanced their pleasures. The honeysuckle and dog roses reminded Wilfred of the scent of Elvina's body and the delicate pink of her soft skin. Beds of primroses softened the ground they lay on. Wilfred made daisy-chains in a pleasantly ineffective attempt to cover her modesty. Both hoped that life would continue like this blissful utopia for ever.

However; requests for Wilfred's healing powers as autumn approached curtailed their activities somewhat. Wilfred knew he must uncover the secrets in his father's papers to cure the infections of approaching cold wet weather.

Searching near the Abbey for assistance with his ancient manuscripts, Wilfred found an alms-house of old infirm men and women. They were no longer able to care for themselves. He entered to find a complete shambles of people and contents. They were in various stages of pitiable undress and uncleanliness; an unpleasant smell of unwashed bodies, stale urine and faeces pervaded the atmosphere. Many had blank faces, unseeing eyes, their bodies alive, but their spirit, their life spark, had departed. One of the side rooms had some ragged grimy children, probably all lonely sad orphans. They all cowered fearfully into a corner when Wilfred looked into their room. Osric and his like-minded few evil monks used to visit for their lewd gratification. Wilfred hoped he and Elvina would never grow old like that.

Amongst them all he spotted a wild looking old lady with dishevelled grey hair sprouting in all directions. Their eyes locked and some strange understanding passed between them. Prior to seeing Wilfred, she had retreated into a little place of peace deep inside her where no one had been for years. Wilfred raised her tenderly to her feet and took her into his house, then asked Elvina to help her to wash and dress in some clean clothes, and finally fed her a hearty meal. An amazing transformation took place. She became a middle-aged attractive woman with well-groomed hair and tidy apparel. She appeared intelligent and well aware of her surroundings. She enjoyed Elvina's good food. She really enjoyed a goblet or two of wine.

She sat back comfortably for a while silently contemplating her change in fortune, then spoke lucidly and gratefully. She smiled gratefully at Elvina and thanked her for the delicious meal and her personal help. Wilfred spoke to her, slightly hesitantly at first in his old Celtic tongue and somewhat surprisingly she responded in the same language with fluent animation. She was an old Druid priestess who knew Wilfred's father, Finnian, her name was Ceridwyn, though she kept all this to herself as she depended on the Christian monks for a little charity these days.

They spent the next few weeks studying Wilfred's documents. Ceridwyn explained all the old words Wilfred had never understood, or could not read, all the cryptic verses with obscure meanings, and then she taught him even more about the old Druid beliefs and medications.

Orva usually sat quietly at the back, absorbing information from Wilfred and Ceridwyn. Her expanding girth revealed that she was with child. She revealed to Elvina that she feared the child was Hakon's as he had raped her on the Beltane festival.

'Not only was he a bully, his performance was a one-minute wonder, then his manhood collapsed. I don't think you were in much danger on the Beltane night, Elvina. I hope this baby doesn't have half a nose. Anyway, the child may not be Hakon's. And no Elvina, it is not Wilfred's. Yes, I asked him. I asked hopefully more than once, but he was always keeping himself in hope for you.'

Elvina and Wilfred exchanged intimate smiles.

Ceridwyn continued her explanations, 'Elencampne is also known as horse-heal or elf dock. Pellitory is a nettle that grows on walls. It did not sting and was known as lichwort. I have not heard of white maring. Wolf's comb, not wolf's tail is an old Celtic term for the camellia.'

'Costmary is also known as the mint geranium, or ale cost as it is used in flavouring ale. Elvina do you know that costmary is mentioned in your bible, it is used as a herb to scent baths and to keep insects away?'

Elvina listening quietly laughed. 'Now I knew that, perhaps sometimes you should ask your wife Wilfred, just because I have red hair, I am not stupid!'

Wilfred looked at Ceridwyn, then at Elvina, 'sorry dearest, do you know what atterlothe is?'

Elvina smiled triumphantly, 'well yes I do, atter means poison, and atterlothe is blueweed or viper's bugloss. It is good for snakebites. Don't forget my mother knew some of this. And no, I have not heard of white maring either. We should have a wander through the forest to see if we can find some of these.'

Wilfred hugged Elvina and said apologetically, 'sorry dearest, I shall always ask you first. We should go with Ceridwyn, so you do not distract me from the task!'

Ceridwyn and Orva laughed and Elvina kicked Wilfred's shin.

Wilfred looked at Ceridwyn thoughtfully, 'my father said his life mission was to cure a cancer, but he gives few ideas in his papers, do you know Ceridwyn, how that may be done?'

Ceridwyn responded, 'Wilfred, I understand that your father had progressed his ideas further down that path than anyone else in the country. He obviously did not write that down unfortunately. I don't know, but to me it must be with the right herbs in the right dose at the right time for the right person with the appropriate cancer. We know nettles, mistletoe and bilberries have some effects on cancer. Finnian also mentions watercress and mugwort as possibly being helpful.'

'One thing I can add to Finnian's ideas is the right food with the right herbs. He did not try this idea much. I believe a diet with plenty of carrots, cauliflower, onions, peas and broccoli will help. Some foods appear to be good for one sort of tumour and some for another, for example dried red grape skins or red wine in moderation appear good for breast cancer, but bad for liver cancer. But a cure, Wilfred? Now that will be a challenge for you. One I sincerely believe you will achieve one day, for I see it clearly in your stars.'

Wilfred thanked Ceridwyn gratefully for all her help and knowledge, then asked about another topic.

'In my father's papers, he mentions the healing powers of gem stones, but does not say any more about them. Do you know about them as well?'

Ceridwyn smiled knowingly. 'Yes. That is another long complex subject. Many stones have healing powers, especially if it is your birthstone. All the birthstones are most effective during your own birth month. Elvina, many Christ-followers think birth-signs are pagan, but in your first chapter of Genesis it says God created the heavenly bodies to give light upon the earth and to be for signs, and for the seasons, and for days, and years. Even your bible believes the heavens give us signs of what is about to befall us. Some of the stones are extremely rare and costly, especially those found only in distant lands. I have no experience of those. I will tell you what I do know. See here, I have some of them, the less expensive or rare ones, in a necklace around my neck.'

Ceridwyn removed her necklace and placed it on the table in front of them. 'This one is garnet, it is the January birthstone. It can enhance passion and pleasure not that you two seem to need that. It increases energy and helps to keep travellers safe. Elvina, you look at me with scepticism, but in your bible, it says Noah used a garnet as a night light to guide him when his arc was floating on the floods.'

'The royal amethyst, this one,' Ceridwyn continued, 'is the February birthstone. Royal because it used to be for kings and queens only. It gives courage and gives relief when intoxicated or stressed. In Greek, amethyst means without drunkenness.'

Wilfred secretly wished he had worn one on the over-indulgent night of Alfred's wedding, and on the embarrassing day Alfred, Sunniva and Alodia took him to the 'Plume of Feathers.'

'And Elvina,' Ceridwyn continued, 'the amethyst is known to Christians as the Bishop's stone because it represents piety and humility. Every bishop I have ever seen wears one, even Osric, the prior has one. Osric actually believes he is pious, so I see it a symbol of self-deception as well for many of them.'

'Wilfred, the amethyst is said to be good for diseases of the blood and lungs.'

Ceridwyn pointed to the next stone on her necklace, 'Aquamarine, this one, is the March birthstone, it will interest you Wilfred. It is thought that if you drink water in which an aquamarine has been soaking it will heal diseases of the heart, liver and stomach. Roman sailors used to carve an effigy of Neptune, their sea god on aquamarine, and carry it on voyages to keep them safe.'

'Diamond is the April birthstone. I have not seen one, but it is said that if you give one to your wife, it guarantees eternal love. It should at the price of them. It also gives courage.'

'Emerald is the May birthstone. I don't have one of them either. Ealhswith wears one given to her by Alfred when they married. Being the month of the Beltane festival, you will not be surprised to know it promotes fertility, love and rebirth. The Romans dedicated it to Venus, their goddess of love and beauty.'

'Pearls like this one,' continued Ceridwyn pointing to the next jewel on her necklace, 'are the June birthstone. The Greeks thought they were formed from the tears of Aphrodite, their goddess of love. Others say they are formed from tears from heaven. They are said to represent purity. Your hypocritical priest Osric also wears one of these, but there is little pure about him. He used to sneak into the alms-house at night and go into the orphan children's room. I saw him with my own eyes. When he left soon after, there would always be some little boy in tears.'

'This next one is ruby, the July birthstone. The deep-red colour, like a woman's lips and nipples signifies love and passion. Some believe it protects from evil.'

Wilfred wondered silently, the red colour of nipples and lips seemed unlikely to protect any man from evil! Elvina caught his eye, she always knew exactly what he was thinking.

Ceridwyn continued, 'The August birthstone is this one, the peridot. See, it is a lighter green than emeralds and represents strength, both physical strength and courage.'

'Sapphire is the September birthstone. It is said to protect against evil and poison. It also symbolises purity and wisdom. Perhaps that is why I do not have one. Alfred should wear one, he is the wisest most pure person we know. But sadly, again that scum, Osric wears one. If a venomous snake is placed in a vessel containing a sapphire, it will die.' Ceridwyn looked at Elvina, 'perhaps your god can explain why it does not kill Osric, he is more venomous than most snakes!'

'This one is an opal, the October birthstone. It protects vision and repels evil.'

'This one, next to last, is a topaz. It is the November birthstone. It symbolises love and affection and improves the physical and mental strength of the wearer.'

'Finally, this one, a ruby, is the December birthstone. It is supposed to be a love charm and to give good fortune and success, as well as keep off evil spirits.'

Ceridwyn paused looking at Elvina. 'Well I had this necklace from my mother with my first moon blood. She said it would bring good fortune. It hasn't done me much good, well not for several decades till you found me in the alms house, Wilfred. Perhaps if I had a diamond, sapphire and emerald it would have been more beneficial, I certainly would have been wealthier! But then those beasts who kidnapped me when I was a young virgin would have stolen them. I will tell you about that shortly.'

'Wilfred, I will tell your more about the healing properties of other stones next time. Elvina and Orva look bored!'

Orva responded, 'no I am not bored, I am fascinated, where did you learn so much?'

Ceridwyn continued, 'well I will tell you my personal story. You must wonder how a silly old lady in an alms house can know anything! I lived in Mona, or Anglesea as the Romans had renamed it, when I was a young woman. Despite the Roman occupation and their heavy-handed law, my family were able to live secretly with the old beliefs. My father, while ostensibly a carpenter, had been a Druid priest.'

'He had been teaching me all about the role of a high priestess. On my tenth birthday I was taken to the west coast of Mona and into the sea on the dawn of the longest day to be immersed by the seventh wave, the seventh wave to promise health and long-life. I was dedicated to the Welsh Goddess Bloddwyn who was born of the foam of the seventh wave.' Ceridwyn explained.

'At the time of my first moon blood, my father and my mother took me to llyn Fan Fach waters, a dark lake high in the Welsh mountains. It was a sacred site for the Druids notable for the ashes of a maiden buried there, buried with meadowsweet which had become a floral tribute at burial sites. The Irish have a similar legend about the Celtic Goddess Brighid.'

'The lady of the lake, Nelferch, a Celtic Goddess, had taught the local physicians of Myddvai about herbal lore in the distant past. The first physician was Nelferch's son by an earthly father. Herbal healing powers have been passed down by word of mouth for centuries there. So that is where I learnt a great deal about herbal healing.'

Ceridwyn turned to Elvina, 'So you see that the herbal lore we use today, the treatments used by your Christian monks, originated from a Celtic Goddess. The Irish Christians have taken over Brighid to become their St. Bega. Our beliefs overlap extensively and are not mutually exclusive.'

Elvina looked thoughtful but remained silent.

Ceridwyn continued her extraordinary story. 'I was initiated as a Druid priestess on my sixteenth birthday. The only three days later I was forcibly abducted by four Saxons. After weeks of group rapes on the journey, they had arrived with me at their village near Sherborne.'

Ceridwyn continued, her voice alternating between anger and sobs. 'They were big brutal men, there was nothing I could do to fight them off. I had to tolerate their lechery, but I was able to curse them. I cursed them on a black moon, and I cursed them on a Hunter's moon. They all died within three years. Although three were married, they were unable to have children, and two were widely known by everyone else to have been cuckolded by their wives. As time went by, people suspected that I had the powers that sickened those four men, powers to make men impotent, even powers to kill with curses. Nobody ever harmed me again, but I lost my mind over those awful weeks.'

Ceridwyn's power sent shivers down her audience's backs

'I have some things for you, Wilfred. I have kept these hidden since I was a novice priestess, but you should read them. My captors looked in my bag and stole a few trinkets I had. They left me my necklace, if it had included a sapphire, a diamond and an emerald, they would probably have ripped it from my neck. However; they were illiterate savages who could not read one word and they ignored my books. This is Pliny's Natural History Chapters 12 -29, all the chapters about medicine, some pages from the Herbal and the Medicina de Quadrupedibus both of Apuleius. They are in Greek and Latin which I learned when young. They have many good ideas and treatments, but many of the plants they use only grow in their hot climate. You should know the contents.'

She turned to Elvina, 'I am eternally grateful to you for your hospitality; you are a much better person than the monks supposedly in charge of us in the alms-house. Some of them abuse the poor little orphan children in the alms-house. I hear you care for many of the young children while their parents work in the fields. If you and your group of young women were able to do so, someone should take over the care of the old people and especially the little abused orphans. They have never known love, or a nutritious diet or cleanliness since their parents were killed.'

'For you, Elvina, I have an old book of the poems of the bard Taliesin. He lived some three hundred years ago and wrote poems of King Urien of Rheged. He was partly a Druid bard and wrote of the wind and the trees. He loved nature. He also wrote of Moses and your Jesus. He could blend the old and new religions in his mind. Both believed in peace and the beauty of nature. Taliesin saw little difference between the old and new beliefs.'

Elvina received her gift with interest, turning it over and over in her hands. She appreciated the age and value of the gift. The leather binding was old and worn. The pages were all yellow around the edges. 'Thank you, Ceridwyn, it is truly beautiful, and obviously full of deep meaning. Wilfred has told me that you are named after the mother of Taliesin.'

'Yes' Ceridwyn replied, 'She was a Celtic Goddess. She had a son Morfran who was hideously ugly from birth. She decided to make a magic potion to give him wisdom instead as some form of compensation. Three drops of the potion were enough to give wisdom and the rest would be poisonous. However, the boy stirring the cauldron, with the magic potion, Gwion, spilt those three drops on his thumb which he then placed in his mouth gaining that wisdom himself.'

'Ceridwyn pursued him. Gwion tried to hide by shape shifting into different animals, but Ceridwyn followed, a greyhound to his hare, an otter to his fish, a hawk to his bird. Finally, Gwion hid as a grain of corn, but Ceridwyn swallowed him as a hen. She then reverted to a woman's form and soon realised she was pregnant with the spirit and knowledge of Gwion. She had meant to kill the baby, but he was so beautiful at birth she could not do that. She put the infant in a coracle upon the waves of the sea, but he was found on the shore by a Prince Elffin, the male equivalent of your name Elvina, and the child grew up to become Taliesin, the Bard.'

'Elvina,' continued Ceridwyn, 'Some of our herbs enable us to see the future, some of our women do this to give guidance to the people, would you like me to explain these to you?'

Elvina looked shocked, 'Oh no Ceridwyn, that sounds to be a sinful pagan belief, a sinful activity, how could I do anything like that?'

'Elvina,' responded Ceridwyn, 'You may have heard of Cyneheard, he was bishop of Wintan-ceastre over a hundred years ago. He approved the use of all herbs, he even complained that there were many in his book of herbs that he could not acquire. I have read your bible, in Mona we were taught about the beliefs of all religions. We learnt there was a lot of good in Christianity, we learnt there was even some good in the beliefs of the Norsemen!'

'In your Genesis Chapter one, verse twenty-nine it says, "Then God said, I give you every seed-bearing plant on the face of the whole earth, and every tree that has seed in its fruit. You shall have them for food." Christians in Germania again over a hundred years ago sent pepper, cinnamon and frankincense to Abbess Tetta Cuniberg in Wimborne not very far from here a hundred years ago. Women use herbs in your Christian Church.'

Elvina looked very dubious, 'it doesn't say you should smoke them.'

Ceridwyn continued, 'on the contrary, in your bible there are ovates or seers, you call them prophets. Their foresight is important to Christians. How do you think they achieved that? The word kaneh-bosm appears several times, that means smoking hemp! If it is used in your bible how can it be sinful? Your monks and priests tell you it is sinful, but I think buggering little boys, and coercing the last coin from the poor is worse!'

'OK, OK' conceded Elvina reluctantly, 'we will try it, but in private sometime later, oh no, do you want me to try it now?'

Wilfred and Orva nodded enthusiastically, they were most curious to see this in practice. Wilfred could add this to his predictions of the future through sheep entrails.

Ceridwyn looked up at Wilfred's shelf of herbs. She picked up a brown capped mushroom pot and another containing mushrooms with red tops and white spots. 'One or both will enable you to see the future. Too much of the red one will turn you into a Viking Berserker! We are frightened enough of you already Elvina!'

'We dry these and grind them to powder, and then dissolve a pinch in hot water. Soon after drinking this pictures will come to your head for a short while. I have done this often and come to no harm beyond seeing the most dreadful things which later came to pass unfortunately. Sometimes I see happy things,' promised Ceridwyn

Elvina held the steaming cup and looked inquisitively, anxiously at Wilfred. He nodded agreement. She swallowed the contents of the cup slowly.

A few moments later she lapsed into a trance like state. Brightly coloured but blurred visions started swirling though her head. Then more clear pictures emerged from the kaleidoscope. She saw herself with three little children, she saw Alfred and Ealhswith with five children, two boys and three girls, she saw Alfred retreating from battles, his army defeated many times, then Alfred hiding amongst some reeds with only a few followers, then Alfred and...and... Wilfred in the front row of a shield wall, Wilfred with his Celtic blade about to be attacked by a man nearly twice his size, then finally a crowned Alfred sitting in a huge hall apparently in triumph. The Wessex Wyvern flew above the Raven Banner. Danes swore fealty to Alfred, their hands between Alfred's. Wilfred was not to be seen.

Elvina awoke in horror. She clasped Wilfred, 'Oh husband, do not fight in Alfred's shield wall. I cannot see you afterwards.' she sobbed.

Ceridwyn watched as Elvina recovered. 'Well it did you no harm, but it is frightening. Wilfred will have a long life, fear not. A similar effect can be achieved with mistletoe and honey mead, but the mushroom seems most vivid. Maybe you could try that one another time.'

Wilfred by now had quite good Latin and Greek now and Elvina was learning Greek. The monks, however, were reluctant to teach women.

They thought that women should learn how to run a household. Cooking and sewing and such chores were what they recommended.

Nevertheless, Alfred believed that men and women should acquire as much classical knowledge as possible. Alfred persuaded the monks to run classes for the females. Wilfred was delighted. He had wondered a few years ago how he would be able to read these ancient texts with all their great knowledge and information. Now he and Elvina together would be able to acquire the knowledge in these old manuscripts of Ceridwyn's. Her abduction unfortunately occurred before she had a really strong grasp of classical languages.

There was no limit to the knowledge that he needed, all sources from any country could be useful, could give new ideas and remedies.

NOVEMBER 28TH 868

E lvina and Wilfred awoke and broke their fast when Elvina said, 'Can I talk to you seriously beloved husband?' Elvina faced Wilfred with her hands on his shoulders. He knew he should listen, this was only when she had something important to say, though it was not guaranteed to be favourable to him.

'Wilfred today is the fourth Sunday before Christmas, it is the start of Advent. Soon we will celebrate the birth of our Lord Jesus Christ.' She paused.

'Wilfred, I know you believe one's own religion is after all a matter between oneself and one's Maker and no one else's, but your old gods are not very different from the new Christ God. He does not only live in sterile stone buildings in Rome. He is the sun that ripens our crops and the moon that guides us at night, he is in the breeze that rustles the oak leaves of the Druid trees, he is in the new life of the young fawn, he is in the gentle rain that falls from the sky at night to feed our wheat, he is a gentle god who says thou shalt not murder. He is all the things you believe in; his life force is what you feel every day in the fields and the forests.'

'Dear Wilfred, you know more about the old folk lore, of healing herbs and the ways of the Druids than anyone living. You have learnt about the cures of the ancient Greeks and Romans from the classic texts. None of the brothers in the infirmaria know as much as you. You are known even by all the honest Christians as the best healer in this part of Wessex. You have so many friends, yet you seem unaware of that. The monks have only one advantage over you; they use the power of prayer to our Lord. Perhaps if you were to add that to your skills you would be an even better lach.'

'Alfred tells me that too,' responded Wilfred, 'but admits that my treatments are usually more effective than his monks' prayers. Perhaps that is because we are all sinners in the eyes of your God. Your monks and brothers, the prior and the bishop like the church's authoritarian structure to control the lives and thoughts of their congregation and to collect their moneys!'

Elvina continued, 'The 23rd Psalm says "The Lord is my shepherd; I shall not want. He maketh me to lie down in green pastures: he leadeth me beside the still waters. He restoreth my soul: he leadeth me in the paths of righteousness for his name's sake. Yea, though I walk through the valley of the shadow of death, I will fear no evil: for thou art with me; thy rod and thy staff they comfort me. Thou preparest a table before me in the presence of mine enemies: thou anointest my head with oil; my cup runneth over. Surely goodness and mercy shall follow me all the days of my life: and I will dwell in the house of the Lord forever."'

'He does not make you lie down in stone cities, he loves the green pastures, the lakes and the rivers, he is not afraid of dark valleys, he is you, Wilfred!'

'Elvina, beloved wife, I understand how you see your faith and I agree with all you say. When I admire the wonders of a sunset or the beauty of the moon, I see a creator who has provided for us all regardless of the name we give him, or her,' he added hastily, seeing Elvina's eyes flash.

'But then Elvina, why does the priest threaten us all the time with hell fire and damnation, your God spends all his time telling us we have been sinful and will suffer. Love is wonderful, but he seems obsessed with how bad it is, he claims to offer peace and love, but from his pulpit he only offers hate and brutality. Why then does Osric accept bribes, bugger choir boys, yet condemn us for the beauty of procreation? Your God has this list of things we mustn't do, especially the seventh one about making love. It is a list of fear not hope, of punishment not beauty, of guilt not happiness.'

'Because Wilfred, that is Osric's Christianity, but you are married to me!' They embraced, and Wilfred said' 'I shall come to church with you today, I believe the new bishop is preaching, not Osric. I will be interested to listen.'

JANUARY 869

Christmas passed uneventfully, happily. It was a time of celebration and the turning of the year for new and old faiths.

Ceridwyn visited Wilfred with a collection of gemstones. 'Here are some other stones that have healing powers, the unfortunate sufferers who see you should wear the appropriate stone to enhance the power of your herbal treatment. Maybe they will help in your quest to cure cancer.'

'This one is the seashell, Abalone. It is helpful for problems with muscles and joints, it will give you strength in battle. It will help with problems from the heart and digestion and cheer you up when you are feeling down.'

'That's useful,' responded Wilfred, 'I could give one to Alfred when he has the bloody flux.' Wilfred actually, privately thought he should wear one next time his cancer treatment failed yet again.

'This one is Agate, it is the oldest healing stone. It is good to wear in battle, especially the black or brown ones. It gives strength and confidence and brings victory.'

'H'm' replied Wilfred, 'from what I hear we might need that soon when the Danes attack Wessex.'

'This is an important one for me,' said Ceridwyn holding out a Blue Agate."

'These honour Ceridwyn, the Welsh goddess after whom I am named. When you are at the bottom of the cycles of life, it will bring you peace and tranquillity until the cycle moves up again. I have been at the low ebb for many years, but you Wilfred have pulled me up, you and Elvina. You and Alfred will make this world a better place.'

'This is a Bloodstone. The ancient Greeks thought it had magic properties. This one comes from the island of Rum in the Scottish Hebrides. It is said to remove poisons from the body and gives more energy. It sharpens the mind when predicting the future with entrails or herbs. It also renders the wearer less visible and can bring rain to the forests.'

'Well that will be good in very hot summers,' replied Wilfred, 'and maybe it will remove the poisons of cancer.' He thought for a moment, then asked, 'is it true that the ancient Druid lords could make themselves invisible, Ceridwyn?'

'Some of the really ancient myths said the old time-lords could do this, but I don't think so. My father did not believe that could be done. Carrying a bloodstone helped. What they could do was to create thick mist to hide in. They made a fire of oak leaves, twigs and logs, sprinkled on a mixture of dried foxglove, thistle and gorse flowers, then covered it with peat. A purple mist comes from the fire and spreads around to hide anyone.'

Ceridwyn continue to explain the benefits of each of her collection of semi-precious stones. 'This is Carnelian. It is a good one for a healer. It increases courage and compassion. It will bring good luck and develop your hidden talents.'

'And this last one is a Moonstone. It is connected to the moon and the triple goddess. It is a stone of destiny for women and determines fertility.'

'So, Wilfred, I do not know if gemstones will help in your quest. It may depend upon which part of the body is involved, but as you say, the blood stone may be worth trying to remove the poisons of cancer.'

Wilfred had more notes to supplement his manuscripts about herbs and some ideas to try. He thought carnelian would give him more wisdom and agate protect him in battle if he had the misfortune to ever be in a shield wall. As a healer he could suggest opals, rubies and bloodstone to ward of evils and poisons.

JUNE 12TH 869

One day when Elvina was busy elsewhere, and after nine months' tuition, Ceridwyn said, 'Wilfred you know everything I ever learned and much more beyond. You have learnt everything in your father's manuscripts and much from the masters of Greek and Roman medicine. You have learnt some of the cures of the physicians of Myddvai, the ones I could remember. Don't however, expect much reward as a healer. The merchants and traders will collect more gold than you. Their greedy fingers are like the tumours you treat, stealing covertly through healthy bodies for their own gain.

Selling slaves is more lucrative than selling herbs. Even entertainers will earn more than you. The kings and nobles prefer to be entertained by fools. They enjoy laughter more than the pain associated with battlefield injuries, death and disease.'

'In the absence of our fellow Celts to confirm this in a proper initiation ceremony, I now declare that you have the wisdom, knowledge and status of a high priest. Undress, then bring me your sword.'

Wilfred handed Ceridwyn Peacemaker, his magic Celtic sword. She anointed his naked body with oil of primrose and vervain on his forehead, over his heart and on his hands. Vervain was believed to enhance male vigour and health. For women, it would enhance breast size and lactation, though if taken when with child it could cause loss of that child. She took his sword and made a small cut below his left nipple. Wilfred did not flinch.

Ceridwyn then recited the traditional words of valor taillaidant, 'You did feel in your flesh the bite of the sword. Now that you know the pain it can inflict, may you use it when only essential without weakening or shuddering, or taking any pleasure. Now go forth and bring your goodness into this changed world.'

'Two more things you must do, firstly, visit the ring stones two days to the East. They possess a power I cannot describe, but you will feel. I heard from Elvina that you walked past them all those years ago after your village was attacked.'

'You must go next week to be there for the sunrise of the festival of Alban Hefin. The Sun god is at the peak of his powers and will be crowned by the Goddess. It is also sad because the power of the sun wanes from this moment. The Holly King is born to be crowned at Alban Arthan. Just being there will give your healing powers a greater spiritual dimension.'

Make sure you wear a garnet and an opal to protect you from the evil eye while travelling. You may be attacked by beings from this world or shadows from the otherworld visiting ring stones at Alban Hefin. Take some red clover and betony before you go and wear a clove of garlic to protect you from evil spirits. Even better if you can find them is some powdered myrrh and frankincense dissolved in wine with some stone shavings of jet first thing in the morning when fasting for three days before you leave to protect you from seduction by an incuba.'

'Secondly you must enter the waves next time you are at the coast and walk out till immersed by the seventh wave. Take a vessel with you for that water of your first seventh wave will make any of your treatments more potent. Save it for special persons or special sicknesses. Any coast will suffice though the west coast of Mona is most potent.'

'Then introduce these militant and miserable Christ followers to the beauty of nature, and the need to exist with all livings things, rather than destroy our land.'

JUNE 19TH 869

W ilfred borrowed a horse from Alfred's stable. He packed some bread, meat and fruit and set off back east towards the Danish strongholds and his childhood home. He avoided inhabited areas. Twice he saw distant smoke, probably from burning houses. It was an unusually wet summer, fire wood would rarely light. Crops were waterlogged, and a winter famine threatened. Once on the great plain he travelled by night, occasionally lit by a pale moon, mostly in pouring rain. Sometimes the stars pointed the way east, sometimes some atavistic memory guided both man and horse. Wilfred saw no other human beings, though the night life scurried secretively around him. Owls and wolves had to eat regardless of the weather.

Wilfred kept mostly dry and warm thanks to the great bear coat Alfred had given him. It was said to have come from Russia and been once worn by a great Viking warrior. On his second night travelling the ancient great ring stones loomed up in the swirling mist before him. The ring stones were built some half a millennium after burials started here as a monument to the powers of the original great lords of the earth, men whose powers could only be imagined today. Wilfred hoped that they would not harm a modern custodian of the old ways.

A summer storm was at its height. The lightning seemed to target the tall stones and flickered around the central stone triads. The stones were old, old long before the collective memory of the elders. Some said the stones had been planted by the gods at the dawn of time. Some said they were planted by Merlin, King Arthur's Druid priest to commemorate a fierce battle between the Britons and Saxons. They said Merlin took the stones from Ireland after a fight in which thousands of courageous Irish warriors died fighting to save their mystical stones. The Irish called them the Giants' Dance and believed the gods had taken them from a great hot desert in a country far to the south and placed them in Ireland.

Others said that the Saxon warrior king Hengist invited Vortigen, the Celtic king to a feast there under a truce but treacherously slew all the Celts at night while they slept. Hengist was so ashamed afterwards that he erected the stones as a monument to atone for his appalling deceit.

Ceridwyn said the three stones, two uprights and one across the top represented the triple goddess. The maiden stood on one side representing the waxing moon, a symbol of new beginnings, birth and youthful zest for life. The mother stood on the other side representing the full moon, ripeness and fertility, family life and stability, a symbol of power. Across the top lay the crone representing the waning moon, wisdom and repose, but ultimately endings and death. They stood three or four times the height of a man in a circle, surrounded by many more stones in a greater circle.

A strange feeling overcame Wilfred. It felt as though the door to the otherworld was open and ghostly figures were passing near him going in and out. Wilfred knew about Samhain, the ancient Celtic festival marking the beginning of winter, when the souls of the dead walked the earth, when the Viking bridge of swords to the otherworld was open, but here, today at Stanheng on the summer solstice, the undead seemed to be all around him. The space between the two worlds appeared to have closed, indeed the space between the past and present also seemed non-existent tonight.

Each flash of lightning seemed to be absorbed by the stones, to reinforce their radiant power. Each flash illuminated the shadow folk, dozens of vague human shapes outside the larger circle. They seemed to flow in and out of an outer ring of burial holes in the ground. These holes were open and lit by some internal ghostly glow. These must be the original burial mounds of the great Druids of yesteryear that his father had told him about.

Whether these were gods, benign or malignant, come to Earth in human-like form, or the sawol of the recently dead, Wilfred could not say. He wished they would keep their distance. Occasionally he felt things brush past him, invisible entities that terrified him.

Wilfred's horse snickered continually with fear. Wilfred felt very alone and full of trepidation. He felt helpless confronted by powers he had not experienced, powers beyond his control or understanding. There was little he could do except hope for the best. He tethered the horse and settled down for the night sheltering as much as possible under the top stone, an animal skin below him and the bear coat over him. Initially unable to sleep, he swallowed a few drops of dissolved black nightshade berries and leaves. His father had taught him to distinguish the black berries from deadly nightshade by the shape of the leaves. Wilfred soon fell asleep but bizarre dreams filled his head through the short night. Coloured shapes, some humanoid, some like monsters swirled before him. Cries of anguish and pain accompanied them.

Wilfred awoke before the dawn. He was totally alone in complete silence. Not even the birds chirped here for the rising son. The shadow walkers and spectres of the night had gone. He looked to the East where the bright sky indicated the impending sunrise. It was about to surface behind a stone. Ceridwyn had told him that was the Devil's stone. Apparently, the Devil bought the stones from an Irish woman, and dropped them on the plain, one of them killing a priestess underneath it hence it was called the Devil's stone.

The sunrise brought a feeling of hope and peace, the warmth reaching into Wilfred's soul. He felt empowered to see into other's minds, to understand their needs, to give hope with his healing. It was a complete reversal of the fears of the night. Wilfred broke bread and ate; he gave an apple to the horse that was grazing contentedly. After an hour unsuccessfully trying to understand and analyse his feelings, Wilfred mounted up and headed for home feeling that he was somehow, inexplicably changed.

Shortly after he returned home, Alfred sent a messenger to their door. Elvina, delighted to have Wilfred home said, 'ignore the knock on the door, stay here with me.' On the third occasion, an hour later a more contented Elvina opened the door. 'Prince Alfred would like to see Wilfred; would he be able to come to the Royal Pavilion?'

Wilfred and Elvina were ushered into the royal presence. Elvina believed that an invitation to one of them was an invitation for both of them. Even Alfred knew not to disagree with her. King Æthelred and Alfred were pouring over a map of Mercia. Æthelred looked up. 'Ah Wilfred, Alfred tells me that you are skilled in the art of healing, though I understand that some of your methods do not have the full approval of our bishop. We are taking an army to Mercia at the request of King Burgred, my brother in law. Burgred is married to our sister, Æthelswith. A Danish army has invaded his kingdom.'

'One of the kings of Mercia, Offa,' Æthelred continued, 'built a huge dyke to keep the Welsh out, perhaps he should have built it the other side of Mercia to keep the Danes out! Burgred tells me his soldiers cut of the ears of any Welshmen found on his side of the dyke, and in return the Welsh hang any Mercian found on the Welsh side!'

Elvina was not one to be left out. 'My lord king, you would be aware then that Offa was married to Cynethryth, a descendant of King Penda, and that they ruled together. Her head was engraved on coins and she endowed many churches. She finally became an abbess at Cookham after the death of Offa. My mother said Cynethryth had suggested a wall on the other side to keep the Danes out. Sadly a woman's wisdom was ignored yet again to the detriment of all Mercia today!'

Alfred took over the conversation, 'Thank you for that idea, Elvina,' he was not going to disagree, but he did change the topic of conversation, 'I was only four when Æthelswith married Burgred. The Great Heathen Danish Army has increased in size and warlike intent since they first started landing here three years ago. They are no longer a raiding party; they seek to take Northumberland, Mercia and finally Wessex with fire and sword. They bring their women and children, a clear indication they intend to stay here. This is a much nicer place than Sweden or Norway, I would much rather be here too, but we shall have to fight them resolutely to retain this land.'

'The Danes have persuaded many Swedish and Norwegian men to join them because they see our country as low hanging fruit, easy to pick. It is said they are led by the three sons of Ragnar Lodbrok. Ragnar was the son of the Swedish King Sigurd Hring. I have read the ode to Ragnar, written about his life as he lay dying. It describes his many battles over lands near and far. In it he sneers at Christianity.'

'He was a cruel barbarian, but a great warrior general. It is said he slew a serpent as big as a house to claim his first bride. He sacked Paris and defeated the French Army. He was married three times and has many sons. I am told three of them, Ivar the Boneless, Halfdan Ragnarsson and Sigurd Snake-in-the-Eye are here leading the army. If they have half of his skills we are facing a formidable foe. They seek vengeance because King Aella of Northumberland captured Lodbrok and threw him in a pit of poisonous snakes to die.'

'St Paul was bitten by a poisonous snake on the island of Malta while collecting firewood but came to no harm because of his faith in Jesus. Ragnar died because he lacked that faith. His sons are determined to kill King Aella slowly, painfully in revenge.'

Æthelred announced, 'We will show them the Saxon warrior is more than a match for any Dane. We will also have the pleasure of seeing our sister Æthelswith. Their hospitality is legendary.'

'There may be some casualties, especially amongst the Danes. We would like you to come along Wilfred and demonstrate your accomplishments. There will be our army to keep strong and healthy. You can keep an eye on their provisions, check that our troops are well fed and fit for battle and ensure our water supply is unpolluted. But you know all that. You can tell my engineers where to place the dunnykins. We will give you a wagon and a couple of horses for the trip. You may keep them in the royal stable, they are all yours for your future needs.' continued Æthelred.

Three days later the army of Wessex was assembled ready to move out. Wilfred had packed his new wagon and hitched up the horses, a fine pair of dragan horses, built for endurance, not speed. He went to say his fond farewells to Elvina. A search failed to locate her. She was not in the house, nor in the garden. Wilfred was scratching his head at the front door when he spotted Elvina now sitting at the front of his wagon, next to Orva and her baby, with the reins firmly in her hand.

Before he could open his mouth, she said, 'Don't argue, we agreed when we were married to "in sickness and in health". Well we are off to do the sickness part. The king's request obviously included me. I could tell that even if you could not.'

'You have taught me a lot about healing and you say I am indispensable so here I am. If there is a big battle, there may be many wounded warriors. Remember you once quoted Hippocrates to me. He said, "war is the only proper school for a surgeon." Well since you men have not yet learnt to solve disagreements without war, here I am to learn. You will need Orva as well. Get up!'

Elvina flashed her green eyes at him and shook her flaming red hair. Wilfred recognised the danger signals. He had already learned there were times when he would not win an argument. This looked like another such time. He hopped up beside her to be rewarded with a kiss and a triumphant crack of the whip. Wilfred could see the horses also knew who was the boss!

Elvina continued, 'Do you remember Seaxburh, she was Queen of Wessex for a year some two hundred years ago, after her husband Cenwalh died. If a woman can be Queen of Wessex for a year, then I'm sure I can be queen of a wagon for a week or two!' Or queen of a house for many years thought Wilfred to himself.

Elvina persisted, 'besides, the Vikings had shield-maidens, warrior women. They could fight as well as men. I hear they were buried with their swords and shields. If the enemy can have shield-maidens, then the Anglo-Saxons should have one as well! Me!'

Wilfred could only disagree weakly, 'Yes, but your Christian Church thought women should be more submissive and have a passive role in life. The term 'peace-weaver' is preferred by your priests!'

'That's the part of the church designed by men; it's bound to have some serious intrinsic flaws. Women should choose their own role in life, and have a significant say in running the country,' flung back Elvina. 'I shall be a peace-weaver when the battles are over, well maybe! Now I am a shield-maiden!'

Elvina gave him another kiss while Orva laughed. Even her baby's laugh sounded amused. Wilfred sat in silence. The gentle does, yes, and even the wolves in the forest were less combative, less intimidating.

They followed Æthelred's army, some three or four thousand fierce warriors, helms and swords gleaming, following the Wessex Wyvern banner and thirsting for Danish blood.

Elvina watched them marching ahead of their wagon with some sadness and some disbelief. Turning to Wilfred she asked, 'do they all expect to be heroes, do they all expect to return unharmed to their parents or wives or children. Some will never come back leaving widows and orphans, some will return with severe wounds, perhaps they will lose an arm or a leg and be a burden on their families for the rest of their days. Yet at this stage they are full of swagger and excitement, feelings they will not have when the swords and axes start to bite.'

'The Danish army will be just the same, full of strong young men bursting with bravado, all convinced that disagreements can only be solved on a battlefield, all convinced of their own immortality and the frailty of the enemy.'

Elvina continued, not pausing to give Wilfred a chance to speak. 'When will men learn to find other ways to settle arguments. When will they think of the folks left behind to worry and fend for themselves. One day I am going to give Æthelred and Alfred a good talking to! Why is it that some things are obvious to women from leagues away, yet men can't see them when they are under their noses?'

Wilfred thought privately that the two royal brothers would have a better idea of how to deal with the three sons of Ragnar Lodbrok than with Elvina.

The men of Wessex joined Burgred and his Mercian army in Tamworth. Burgred hosted a magnificent feast for all the nobility of Mercia and Wessex.

Alfred presented Æthelswith a ring he had commissioned at the jeweller's in Cheap Street. It was a simple gold hoop expanding at the shoulders into a circular bezel all composed of a fine intricate network of gold lace in an ancient Celtic pattern. The shoulders and bezel were studded around with fine pearls. The centre of the bezel was decorated with the Wessex Wyvern, and the shoulders each with a bear. Inside the hoop was engraved Æthelswith Regna. The ring was the most exquisite piece of craftmanship Æthelswith had ever seen. She stood silently tears running down her face as she studied the ring on her finger. Finally, she gave Alfred a big brotherly hug and turned to show her gift to Burgred.

The jeweller had shown the design to Wilfred and at Wilfred's suggestion made slight changes to the central animal, so it resembled more the Wyvern than the Agnus Die lamb originally suggested by Alfred. Neither could be sure if Alfred had noticed the difference!

Æthelswith stood up again. 'Æthelred and Alfred, thank you again for this precious gift, now it is our turn, my husband, King Burgred and I have a gift for each of you. A gift to thank you for coming to help us repel the pagan hordes. You will be aware of St Chad who brought Christianity to the Litchfield area of Mercia when he was bishop there two centuries ago.

He developed a scriptorium there and to this day they produce the most beautiful books.'

'We have copies of their Gospels, one for each of you. Thank you.'

Æthelred accepted his with astonishment and looked appreciatively through the pages. 'Why it is exquisite, the decorations on the carpet pages are unsurpassed. I have the Gospels of Matthew and Mark. Oh, and here is part of the Gospel of Luke, have I received a bit of Alfred's?'

Alfred and Ealhswith were perusing his gift. Alfred was struck dumb. He could not have received a gift of more significance, a precious item bringing him closer to his lord. Ealhswith stood up to speak for Alfred, 'My lord Burgred and Æthelswith, my husband is unusually lost for words at this precious gift, he will treasure it all his days. St Chad is one of his most admired saints, he was a truly great man bringing the faith to our ancestors. And yes, my lord Æthelred, we have the Gospel of John and most of the Gospel of Luke. We will not argue as long as we can sometimes exchange copies.'

Burgred also provided entertainment for all the warriors of both nations. A few days feasting, drinking, music and dancing girls, and then swordplay followed. As Elvina had observed, the men of Wessex were full of swagger and bluster. They boasted they would kill many more Danes than the Mercian men. Burgred's Mercians disputed this. Again, while other men were still able to listen and remain conscious, the boasts of heroism in battle increased in noise and valour as ale and mead were consumed in heroic quantities.

Warriors of both armies were not in a fit state for some weapons training till midday. Practice between allies was supposed to be to first blood, though Wilfred had a few deep wounds to suture. An advance guard proceeded to Nottingham Castle to besiege the Danes.

The chance of a major battle was already receding as Burgred had previously paid off the Danish army and most had left for York. The men of Wessex and Mercia professed disappointment. Burgred and the Danes had agreed to a two-year truce, but Alfred expected that the Danes would be back after the winter following the coming one, when the treaty expired, and the blood money was gone.

The men of Wessex on the other hand were fairly convinced the Danes had heard they were coming and fled in fear for their lives.

A few hundred Danes were not prepared to leave without any honourable conflict. Thor's blood lust outweighed discretion. However, they were rapidly crushed by the larger combined Saxon force. Few injuries ended up on Wilfred's wagon as there were not many Danish survivors. There were some wounds to suture, and apply Wilfred's salve of yarrow, tansy and scarlet pimpernel boiled in lard. Some had severe abdominal wounds where death was inevitable. Some wine, eryngo, poppy and henbane eased their passing.

Ceridwyn had told Wilfred about Wolfsbane, thus named because it was widely used to poison wolves. The purple flowering plant was mentioned in his father's papers as one to avoid. He said it had been used in ancient times by Medea to poison Theseus, and by Livia, the wife of Emperor Augustus to poison anyone who thwarted her ambitions.

However, in Myddvai they also called it Monkshood. The plant grew well in the Welsh mountains. They used extremely diluted powdered root to relieve pain. It was also used in slightly larger quantities by their seers in combinations with mushrooms to look into the future. The church considered its use a mortal sin and named it witches flying brew. Wilfred tried it in very small quantities on a few Danes with mortal wounds and founds it aided their passing into the other world with little distress. They seemed able to see Valhalla even before getting there.

It was the first time Elvina had seen mortal wounds, with blood and excreta covered bodies, since the horrendous massacre of her childhood. She busied herself with cleaning wounds, then applying bandages and words of comfort. Her composure facing gruesome injuries endeared her more than ever to Wilfred. He had found a perfect partner in so many ways.

Poor Orva was made of less resolute clay. She had disappeared vomiting and crying at the sight of so much blood and gore.

Wilfred surveying the bodies thought to himself, 'It is nearly Samhain, when the bridge of swords to the other world is open, when spirits walk the Earth, when the seven sisters can be seen from dusk to dawn and reach their zenith in the sky. Hopefully these warriors will enter their afterlife without problems.'

After some more feasting and boasting of the minor skirmish they had experienced and even greater imagined battlefield heroics, the men of Wessex under Æthelred and Alfred returned reluctantly home. Alfred thought with greater certainty they may be back again when the Danes returned to Mercia. Money would simply delay the final blood-reckoning between Saxon and Dane. Ultimately, they would be stopped by strength, not weakness, not by blood money, but blood on the field of battle. Preparations needed to be made well in advance of that day.

Wilfred, Elvina and Orva returned home with the army. Like Alfred, they foresaw more battles, more deaths, more widows and orphans. Unlike Orva, Elvina and Wilfred were reluctant to bring a new child into this world. Orva's child had not really been planned either. No man in Sherborne acknowledged fatherhood. If Orva knew the father for certain she remained silent.

Elvina drank mugwort tea daily to maintain regular moon blood and inserted moss to prevent conception. Wilfred applied dilute pennyroyal oil to his pintle to prevent fruitfulness before they were ready.

Ceridwyn came to visit Wilfred bearing a large pile of manuscripts. 'I have been I touch with the healers of Myddvai. The high priestess was one of the acolytes with me many years ago. They were delighted and astonished to hear I am still alive. They had given up all hope for me when they saw me disappearing with those Saxon brutes, already tearing rapaciously at my clothes. I told them about you and our studies. These are written copies of their medical knowledge and forms of treatment. I have translated them for you. I hope you find some good ideas. The old Druid knowledge and philosophy is incorporated into a healing manual.'

Wilfred accepted them gratefully. He devoured them slowly over the next few weeks. The information added greatly to his facts garnered from the classical tomes of ancient medicine and from Finnian's manuscripts. The Welsh laece or healers recommended peaches, plums and grape skins dissolved in red wine for breast lumps. They advised walnuts for bowel cancer and the application of foxes glofa salve to the skin over any tumour. They advised a diet with plenty of onions, carrots, peas, and broccoli for any tumour. They wrote that a combination of watercress, mugwort, plantain, chamomile, nettle and fennel would help tumours. Watercress should be given in an especially large dose.

The great physicians of Myddvai recommended that any person really sick with infection would benefit from a mixture of powdered black pepper, cloves, geranium, nutmeg and thyme dissolved in small ale. Meadowsweet was advised for painful joints and fevers. Dandelion was given for abdominal pain and for swelling with fluid. Butterwort was prescribed for kidney stones, and Sage for sore throats.

The Myddvai physicians knew of herbs used in distant countries, such as frankincense and myrrh. They mixed a concoction of orpine, eryngo, poppy, mandrake, ground-ivy, hemlock and great lettuce dripped into the nostrils to relieve pain before operations.

Here were ingenious therapies worth more than fields of gold to Wilfred; here there were practical details of how to use the remedies mentioned in somewhat obscure terms in the ancient Greek and Latin therapies. Here were details of preparing herbal mixtures and safe doses. Nutmeg for example was a beneficial herb for infections, but too much was poisonous and caused hallucinations before death. Here were the ideas to take his skills to a higher level. He thanked Ceridwyn profusely and hugged her tightly, the first friendly non-threatening contact with a man she had permitted and experienced since before her sixteenth birthday.

John, the widowed carpenter had taken a fancy to Ceridwyn over the last few months, but she gently, ever so gently, declined his polite requests. Elvina and Wilfred thought she was unlikely to ever be intimate with a man again after her past traumas

The Welsh healers also had some novel ideas about examination as well as treatments. In Myddvai the physicians examined the prostate by covering a finger with some animal intestine and inserting it into the anus. It should be a small soft lump at the front of the rectum. If it was large and hard it indicated a tumour.

Finally, Wilfred had adequate information to take him forward in the fight against cancers. Wilfred planned to combine all this knowledge into one volume, one volume of practical therapies supported by experience. It would be written in current Anglo-Saxon English and he called it the remedies or Lacnunga, the old Saxon word for remedies. He would one day be able to pass it on to Orva and any others of his acolytes should he gain more acolytes.

JULY 869

Wilfred and Orva were busy endeavouring to heal the many sufferers arriving outside his house. Betlic, a young man complained, 'look I have all these spots. Girls avoid me and laugh at me!'

Betlic had severely infected acne.

Wilfred pulled a brass vessel from his shelf. 'Betlic, this is a mixture of garlic, leak, wine and ox gall. It is very powerful for skin infections. I shall apply it to your spots today. You must do the same with this mixture I shall give you to take home every day for seven days. By two weeks, the women will be pursuing you!'

Cwene, a very thin lady entered next. 'Wilfred and Elvina, my moonblood had ceased although I was only thirty years old. I have just found the love of her life, truly the one and only love of my life, and I want to bear a child with him. I went to see the priest in the monastery, but the fat one said I must pay the church handsomely and lie with him to prepare my body for childbearing. He said after I lay with him God would make me his vessel and a baby would follow shortly. I walked out.'

Orva and Elvina were aware that Cwene had a new true love every year, to replace the previous love of her life, and the ones before that. She had desperately wanted a child with each but so far had been unsuccessful.

They identified Osric's undesirable practices and his use of his God for emotional blackmail

Wilfred gave her brooklime, and advised her to find some half-ripe mulberries, pluck them and eat them at night. Both would promote her cycles. He also advised her to eat more food in general, at least two sizable meals a day, for she appeared far too thin.

Woodrow, a farmer with a leathery tanned skin had several neck and face ulcers from many years in the sun was treated with milkweed sap on the lesions. Wilfred said, 'I know you must be out in the sun a lot on your farm. Wear a hat when outside. This salve is pulverised ivy twigs dissolved in butter, put some on any areas of sunburn.'

Hollis, the mother of the metal worker had a breast lump. She said to Wilfred, 'Ellsworth was my friend; she told me how your treatment made her better for months. I think I have the same problem.'

Wilfred examined her breasts. Again, there was a hard lump, this one in the left breast. It was fixed to the skin and to the chest wall. Again, there were lumps under her arm. This time the whites of her eyes were yellow and there was a large hard mass in her abdomen high on the right side. This was another cancer, but more advanced than Ellsworth's. It had invaded the liver.

'Hollis, I am sorry to say that I think you are completely correct. You should prepare yourself and your family for the worst. I have some herbal therapy that will give you improvement, but so far no one has ever been known to cure a tumour.'

Armed with his new knowledge from Ceridwyn and Myddvai, Wilfred prescribed powdered plum tea twice daily, a regular diet of carrot, onion, broccoli, peas and cauliflower plus two drops of mistletoe oil in a goblet of red wine nightly. Wilfred had prepared a large jar of a blended tea composed of dried pulverised watercress, mugwort, plantain, chamomile, nettle and fennel as listed in the Myddvai documents. He gave Ellsworth a supply, to take two spoons nightly in hot water.

Finally, he gave her an amulet of bloodstone to wear at all times.

Durwyn from the Half Moon arrived next. 'Wilfred,' he whispered,' I am passing blood in my piss and I have pain in here,' indicating his right loin. Durwyn was embarrassed that Orva was listening to his male problems. 'I have been drinking more fluids, well, er, especially mead, but it does not seem to help!'

'Durwyn,' Wilfred responded, 'I suspect you have a kidney stone, probably from drinking far too much mead. This is a solution of butterwort and dandelion, drink it with lots of water.'

A few days later Durwyn pissed out a small stone with acute transient discomfort, then total relief of his pain. He sang Wilfred's praise to all in the tavern and returned to liberal quantities of mead.

Soon after, John's older brother, Acwel, arrived to seek Wilfred's opinion. He was an old man bent with arthritis. 'Wilfred,' he wheezed, 'everyone in the Half Moon says you can cure everything, can you fix my knees?'

'Acwel, I can try, here is some herbal tea of Meadowsweet tea plus chervil, have a big spoon full every night dissolved in hot water. Also, here are athelfarthingwort poultices for your knees, put a hot one on your knees every night for half an hour before you go to bed.'

Three days later Acwel was seen walking around town with a youthful spring in his step that he had not enjoyed for a few years.

Next person seeking Wilfred's help was Eagdyth, wife of Woodrow the farmer, arrived quite breathless with very swollen legs. 'Wilfred, I am still puffed on walking just a short distance and my swollen legs are no better,'

Previously Wilfred had applied henbane alone, but the Physicians of Myddvai also recommended mixing the henbane with powdered lupin and blending the two with fine wheatmeal. Once blended into a dough, Wilfred applied the mixture liberally over the lower part of her leg and bound the leg tightly. 'Eagdyth, that mixture is used by the physicians of

Myddvai. Put a dollop every morning on your leg and bind it in to your leg with a tight bandage.'

'In addition,' continued Wilfred pounding a mixture of crushed dandelion and foxglove flowers and hawthorn berries. 'Dissolve a spoonful of this in hot water on awaking and drink it, come back and see me in three days he advised.

As Eagdyth departed, Wilfred puzzled over poultices for swollen legs. His various sources of information recommended henbane, oak bark, seal's hide shoes, elder tea, waybread, goose droppings, cabbage and many many others. Was that because they all worked, or because none of them worked? Could it be there were many different causes for swollen feet, and each required a different cure? He wished his father were here to discuss the problem. Ceridwyn didn't seem to know which was best. Perhaps he should visit Mydvvai. He would keep notes of his various customers and which worked in each case.

Four men arrived bearing a fifth man on a stretcher as Wilfred ruminated. A sixth man preceded them bearing a white flag above the Raven Banner mounted upside-down, a flag of truce. They were all Danes, everyone with armband engraved with Viking runes, everyone with an amulet of Thor's hammer round their neck, yet none carried arms. They had requested to come in peace to see Wilfred.

'Wilfred,' one spoke, 'I am Hjalmar. We bear our leader to you, a warrior of great courage, a man of many victories in battle. He has been sick for several months and none of our healers can make a difference, he gets worse every day. We went to the Abbey looking for the great healer of Sherborne, but we were not allowed in. We thought that we would find a man of your reputation in the abbey, but a fat very rude man told us we were cursed by god, and to go away. He said we were condemned to hell and he could do nothing about it. He did say putting gold coins, lots of gold coins, in the collection box might just help to save our souls.'

Wilfred and Elvina had no problem recognising Osric. Why the abbey kept him on as prior was a mystery to most of the town.

Hjalmar continued, 'However; as we walked away another monk, a really nice old man told us to go to Wilfred in Cheap Street, that you are the great healer of Sherborne, so here we are. Your reputation is known in amongst the Danes in Mercia and Northumberland, your reputations for treating battle injuries of either side, so we beg you to help, although he is your sworn enemy.'

Wilfred recognised their descriptions of his friend and loyal colleague, Brother David. He said, 'I have only one sworn enemy, but that is another story from long ago, allow me to see this man.'

The Danes hoisted the stretcher onto Wilfred's table. Wilfred looked at the Dane, he was clearly prematurely aged, and thin grey hair straggled over his grey sweaty face. He appeared semi-conscious and groaned intermittently. His facial bones were prominent, a marker of weight loss. He had several red marks with pale centres on his face. Wilfred pulled off the woollen blanket covering him and looked at his hands. The little finger was missing on both hands! Wilfred gasped and looked at the Danes. 'This is Ragnar Fourfingers?'

The Danish leader spoke proudly, 'Yes, you have heard of his heroic prowess?'

'Prowess? Hero? This man attacked my village a decade ago; he murdered my father and all the men., young and old. One suffered the unspeakable agony of your blood red eagle. My father was cut down ruthlessly before he could find his sword. With his brave warriors, oh so brave warriors, he raped and then murdered the old ladies. Next, he abducted the young women including my mother and sister, and my wife's mother and sister. They stole our only horse and all our cattle and burnt the houses. How courageous is that?'

Ragnar opened his eyes and looked at Wilfred. His voice was croaky and weak. 'That was not a great battle; we were unspeakably cruel to the women. The Saxon men were armed, well some of them were, but they were not warriors, some were old men. They tried to form a shield-wall, but they were too weak and untrained in the arts of battle. We butchered them all. Now I realise we did a cruel and evil thing, not one that will gain us entry to Valhalla. I am sorry.'

'However; your mother and sister and the other women had their revenge, when we left with them, they were singing. Singing and chanting quite fiercely. We thought they were trying to keep their spirits up, but when we returned to our home, we were told they had been cursing us. Just after we left your village, a hare ran in front of my horse, well your village horse. The horse bucked, and I nearly fell off. All the women laughed, apparently to see a hare is a sign of bad luck coming.'

'They grew dog's tongue in our herb garden and put some in our houses. We only discovered later that brings bad luck. They planted an elder tree in my garden and told me that the Saxons used elder for boat building and children's cots. Only after the first boat was lost in a storm, and the first child in an elder crib died, did we discover that the wood was an evil bringer of bad luck. Apparently, the fruit and flowers however, can be good for healing. Apparently, you believe that a hearse driver should have a whip handle made of elder wood to protect himself from the spirit of the newly dead. We did not know these things.

Within weeks the first of our raiding party became ill. He had pain in his guts and the bloody flux. He could not eat, lost weight and died slowly in terrible pain. Then a few months later another became ill. Slowly one by one over ten years, all thirty of my band became sick and died, usually in agony. I am the last survivor.'

'No one dared touch your mother or sister, neither did we dare kill them for fear of their spirits remaining on earth and following us for vengeance. We finally took them all untouched to Ireland five years ago and left them in a convent unharmed. Well Wilfred, I did not know you were from there, I did not know the little boy peering round a burning hut had become a great laece. I may as well plunge a knife into my heart as hope for help from you. I expect I am your one sworn enemy?'

Wilfred looked Ragnar in the eye, 'Indeed, you are Ragnar, but it sounds you have suffered enough pain and grief. The fates, or rather the women's curses, have dealt you a crueller blow than I could with a sword. Indeed, to see a hare indicates bad luck, while to see a sow or a wolf usually brings good luck. Beware the powers of the old people of this country; they may connect with unknown forces greater than your Woden or the Christ Lord.'

Wilfred examined Ragnar carefully; he had red spots over his body, all with central pale areas that were insensitive to a gentle then a firm prick from Wilfred's finest blade. The nerves running down the back of his arm below the elbow were like thick cords; his feet could not feel Wilfred's touch not a light prick with the blade. He had one deep smelly ulcer on his right ankle.

'Ragnar, you have been cursed with leprosy, it is usually a mortal disease, your body slowly falls apart, starting with your toes and fingers. Everyone shuns you; young brave and loyal warriors avoid you, no woman will share your bed, and even your slaves walk as far as possible from your rotting body. No one will bury your body for fear of catching the disease. Lepers are left to decompose where they die, or become food for the dogs and crows, unless a slave can be forced to dig your grave and throw you in.'

'Any warrior would prefer to be cut down in the shield wall or even suffer the blood red eagle. Your pain and distress may last years. I cannot think of a more deserved punishment. Such an inglorious death rules out entry to Valhalla. My mother's curses are more lethal than your sharpest blade, she has assigned you a much slower more ignominious painful death than anything you did to my father.

However, our old ways advise help and forgiveness for your enemy. I shall treat you to the best of my ability.'

Elvina watched all this silently, thinking Wilfred was one of the most Christian people she knew if he would only recognise the fact.

'I have some medication that may help. Salve of wallwort, burdock, cocklebur and five fingers applied to the spots is the standard treatment, it is only moderately effective. This bottle contains powdered oak bark and the inner part of blackthorn root; it should be sprinkled into the ulcer on your ankle daily. This bottle contains powdered holly, both leaves and berries. You should have half a cupful daily in a bath. Do not drink any, it is poisonous. This is a mixture of powdered black pepper, cloves, geranium, nutmeg and thyme dissolved in small ale. Drink one cup nightly.'

'There is another therapy your people brought to this country, possibly having learnt it in Russia. Few know of it and it is hard to find, but it is very effective. It is an extract of beaver lymph gland. You are fortunate; I have a little and will give it to you for free. Have three drops dissolved in mead each night. I will need your men to find another beaver or two.'

Wilfred continued, 'however, you should be totally isolated from all other people. My wife and I have a hut out in the back garden where we will keep you in isolation and treat you to the best of our ability. Elvina, Orva and I should be your only visitors. We are protected from infections by the powers of our various Gods. We will hang an onion over the doorway to protect those who visit you. Each morning before breaking your fast, eat a radish root. That will at least protect you from the curse for that day.'

'Finally, I think, as my mother's son, I think I can lift her curse, I will need to read some of my manuscripts. We will start by putting some hawthorn, vervain and holly in your room and nail some primrose to the door that will provide some protection against curses. It is said vervain and dill hinder witches from their will, though only unreasonable Christians would see my mother as a witch, or her curse as undeserved.'

Elvina interjected, 'I know how to lift curse, and it requires a Christian incantation, Wilfred and Ragnar, are you happy if I recite this?'

Both nodded affirmatively, anything to relieve this dread disease.

Elvina knelt beside Ragnar and placed her hands together. She began, 'My Lord, I ask you, Father I beseech you, Son I beg of you, Lord and Holy Spirit, Holy Trinity, that you remove all the devil's works from this man. I invoke the Holy Trinity to my assistance, that is the Father, Son and Holy Spirit. Lord, turn this man's thoughts and his heart so that he may confess all his evils and all the sins he has, so that he may give up all his gods and his will.'

'Therefore, curser, recognise your doom and give honour to God, and turn back from this, God's servant so that with a clean mind he may serve, following grace.'

Wilfred and Ragnar were dubious if the curser would give honour to Elvina's Christian god, but it was worth a try, anything was worth a try as far as Ragnar was concerned.

Wilfred looked at Ragnar with a mixture of anger and pity. 'Fate has wiped your slate clean Ragnar; providence has caused you more suffering than I possibly could. Perhaps your greatest humiliation is to depend helplessly on one of your victims for assistance and forgiveness. Should you survive, we expect you to return to your people. Not only will you fight no more, but you will encourage Guthrum to live in peace with the Saxons.'

After Ragnar's needs were attended to, Wilfred opened his papers wondering if he could do more for Cwene. A recommendation for unsuccessful breast feeding was to spit some milk into a river and say, "everywhere I have carried the splendid stomach-strong with this well-fed one which I wish to have for myself and go home."

Wilfred understood that herbs and perhaps gems had powers to heal, but these sayings seemed a load of nonsense. 'Oh well, father used these, I will have to try them all and keep notes,' he said to himself.,

Three days later Eagdyth arrived back at his door; her leg swelling had all gone. She gave Wilfred a hug and a wet kiss on his cheek, and then gave him a basket of fresh fruit and vegetables from the farm garden. 'I have been peeing and peeing the last two days, I have hardly been able to go out, but I can get my stockings on again, and I don't feel as puffed. Woodrow says you are welcome to a patch in our farm should you wish somewhere else to grow more herbs.'

Wilfred appreciated the fresh produce and the offer of another herb garden. Farmers worked long hours often in the cold and dark for little reward compared with other merchants, middle-men wearing rich robes, sitting in great houses who became rich selling workers produce for large personal gains.

A few days later Wilfred and Elvina were taking lunch with Alfred and Ealhswith. Wilfred was smiling at Alfred after losing two games of hnefatafl. 'So, Wilfred, why are you smiling inanely at me after losing two games?' enquired Alfred curiously.

Wilfred raised his goblet of wine to Ealhswith and Alfred and surprised Alfred by saying, 'Because, my prince, I know you have some good news, but I am not sure if you do.' Wilfred was smiling even more. 'Congratulations on your good news!'

'What is good these days, bad news always seems on the horizon?' responded a perplexed Alfred.

Wilfred and Elvina looking askance at Ealhswith who blushed.

Alfred catching Wilfred's drift, looked askance at a blushing Ealhswith and asked, 'what good news?'

Ealhswith turned to Alfred and confessed, 'Wilfred is right, my moon blood is two months late, we are going to have a child! I was going to tell you shortly. You will be a father before Easter next year. Wilfred, no one else knew my last moon blood was two months ago, how do you know such things?'

Alfred jumped up, hugged his wife and two good friends, then surveyed Wilfred, 'so, yes how do you know that? Trade secrets I suppose.'

Wilfred added, 'Indeed, my prince, I don't always know how I know but it will be a daughter, she will be a fierce shield maiden after her father and uncles, a characteristic she may have caught from my wife, or her father.'

Elvina hugged the expectant couple. Alfred said, 'this is an omen from God, this is a harbinger of better news, how wonderful!'

Three months later Acwel arrived at Wilfred's door. His arthritis was not too bad, but he was having trouble having a pee.

Wilfred asked him, 'do you get up at night to pee?'

'Yes,' replied Acwel, 'several times.'

'Does it flow well or slowly with dribbles?'

'Very slowly with dribbles,' Acwel confirmed.

Wilfred examined Acwel's abdomen carefully finding a distended bladder, and to Acwel's surprise some marked tenderness over his lower spine. Wilfred found some length of cows intestine and slipped his index finger into the tube. Then he inserted his covered finger into Acwel's rectum, even more to Acwel's surprise. Sure enough, as the physicians of Myddvai instructed, at the front of the rectum was a brick hard lump where the prostate sits. Wilfred was sure this problem was caused by a large prostate, almost certainly one with a cancer in it.

'Acwel, you may have a serious problem. I think you have a tumour in your prostate. See the priest and make sure your confession is up to date, for you may die with this problem in a few months. However, I will do my best to cure you. This is a solution of dandelion in mead, drink half a goblet daily in the morning. I will make more for you. This one is powder of nettles, mugwort and watercress, dissolve one small spoonful in hot water and drink it at bedtime. Also tell your brother John to allow you meat and mead only on Wednesday and Saturday. You should eat plenty of peas, broccoli, carrots, onions and cauliflower.'

Later that day a robust spotless plumper Ragnar emerged from his hut and clasped Wilfred's wrist tearfully. 'I cannot thank you enough Wilfred. I do not deserve your unbelievable kindness and brilliant healing. I am totally humbled by your great wisdom and compassion. The Norse Gods see only one lifestyle, one only of violence, Odin supposedly acquired wisdom in exchange for an eye on Yggdrasil, but not compassion. Your Gods see much more than mine. They also see a lot further. Not only will I fight no more, we will sail to Ireland on the tide and seek to return your kin as the best recompense for our past brutality that we can do. Thank Elvina for me too, her removal of that curse must have helped.'

He dropped his voice, 'Elvina says your healing come from Jesus, but a scatty old lady I have seen in the market tells me your skills comes from the old knowledge, old long before the Romans came here. She said your mother's curse also comes from the ancient power of the land. Which is true, what should I believe?'

Wilfred winked and replied obscurely, 'Indeed, the Romans said all roads lead to Rome.'

'We Danes hear the Druids used to sacrifice children, is that true?' asked Ragnar.

Wilfred laughed. 'Do you know how that story came about? There is an old English word 'cythth' for one's family, one's relatives. That is sometimes changed to kids for young relatives. In no time, the Romans spread the word that our sacrifice of a young goat or kid was a human sacrifice.'

'The Romans! Did they not sacrifice innocent humans in their Coliseum? Women killed by lions; unarmed slaves killed by gladiators! How dare they criticize the Druids!' Wilfred responded scornfully.

'We did not take captives; any Romans we captured were all killed. Bear in mind they had invaded our country and attempted to eliminate our old culture, as you Danes have also tried and failed so far. Bear in mind they butchered Boudicca, Queen of the Iceni, and raped her daughters. They attacked our holiest centre in Mona and killed all our defenceless high priests and priestesses. Death was what they all deserved.'

'Children were not a sacrifice, and we did not eat them. My father once went to the Summer Temple in the Orkney Isles to the ancient Druid

Festival. There are sixty standing stones in a circle surrounded by a deep ditch at Brodgar. On the summer solstice, a young goat is sacrificed. If there is a Roman prisoner, he is executed. His throat is cut so his blood soaks into the soil, his body is buried to fertilise the land. Romans must be useful for something. It is all they deserve.'

'The community maiden girls all dressed in white lead a kid into the centre of the circle where the high priest and priestess await. An unmarried man stands at each of these sixty surrounding stones. Married men and women who are no longer virgins are outside the ditch.'

'The animal's throat is cut by the high priest and its blood collected in two vessels. The eldest virgin takes one bowl around the sixty young men and daubs their forehead with blood. She chooses one of these young men, her favourite and they cohabit in the middle of the circle, while the maidens gather round to watch. The year my father watched, the girl had clearly chosen her partner before-hand, but to tease him, she went around the whole circle while he watched anxiously, hopefully. Finally, she took his hand and led him to the centre. In the meantime, the people outside the ring start singing and chanting, singing and chanting. They reach a climax at the same time as the couple, well aware that a young couple lack the skill and patience for a prolonged first event.'

'The young man and his virgin are usually too engrossed with their first time, their first time together to worry about an audience. They don't even notice the cool breeze or the prickles in the gorse.'

'It was the most powerful affirmation of man's connection to the land that my father had seen. It is educational for the young ones, especially for the second eldest girl before her turn to lose her virginity the following year. The older men cannot see into the circle, but they have a fair idea of what is happening! The other container is mixed with a large amount of wine and passed round the outer circle for all the spectators to drink a little. Every man, woman and child participate. The remaining virgins were then removed by their parents to a secure place in case they were tempted to have a foretaste of next year's festivities.'

'Later a huge fire was built in the center and flares of peat on either side of each standing stones. The people then share the friendship of the thighs with as many friends as they can find on that night. Like Beltane here it improves the fertility of the land. We confirm our bondage with the land and its living entities. We love the land in all its appearances and structures, we love all life in every form. Nobody is killed but most people have fun. Virginity is lost at an appropriate time, and the young maidens see what is in store for them. Human sacrifice? definitely not!'

'Hm,' said Ragnar, 'do you think some young maiden might now be happy to cohabit with me. Thanks to you I don't look as ugly and undesirable as I did a few months ago.'

'Good luck, Ragnar,' chipped in Elvina, who had just arrived, 'remember real men don't use force! Wait till you are invited. And don't forget to thank our Christ Lord in your prayers, he was partly responsible for your fantastic recovery.'

Two months later Acwel met Alfred at the Half Moon. 'I am feeling fine, I can sleep all night without getting up to pee, and my back pain has gone. Thank you so much, you are a great healer.'

Sadly Wilfred could visualize Acwel in his winding sheet.

870

Just after the Christmas festivities, Alfred and Wilfred were concentrating over the hnefatafl board.

Alfred announced, 'I have just heard my step-mother and sister-in-law Judith died. I fear the country is up for some penance after her scandalous marriage to my brother Æthelbald, when my father Æthelwulf died, in defiance of an ecclesiastical prohibition. Not only did she do that, but after my brother's death she was sent to a convent. She escaped from there and eloped with Baldwin of Flanders and had a child or two with him.'

'God will punish this country for her immoral sins and promiscuity. Thank God, her marriages to my father and brother were barren. We would have some child of dubious legitimacy to lead us in a time of crisis. The Danes will make us suffer dearly. Our punishment will be at their cruel hands. We will only overcome them through prayer and penitence, as well as courage and resolve on the battlefield.'

Wilfred made a winning move to the surprise of a distracted Alfred.

A month later Wilfred and Alfred met to discuss the news over another game of hnefatafl. Wilfred's first four moves as was his usual tactic these days as black, was to block the four corner squares to prevent Alfred doing a sudden breakout with his king. He had defeated Alfred twice running with this play. However, this time Alfred feinted to attack one corner drawing Wilfred's blocking pieces, and then shot off to the opposite corner. Wilfred was caught unawares and shortly Alfred had captured a Viking base terminating the game.

'My turn to win,' smiled Alfred.

'So, Wilfred, have you heard that the Danes are threatening Wessex again. They have conquered East Anglia and killed King Eadmund. They have currently retired to Thetford for the winter, but I have little doubt they would be aiming for their final conquest of Wessex come spring. Do you think I could settle the dispute between us and Ivar the Boneless and his Great Danish Army with a game of hnefatafl? It would be a much more civilised way to solve disputes between kings that the blood-spattered battlefield. There would not be dismembered corpses with many weeping widows and orphans everywhere.'

'Besides that, I have a great tutor, I don't think Ivar would beat me. What do you think Wilfred?' teased the young prince.

'Well, my prince, I could always pretend to be Alfred and play for you to ensure victory,' responded Wilfred cheekily.

'Do you know about the history of Thetford, their winter quarters, Wilfred?' asked Alfred, 'Eight hundred years ago Queen Boudicca led the Iceni tribe in their brave revolt against the Roman invaders. They killed thousands of Romans, but ultimately the greater strength and discipline of the Roman army defeated her and the Iceni leading to her death. Now she was a great shield maiden, we could do with her now to inspire our warriors and fight the invaders again but combined with the organisation of the Roman's battle plans!'

Wilfred responded, 'The spirit of the Iceni lives on in the countryside, it just needs to be harnessed. Boudicca and the violence her daughters suffered at the hands of the Roman invaders has not been forgotten. The people of this country have long memories. To the old inhabitants of this land, families here before Stang Heng was built, one invader is the same as the next. I will show you how, where and when at the right time to raise the spirits of the Iceni.'

MARCH 870.

A few weeks later Wilfred and Elvina were awoken in the early hours of the morning. Alodia was at the door. Somewhat surprisingly she had the position of head lady-in-waiting to Ealhswith on the dubious qualification that she could advise the queen on Alfred's requirements!

'My lady needs you immediately, can you come at once?' puffed Alodia.

'I shall come immediately,' said Wilfred hastily grabbing his bag.

'No, you fool, not you,' responded Alodia, pushing Wilfred firmly back, 'the queen obviously wants Elvina, she has gone into labour!'

Curious thought Wilfred, once Alodia wanted me for an activity in which I had no expertise, now she has rejected me for an activity in which I have a lot of experience.

'I'm coming,' responded Elvina, taking the bag from Wilfred.

Wilfred was however also summoned to the royal pavilion by Alfred in case there were problems with Ealhswith's labour. Wilfred was confronted by Nelda, the royal midwife stoutly blocking his entry.

137

'So, Wilfred, do you think you really know better than Elvina and I do how to deliver babies. How many babies have you had personally? Just wait outside. I will call you when I want a man's advice!' scolded the midwife.

Wilfred backed off feebly, he did not think he would ever win a fight here. Even if he overcame Nelda's objections, he would be confronted by an equally feisty Elvina. 'Er, I have some syrup of henbane to relieve pains and a bag of coriander to apply to the inner thigh to aid in the delivery and the afterbirth, but it must er then be removed immediately,' he offered weakly.

'You think I don't know that? I will take your herbs though, thanks. Sit outside and wait patiently with Prince Alfred. You can comfort him.' ordered Nelda.

By mid-afternoon, the lusty cry of a baby girl was heard. Alfred and Ealhswith had their first daughter Æthelflæd, after an uneventful first labour competently supervised by Elvina and Nelda. Alfred kissed and hugged Ealhswith, then Nelda, then Elvina and Wilfred and everyone else in the pavilion. Then Elvina and Wilfred hugged and kissed. 'Thanks for teaching me all about birthing babies,' Elvina whispered in his ear

Toasts in royal mead were proposed to the future of little Æthelflæd. Wilfred and Alfred well and truly wet the baby's head with second and third goblets of royal mead, though Alfred then developed his thoughtful far-away look. He was wondering about his first-born's future and hoped that she would grow up in a more peaceful country.

Wilfred hoped her future would be bright. Alfred in his extreme happiness had briefly forgotten the problems besetting Wessex. Looking at the healthy baby, Wilfred could see an aura of strength and success around her, a vision of a beautiful sword-bearing maiden before hundreds of adoring fighters. He felt quite as optimistic as Alfred.

MAY 870

A cwel knocked feebly on Wilfred's door. He looked terrible. He was very thin and in severe pain from his back. He had been well for nearly a year, but in the last two weeks he had been suddenly increasingly unwell. Wilfred doubled the dose of nettle tea, but within a month Wilfred attended Acwel's funeral. His unwanted vision of the winding sheet seemed sadly correct every time.

John and little Meghan approached Wilfred standing sadly at the back. 'Wilfred, we thank you for making Acwel well and free of pain for almost a year,' said John.

Meghan gave him a hug and a kiss on his cheek. 'Wilfred, you are so clever, you made me well when the adder nearly killed me. When I am big, I want to be your assistant and learn how to make people better. Women can be healers too, can't they?' she asked looking so seriously at Wilfred with her big brown eyes.

Wilfred smiled sadly and patted her hand, 'you can start to help me when you are eight like I did with my father.'

However, inside Wilfred only felt frustration. He slipped quietly away from the graveyard as hollow laughter echoed in a corner of his mind. The black badger was still pestering him. Elvina caught up with him and hugged him as he shed a few tears of failure on her shoulder. Usually he managed not to betray his inner feelings to anyone. Again, his treatment had shown initial promise but then the poor sufferer had died. The nettles had worked better for prostate cancer than breast cancer. He was starting on the right track, but he needed to be a lot more shrewd and knowledgeable.

AUGUST 870

 The four friends were dining one evening after a couple of games of hnefatafl. Alfred and Wilfred had won one game each.

Alfred announced, 'well my assessment unfortunately turned out to be over-optimistic. I had hoped for a longer period of peace. However, our network of spies tells us that the Danish Army left Thetford a few months ago and marched to Reading establishing a base camp there. It is well defended on two sides by the Thames and Kennet Rivers, and on the western side by a rampart. A direct attack on Reading would be foolhardy. We will wait till they move out and attack in a more favourable site.'

A few months went by. Wilfred and Alfred met a few days after Christmas having believed the Danes seemed to be consolidating their position for winter.

'Hi Wilfred, well the Anglo-Saxons hope for a longer respite from warfare again was over optimistic. On December 31st a small party of Danes attempted a surprise breakout of Reading. We were ready for them. They met a strong Saxon army under Æthelwulf, the Ealdorman of the shire, at Englefield. We outnumbered them. Many Danes were killed including their Earl Sidrac and the rest fled back to Reading. We will have stirred up a hornet's nest, they will be back in larger numbers.'

871

The year of battles had commenced after Englefield with the Danes intent on bloody revenge. Alfred stood beside Æthelred in a series of conflicts with the Great Heathen Danish Army under Ivar the Boneless and Halfdan Ragnarsson. Both sides would take many casualties with the Saxons suffering to the greater extent.

A few days after Englefield on January 4th a more hopeful but ill-advised Saxon Army attacked the secure fortification around the Danish Camp in Reading, only to be repulsed in a bloody and predictable conflict in which the Saxons took most casualties including Æthelwulf, the victor at Englefield.

6TH JANUARY 871

Wilfred found Alfred looking thoughtful. Alfred always looked thoughtful. He was reading from the little book he always carried, his book of favourite prayers and psalms, perhaps seeking solace or inspiration.

'Hello Wilfred, I suppose you heard about Æthelwulf. His victory in a minor skirmish went to his head. Silly fool, silly dead fool. Without discussing this with Æthelred, he was reckless enough to attack the main Danish stronghold. Inevitably it was an unmitigated disaster. We had lost many men we cannot afford to lose at Reading only two days ago That will give the Danes sufficient confidence to break out in large numbers imminently.'

Wilfred approached him and whispered quietly so Alfred's warriors and nobles could not hear, 'my Lord Prince, I beg you to come up yonder hill, I have something important I must show you. Something that will help you defeat the Danes.'

As they climbed slowly on horseback, Alfred following reluctantly, Wilfred continued, 'in two days' time it is the start of the Druid New Year. It is always a propitious day for a new venture. Come and see this.' At the top was an old sarsen stone, like those found at the mysterious and ancient ring stones at Stanheng.

Wilfred showed Alfred a perforation in the stone. 'My prince, this is the blowing stone where the tribal leaders in the old days called their warriors to battle. Only great leaders can produce a sound. Both my father and I tried without success; would you believe it was silent even for Elvina,' he said with a wry smile.

'Those who can sound it are assured of victory by the ancient mystical unseen forces of this land. Boudicca came here twice, first time her battle cry echoed round the land. She had a great victory over the Romans. Second time she came, it did not work, and the Iceni suffered a terrible defeat. None could understand why the gods did not support her on the second visit.'

Alfred said, 'Rubbish!' with a scornful smile, but he bowed down, took a great breath in and blew with all his might. They were both surprised when it emitted a deep booming noise, a sound from the distant past, a sound for tomorrow from deep in the earth, one that seemed to make the ground vibrate, it echoed over the hills and was detectable as a strange disturbance in the air and in the ground far away in the West Country. One that woke men from their sleep, one that summoned them from the fields to collect their swords. One that reminded men of Boudicca, the first great shield maiden, and her Iceni warriors fighting invaders. They felt her courage marching with them.

Over the next few days, armed young warriors poured into Alfred's camp, some from fifty leagues or more away. Every man carried a razor-sharp spear, battle axe and short sword, the seaxe with its angled back. Broad bladed spear-heads with moulded sockets were mounted on toughen ash staves taller than the height of a man. Weapons had sat concealed for years till the call to arms was heard.

'We heard our country call us,' they said to Alfred, 'it was the clarion call of all the ages, from long before the Romans up to today, it said our country was in danger, it said a great warrior king needs our help, or he will be called to the otherworld. It said the spirit of Boudicca is on the march again with us. So, Prince Alfred if you are our man, then we are your men.'

Alfred looked bemused but exceedingly grateful.

Two days later Æthelred and Alfred mustered the entire Saxon army. It was a gloomy day, grey with intermittent showers. Even the high ground was boggy underfoot. Alfred wore a new helmet gifted to him by his brother the king. Three iron bands were rivetted together, one around his head, and two over his head, one from front to back, the other from side to side. Thick slices of horn filled the spaces, and the nasal plate descending from the iron plate extending from back to front was decorated with a large cross. The royal smiths had also created suits of chain mail for the two brothers, made of copper, they were light, flexible, and strong, it provided good protection from all but the most violent of blows. Wilfred's helmet was somewhat more battle-worn and decorated with a wild boar, a pagan symbol.

Æthelred and Alfred assembled the Saxons on Lowbury Hill. The rear half of the army crouched down on one knee such that they were not visible to the enemy who underestimated the force opposing them. The approaching Danish hoard appeared numerous and threatening, but as they drew closer it appeared many were not fully armed and armoured, many were singing and staggering. Their force however, was not as numerous as the Saxons. They were clearly overconfident and suffering from too much celebrating after their triumph four days ago, at Reading. Alfred and Æthelred had divided their army on either side of a ridge on Lowbury Hill. The Danes sobering rapidly divided their force and began a flanking movement to reach the higher ground.

A messenger reached Alfred to announce that Æthelred was still at prayers and not to commence battle yet. However, Alfred could see that delay would yield the high ground to the Danes; therefore, he ordered an immediate charge downhill at the Danes on his side of the ridge. Wilfred stood beside Alfred, Peacemaker in his hand. 'My prince, I am here for you and for Boudicca. The two of you command my help, your wishes are stronger than my preference to avoid violence.'

The Danes formed a shield wall and the two armies crashed together at the bottom of the hill with awful violence. Wilfred and Alfred stood resolute shoulder to resolute shoulder, shield to shield. Alfred's largest housecarls stood on either side, ready to take an axe for their prince. Neither needed to have worried. To their surprise they stood either side of the two fastest blades in Wessex. Larger Danes hoping for the glory of killing the royal prince, armed with heavier weapons were too slow to resist and, to their surprise as well, went down before their slighter opponents flashing steel. The Saxons were inspired by Alfred's leadership. Numbers and momentum enabled his warriors to crash through, and push the Danes back up hill.

The battlefronts separated briefly. Water bottles were passed rapidly around the Saxon army, on Wilfred's instructions. Running through the forests in high summer had taught him the need for plentiful fluids to maintain stamina. He knew the locations of all the little streams in the woods. However, the Danes, lacking a warrior-healer knowledgeable in the needs of warfare, were unprepared and dehydration added to their exhaustion.

The battlefront had moved up the hill to a five-way junction marked by a stunted thorn tree. Wilfred knew it was a sacred Druid site of yesteryear. He called out some old secret Druid war chants, surprisingly echoed by many of the Saxon warriors. Whatever the cause, though now fighting uphill, the Saxons found new energy. The Danes looking over their shoulders, could see some ancient funeral barrows up on the hill behind them, old long before the Romans. Some swore afterwards that they could see open doors with the fires of damnation glowing inside awaiting them.

Soon Danish morale and resolve collapsed before the freshly motivated onslaught. Soon the survivors were in full retreat. Shortly after Alfred's charge, Æthelred arrived and ordered an attack on his side against Danes already somewhat dispirited by the action on the other hill with a similar result. Shortly the brothers were united at the base of the hill with the enemy routed, though both sides had taken many casualties. Bagsecg, one of the Danish kings was amongst the dead, as were five of his jarls.

It was the first Anglo-Saxon victory in a major battle against the Danes. Perhaps it was Alfred's Christ protecting them, perhaps the largest of Alfred's body guard on either side of them. Perhaps the mystical powers imbued in Wilfred's Peacemaker prevented injury. Perhaps the size of the Anglo-Saxon army outnumbered the Danes. Perhaps even the agate pendant they both wore, and the spirit of the Iceni summoned by the blowing stone helped.

Æthelred hugged his brother. 'Young Alfred, you nearly spoilt my fun. There was I still at prayers, when I heard that you had half destroyed the Danish Army. I will have to finish prayers later with a thanks to God, rather than a plea for help to finish off these blood-thirsty pagans.'

'With God's help and your leadership, it has been a great day for Wessex,' responded the modest younger brother.

Wilfred caught the corner of Alfred's eye, and they exchanged a conspiratorial smile. His brother would not have noticed that Alfred's statement could have applied to more than one god belonging to more than one faith and more than one person. Alfred wondered at the inexplicable powers of his Druid friend and his Druid new year, his God said it was nonsense, but curiously it seemed to work together with his Christian faith.

Æthelred looked again at Alfred. 'You are covered in blood, are you wounded?'

Wilfred and Alfred although covered in blood, were uninjured. 'Nay my king, young Wilfred here is nearly as good with a blade as I am. We were too fast for their dull monster warriors, we had swords in their guts while they still had their axes held aloft, isn't that so Wilfred?'

Wilfred smiled and headed back to the battlefield to see if his services were of need to Saxon and Dane alike.

The Saxon warriors had found the Danish wagon carrying meagre fluid replacements. The small amount of water was untouched by the Danes during the battle and remained untouched by the victorious Saxons, but the honey mead and the mealtealoth revived parched throats as shared tales of personal valour and heroic deeds became progressively more exaggerated and improbable.

22 JANUARY 871

 L ong-term victory did not follow Ashdown. The humiliated Danes returned soon with reinforcements for revenge. Defeat did not deter them; it guaranteed a place in Valhalla. The supply of reinforcing warriors seemed limitless.

Wilfred observed yet again the lines of battle before him, this time in the rolling hills of north Hampshire, the Saxons on a nearby rise, and the Danes across the valley. To their left was a woody dell called the Lychpit. Wilfred knew this was an ancient graveyard used long long ago by the early Druids. The local villagers shunned the place, believing it to be haunted. Wilfred wondered whose bodies would rest there at the end of this day.

Ashamed of the blood he had spilt at Ashdown only fourteen days ago against his personal beliefs, he insisted of remaining behind the army with his wagon to treat wounded fighters. Nearby he saw Brother Sam, still in his monk's robe with a sword strapped to his side, and some chain mail underneath his robe, with a small band of housecarls to protect Alfred should the day turn against him. Sam appeared to be studying a small book rather than the battle front. Presumably his favourite Caesar's Gallic War was hidden underneath his robe.

The little village of Old Basing was half a league down the valley. The young men of the Basinga's, the local Anglo-Saxon tribe had already joined

Æthelred's army. Otherwise there was no sign of life there. Presumably all the remaining inhabitants had fled at the first warning of approaching armies. Wilfred was astounded at the sheer size of the opposing Danish army. Every time they were defeated, they soon returned with larger numbers. Unfortunately, many of the victorious Saxons had returned to distant homes after the battle at Ashdown, believing the war to be won.

Horns blew on both sides to signal an advance. Soon both shield walls were hacking viciously at each other. Shortly casualties started arriving at Wilfred's wagon. He was busy suturing and amputating when he became aware of Saxons streaming back past his wagon, some running, some in Brother Sam's organised fighting wall tight around Alfred. They were resolute, undefeated, bonded together in strength, ready to die for their prince.

Æthelred was also slowly retreating before the victorious Danes. The invaders had won the day. The Royal Guard gathered in larger numbers around the king as they retreated in an organised group. The exhausted Danes downed their weapons and picked up their drinking horns. Pursuit required more energy than they had left. A few fills of water were soon replaced by celebratory ale and victory toasts to Odin and Thor.

Some Danes spotted Wilfred still working away on his wagon at he edge of the battlefield and drew swords to investigate. There lying on his wagon was a bloodied warrior with Thor's hammer around his neck having a deep bleeding wound sutured and dressed. One of the Danes cried out, 'That is Wilfred, Ragnar Fourfinger's healer, don't you harm one hair of his head or you will answer to Ivar!'

The Dane offered Wilfred a horn of ale. He was Ragnar's Fourfinger's friend, Hjalmar. They clasped wrists and locked understanding eyes. Having worked till sundown on wounded warriors of both sides Wilfred packed his wagon and withdrew. Although the Saxons had lost, the field was littered with corpses of both armies.

Ivar the Boneless surveyed the field nearby. 'We cannot afford many more victories like this! Perhaps the best part of this victory is that those wagons next to Wilfred's contain Æthelred's winter supplies. See my men around one of them, that one was full of ale and mead. I think there is little left unfortunately. The Saxons may face starvation. We must regroup and find reinforcements for the next battle and the next battle until we finally drive these troublesome Saxons into the sea.'

MARTIN, DORSET
MARCH 21, 871

Alfred and Æthelred sat silently around the camp fire contemplating tomorrow's conflict. Every two months the Danes came with a new army, their man-power seeming inexhaustible. The mood in the camp was subdued. The glorious memories of Ashdown had faded. The Saxons seemed to be hoping for the best rather than confident of victory as they had been before Ashdown. Alfred was frustrated. Fighting for Jesus and Christianity did not seem to motivate the Saxon warrior as much as fighting for both the new and old faiths together. Somehow the blowing stone to which Wilfred had taken him combined both.

Æthelred said morosely, 'well Alfred, if I am killed, you will become King. Should we both be killed, my young son, Æthelhelm would be next in line. He is a little boy, quite unsuitable yet for a leadership role. I fear he would disappear violently somewhere beneath the marauding hordes of pagans having had no chance of a life. Make sure that you withdraw if I am among the fallen.'

'Nonsense my brother, tomorrow you will lead us again to a great victory,' replied Alfred. He did not sound convinced.

Wilfred had a momentary unwanted vision of Æthelred in his winding sheet and was even more pessimistic about the king's future. At least he saw an aura of greatness and long life around Alfred's head.

THE BATTLE OF MARTIN
MARCH 22, 871

The Saxons initially drove a wedge between the Danish forces of Halfdan Ragnarsson and his brother Sigurd Snake in the Eye, but the Danes regathered their forces and attacked the Saxons from both sides with much slaughter. Wilfred awaited casualties just behind the front line. For many he could only give henbane or wolfsbane to relieve pain. After midday, a litter arrived bearing Heahmund, the bishop of Sherborne. One look at his deep chest wound confirmed to Wilfred that he was beyond care. Heahmund was unconscious and had only very shallow breathing. His pulse was weak and thready, and as Wilfred stood there with a finger on the pulse in his neck, both heart beat and breathing ceased. Heahmund had gone to his otherworld. The poor man had only been consecrated as bishop three years previously. Surely Rome would recognise his piety and make him a saint one day.

Then another litter arrived born hastily by six anxious men accompanied by many leading Saxon lords. It was Æthelred; he appeared pale with a cold sweat on his brow. His pulse was also thready and when Wilfred pulled back the robe covering him, he could see an abdominal wound leaking blood and an open fracture of his upper leg.

'Here my Lord King, drink this,' said Wilfred, 'this is syrup of henbane, it will give you some relief from your pain. There is also some of my concoction of leak and onion to see how bad your wound is.'

This was an old trick taught to him by the Vikings. If the leek and onions could then be smelt at the abdominal wound site, it confirmed gut damage and inevitable slow painful death. Æthelred's wound did not smell of leek and onions. Wilfred turned his attention to the leg wound. A heavy weapon had ripped through flesh and smashed the bone beneath just below the groin. The wound appeared contaminated with earth and probably human excreta. Such wounds were usually fatal. A more distal wound could have been treated with an amputation, this was too high.

Wilfred washed out all the dirt and blood. Then he placed a concoction of ox gall, onion, leek and garlic in the gaping wound and bound the edges together. It was too infected to be sutured together, for any pus would need to drain out. He caught Alfred's eye and bowed his head sadly.

Alfred called for a fighting withdrawal of his force leaving Halfdan Ragnarsson in command of the field. A deep voice echoed around the retreating Saxon forces, 'Noli illegitimi carborundum!' It was brother Samuel's Latin war cry, don't let the bastards grind you down. The exhausted Saxon army drew on its last vestige of resolve and strength to make an organised retreat and to protect the wounded king and his brother.

Brother Samuel and his collection of Alfred's housecarls stood between the royal brothers and the Danes slowly walking backwards while still striking down many pursuing Danes. Halfdan called a halt to the fighting, the field was his. There was little possibility of capturing or killing Æthelred without great loss of his own warriors. He had observed the Saxon fighting retreat before. He had seen a robed brother holding the remaining men together in a disciplined shield wall slowly moving backward, while carefully protecting their leaders. There was never a trace of panic, no heads nor swords dropped, no backs were turned. Halfdan reflected it was as well that that monk did not organise the original attack.

Æthelred was carried away from the field first on a stretcher. He was a strong young man, not yet twenty-five, death would not come easily or quickly. Wilfred gave him sips of peppermint and garlic tea slowly. He washed out the leg wound again more thoroughly now away from the site of combat and applied poultices of garlic, ox bile and lavender to it. Alfred prayed optimistically for his recovery. Elvina, never far from the site of battles, joined the shattered remnant of the Saxon army and prayed for him.

Alfred looked down on the battlefield from the nearby hilltop to which they had retreated and the casualties of his army. He could see the Danes sifting through the corpses for weapons and armour, especially helmets and chain mail. They scavenged any trinkets or treasures of any value they could find. In the meantime, the scavenging ravens and hawks were picking at dead eyes, and a few wolves had emerged from the nearby woods to feast on the entrails of the gutted warriors. Dane or Saxon made no difference to them, battlegrounds were easy pickings.

Alfred wept. 'Tomorrow when those heathens have left, we must give our slain warriors a Christian burial with full honours to ensure their passage to the care of Jesus in heaven. That is our sacred commitment to every man who fights under the flag of Wessex.'

Wilfred by his side nodded agreement, 'There is an old poem about the Danes.'

> *"They left behind them corpses*
> *for the dark black-coated raven, horny-beaked to enjoy,*
> *And for the eagle, white-backed and dun-coated,*
> *The greedy war-hawk, and that grey wild beast,*
> *The forest wolf."*

He and Alfred surveyed the carnage sadly, silently for a while and returned to the camp.

Æthelred lived for nearly three weeks teetering between life and death. He looked pale and had episodes of cold sweats and high fever. Wilfred gave him the mixture of powdered black pepper, cloves, geranium, nutmeg and thyme dissolved in small ale that he used previously for severe infections. He gave the king syrup of henbane when he appeared in pain.

Wilfred sent a rider back to Sherborne to ask Ceridwyn if she had any further ideas. A message came back via a chain of riders who had ridden day and night to bring back a message to Wilfred.

Ceridwyn said that the physicians of Mydvvai believe the most effective potion for severe deep infected wounds was a mixture of powdered sticklewort, cuckoo-button and five fingers taken both a drink dissolved in red wine and applied to the wound as a poultice. Ceridwyn also suggested ox bile in leek and onion as Wilfred knew from previous experience.

Wilfred had heard that five fingers was also used in love potions, and that witches used to dig up dead children to mix their fat with five fingers, smallage and wolfsbane to cure the marsh fever. He would not be doing that!

For the first time, he added some water from his seventh wave to the mixture recommended in Mydvvai. Wilfred suspected Æthelred had deep infection in his thigh bone. The skin healed slowly with Wilfred's various therapies, but the upper thigh remained hot and swollen as though there was still infection deep inside. Perhaps it was the thigh bone itself had become infected.

Perhaps amputating the whole leg at the hip would cure him, but that was a big operation that Wilfred had not done before. Should he operate unsuccessfully he would not only face the omnipresent black badger but have to answer to Alfred. Æthelred did not appear well enough to countenance the idea. Æthelred survived till just after Easter, then deteriorated as the night fell. Alfred called the priest to give absolution to his brother, whose dying act was to grasp Alfred's wrist and say, 'may God go with you and the people of Wessex.'

Wilfred said, 'Heahmund and Æthelred were good men, too good to lose, may they find relief in the otherworld.'

Alfred was too grief-stricken to disagree. Not only was he grief-stricken at the loss of his brother leaving him the last survivor of five brothers, but he was aware of his nearly hopeless role as the last defender of Wessex.

Wilfred could read his dark thoughts clearly, 'You may feel anxious, even unprepared for the throne of Wessex, but I have seen that you will fill that seat with courage and wisdom. This may seem silly to you Alfred, but this flask contains special sea water to me, it is water of a seventh wave. Dip your finger in the little sea water in this goblet and make the sign of the cross on your forehead. You will be doubly protected by the heavens. It will guarantee your survival. By the end of your long reign, Wessex will be a country at peace, a country of learning and Christianity, A country of wise laws and justice for all men and women.'

Alfred smiled uncertainly, but obliged wondering about the significance of the gesture. He was not in a position to reject anything that may help.

The next call for medical assistance was two days later at a more sociable hour of the morning. Wilfred and Elvina were pleased to have a visit from Hollis. Not only was she still alive, but her lump was smaller, her eyes were no longer yellow, and her liver was normal in size and consistency. She thanked Wilfred, hugged them both and put two silver pennies in Wilfred's box.

Elvina hugged Wilfred, 'your treatments are improving, you are getting close to curing cancer, you are so clever Wilfred!'

Wilfred smiled hopefully, 'let's see how she is in another six months.'

APRIL 21 871

A lfred was leading the funeral and burial rites for Æthelred in Wimborne Minster south of Sherborne. The event had been delayed by the need to ensure that another battle was not imminent. The body had been eviscerated and embalmed pending an appropriate time and place where his memory could be duly honoured.

Alfred sat pensively in the front pew, contemplating on the gravity of his inheritance. Æthelred had two sons Æthelhelm and Æthelwold, but they were infants. The Anglo-Saxon Witan had decided unanimously that Alfred should become the King of Wessex; it was indeed their only choice with the imminent threat of complete conquest by the Danes. Alfred reflected that his brother's five-year reign had as a minimum given him a chance to become a man with at least the victory at Ashdown to his credit.

Wilfred read the ancient bardic tribute to a fallen warrior.

'Then Æthelred drew sword from sheath,
Broad and bright-edged and on the byrnie struck.
Too swiftly one of the Danes hindered him,
Smashing the king's right leg.
So fell to ground the gold-hilted sword
No longer might he hold the sharp weapon

163

Nor might he longer on his feet stand fast
He looked to heaven
Then heathen warriors hacked him down
Then departed from the battle those who wished not to be there
Nor caring for war
They turned from battle and sought the wood
And its safety and kept their lives
To avenge their king another day.'

While the chanting of the black robed Benedictine Monks was bringing the service to the warrior king to a close, a dust-covered breathless rider slipped into the pew beside Alfred, his arms clasped firmly behind him by Alfred's personal bodyguard. They were very careful to protect the king from a Danish assassin masquerading as a messenger.

He gasped, 'Your majesty, the Danes are only thirty leagues away, they have just routed your defence force near the border with the Danelaw, the border gets closer by the day. As soon as this service is finished we must all flee further west till we can train and assemble another army'

Alfred and his bodyguard mounted up moving further westward. Alfred was aware that if anything untoward happened to him, there was no other suitable leader on the horizon. Christian Wessex would almost certainly be lost for ever to the Danes and Thor.

In May Alfred reassembled his diminishing resources at Wilton, but after initial success, the Danes counter-attacked and inflicted another severe defeat on the Saxons. Alfred realized he could not defeat the Danes currently, fortunately after nine battles in one year; they were both equally exhausted and depleted of fighting men.

Alfred sent his emissaries under the flag of truce; the Wyvern of Wessex held upside-down, to Ivar the Boneless and Halfdan Ragnarsson to sue for peace. A concept equally welcome to the battle-weary Danes and their depleted ranks. The brothers were pleased that Alfred was unable to see the small number of fit fighting men they had at the command. Alfred surrendered nearly all his available treasure to persuade the Danes to withdraw from Wessex. The Danish army withdrew to Reading until later that year when they retreated to their winter quarters in London.

It was the start of five years relative peace, but Alfred knew they would come again. A truce would only last till the blood money ran out. Alfred had seen the same happen in Mercia. News reached Alfred that the new king Guthrum was slowly rebuilding the Danish Army. They would only be stopped with a total defeat in battle. The battles of the year with sometimes the Saxons winning, more often the Danes winning, but neither side fully conquered had not resolved conflict between the warrior nations.

871 DECEMBER

A knock on the door revealed Alodia, now Sigbert, the metal smith's wife. She had been married only a few weeks ago, yet her advanced abdominal swelling suggested a pre-view of the honeymoon night had occurred several months earlier. Wilfred hoped the child resembled Sigbert.

'Hello Wilfred, hello Elvina, I dropped by to say my poor mother-in-law, Hollis, died last week. She was sixty-nine when she died, pretty good eh. She did really well on your treatment for over two years, but suddenly two weeks ago lumps came back all over her body. She went down very quickly. We were all so grateful for all you did for her.'

Alodia hugged Wilfred, dropped a couple of pennies in the box and departed. Wilfred again felt frustrated. Again, he saw himself as a failure. The black badger crept into the corner of his eye. Hollis had done much better than Ellsworth, but he had not found a total cure. Elvina could not cheer him up, as he sat morosely by the hearth overnight.

872-3

News reached Alfred from his network of spies all over the country that the Danish Army had returned to Northumberland, apparently to deal with a minor revolt by the lackey left in charge while the army fought for Wessex. That winter they established quarters at Torksey in Lincolnshire. Mercian money purchased peace, though all knew it would not last. By the winter of 873, the army decamped and advanced south-west to Repton.

Wilfred and Elvina were dining with Alfred and Ealhswith in the royal pavilion. 'Wilfred, dear friend, news has reached me of a plague affecting the great heathen army; apparently several hundred young warriors have died. We believe this is God's curse on the pagans, will they all die, and is there a possibility that the more godly in Sherborne are also at risk?'

Wilfred smiled, 'My Lord King, such rumours come along the healers' network as well. Indeed, God will curse pagans or even Christians who place their dunnykins near the river from which they take water, and where they wash, who do not wash their hands before food and after excretions. The Danes are dying of the bloody flux due to their own lack of knowledge about hygiene. You will have seen I ensure your armies do not build dunnykins next to rivers. I have always ensured your men are well supplied with fresh water. Repton is sixty leagues from here, at the moment there is no danger to us from the Danes flux.'

'However, the neighbouring town of Yeovil remains in danger of contaminated water as long as the abattoir throws animal waste into the River Yeo. Fortunately our town water supply is upstream from the point, but may I suggest that your legislation includes a requirement for the abattoir to bury offal and waste at least a hundred paces from the water.'

Alfred nodded to an attending clerk in the corner. Alfred always had a scribe nearby to record the king's current thoughts, prior to developing new laws on that topic.

Wilfred turned to Ealhswith. 'Thank you for your kind hospitality, may I congratulate you and Alfred on your good news. I think you will have a son this time.'

Alfred and Elvina looked at Wilfred in amazement, how had he known that. Alfred swept a blushing Ealhswith up in his arms. 'Is it true dear wife?'

Ealhswith paused and said, 'Yes my King, my moon blood is again two months late, I was going to tell you soon. I hope to present you with the next king of Wessex. How can you tell, Wilfred when I am still so early and not yet spreading outward?'

Wilfred just smiled.

874

Another knock on the door was a summons for Elvina to perform her midwifery duties for Eahlswith. Nelda was unfortunately in poor health and retired after delivering many hundreds of infants. After some six hours labour this time, a lusty child was born. As Wilfred foresaw, Alfred and Ealhswith had their first son, Edward. Although a baby Edward was now the heir to the throne, the ætheling. Alfred would need to shore up his kingdom against the Danes to ensure there was a throne for baby Edward to inherit in the fullness of time.

'Congratulations my lord king,' said Elvina, giving both Ealhswith and Alfred a kiss and a hug.

'Congratulations on the birth of your son and heir, he will be a mighty king in his time, but not for at least twenty-five years, not till his father has won Wessex,' added Wilfred.

Alfred looked both happy and concerned. 'I wonder how much of a kingdom I will be able to bequeath to my son. I hear the Danish kings give their first-born son only a naked sword, a gift to say I have nothing else to give you, you will have to carve out a kingdom for yourself!'

'However, look at this Wilfred and Elvina, this is a special gift from me to Ealhswith on the birth of our first son.'

Alfred showed Wilfred a gift he had commissioned for Ealhswith. It was a piece of polished clear quartz crystal as long as a man's thumb set into cloisonné enamel from Gaul all set into filigreed gold. Wilfred peered at it. There was an enamelled image of a man under the crystal holding floriated sceptres, and it was engraved to Wilfred's surprise in old English. Alfred usually preferred Latin for formal things. It read 'Alfred ordered me to be made'. The whole jewel was attached to a small stick of polished wood.

Wilfred exclaimed in amazement, 'why it is quite exquisite, in a thousand years people will be jealous of the craftsmanship, what is it for?'

Alfred smiled encouragingly, 'it is a bookmark and a pointer for Ealhswith's bible, and you may care to look at it with her and Elvina.'

Two days later Ealhswith knocked gently on Wilfred's door. She held little baby Edward closely in her arms. Wilfred and Elvina welcomed her in and offered food and drink. Ealhswith chattered on aimlessly for a while about the weather and the colour of Edward's eyes, but appeared to have something else on her mind. When Elvina went out for a moment, she leaned forward to Wilfred, and said in a conspiratorial whisper, 'Alfred told me once about you reading his future in the entrails of a sheep, he wondered vaguely what it would show for Edward, then said of course it's a load of pagan rubbish. I think he would really like to know, as times are so difficult and the future uncertain. Obviously, we mustn't let the bishop, or the brothers know, but would you do that for me?'

Wilfred looked surprised but amused. 'Next week there is the Shrove Tuesday feast in front of the Abbey, the night before Ash Wednesday. I will open one of the sheep before it is roasted over the fire for you.'

874 SHROVE TUESDAY
FEBRUARY 28

As dusk fell, flares and fires were lit outside the Abbey. A good-humoured crowd gathered around the fires to enjoy the food, ale and wine. It was the last chance for the poorer people of the town to enjoy a free feast till Easter. For forty days food would not be permitted till early afternoon. Ealhswith led one of the sheep behind the houses to where Wilfred awaited discretely under a flare.

Wilfred sang some ancient incantation he had learnt from Ceridwyn, unintelligible to Ealhswith, in the Gaelic tongue for a while, and then deftly opened the animal's carotid arteries. The sheep appeared un-distressed by the procedure, but rapidly collapsed. Once the blood flow abated he rolled the carcass onto it back and cut open the abdomen, steam rose from the intestines into the cold air.

Wilfred looked into the abdominal cavity for a short while before announcing, 'this is very good Ealhswith, even better than Alfred's. This liver is large; Edward will have a larger kingdom, perhaps including Mercia. There are no large red marks on the liver. Edward will have a successful reign as king after Alfred without the wheel of life languishing at the bottom for long periods. There is only one shallow division in the liver, perhaps indicating a unified kingdom at least up to Northumbria.'

'Again, the spleen edges are unusually sharp; your son will be a successful warrior, a great fighter. The appendix is in front of the bowel, as Edward will be in front of his people. He will be a leader of men like his father. His character will not be so severely tested as Alfred's has been and will be again. Again, this is one of the best I have seen,' said Wilfred smiling at Ealhswith.

'Thank you, Wilfred,', whispered Ealhswith gratefully 'I shall tell Alfred at an opportune moment, he will be pleased to hear this, though he will pretend to be shocked!'

A figure emerged from the shadows as Ealhswith departed. At first Wilfred feared it might be Osric and his bully-boys intent on burning Wilfred at the stake for his pagan blasphemies, but it was a girl. She walked up to Wilfred and said, 'do you remember me, I am Meghan. You saved my life when I was bitten by an adder nearly ten years ago. Am I old enough to help you now, you said eight was enough? Can you teach me how you do that, how you treat people, can I be your apprentice like Orva, please, please? If there are more battles you might need some more help. I'm not squeamish, I help the farmers deliver their calves lambs and piglets. please, please let me help and learn.

Wilfred smiled and grasped her forearm, man to man. 'You start tomorrow!'

875

A lfred sat in his royal palace worrying about the future when a rider arrived at the gallop. He leapt from his horse and entered the king's apartments. It was Enevold, or at least that was the name he used in the Danelaw, dusty and breathless. He went on one knee before Alfred who raised him to his feet and took him to the table laden with food and wine. Alfred filled him a goblet of wine which Enevold downed without a breath.

'My lord, I come from the court of Guthrum, the Danish King. The great Danish army has left Repton after a year there. The plague which killed so many has resolved, perhaps because their healers belatedly established the precautions described by Wilfred, they moved the dunnykins well away from the river and they wash more often.'

'The survivors have regained their strength and they have been reinforced by the arrival of many warriors from Denmark, Sweden and Norway. Guthrum seduced them here by promises of battles and wealth, women and land.'

Enevold paused for breath and another goblet of wine. 'Guthrum had sent emissaries to his homelands claiming that Wessex would soon fall to the Danes after some glorious battles. He had claimed that the Danes were better fighting men than the Saxons, and that beautiful willing Saxon women would be available for them after the battles. By spring they were fit to resume campaigning. Weapons practice was in full swing. Most of the warriors were keen to join a shield wall for the real thing. The Danes are confident in Guthrum's leadership and promise of victory.'

'Guthrum guaranteed entry to Valhalla as always for the fallen. They have conquered Mercia, driving out your sister Æthelswith and Burgred into exile and crowning Coewulf as their puppet king.' Enevold continued, 'There is some good news. Guthrum has divided his army. Halfdan had taken half the army north to Northumbria where they had wintered on the River Tyne with a view to attacking and subduing the Picts and Britons in Scotland. Apparently, his aim was to establish a Danish kingdom in Northumbria. His men would receive land for military service. They would plough the lands and grow crops. They would make a Danish kingdom under the Danelaw. Halfdan discovered that Frithlef was also your spy, I am sorry to say he suffered the blood red eagle.'

Alfred gulped and crossed himself. Every man would prefer a painful but rapid death sword in hand to that unspeakable cruelty.

Enevold continued, 'Guthrum moved the other half south preparing to attack Wessex. After moving west to winter in Cambridge, he is moving west planning to set up his base very soon in Wareham only ten leagues distant on the south coast. Small groups led by Oscetel and Anwend, Guthrum's chief lieutenants are ahead of the main army and will commence raids on the surrounding area any day now. I was with Anwend's group and managed to slip away before dawn seven days ago. I will not be able to go back ever again. Guthrum thought I was one of his bravest warriors but now they will all know I am your spy. Grimkil, your other spy with Guthrum was caught trying to leave three weeks ago, he was caught by Guthrum's outer ring of scouts and was fortunate to die with his sword in his hand. That is why you have not had much news from inside their army recently.'

Alfred knew that sometime in the future the Anglo-Saxons would have to fight the northern Danes to the death if ever this country was to become a unified Anglaland under the true God, under the Anglo-Saxons. For the moment, he would have to deal with the other half of the Danish army coming menacingly to Wessex.

Once Guthrum and his army arrived in Wareham, Alfred's emissaries approached him to negotiate. Guthrum agreed to a truce in return for most of Alfred's remaining treasure. He took most of the army and returned east, however intermittent raids and skirmishes continued for three years.

Wessex remained under a black raven cloud of half peace. Seeking a temporary relief from anxiety, Alfred and Ealhswith again sought the company of Elvina and Wilfred. Ealhswith held up her hand smiling and said, 'No need for comment, even my husband can see a child on the way. I have three months to go.'

Elvina looked at Ealhswith and back at Wilfred. 'You will have a daughter this time,' she pronounced. Wilfred nodded in agreement.

Ealhswith looked at Elvina, then at Wilfred, then back to Elvina, 'so he has taught you some tricks, I don't suppose you would like to explain how you know to me?'

'I can't explain,' Elvina responded, 'it just sort of happens!'

Alfred had other concerns.

'Wilfred, saviour of my army's health if not their souls,' commenced Alfred, 'we will be marching soon, perhaps this year, certainly by next spring. My sources of information tell me Guthrum is planning to attack Wareham again. Wessex needs your knowledge to keep my army free of plagues as well as to patch up the wounded. The deadly scourge in Repton certainly taught me about having an expert in medicine and hygiene with the warriors. I know you prefer to relieve pain rather than inflict pain in the shield wall, though I would love to have you as my wing man at the front, your speed with a blade is well known, and the Danes have heard of your magical sword. They also respect your fearless courage in remaining on the battlefield healing the wounded of both sides after the fighting regardless of who wins.'

Wilfred bowed, 'I am honoured to serve all of mankind and your kingdom.' Wilfred saw Elvina scowl out of the corner of his eye, 'And womenkind of course,' he added hastily.

Alfred responded, 'Some of my nobles and all the clergy tell me I should exile you for your pagan beliefs, but how can I throw out a loyal friend, one who expects no gifts, no honours, nor land nor titles, one who is the best healer and the second-best swordsman in Wessex?'

Wilfred smiled, 'Second best? Remember my king that we have not duelled since I was only eight and you were ten!' They both laughed amicably.

Later that year, Alfred and Ealhswith were not too surprised when their third child was a daughter, their second daughter. They looked at each other and wondered how Wilfred and Elvina knew every time. They named her Æthelgifu.

876

Alfred summoned his ealdormen and thegns of the Witanagemot to the royal hall. 'Fellow Anglo-Saxons, as we expected the oath-breaker Guthrum had led his soldiers back into Wareham. He is sending out small raiding parties into my kingdom causing death and destruction in typical Danish style. My spies do not think he has a large enough army to risk a major battle. We must reclaim Wareham. It is a royal Saxon burial ground. Amongst others King Beorhtric, the magnificent Anglo-Saxon ruler is buried there in the church Lady St Mary. He was the successor to Cynewulf and he defeated the early Danish raids.'

Elvina at the back whispered into Wilfred's ear, 'Beorhtric was ruling really well till he was poisoned by his wife Eadburh, supposedly accidentally. Did you hear she fled to a nunnery in Francia but was ejected from there when found in bed with another man! Just goes to show a man even a king should not offend his wife, or she may poison him and find another!'

Wilfred whispered back, 'And did you know that is why from that day onwards Anglo-Saxon kings' wives are not called queen because they can't be trusted!'

He pinched her bottom and she kicked his shin. They refocussed on Alfred who called for an assembly of his fyrds in three days' time. Another indecisive battle followed. After two hours fighting the two shield walls drew apart leaving a mass of dead and dying warriors. Neither wall had broken, and the surviving warriors withdrew in exhaustion. Wilfred at the rear of the conflict on the city walls had his usual number of severely wounded warriors. After fighting ceased, each side reclaimed their many bodies under a white flag of truce for a formal funeral. The Danish corpses were piled onto a longship which was then pushed out under sail and ignited with a flaming arrow on its final voyage to Valhalla.

Alfred sent emissaries to Guthrum who agreed to meet under a truce. Alfred choose the site of Maiden Castle, near Dornwaraceaster, a hill fort constructed a thousand or more years ago, by the ancient Britons. He thought the sheer size of the ramparts would impress Guthrum.

War parties of Saxons and Danes laid down their weapons on opposite sides of the hill. Six unarmed representatives of each side climbed up to meet where a huge pavilion had been erected.

Wilfred said to Alfred quietly, 'Do you think this is the most propitious place? It is said that one of Vespasian's invading Roman legions defeated the Dumnonii and the Durotriges, old tribes of Briton, here, and then after the victory the Romans put all the surviving men to the sword, and then they slaughtered the women and children.'

Alfred looked surprised, 'Now I had not heard that.' Alfred, despite his knowledge, knew little about the original tribes of ancient Britain in the days before the Roman invasion, or their beliefs. 'I hope Guthrum is unaware of that or sees no connection.' Wilfred was surprised to discover he knew more about the history of the ancient peoples of Briton that Alfred.

Alfred was accompanied by Athelheah, the new bishop of Sherborne, Æthelflæd his eight-year-old daughter, now an opinionated determined true child of Wessex, Wilfred and two ealdormen. Guthrum was accompanied by five nubile scantily clad young ladies much to the disapproval of Athelheah and Æthelflæd, who surveyed him with expressions of forced friendliness, forced by an unsought untrusted accord.

A table sat in the middle of the tent. Athelheah placed on it the Lindisfarne Gospels; a uniquely beautiful decorated manuscript dedicated to St Cuthbert a century and a half ago. It was one of the most sacred icons of the Anglo-Saxon church. Guthrum's ladies placed on the table a raven banner, then one removed a ring engraved with the hammer of Thor from around his finger, and another removed Guthrum's gold armband engraved with Viking runes apparently translated as Odin.

Athelheah looked at Guthrum's icons dubiously. 'Are these you most sacred icons, your most oath-binding symbols?'

Guthrum nodded unconvincingly.

Athelheah looked even more doubtfully at Guthrum. 'I believe you Danes have a saying, cattle die, kindred die, everyman is mortal: but the good name never dies of one who has done well. Your word should be your bond King Guthrum or we Anglo-Saxons will know you forever after as Guthrum Falseoath. Then clasp hands and may my God or your God strike down an oath breaker!' said Athelheah.

Alfred and Guthrum clasped wrists over the table and swore never to raise arms against each other for a period of ten years. Wilfred noted that the two leaders locked eyes briefly before Guthrum looked away. A slippery character was Wilfred's assessment, not one to be trusted. A snake in the grass. They then drank a toast to each other in Alfred's royal mead.

The treaty did not last as both Wilfred and Alfred anticipated. Guthrum organised the murder of all his hostages and sent a small fleet to attack Exeter well behind the front line between the Danes and Wessex. The besieged garrison had little water and could not survive even a short siege, though the Danes were unaware of this. A sudden relieving attack at first light caught the larger force of Danes by surprise and eight hundred of them fell when still half asleep. The Saxons captured a prize trophy, a Raven banner said to have been woven by three daughters of Ragnar Lodbrok. Some even thought it was woven by the three norns sitting under Yggdrasil. It was deemed to have mythical powers. Those powers were now in Saxon hands.

The banner was presented to Alfred as a trophy of the great victory. Wilfred looked delighted at the prize, 'My lord king, I have seen that flag before, the Danes called that flag the Landwaster, now we must call it the Land keeper, both for you to protect your kingdom of Wessex and for me to protect the forests and rivers.

Alfred managed to trap and destroy their fleet near Exeter. A message then arrived shortly through Alfred's network of spies throughout Wessex and beyond. The unfortunate Grimkil and Frithlef had been replaced by many others though none attempted to join the Danish army to provide inside information.

Guthrum had sent a mighty fleet of longships seeking revenge, but a storm near Swanage had destroyed a hundred and twenty ships with the death of five thousand Danish warriors. Wulfbald, Alfred's lookout at Culliford Hill near the settlement of Ogre, came to tell the tale.

'My king, from my vantage point on top of the ancient funeral barrow I can see the sweep of the coast to both the east and west of Portland Bill. I saw this huge fleet approaching from the east pursued by a black threatening sky. Soon they almost disappeared in a fierce wind and pouring rain. I was soaked and nearly blew away as well. One by one the longships vanished under the waves. The beach nearby soon was being littered with corpses.'

Alfred's inviolable fidelity to his God and his son Jesus left no room for any belief that the storm was by chance. He boasted, 'so, Wilfred, how can you deny the bounty of our Christian lord, his storm destroyed the pagans and saved us of the true faith.'

Wulfbald continued however, 'one of the few survivors said the fleet was hit by seven waves, each bigger than the last, till they were overwhelmed by the seventh wave, a monstrous wave sent by God!'

On hearing of the seventh wave, Elvina and Wilfred exchanged glances, perhaps it had been sent by the Welsh Goddess, Bloddwyn. Even Wilfred agreed that some higher force had turned on Guthrum, the oathbreaker.

No god liked oath breakers, but whether it was Alfred's god or Ceridwyn's goddess remained debatable, perhaps they were one and the same.

Again, after the slaughter at Exeter and the loss of a fleet, the Danes' warrior numbers were depleted and Guthrum once more accepted Alfred's offer of another treaty and returned to Mercia. The Saxons still lacked confidence in his word. They were happy to avoid a set battle for the present. Guthrum was secretly relieved as he thought the Saxons could probably raise a larger army than he could at that time.

Wilfred could understand Alfred's faith in his Lord, but not why he had any faith in the word of Guthrum or any Dane. Alfred said to Wilfred, 'I do not trust him, certainly while he remains a pagan believer in Odin and Thor, his oath is of little value. However, I am buying time, time to build up my own army to defeat his on the field of battle, an overwhelming victory, that will start the Anglo-Saxon domination not only of Wessex, but ultimately of Mercia and Northumberland.'

877

However, there were no hostilities the following year. Alfred and Ealhswith decided to increase their family in the hope of having a second son, a spare heir in the event of disaster befalling Edward. Elvina and Wilfred however predicted a third daughter and the child was duly born a little girl. They called her Ælfthryth.

Wilfred and Elvina congratulated the couple on the birth of their third daughter. 'Four children for you my lord prince,' noted Wilfred. Four is a significant number for us both, a good luck number. There are four Anglo-Saxon kingdoms, Wessex, Mercia, Northumberland and East Anglia, there are four days of the week named after our old gods, Tuesday, Wednesday, Thursday and Friday, and there are four virtues still important today, loyalty, generosity, heroism and love. The future looks good for Ælfthryth.'

Elvina added, 'a fourth child is symbolically very important for all faiths, it represents security and structure, our homes have four walls, there are four cardinal directions, four gospels, four seasons, and the four elements of earth, air, fire and water. This child is especially important to your family,' she predicted.

Wilfred predicted, 'she is important for the succession of the house of Wessex, for when brothers fight and the last Saxon king falls, Ælfthryth's children's children will restore the blood of the House of Wessex to the throne of England for a thousand years.'

Alfred and Ealhswith looked askance at Wilfred, 'anyone else stating that would make me laugh in disbelief, but so many things you foresee, Wilfred, come to be. I hope you will be correct about Ælfthryth, though not about brother fighting brother,' responded Alfred

Towards the end of the year Alfred planned to spend the Christmas festivities with his court and his fjord, his personal body guard at Chippenham. He sought Wilfred and Elvina, 'will you join the court and look after everyone's health?'

Wilfred was extremely worried. 'I have a feeling of snakes slithering in my gut at the idea. You should not believe Guthrum. Chippenham is not too far from the nearest Danish stronghold, my prince, perhaps we should put a spy in their camp, or spend the Christmas festival further away from Guthrum's army?'

But Alfred ridiculed his suspicious nature. 'My dear friend, not only do we have we have Guthrum's oath, but we know the Danes celebrate not only their festivals of Odin and Thor, but also ours. They will celebrate anything. They will be drunk for a couple of weeks. Chippenham is a great place. I have a hunting lodge on the edge of the forest. Our hunting parties can catch deer and wild boars, perhaps even a wolf. We shall have some great feasts of venison and boar.'

'It is a special place for me as my sister Æthelswith was married there to King Burgred when I was only four. We will be safe. You must not lose faith in humanity. Humanity is an ocean; if a few drops of the ocean are dirty, the whole ocean does not become dirty.'

Wilfred thought to himself that the Danes weren't celebrating a Christian festival, more that the Christians were celebrating an old pagan Roman one, the Saturnalia which supposedly commemorated the winter solstice. The Romans thought that occurred on December 25th. Both had that wrong, everyone, well certainly the Druids knew that Alban Arthan the winter solstice was a few days earlier on December 21ˢᵗ. The Christians also preferred to ignore the fact that the shepherds were with their flocks of sheep in the fields when their Jesus was born. It could not have been so in midwinter. At least the Christians knew that cancelling a good party would not gain many adherents to their faith.

The king sent most of his army home to enjoy the festive season with their families. Wilfred accompanied Elvina to the religious events which were pleasantly short as Alfred's priests seemed to prefer the abundant food and wine to giving long tedious sermons. Like Alfred, they didn't mind a bit of festivity. More than one was seen disappearing into the woods briefly accompanied by a young lady. The seventh commandment was on holiday as well.

JANUARY 6TH 878

W ilfred and Elvina sat on the edge of Alfred's camp as darkness fell enjoying the day's kill of venison and some of Alfred's best imported wine from Francia. Wilfred felt his suspicions about the Danes may have been misplaced. Last night they all enjoyed a huge feast for the twelfth night. Some of the old Celtic tricks had been played on unsuspecting guests. An empty pie case containing twenty-four black birds had astounded poor Æthelflæd when she cut it open, and all the birds flew past her incredulous face.

The large Christmas cake contained some roll-playing bean tokens. Elvina drew the bean becoming king for the night. Alfred drew the pea becoming queen. Both seemed to enjoy their positions and acted them out with gusto and some change of outer vestments. Osric drew both a twig and a clove indicating he was a villain and a fool to everyone's amusement, and some suspicion that Wilfred had somehow fixed the prior's slice. Osric failed to see the funny side. Finally, Alodia drew the rag indicating she was a tarty female. Ealhswith was not surprised and wondered why Alfred had invited her to the event

The day had been another feast, that of Epiphany, and all were feeling gorged with food and wine. On recovery, Alfred's court would pack to head back to Winton ceastre in a day or two. Only a few hundred of Alfred's personal fjord, now known by all the Saxons as housecarls in

Danish fashion, remained with him to celebrate the Lord's birth. Wilfred and Elvina were a little drowsy from Alfred's wine and the warmth of the camp fire.

The Danes were supposedly celebrating their own festival many leagues away, enjoying the Danegeld they had extracted from the Saxons as the price of peace. Wilfred had persuaded Alfred that the festivities of the night before should include a Lord of Misrule as that old Druid concept had since been taken over by the Christians.

Alfred had accepted that idea but had not been aware that two weeks previously Wilfred had discreetly observed the old Druid festival of Alban Arthan on December 21st, the shortest day of the year, the winter solstice. With a few followers, he disappeared into the forest for a few hours. They decorated an apple tree with mistletoe, so the branches looked silver, a sacred adornment to commemorate the Celtic Sea god Manannan. They decorated an oak tree similarly and under its branches sacrificed a young heifer to the oak god Hu, a sacrifice ensuring sexual vigour for all the men for the year to come. They consumed some steaks from the heifer and a very small quantity of mistletoe.

Wilfred's learning suggested this plant could ensure health and prevent cancers. Athene, the Greek god took mistletoe as a curative. It also gave them visions; some believed they could see transiently into the otherworld. The Greeks said Aeneas took it with him to the otherworld to ensure that he could return safely to the world of humans above.

Now Wilfred and Elvina were observing the Christian version. Even the Christians decorated trees with mistletoe, believing men were entitled to seek surreptitious perhaps not unwilling kisses from the ladies beneath it. Most of Alfred's court had not been to bed till the previous sunrise and had collapsed earlier. Alfred had carried drinks around as inversion of the social order was part of the order of the day. The women, some who were wives, some who were not, looked as exhausted as the men.

Wilfred as always was closely in tune to the sounds of the forest around him. The scuffling of the night creatures was well known to him. The wolf, the weasel and the owl ruled the night kingdom. Their sky mother, Orion, the hunter, looked down approvingly from the frosty sky to the south. Woe betides any smaller creature not in its burrow for the night. Death squeals were heard intermittently. The eternal cycles of life and death continued.

Wilfred appreciated that animals only killed to eat. The Danes appeared to kill for pleasure. Wilfred saw more honour in the fox and the wolf. Other spectres roamed the forest at night, some benign, some malignant, some with unfinished business on earth before passing to the otherworld.

Tonight, they seemed curiously noisier than usual and less like animal noises. Owls could be heard hooting around the camp. A wolf howled nearby. Realisation suddenly hit Wilfred. Leaping up he grabbed Elvina's hand and his sword, dashed into the horse enclosure and grasped four sets of reins. Several horses had been kept saddled for any emergency, and Wilfred foresightedly kept his saddle-bags on one in case his suspicions on the Danes should be correct.

He tossed Elvina onto one horse, leaped on the other and steering the other two, he led them to Alfred. 'Quick my king and Ealhswith, mount and fly, there are Danes in the forest about to attack.' As Alfred mounted dubiously, Viking war cries commenced on both sides as hundreds of Danes bearing weapons and torches poured into the unsuspecting Saxon camp. One of Wilfred's four horses fled in terror, but Alfred's eight-year old eldest daughter Æthelflæd leapt up behind him, and Alfred's wife, Ealhswith mounted behind Elvina. Wilfred, Alfred and Elvina dug their heels into their mounts, Wilfred leading carved a path with his magic sword, and in a moment, they were free of the fight, though unprepared and Alfred unarmed, it became a massacre with few of Alfred's bodyguard escaping alive.

Once a league from the camp, with no evidence of pursuit, Wilfred turned to the king and said, 'we must find somewhere safe for you from Guthrum and his army, while we plan the future. I know a place where they will never find you. We must ride for two nights and a day to reach safety. After riding through the night, as the sun rose they saw half a dozen mounted men in hot pursuit. The leader bore the gold wyvern flag of Wessex. Wilfred turned the party into a nearby clump of trees till they could obviously identify members of Alfred's body guard, some visibly wounded.

When the groups joined, the leader, Godwine, one of Alfred's thegns, dismounted and went on one knee to Alfred. 'My king, thank the Lord you are safe, we were near the horses and saw what Wilfred was doing, we mounted just after you and fought our way out, a few of us were taken off our horses. We don't think any others survived.' He looked at Wilfred, 'you are a weird fellow, how do you sense things others don't, nevertheless we owe the king's life to you, I hope you will see me as a friend, even if our beliefs are different.' He offered Wilfred his right arm and they clasped wrists with a look of mutual esteem and understanding.

Godwine turned to Alfred. 'I fear we are being pursued. On top of the last hill I could see a patrol of perhaps a hundred horsemen following us, perhaps two leagues away, we should keep moving. We will need a good hiding place. They will outrun us within two hours as we have two on some of the horses. If necessary I will lead your remaining fyrd back against the Danes, that should give you a little more time.'

Wilfred said, 'Godwine, we don't want you all to die, Alfred needs every warrior available, there will be a great battle to come, one in which the Danes will be vanquished by Lord Alfred for ever. Just give me a moment.'

Wilfred searched in his saddle-bags emerging with a small bag of powder. It was seed from the male fern previously collected on St John's eve, June 23rd. He scattered a little on each member of the party. 'This will make you all less visible. Alfred, my Lord, you will be pleased to know that collecting this on the day of St John the Baptist's birth gives it special potency.'

Elvina was aware that the date was more important to Wilfred as the old Druid midsummer festival of Golowan, when a man dressed as a horse led a celebratory procession.

Then with the aid of his flint and some dried straw and leaves, plus twigs from an oak tree, he lit a fire, then threw some purple powder from his saddlebag into the flames, muttering some ancient Celtic incantation to himself. It was the foxglove, thistle and gorse dried powder recommended by Ceridwyn. He covered the fire once alight with two pieces of peat. Within a few moments a purple mist grew out of the fire and slowly spread to envelope the whole valley. It grew so thick around them, such that they could only see a very short distance; they could scarcely see each other.

All the others crossed themselves apprehensively. They were fearful of Wilfred's power and the source of that bizarre power. It did not seem the least bit Christian despite the claimed association with John the Baptist. However; they were most grateful that Wilfred was on their side, especially grateful for this cloak of invisibility. It absorbed all sounds they made riding onward. Through the day and night Wilfred lead them through the mist with surety and confidence. No other human being sighted the group all night, nor the following day. They had eluded Guthrum's pursuit. Even Alfred was not convinced by Wilfred's certain vision of the future.

As dawn broke on the eighth of January, the mist lifted to give visibility up to half a league. There was no sign of any Danes in pursuit, there was no evidence of any human beings. None of Alfred's party had any idea of their location. Wilfred knew where he was, he was exactly where he intended to be. Only Elvina was unsurprised by his sense of direction and ability to find a safe haven for them all. Wilfred led the party through tall reeds over boggy ground. They finally reached a wide waterway and a small village of a few families.

The elder approached the party and bowed deeply. He said, 'welcome Lord, you look exhausted, how can we help you. Allow us to take your horses and give you food and drink and some rest.' Alfred on the verge of collapse was about to reply when he realised to his surprise that the man was addressing Wilfred as Lord. Wilfred slid from his saddle, and helped the women down, Æthelflæd was asleep with her arms round her father.

'Thank you, my brother,' said Wilfred, 'we will have some sustenance, but we cannot rest yet. Please accept our horses in exchange for a boat. Can you paddle us to the island of Athelney? Should anyone, especially Danes, come here you must deny seeing us. Our future as followers of the old ways depends upon not being purged by the Danes for this is the chosen one.' The community bowed to Alfred who was a little surprised to be called the chosen one.

Wilfred turned to Alfred, 'unfortunately or perhaps fortunately, there is no ford here, we have to paddle through a network of waterways, and only a few people know which way to go.'

'Fine,' said Alfred, 'it is said that in every river, the worse the ford, the better the fish!'

After a short break, the party boarded a little boat. Godwine and three of his men took the oars as directed by Wilfred. Their bulging muscles and fitness made light work of their travels. Wilfred could see these were men selected personally by Alfred for their inviolable fidelity and physical prowess. After an hour weaving in and out of a totally confusing maze of waterways, they arrived at a landing where again there were a few families. Again, they bowed to Wilfred and led the party ashore into a hut made of a wooden frame and woven reeds.

The eleven crashed on the floor and did not wake till nearly dusk. Alfred slept restlessly, the dark rivers in his brain always seemed infested with Viking longships looming out of the morning mists, the pounding of their oars getting ever closer. However, on awaking, they finally enjoyed peace and safety with a generous meal provided by their hosts.

Alfred then turned to Wilfred in amazement and gratitude. 'Thank you, you saved my family and some of my friends. How come I am surrounded by warriors, nobles and clergy, but it is you Wilfred always coming unexpectedly to be my saviour, yet you seek no reward? Where are we?'

'My dear king, this is Athelney, we are where no one can find us, we are protected by people who will give their life for us, who will never reveal our presence. The spirits of the old ways are strong here; we are near Ynys Witrin or as you name it, Glestingburg. This is the sacred island of Avalon. On the summit of the tor was a glass mansion which received the spirits of the dead going to the otherworld. We believe King Gwyn lived there on a throne of gold surrounded by exquisitely dressed courtiers. If I tell you he was king of the fairies, you will laugh at me, but while you live here, keep an open mind about the inner feelings you experience here, you may be surprised.'

'You Christians believe King Gwyn summoned St Collen, and then St Michael to make it a Christian site, but here the air is full of phenomena you may not understand, you will feel strange sensations and strange presences your God can not explain. Tomorrow I shall take you to the Chalice Well.'

The next morning Wilfred rowed Alfred accurately, inexplicably through an intricate maze of reeds and waterways to the foot of Glestingburg Tor. Only the twittering birds disturbed the aura of peaceful tranquillity. Snipe and curlew flew around seizing fish swimming too close to the surface. They reached a half-hidden wooden jetty and disembarked. A short walk took them to a hidden well where water gushed up from the ground and flowed into the waterway by the jetty. The water was stained a red colour and was warm to the hand.

Wilfred said, 'This is the Chalice Well, a special sacred well in the old beliefs. It has flowed since man arrived here and will continue till the end of time. The red colour represents life's blood and women bathe in it or drink it to give fertility. It is said that a local villain Melwas kidnapped Arthur's Queen Guinevere and hid her on the tor, but Merlin could see all things hidden with his magic and led Arthur here to confront Melwas and reclaim his wife.'

'Sometimes balls of coloured light are seen in the sky circling around the tor, some of the old folks here report balls of green, purple and white lights. At night, the whole area can be lit up, brighter than the brightest moon.

It often foretells of disaster; it has been followed by storm and tempest or even a raiding party of Danes.'

Alfred responded, 'I have never been here, but I know of this place. Thank you so much, Wilfred for bringing me here. St Gildas came here with Arthur and was able to mediate between Arthur and Melwas to achieve a peaceful solution and return Guinevere to her rightful husband without bloodshed. When Arthur died, it is said Sir Lancelot became a hermit in the grounds of Glastonbury Abbey to meditate and seek forgiveness for his adultery with Queen Guinevere. Alas it is also said that the first Saxons here destroyed the abbey a few centuries ago.'

'Even more important in our Christian faith, this is the very spot where Joseph of Arimathea buried the Holy Grail. That is the Chalice used by Jesus at the last supper, that is the vessel that caught the blood of Jesus Christ as he was bleeding and dying on the cross. That is why it is named the Chalice Well. When Joseph arrived here exhausted from his travels, he thrust his staff into the ground and fell asleep. In the morning, he found it had grown into a hawthorn bush.'

Alfred looked around, 'see like that one there, it flowers twice a year, once on Christmas Day, and once in summer. It is a unique reminder of Joseph's visit to Wessex, it marked Wessex as a holy place to Christians. Pilgrims come here to see the miraculous flowering as Christmas.

'Can your old faith explain how it can flower twice a year? Somewhere hidden under the ground here is buried our most sacred relic. The red of the water is said to come from the rusty nails used to nail Jesus to the cross or from the blood of Jesus staining the bottom of the chalice. I shall explore here when the land is won from the Danes and at peace to search for the Holy Grail as Arthur and his knights did.'

'Hm,' said Wilfred, 'the hawthorn is a beautiful plant, but also thought to be a bringer of bad luck. If it is taken inside by a husband or wife, then the spouse will be beguiled by an illicit lover in the fields.'

'Glestingburg and the Vale of Avalon is truly an enchanted place. It is a sacred site for both of us. It has strange powers, it will transform your fortunes. The earth's energy flows out in wells like this. It is going to energise you to defeat the Danes and turn your wheel of life back to the top.'

Alfred looked thoughtful. 'I am forever in your debt Wilfred, there are things about you I cannot comprehend, but do not ever underestimate my gratitude. We seem to achieve great things only when our beliefs are in harmony, when they work side by side. The old and new faiths. Don't you ever dare tell my priests that I said that. While our fortunes seem at the lowest ebb I can recall, I must send out my men to discover what is happening, to tell the Saxon people I am alive and will return as King of Wessex. I will need your people to help us in and out of the marshes. A small body of determined spirits fired by an unquenchable faith in our Lord, Jesus Christ will alter the course of the history of Wessex.'

'One day I shall found a monastery here, a quiet place of spirituality, of learning and contemplation. I hope you friends will support the idea. I may dedicate it to Neot. He will be beatified soon. I met him when I was young. Although smaller than me, perhaps four feet tall he was a warrior, but he renounced violence to become a monk. I had a dream about him last night. He begged me to seek peace, but only after my next great victory Wilfred. He though our next fight would be a great victory and lead to peace between the Danes and the Saxons!'

'He was a great example, an inspiration for me. Once he had a well with three fish in it. God promised him that there would always be three fish in the well so long as he ate not more than one a day. Once when a servant took two, Neot prayed to God for forgiveness and God replaced them the missing fish. A strange miracle you may not understand Wilfred!'

Wilfred shook his head unenthusiastically.

Alfred sat silently for a while, his head in his hands. A few tears ran down his cheek.

Wilfred said, 'come on my prince, remember your wheel is about to head up.'

Alfred replied, 'no, it's not the wheel. It's what Neot said to me. He said I would learn courage from cowardice. He said I would one-day desert my people, I would leave them to die for me while I fled the battle field and fled my kingdom. I did that at Chippenham. I was terrified of the blood red eagle. I shall never desert my people again. I would rather die on the battlefield than earn the scorn of Neot again! I wonder if I deserve to have the support of the people of Wessex on the battlefield again.'

'At night I feel like St Guthlac. He lived over a hundred years ago. He wrote a poem about the monsters that tormented him at night. He said they had yellow complexions, shaggy ears, foul mouths, horses' teeth, throats vomiting flames, scabby thighs, and such terrible mighty shriekings that filled the space between earth and heaven. The same demons haunt my dreams.'

Wilfred grasped Alfred's shoulders, 'nay my Lord, Neot's scorn should be directed against me. I led you from the field at Chippenham. I was the coward. I don't fancy the blood eagle either. We had to save you for your people. You lived to lead your army on another day. Without you all Wessex will die under the Danish onslaught. There is no grown man with the royal blood of the house of Wessex left should you be killed. Your Neot had promised you a great victory, then peace. You alone carry the hope of the men and women of Wessex, not their scorn.'

Alfred sat sullenly, unconvinced. 'You know Wilfred, some days I think I feel a tap on my shoulder. It is the cold dead hands of my father and brothers emerging from the grave to remind me of our desperate situation, to tell me that I am the last hope for Wessex. They tell me it is my duty to my family, past and present to win the next battle. They seem to threaten me with rejection from heaven, rather than encouragement on earth.'

That night the small party sat silently, morosely around a camp fire. Wilfred suddenly leapt to his feet, 'This is no good, the spirits need a sign of hope for the future. Alfred, your proverbs say, when it is most dangerous, then find comfort and good fortune. Can you hear the bull frogs all round us, their roars are to attract a mate, and their splashes suggest success? They have the right idea, much better than sitting around feeling sorry for ourselves.'

He went to Elvina and lifted her to her feet. He placed his hands on her shoulders, looked into her green eyes, and said, 'Our situation needs new life to bring hope, tonight you and I are going to make a new life to show our belief in the future of Alfred and Wessex. Here is some water from the Chalice Well, mark your forehead and breasts with some and drink the rest. It will ensure our fertility. When the wheel of fortune is at the bottom, hold on tight because it is about to go up!'

Elvina blushed briefly, then accepted his hand with enthusiasm to disappear into the reeds accompanied by cheers from the rest of the party, their spirits uplifted by such optimism and good cheer.

Ever since their unexpected wedding, Wilfred and Elvina had preferred not to bring a child into this turbulent world. Their faith in Alfred's most commendable desire for peace was limited. Elvina had consumed a tea of houseleek, black hellebore, thyme and rue to ensure her moon blood arrived regularly. She inserted a little internal moss to block Wilfred's seed.

Wilfred had anointed his pintle with oil of pennyroyal to reduce the chance of conception. This was now a sudden prediction for a more optimistic future that seemed highly improbable to the rest of Alfred's little party. However; they were all aware of Wilfred's uncanny ability to foresee the future and were much cheered by it.

On the morrow one of their hosts approached Alfred. 'I am Wulfgar, the hunter. Do you see that bird flying overhead?' Then with a swift action he raised his bow, placed an arrow on the string and fired bringing down the bird before anyone could move. The bird fell at Godwine's feet before he could so much as draw his sword to protect Alfred. Wulfgar continued, 'I will teach your warriors this skill; Danes are a much easier target than a flying bird. You can kill quite a few before the shield walls clash.'

Alfred thought briefly, and then said, 'I had a vision last night of St Cuthbert. He said even in my darkest hour, God will grant final victory, but I should avail myself of improvements in warfare. This is what he meant. We will all learn this, even Wilfred for when he hunts for food in the forest for his family.'

A few days later, the people of the village went out in their boats to go fishing. One of the ladies left some bread on a griddle pan over the fire to bake, asking Wilfred and Alfred to remove them when cooked. Unfortunately, the two were too engrossed discussing the future and how their different spiritualities might combine to defeat the Danes. The use of bows and arrows had captured Alfred's imagination. Many trained archers could seriously deplete a Danish shield wall before they clashed. They failed to notice the bread burst into flame, earning a severe reprimand for Alfred when the fishing party returned. The lady vented her wrath on Alfred believing Wilfred to be too high above her status for criticism.

'Alack man,' she cried, 'why have you not turned over the bread when you see that it is burning, especially as you so much like eating it hot!'

Alfred apologised humbly reflecting that his status here compared to Wilfred's was fairly minimal!

FEBRUARY 2ND 878

Alfred sat by the camp fire looking sorrowful as usual. He looked up at Wilfred and Elvina.

'Elvina, you know we should be celebrating Candlemas today, to commemorate the day Mary first presented Jesus to the temple. We should be lighting all the candles tonight, but we will be lucky to find one or two.'

'Well,' responded Elvina, 'the weather is dull and rainy, which is making us all a bit miserable. However, do you remember the old saying, "If Candlemas Day be fair and bright, Winter will have another fight. If Candlemas Day brings cloud and rain, Winter will not come again." So, it should warm up soon with an early spring.' None of those huddled around the fire looked encouraged.

'Don't despair, my prince,' replied Wilfred, 'today is also our festival of Imbolc, as Elvina says, to commemorate the coming of spring. The Christians have taken it over as with other festivals. It used to be to celebrate Brigid, the goddess of fertility. Elvina and I were a little premature on that score.' A little laughter rippled around the group.

'You have made her a saint, so you now remember Saint Brigid today. We share some ideas, we can make a St Brigid doll and take it round the houses to protect our homes and livestock. We can make a bed for her and leave her food and drink. We can leave items of clothing outside and she will bless them. We should also visit the holy well, you know, the Chalic Well. So, let us get busy and share some fun.'

Before bed, Alfred reflected that the day of a combined festival had been fun.

Four months went by. One day, Orva and Meghan arrived at the encampment unexpectedly.

'How did you find us?' asked a worried Wilfred. If they could be found easily, the Danes might also come before the Saxons were fully prepared.

Meghan responded, 'we went to Ceridwyn to ask if she knew where you were. She had no idea, but said she knew how to find you. She put a cauldron on a fire and filled it with some herbs, mainly mushrooms and wolfsbane, while she chanted something in a funny language we could not follow. After a few minutes when it was steaming, we all looked into it. The surface was black, black as the darkest night and deep, deep to the bottom of the world. It was terrifying. Then we saw some marshes with a big tor in the middle, and people, you and Elvina. Ceridwyn said that is Ynys Witrin. So here we are. We came on one horse stopping often in the forest to ensure we were not followed.'

The word that Alfred was alive in hiding and would return went secretly round the towns and villages, the word went across the sea to France where many of the Saxon warriors were in hiding. All rejoiced. The word was that the old and the new gods supported Alfred. Many believed that the spirit of Arthur and his knights of the round table were awakening from their slumber and their shades would be in Alfred's shield wall. Swords hidden under mattresses were kept sharp. Men practised their swordsmanship when unobserved.

Their appeals for support in arms, money and warriors from the French King were unanswered. He had no wish to bring the longboats back to Paris. A few dozen Saxons joined Alfred's party all learning how to draw a bow. Alfred excelled as he did in all forms of hunting and combat, though he would rather be in the library of the nearest abbey, studying old Latin texts. Helmets and armour were patched and polished but kept hidden awaiting the day when Wessex would call its people back to save their land, when the shades of Arthur and his knights would stand in Alfred's shield wall.

Alfred's warriors launched occasional swift and ruthless raids on nearby Danish camps, always at night. Sentries were found in the morning with their throats cut, yet no warning had been heard. Buildings were set on fire, yet no enemy was seen. Alfred's Wessex Wyvern flag left behind after each incursion was the only evidence of an assailant. Rumours went around the Danes that Alfred was dead, but his indestructible shade would wreak vengeance till they were all dead. Only then would Alfred progress to the otherworld. He had become a shadow walker, an undead wolf's head, a vengeful malign spirit, occupying a space between life and death.

The Danes had no fear of an armed foe on the battlefield, but phantoms of the night undermined their courage.

One night as darkness fell, Alfred was missing. Hours went past. Search parties failed to find him in the immediate area. Had he drowned in the waterways, was he lost, had a raiding party of Danes kidnapped him, could he have suffered the dreaded blood red eagle? As everyone prepared to sleep restlessly prior to a search again in the morning at first light, Alfred suddenly appeared carrying his harp and looking very pleased with himself. 'I have been in Guthrum's camp. I pretended to be a Danish Minstrel.'

Elvina recovered first, 'My king, that was crazy and brave. We were so worried about you. However, the Norse people are mesmerised by the harp, they think the strings represent the pathway to Valhalla, or to the heart of a woman beguiled by lyrical poetry set to music. Like the Celtic people they see it as a symbol of love because it is played close to the heart. You chose the right instrument. Not much else however, touches the hard Viking heart.'

Alfred responded, 'more than that it became a Christian symbol of devotion to the Lord after King David played his harp to express his love of God. Whatever the reason, the Danes were more than happy to relax, drink and discuss their battle plans while I played. I sang them some of Wilfred's pagan songs while they discussed their plans quite openly in front of me. Our time is short I discovered. Guthrum is planning to drive the Saxons from Wessex very soon. He has reinforced his army. His warriors will burn and pillage and destroy our army till we are finally forced into the waves at the Land's End. We must mobilise in secret and confront his forces when unexpected.'

'I shall send out riders to every town, every hundred, or wapentake as certain of the areas under Danish influence at some stage call them. We will raise the fyrd to muster at the border of Somerset, Dorset and Wiltshire at the start of May. Wilfred, we must seek the help of my God and your Gods to mobilise every fighting man in Wessex under the Wyvern banners. The Wyvern will then eat the Raven!'

Alfred then whispered in Wilfred's ear, 'And I took some fern tea, and wore a bloodstone which you said made one less visible, not that I believe that for one moment, but the Danes did not notice me walking in and later out of their camp! They must believe you!'

Wilfred spoke urgently to Alfred. 'You must raise the flag of Wessex at Ecgbryhtesstan, Egbert's stones. That is close to the border of those three counties. Not only was Egbert your forty-second grandfather, but he is the last king to defeat the Mercian's, and the stones where he kept his court were the remains of ring stones placed there many centuries ago by the Druid guardians of this land. You will feel their presence though you will not see them. Like Ashdown, if you combine the old ways and your new Christ, people will flock to your banner in the sure knowledge of victory. We will both wear a black agate, it gives confidence and courage in battle, leading to victory. I will stand beside you in your shield wall for I will be protected by the old spirits of the land.'

Alfred was momentarily stunned then grasped Wilfred's arm in mutual respect. 'Have your skills improved since you were eight?' he jested.

Wilfred smiled, 'Hakon Halfnose thought I could handle a blade a bit. Why do you think you were not wounded at Ashdown? I was beside you to protect you and take down the Danes after your royal blood. Here, wear this agate pendant, but put it under your clothes so you don't upset the priests.'

Godwine had seen the two brilliant swordsmen at Ashdown, a fight to first blood between Alfred and Wilfred would be a battle for the ages, the championship of Wessex and the Danelaw. Godwine knew that would never happen.

MAY 878

The word was put out to meet at the ring stones of Ecgbryhtesstan. The fyrds of Somerset, Wiltshire, Dorset and Hampshire, led by their ealdormen, royal reeves and thegns gathered at Egbert's stones. Thousands upon thousands of warriors arrived at the mythical site, strong, armoured, proud to do their duty for Wessex. There was a buzz about the gathering, an aura of victory, an atmosphere of honour and of duty to Alfred's Wessex. A responsibility to king and country, a responsibility to their women and children. There was an unspoken perception that the inviolable shades of King Arthur and Lancelot, even of Boudicca and all the Iceni, would march with them. It was the same feeling Alfred had assembling his army before Ashdown.

Alfred looked at Wilfred, 'why can you totally rely on the men of Wessex only when the cycle of life has taken you to the bottom, and Wilfred, why do the old stones attract so many?' Wilfred shrugged in feigned surprise and said, 'Perhaps it was your prayers to Neot!'

Alfred divided his force. He led a third of the men, the wyvern flag of the King of Wessex fluttering proudly in the breeze, while the other two thirds followed two hours behind. As they marched north-east, they saw horsemen on distant hills shadowing their progress, presumed Danish scouts. As the approached Ethandune, Alfred's scouts reported a Danish army of similar size to his vanguard was a half hour ahead in battle order.

Alfred sent a messenger to his rear-guard to close-up quickly while delaying his advance. Alfred paused just over a hill. Alfred and his mounted warriors sent their horses to the rear and he lined up his shield wall opposite the Danes. They appeared similar size armies; The Danes crashed their weapons against their shields in unison and chanted their war cries. The Anglo-Saxon men stood in an ill-omened silence, unintimidated.

Alfred, Wulgar and his trained group of fifty archers stepped forward to release a dozen arrows each at close range. Perhaps a hundred or more Danes fell wounded or killed while the rest evaded the missiles behind their shields. The attrition was limited, but the effect on Danish morale was significant. They had arrived on the battlefield aware that their leader was an oath-breaker. They feared that Odin would desert them and entrance to Valhalla be denied to fallen heroes. Anxiety sat in their hearts along with valour, but they were uneasy with the imbalance of thoughts. Now here was a force able to kill them at a distance before they had engaged in hand-to-hand combat, even before their uncertain chance to enter Valhalla if killed in hand-to-hand mortal combat.

Alfred ordered an advance just as the remainder of his force came over the sky line to the dismay of the Danes. Their war cries died out in a desultory fashion just as the previously ominously silent Saxons began theirs. The Saxons held their shields in front of the mouths to amplify the reverberating chants to a deep crescendo, a terrifying volume that sounded like a huge army of tens of thousands of warriors. The Saxon army now overlapped the wings of the Danish army and the main body of the Saxons was twenty ranks deep compared with the Danish army which was only eight ranks deep. The shield walls crashed together, but the horns of the longer Saxon line wrapped itself around the flanks of the Danish force.

Although they fought valiantly the outcome was inevitable. The battle, so exciting in prospect, so heroic in retrospect, was as always, brutally horrific. Twenty or thirty blows with sword or axe would usually see one combatant dead or severely wounded. Husbands and fathers, lovers and sons went down in the stench of blood and guts. The crossroad between now and the eternal hereafter was very short. The ground was soon discoloured

red and brown, and littered with dismembered body parts. Grown men gasped in agony for their mothers as the last breath left their body. Alfred and Wilfred stood shield to shield, their flashing blades again more than a match for larger, stronger, but slower foes.

Immediately behind the front line, Alfred had positioned his spearmen. Should an opponent raise his shield to parry a blow, or raise a weapon to inflict one, a spear would slip out almost unseen between Alfred and Wilfred, and slip between the Danes ribs, or into the eye holes of his helmet. Few withstood this double front line for long.

Alfred was wielding a new sword left to him by Æthelred seven years ago. He had not the confidence to use it before. The hilt had a guard at the top and bottom, both decorated with a gold engraving. One labelled Alfred Rex, the other Wessex. The hilt was engraved with a cross. Æthelred may have had the same premonition before the Battle of Martin as Wilfred. After two hours ferocious fighting, warriors on both sides were flagging with exhaustion, but the Danes had suffered much more severe losses, Alfred was breathing heavily, but Wilfred had barely raised a sweat. His hours of training in the forest stood him in good stead

After a short pause in which both sides could see the power and probably success of Alfred's army, they crashed together again. It was not in the Danes' nature to surrender, death before dishonour was their creed. Outnumbered, nearly surrounded, they fought on valiantly, hopelessly. Their shield wall fragmented. Each Dane was confronted by two or three Saxons. Several thousand went down. In a few hours the flower of the Great Danish Army perished, never ever to be as fearsome a fighting force again. Scarcely a Dane survived, and the Saxons also had many casualties. The Danes finally broke completely with the few unscathed warriors managing a fighting retreat. They persuaded Guthrum to leave the field, that there was perhaps more honour in achieving victory at a later day, than to die today with a sword in his hand.

Wilfred walked sadly amongst the mutilated corpses on the battlefield, clearly a few would have had a sudden death, but most would have suffered a slow painful death, especially those with missing limbs who bled to death, and those who were disembowelled. Already the smell of burning flesh contributed to the battlefield stench as the funeral pyres of corpses began to burn. One of the Saxons indicated to Wilfred that there was a wounded warrior lying just behind him. 'He may be important; he had four Berserkers protecting him till they were all cut down.'

Groans reached his ear; a man was lying with his upper arm bent in the middle, clearly broken, and a deep cut in his thigh. His skin over the fracture was intact; he had a chance of survival without an amputation. Wilfred gave him some syrup of mistletoe and madragora which soon changed his groans to mumbled songs of Viking Gods and heroic deeds. Wilfred straightened his arm, feeling the bones crunch under his hands, causing the man to scream briefly in agony before lapsing back into his jumbled songs.

He applied a slab of wood to either side of the arm and bound it lightly. Wilfred had him carried back to his tent where Elvina, visibly pregnant was already working amongst the wounded with Meghan and Orva. A gentle female hand and soothing reassurance seemed as good as henbane for relieving pain. Wilfred and his assistant laid the Dane on the treatment table where he loosened the splint, applied a poultice of boiled bran and potato with added comfrey, the standard Druid remedy for broken bones, then reapplied the splint firmly.

He checked the deep stab on the outer thigh, it was bleeding a little but had no bits of metal inside. He washed it out with water, then sutured the edges together, and applied some tincture of nettle to stop bleeding and his concoction of burdock, cocklebur and dandelion to aid healing. Finally, he covered the wound with strips of bandage, as he recited the nine-herbs charm, *'If you were a skin-shot, or if you were a flesh-shot. Or if you were a blood-shot, or if you were a bone-shot, or if you were a body-shot, as never before in your life.'*

By now the mistletoe had worn off, and the man had largely regained his faculties. He looked at Wilfred with a mixture of surprise and suspicion.

'Do you know me, I am Brynjar?' he asked.

Wilfred looked at him uncertainly, 'I know Thor's hammer when I see one,' he replied.

'So, you know I am a Dane, why not cut my throat when I am helpless?'

'Because we of the old folks care for everyone wounded on the battlefield regardless of race or creed. It is a privilege for us all to walk on this earth and when you are recovered, you can go and see Guthrum, tell him from one of the old Britons, the ones here before the Romans, that there is room for all here in peace, that a strong man cares for his wife, that a real man provides for his family, he does not leave a widow and orphans, tell him from Wilfred to seek Alfred to talk peace. A man who breaks his oath three times will not enter Valhalla!'

Not for the first time, Elvina saw her husband as the most Christian disbelieving pagan in Wessex, a mixture she found hard to fathom, but easy to love and cherish.

The Dane surveyed Wilfred with a mixture of surprise and gratitude. Two of his fellow Danes arrived, one bearing a white flag, one bearing a raven flag upside down, signs of a truce. They bowed deeply to the wounded Dane, nodded respectfully to Wilfred and asked if they could escort their lord back to the Danish camp. Wilfred nodded acquiescence.

At the end of the day, Alfred had won the most decisive battle of the last decade. The next day he gathered his army together to address them. They stood in their ranks, hundreds upon hundreds, the Wessex Wyvern fluttered proudly, victoriously in the front ranks. 'Men of Wessex, you have won the greatest battle in the history of this country, never before have invaders been so comprehensively defeated. Your courage this day will be remembered in a thousand years. I suspect the Danes were frightened to be confronted by your unconquerable spirit, I thanked my god that I was privileged to command you not oppose you. I would have run away in fear. From this day forward, this will be a Christian Anglo-Saxon country. Your wives and children, even the families of the fallen will live in peace. There is a little more to do. Guthrum and his few remaining warriors are holed up in Chippenham. We go to accept their final surrender or destroy them.'

His rows of warriors stood still for a moment, then started thumping their spears and swords on their shields, then started chanting 'Alfred, Alfred!' Cheering echoed around and around the land, even reverberating around the distant hills. Godwine emerged from the ranks with two house carls. They went on one knee and presented Alfred with Guthrum's captured raven battle standard and his battle axe as trophies of the battle, and finally a new huge Wessex Wyvern Flag as long as three men. 'My king, this will be visible to friend and foe alike from leagues away. They will know the rule of the greatest king of England reigns here, none will want or dare to challenge your authority. It has been the privilege of all of us here, and of those who fell beside us to have served under a great warrior king!'

More cheers echoed around to Alfred's surprise, gratitude and embarrassment. From the rear ranks, Alfred appeared a young man, almost boyish, with a silly smile on his face. Those who knew him or were nearer could see his expression was shaped by his experiences not his years, the creases around his eyes were sentinels to the vicissitudes he had experienced, his ride around the cycles of life. Alfred had been to the bottom of the cycle enough times to know he would need to prepare well to remain at the top. Finally, the cheering quietened, and he persuaded them to move to Chippenham surrounding the remaining Danes in their stronghold. The Danes in there were mainly women and children, the aged and battle scarred. Most of their warriors had fallen at Ethandune. Guthrum had escaped and joined the besieged survivors. Alfred sent a messenger to Guthrum announcing his terms required an unconditional surrender and an oath on Christian relics with Guthrum's son as a hostage.

Guthrum called the men together to outline the choices, to surrender now, for many to starve to death then the remainder to surrender, or to attempt a fighting withdrawal to Mercia while surrounded by a much larger army.

Ivar One-Eye, one of Guthrum's most experienced and scarred fighters stood up. A fierce red mark ran from his sightless opaque left eye to his chin. 'My lord Guthrum, may I speak?'

Guthrum nodded ascent.

'I have fought beside you and other Danish kings for ten years now. I have stood in many shield walls. I have killed many Saxons, and regrettably yes, women and children when my blood lust was up. A Saxon axe took my sight in this eye. Odin and Thor were my inspiration, Blood was the Viking wine of manly virility, we had the blood of wolves in our veins. Valhalla an exciting prospect. I have spread my seed over this land, women have fought me or endured me, and none have loved me. I have never experienced the friendship of the thighs. I have never seen desire in the eyes of a woman, only hatred. I have drunk too much in men's mead halls, but never with women other than in brothels.'

'I have lived a lonely life with my fellow warriors. We have enjoyed the grandeur of the angry sea and the relief of safe arrivals on foreign shores. We have survived the hardship and loneliness of long cold voyages. We dare not show the weakness we all feel inside to our fellow Vikings. But I have had enough. I have no known children, no house, no home, no crops, and no hearth for my old age. I own only my shield and axe. Today our women and children here are frightened, hungry and cold. They are fearful for their virtue and their lives with a victorious Saxon army outside the walls. An eye for an eye only ends up making the whole world blind.'

'The Norse Gods are for fierce young men. We have become violent bearded warriors who chop the heads off innocent people for a flawed religion. Our Odin has many names like Skollvaldr, the lord of treachery, or Bolverkr, the evil worker, or Glad of War. There is a shadow of violent death and destruction always following him. I am no longer glad of war. Ultimately our faith is going to end at Ragnarok, some frightful Armageddon of fire and destruction, and what happens to our otherworld spirits then?'

'Alfred's Christ Lord stands for peace and kindness, but not weakness. It seems to have a more optimistic outlook.' Ivar paused and continued, 'mind you, both Odin and Christ offer us some afterlife paradise, but nobody knows where it is, nobody has ever come back to tell us about the place. Perhaps it is a pie in the sky! Last village we raided the women fled leaving a plate of Saxon beef and onions pies, they were delicious. I think I prefer to be sure of a pie on earth!' The Danes laughed before Ivar continued in a serious vein.

'Sometimes after losing battles, I have endured the Christian baptism. It was that or execution. It meant nothing to me; I lived to fight another day. I have had this washing twenty times, the twenty-first time I shall pay attention, it may be a good idea. I am not a coward, but the world is changing. I do not know Alfred, though I have been close to him in the clash of the shield walls. He is not a large man, but his blade is lightening, like one of Thor's thunderbolts. I have seen him take down some of our larger warriors. There is another beside him, a slight man as well but with the fastest blade I have ever seen. That sword is said to be imbued with ancient Celtic mysticism and powers, and the man is said to be a great healer.'

'Those two will inspire the men of Wessex to invincible heights in defence of their land and their families. However; Alfred seems an honourable man who would rather live in peace with us than be forever fighting. He has a beautiful wife and children. I would like to accept his offer of peace. I would like to embrace the Christ Lord, who apparently favours peaceful sharing of the land. I would like a wife and family. I want to share the friendship of the thighs with a woman who wants me and will provide a hearth for my old age.' Ivar sat down.

His words moved the whole audience and the group sat thinking in silence and awe at his eloquence. He had summarised the feelings of all. Not one disagreed. After a while they thumped their weapons on the ground in unison to denote approval.

Guthrum stood. 'Thank you, brother Ivar One-Eye, you speak with the maturity and wisdom of an esteemed battle-hardened hero who has reached a turn in the road and seen a better way. No one could ever doubt your courage. Ragnar Lodbrok, the greatest warrior of our time, said war was the best teacher, but as Ivar says, war never taught us to love a woman and raise a family, war never taught us to plough the fields or milk a cow. War taught us to burn a village, not create a town.'

'Our lives are about to change totally. Alfred's terms included converting me to Christianity which I thought I would never do, but you have made me see a better way for both our peoples, thank you Ivar. I shall send emissaries to Alfred now agreeing his terms.'

Another silence followed, then one of Guthrum's jarls started banging his drinking horn on the table, slowly quietly, then faster and louder, one by one, all Guthrum's men followed to show approval.

Three weeks after the battle at Ethandune, Guthrum and twenty-nine of his leading warriors arrived at Alfred's court at Aller, near Athelney, clad in their finest outfits, but unarmed to be baptised. Alfred's army stood, row upon row of strong virile and very proud young men, in their finest ceremonial robes, armour shining, swords sheathed, but ready in the event of another betrayal.

Ivar One-Eye walked to the front of the Saxons, saluted the massed regiments, then, looking him in the eye, handed Godwine his sheathed sword, handle first. The two clasped arms in mutual respect. Godwine recognised a fellow warrior, a courageous honourable veteran who would never never break an oath. He returned Ivar's sword, handle first, to thunderous cheers from the Saxon and Danish soldiers alike. It was an important gesture of peaceful cooperation.

Ivar called for his blacksmith, 'take my sword and beat it into a ploughshare for me and then return it, I will have more need for that from henceforth.'

More cheers followed.

Alfred then welcomed all the Danes to his Royal Villa at Aller. 'King Guthrum, jarls, nobles, warriors, welcome to the peace of our Lord Jesus Christ. Guthrum, your spiritual name in Jesus from henceforth will be

Athelstan, my first-born brother. I wish to give you a gift as a symbol of our treaty and as a symbol of your life's journey from your Norse Gods to Christ.'

Alfred held out a carved whalebone casket as long as a lady's foot, as wide as the span of a man's hand, and as tall as a lady's hand. It was exquisitely carved. One the front panel there were two scenes, one of Weyland the Norse blacksmith, and one of the adoration of the Magi. On the left panel was the scene of Romulus and Remus being suckled by a wolf. The rear panel depicted Titus and the capture of Jerusalem in the first war between the Jews and the Romans. The lid showed the Norse warrior Egill, identified by the runes above his figure, defending a fort with his bow and arrows from his foes. The right panel showed a warrior with his horse surrounded by runic writing. All the warriors were attired as today's fighting man with helmets, breast plates and shields, while carrying swords and spears, bows and arrows.

Alfred continued, 'My brother-in-law, my sister Æthelswith's husband Burgred gave this to me as a token of appreciation after King Æthelred and I fought for him in Mercia some ten years ago. Inside is a Holy Bible for you King Guthrum, I suspect you may not have one?'

Guthrum rose and responded 'Alfred, son of Æthelwulf, son of Egbert, son of Ealhmund, son of Eaba, son of Eoppa, and son of Ingild, son of Coenred, son of Coenweald, son of Cutha Cathwulf, son of Ceawlin, son of Cynric, son of Crioda, son of Cerdic, son of Elesa, son of Elsa, son of Gewis, son of Wigg, son of Freawin, son of Frithogar, son of Brand, son of Baldur, son of Odin, son of Borr, son of Buri, we recognise your great royal blood line, not only to the ancient Kings of Wessex and your rightful heritage, but also to Odin, the King of our Norse Gods and to the first Norse God Buri. We shared a common ancestry only a few hundred years ago. However, our paths and our gods had diverged with unhappiness to both our peoples.'

'Danes and Saxons, nobles and warriors, the strength of a single man through his unconquerable devotion and decency has raised the conduct of our two nations to a much better place, a place of gracious civilisation, Alfred, we respectfully salute you, we thank you sincerely for showing us our faults, for making us all better people.'

He accepted the gift in subsequent prolonged stunned silence as he turned it around and around. 'This is too much, more than I deserve. I have heard of this, Frank's casket we call it. It was made in Northumbria by a Viking warrior and craftsman after his conversion. He was unjustly executed by some of my warriors as a traitor. The casket was lost though we searched high and low everywhere especially in your churches. The carving is perfect, unmatched. I can read the runes to you. The symbolism of ending with the adoration of the Kings is my journey. We still respect the Norse heroes shown here, but we have moved on.'

'This is a great treasure beyond the price of gold, the greatest treasure you could give to a Viking warrior. It is a mark of your trust in us, I must insist that we share ownership of this and that it stays in your Royal court. I have been an oathbreaker to my humiliation and sorrow. It will not happen again.'

The Danes were all baptised and Guthrum became Alfred's spiritual son thought he was only a few years younger.

A few days later, the two kings and their followers assembled in the Bishop's Hall, now to be used as the King's Hall, at Wedmore. Prior to feasting, Alfred addressed the gathering, 'King Guthrum, jarls, nobles, warriors, friends in Christ from Denmark, men of Wessex, princes, earls, ealdormen, house carls, warriors and citizens of Wessex. Welcome to this gathering of former bitter foes, now friends. This is the most important meeting in Wessex since St Augustine converted Æthelberht to Christianity over two hundred years ago. The land will have a peace like Northumbria some two hundred and fifty years ago under King Edwin, the first Christian king of that nation. It was said that a woman and her new-born baby could walk from coast to coast in safety at that time.'

'A year after Edwin died, Oswald became king of Northumbria. With the guidance of St. Aidan, he gave liberally to the poor, not only food, but the silver plates from his table. When he was killed, the place of his death and his bones became associated with many miracles. Like Oswald, Guthrum and I wish to ensure that no one goes without now our kingdoms are at peace.'

'King Guthrum and I met yesterday to agree to the terms of a treaty. I will read to you the clauses.'

'This is a treaty between King Alfred and King Guthrum and the councillors of the Witan of all the English race and all the people, Saxon and Danish, which is in East Anglia and Wessex, have agreed on and confirmed with oaths, for themselves and for their subjects, both for the living and those yet unborn, who care to have God's grace upon ours.'

'First clause concerns our boundaries between Wessex and King Guthrum's Danelaw; London now being a part of Wessex. The boundary will go up on the Thames, and then up on the Lea, and along the Lea unto its source, then in a straight line to Bedford, then up on the Ouse to the Watling Street.'

'This is next, the second clause concerns the Wergeld; if a freeman is slain, all of us, Englishman and Dane will be valued at precisely the same amount, at eight half-marks of refined gold, except the eorl who occupies rented land, and the Danes' noblemen; these also are estimated at the same amount as each other, both at two hundred shillings. We trust these figures place a high value on life, such that all men will bring disputes to the courts of law, rather than imposing a violent unilateral solution to personal grievances.'

'The third section sets out regulations on the number of oaths a plaintiff and defendant are required to produce in a case of manslaughter.'

'The fourth clause stipulates that a man must know his warrantor when purchasing slaves, horses or oxen.'

'The fifth clause establishes the nature of peaceful relationships between the English and the Danes. And we all agreed on the day when the oaths were sworn, that no slaves nor freemen might go without permission into the army of the Danes, any more than any of theirs to us. But if it happens that from necessity any one of them wishes to have traffic with us, or we with them, for cattle or goods, it is to be permitted on condition that hostages shall be given as a pledge of peace and as evidence so that one may know no fraud is intended.'

Alfred paused and looked at his audience. He knew the future of Wessex and indeed the whole of England would depend upon cooperation between Dane and Anglo-Saxon, an unlikely concept despite the current treaty. Peace would depend largely upon his eloquence today persuading all men and women of the value of his proposals for the future.

He continued, 'men and women of Wessex, this may surprise you, but we should from now onwards consider the Danes as our blood-brothers. We were neighbours from adjoining states of Saxony and Denmark nearly half a millennium ago. We are both from brave warrior cultures. My fellow Anglo-Saxons, the Danes are not just fiercesome warriors, they are great builders of halls and ships, they are intrepid travellers across the seas and to the ends of the world, they have a rich oral tradition of heroic sagas and poetry.'

'Odin, the All-Father of the Norse people, recognised the importance of knowledge. According to Danish legends he sacrificed an eye while hanging on the tree of life, Yggdrasil for nine days. Knowledge is power and destiny. Together we can seek the true wisdom of our Lord.'

'Our two peoples will benefit from sharing our skills under one Christian faith. Together we will make this country into a mighty state, one to be honoured and feared for a thousand years. We will be stronger, even unbeatable, together in a united shield wall. Imagine the power of us all side by side. I ask you all to consider these ideas and work with me towards a harmonious coalition.'

Alfred sat down hopefully to silence for a short period, then one by one Viking and Anglo-Saxon started cheering and banging on the tables till the hills echoed.

Guthrum stood up to address the assembly. 'Friends and brothers, King Alfred has dealt fairly with the Danes. In victory, he has shown magnanimity. His hand of friendship is sincere and attractive, it is something for us all to consider deeply. I King Guthrum sign this treaty before you. I King Guthrum will return to my kingdom in Mercia, and I will never attack Wessex again.'

Then Wilfred received a summons to the King's Hall. Feeling that he may be in trouble for some misdemeanour such as worshipping the old gods or seeing the future, Wilfred walked in with some anxiety. On entering the Royal Tent, he saw Alfred sitting on a dais at the far end with... with, yes surely that was Guthrum, the King of the Danish Army. Alfred summoned him to the front where he bowed at the two war lords, mighty men with mighty armies. Wilfred bowed again and looked askance at Alfred.

'Welcome Wilfred, dear friend,' said Alfred, 'Firstly I wish to give you a gift of something that is very special to me to mark my appreciation of your support both in good times and bad, both in health and sickness, both in peace and war. I would not be here today without your many skills, as would not one else in this room. However; more of that shortly.'

Alfred removed a ring from the fourth finger of his right hand and placed it on Wilfred's. It was made of gold with a head inscribed. Underneath the head was inscribed Æthelwulf rex 828 to 858. It had a mitre shaped bezel decorated with a central tree flanked by two peacocks. A rosette adorned the tree and foliage filled the corners. Another rosette decorated the back of the hoop. The Saxons really knew how to make beautiful jewellery.

Wilfred gasped, 'This was your father's, it is too much!'

'Quiet friend, it is too little.' responded Alfred and they grasped wrists in silent acknowledgement of all this meant. 'Secondly, I want you to meet Guthrum, my friend now, but my former enemy. He specifically asked to see you.'

Wilfred bowed to Guthrum and waited expectantly, anxiously.

'My dear Saxon, Wilfred, I expect you remember Hakon Halfnose, you may not be surprised to know he was my spy in your camp. He claimed to be a great Viking Warrior, though we suspect the scar on his face was inflicted by a woman he raped, then murdered. He had never been seen in a shield wall. I heard you took him down with your magic sword, though he is nearly a foot taller than you, to defend your lady's honour. I heard you were going to rename him Hakon Halfpintle, that you spared his life.'

'Lord Guthrum,' Wilfred replied, wondering where this conversation was going, 'Hakon's courage was such that at the time he was Hakon Quaterpintle, and there was almost nothing for a surgeon to operate on.' Laughter from both Dane and Saxon echoed around the hall.

'Well,' continued Guthrum, 'you may not be surprised to gather his body was found after the battle at Ethandune, dead with an arrow in his back, quarter of a league from the shield wall, he had been running away. You were correct about his courage. May I see your sword?'

'No Lord Guthrum,' Wilfred refused, 'My sword should not see the light of day in my hand unless it is to defend Elvina, or Alfred and his kingdom.'

Guthrum looked at him thoughtfully. 'Do you recognise this young man?' The Dane sitting next to him threw back his hood; it was the young Dane with the broken arm he had treated after the Battle of Ethandune. 'This is Brynjar, my son, my heir; I thank you most sincerely for saving his life and would like you to accept this gift.'

He gave Wilfred a small wooden box, edged with gold leaf, with a large ruby on the lid. Wilfred took it, totally amazed by the turn of events. Having expected some sort of punishment from the two kings, he opened it in amazement to find it full of dried bilberries. They were one of the best healing herbs known. They grasped wrists in a gesture of friendship and respect.

'Lord Guthrum, I am unworthy of your generosity, but I am most grateful for the contents, they grow better in your country than mine. Bilberries have tremendous healing powers.'

Elvina suddenly appeared at his side, having crept in the back in trepidation at what may be about to happen. 'Lord Guthrum,' she said, never one to be overawed by a man, any man, 'I am Elvina, wife to Wilfred, we agreed to share all our worldly goods when we married, so Wilfred will use the contents with benefit to all he treats, while I will have much pleasure, with your permission in owning the box.'

Guthrum nodded acquiescence to gales of laughter from Dane and Saxon alike in the room, so Elvina took the box from Wilfred who looked half amused, half embarrassed.

Guthrum continued, 'so Wilfred, my precious son is the enemy of your blood, you obviously could have killed him with a flick of your wrist, why did you save him, and earn my enduring gratitude?'

Wilfred responded, 'Brynjar is not the enemy of by blood, my blood has no enemies, or had no enemies till the Romans nearly destroyed our culture. We worship an old god, older than Alfred's Christ Lord, older than your Odin and Thor. We worship all life and would not take life unnecessarily. My reward is to see him well; perhaps we could have a round or two with a wooded sword to check the healing of his arm.'

Laughter echoed round the room again, Guthrum's son replied, 'Wilfred, you are a powerful Druid lord, though you prefer to keep this a secret. There is somehow more strength in your head than in your arm. I have not used a wooden sword since I was a small boy of six years. Thanks to you, I can wield a blade again as well as the next man, and would love to accept your challenge against this mythical Celtic blade perhaps to first blood?'

Wilfred shook his head, bowed to the assembled kings and war lords, and walked out.

Elvina stood in front of the kings, nobles and warriors, angered by their laughter, hands on hips, eyes afire, as fiery as her vibrant red-hair. Alfred wondered if Æthelflæd was influenced by Elvina. They were a pair of intimidating females. Neither for one moment considered that men were more important than women. His surmise was correct, the two often discussed the incompetence of menfolk.

Elvina spoke contemptuously, 'You men think a man should be manly, and a woman should be womanly. Sadly, all you men with one exception, only know one way to be manly, the way that leaves destroyed communities, widows and orphans. The exception is my Lord King Alfred, the bravest and best warrior of Wessex, but a man who prefers justice and learning to fighting. Women on the other hand know many ways to be womanly apart from lying on our backs which seems to be the only one you men know or desire.'

'Wilfred is twice the man of any of you,' she said, 'if you listened to his wise council, wise beyond his years, I would not now be caring for so many broken widows and so many tearful orphans. The women of Wessex and the women of the Danelaw could have told you men many years ago that we must co-exist or co-destruct. If women ran the country it would be a better place! It may be the cock that crows, but it is the hen that lays the eggs! Make peace between our peoples or fight a personal duel your selves, king against king, to solve your differences!'

'Incidentally, until I married Wilfred, I carried a dagger attached to my thigh. I would not have been as magnanimous with Hakon as Wilfred. He would have regretted the moment he removed his breeches. However now I doubt if the devil would soil his toasting fork on such scum.'

Elvina then followed Wilfred out of the tent, announcing over her shoulder, 'and Wilfred is most definitely not a halfpintle!' leaving some stunned silent fighting men.

Guthrum's son broke the long reflective silence. 'I would rather fight Wilfred and his Peacemaker, than have a round with that firebrand; she scares the hell out of me. She makes me double and quarter pintle at the same time. Thank Odin my wife is more timid, Lord Alfred, I think they both should be on your council, if not your shield wall.' Laugher broke out again around the room.

The land was at peace after ten years warfare. Alfred's trust in Guthrum's oath as a Christian seemed justified. Alfred had much more faith in his word this time than on the previous occasion when Guthrum's oath was to Odin and Thor. Warm summers and bountiful harvests followed, a sign the Danes saw as approval from the heavens of their change in beliefs, though many had merely changed the priority order of their gods. The Christian Lord was now the head of the gods, while Thor's amulet sat around their necks hidden by their tunics.

Only minor raids occurred in the next few years. A small Danish army occupying Rochester in Kent fled before the advancing army of Wessex. Guthrum withdrew to Cirencester and then to East Anglia. He never fought again against the Anglo-Saxons up to his death twelve years later.

JULY 878

A lfred approached Wilfred to run his latest thoughts past his dear friend. 'Wilfred, I have not thanked you for being my right-hand man twice in the shield wall. I am still overcome with gratitude that you, a man who hates fighting, should do me that honour. I am still in awe of your speed with that Celtic sword. Any king would love to have you as his first warrior, but money would not persuade you I know.' He smiled at Wilfred. Their bond of fellowship was stronger than life itself

'I must discuss something different and dear to my heart as a man of peace, as it is to yours. I see Elvina there, such a beautiful woman, and even more so now she is near her time with your child, your sign, your inspiring spirit to us all of a better future only a few dark months ago. Our children need education, my four children are now aged three to nine. Owing to the variable fortunes of those years they have run wild for much of their life. All forms of learning have declined in the last ten years. Few Christians in Wessex or Mercia can understand divine services even in English. Most cannot understand simple Latin documents. We should live as if we were to die tomorrow. We should learn as if we were to live forever.'

'I shall remind the men and women of Wessex that there were formerly wise men among the English race. Some were in sacred orders, other had secular roles. They were happy and peaceful times for the English people.

225

The kings who ruled the folk in those days obeyed God and maintained peace and morality through the land. They prospered in war adding territory abroad to their kingdom and were able to bring peace and wisdom to their new subjects. Then foreigners came in peace to this country to learn at the feet of wise men. Churches were full of God's treasures and books.'

'Then the pagans came and ravaged and burnt our houses of religion. Gold icons were melted down for jewels, monks were butchered at the altar.' Alfred paused, 'but you know all that Wilfred, sorry to bring back bad memories. Now few men living south of the Humber can read their prayer books in English or Latin. I am told that north of the Humber is even worse. Those unfamiliar with the word of God risk eternal damnation.'

'The men and women of Wessex should be familiar with the law of the land, so they know their own rights. We will have yearly meetings to discuss the great affairs of state and to settle grievances. Each year a third of our laws will be read to the community so all are familiar with them, and to ensure that improvements in the law are known to all men.'

Alfred was in full flow and full of passion, 'Even the monks in Sherborne Abbey cannot now produce manuscripts like the Lindisfarne Gospels penned by the monk Eadfrith. That beautiful gospel fortunately avoided being destroyed by the Danes when they slew saintly men at the altar. Lindisfarne is one of the most sacred places in all England. I pray to visit there in peace before I die.'

'I am establishing a court school for my children and those of my nobles, my advisers on the Witan and all my camp followers. They will learn English and Latin. Brother Samuel did a mighty job with little assistance, but he is old now and wishes to spend his final days in solitude and prayer. You may be pleased to hear he has broken his canes!'

'The people of Wessex will study our Lord's teaching under the hermit Plegmund, the next Archbishop of Canterbury, Bishop Werferth of Worcester, and my royal chaplains Æthelstan and Werwulf, from Mercia. I will establish the largest library in the whole country. Books will be welcomed from all sources. Also, I believe you know the Welsh monk Asser, from St David's who will become the next Bishop of Sherborne. I gather you and Asser have discussed the traditional beliefs of the Welsh people!'

'One of the monks here I have just discovered is an expert in new sciences. He has studied the work of Aristotle, about size and weights, about movement and speed. He has studied the stars and other earths in the heavens. He has a new book written by one of the Moors, although they do not worship the same God as us, they are advancing knowledge and we must keep up. Do you remember him Wilfred, it is Brother Parsifal?

'The other monks call him Peaceful Parsifal because he will never fight. He is always too engrossed in his books. Some say he was knocked unconscious in a previous battle and had a changed personality afterwards, one that refused to ever fight again. Did you see him just before the battle at Martin? He walked between the two battle lines, buried in a book and quite oblivious of any danger. Both side stopped beating their shields and chanting war cries in amazement at Peaceful Parsifal, before charging at each other once he disappeared to the side.'

'One of Guthrum's jarls, David, a knowledgeable man has offered to teach all aspects of the Viking culture, apart from the Norse gods. He will teach about distant places and their cultures. He will teach about travel, about building ships and navigating them across the oceans, and what crops grow best where. Jarl David will be a useful addition to our teaching staff.'

Alfred paused and looked at Wilfred. 'They must also learn about the beauty of peace and the beauty of nature. The boys must learn self-defence, and the girls must learn about supervising a household, including healing, cooking, sewing and embroidery. I wondered if you and Elvina might see a place for yourselves to help with some of that?'

Wilfred smiled, 'well certainly yes, as you know my wife is now six months carrying our child. The babe will now be covered in skin and have growing bones and is due in three moons. Elvina however is a shield maiden, not a peace weaver, she will happily teach the girls some swordsmanship, and

I will teach the boys how to do camp cooking, though my skills at bread making have not improved. Is that what you have in mind?'

Alfred smiled, 'well something like that, perhaps I should have asked Elvina first! I have also asked two scholars from across the South Sea to join us. Grimbald, a Benedictine monk from Saint Bertin Abbey and John of Saxony have consented to come to Wessex to teach us about God and Caesar. They are men of great intelligence and learning, of tolerance and tranquillity, you may find them interesting. They will improve the standard of Latin for us all, particularly those taking holy orders.'

'We also need great books to be translated into English for the less learned members of the Wessex community; I am working on the Dialogues of Gregory the Great and Pope Gregory the Great's Pastoral Care. I shall give my translation of Gregory to my Bishops to help them train young priests. Then I shall translate Boethius's Consolation of Philosophy and St Augustine's Soliloquies. It will be a great pleasure to have some quiet time to myself in the library, away from the battlefield and royal duties, to commune with these great men of God.'

'You know Pope Gregory was interested in sickness and cures. There were outbreaks of plague in Rome while he was Pope. He thought it was far more difficult being a spiritual leader than being a physician, for he must cure souls, not bodies only; it is not the physical man he cares for, but the inner, hidden man of the heart.'

'Our scholars can also translate Bede's Ecclesiastical History and Orosious's Histories against the pagans. Bede wrote about the miracles of St Augustine. Once a blind man was brought before him. The Celtic bishops had tried all their remedies unsuccessfully but when Augustine knelt and prayed the blind man recovered his sight.'

'Bede also wrote a story of St Benedict. Once a young monk had not only his arms and legs broken, all the bones in his body was crushed when a wall under constructed fell on top of him. Benedict asked for the boy's body to be brought in so that he might pray over it alone. Within the hour he sent the boy back to his work as sound and healthy as the day before.'

'And Wilfred, I hoped you could translate the old Bald's Leechcraft and add to it some new remedies for internal disorders that have been sent to me by the Patriarch of Jerusalem, Elias? The old ones were not as effective as your remedies for my sore guts, you may well remember!'

Wilfred smiled, 'I have translated Bald into the old Celtic language already. I would be most fascinated to see the new recommendations from Elias. It would be a pleasure to translate it all into English for all to read.'

Alfred replied, 'The great St Augustine said many wise things. One of my favourites is in my little book, listen to this, "*Therefore, he seems to me a very foolish man, and truly wretched, who will not increase his understanding while he is in the world, and ever wish and long to reach that endless life where all shall be made clear*".'

'A king has a divine duty to promote learning or earthly punishments will befall his people. Kings are entrusted by God to care for the physical and spiritual welfare of their people. Even Guthrum can now see the wisdom of that.'

'I once said to you that I would found a monastery at Athelney. Bishop Asser has visited there and, as you thought, not found much enthusiasm for Christianity amongst the people there. They seem more interested in tending the land, or amongst the young men, becoming warriors in our army.'

Wilfred thought to himself the locals in the marshes, especially the men, were more interested in the old beliefs than Christianity, though he kept that to himself. Alfred had an inner conflict between his totally committed belief in Christianity, and his observation that followers of the old Druid beliefs were his most courageous supporters in times of crisis. There was a strange power associated with the ancient stones of the country that had twice come to his aid.

Alfred continued, 'Grimbald is interested in finding somewhere to go back to the life of a hermit and will help establish the foundation at Athelney. John of Saxony will be the first Abbot. Many women, especially the widows with grown children, seek a retreat to a more spiritual life. There should be more nunneries for both young and old women seeking contemplation and forgiveness. Young virgins and older widows will all be welcome. The convent of St Mary's in Wareham was nearly deserted during the Danish occupation. It must be revived. I shall also found one in Shaftsbury, where perhaps my daughter Æthelgifu might find an alternative to her unruly youthful mischief.'

'Apart from education, I must look at the laws of the people, and the organisation of society so we are ready should war come again to this land.' The two grasped wrists, a sign of deep warmth and reliance, but not agreement in belief.

878 OCTOBER

Three months passed, and Elvina's waters broke. 'Dear Husband, can you send a messenger to bring Synnove to our house, she is a skilled midwife. You can wait outside!'

'First can I give you some henbane or mandragora to ease your pain?' asked Wilfred.

'No dear husband remember in my bible, in Genesis chapter three verse sixteen it says, "In pain you will bring forth children." My Christian God says it is alright for strong male warriors on the battle field to have your herbs to ease their pain, but not for women in childbirth. Unfortunately, the bible was written by men only. It is a good job we are the stronger sex.'

Synnove arrived and pushed Wilfred roughly out of the door. A little later she allowed him back in for a while. Wilfred gave her a small bag of coriander. 'Apply these herbs to Elvina's upper inner thigh to aid in the delivery and to draw out the after birth. They are best applied by a virgin midwife.' Wilfred looked at Synnove quizzically, but she only poked her tongue out at him. 'They must then be removed quickly to prevent guts following.'

Synnove escorted him back out of the door. 'Do you remember me Wilfred?' Synnove asked.

'Why yes, you have been a friend of Elvina's for years.'

'But what is the first you remember of me?' she continued.

Wilfred shrugged, trying to recall her.

'I owe you and Elvina my life. After the Danes attacked our village, you and Cerdic carried me for days. I was only two and could do no more than toddle short distances. You two carried me, mile after mile, day after day. You fed me with whatever food you could find, you fed me before yourself. After Cerdic died, Elvina helped carry me. I do not remember any of this, but Elvina told me about your kindness.'

'I remember now,' replied Wilfred, 'you clung tightly around my neck and wouldn't let go!'

'Did I?' sighed Synnove, 'I wish I could remember, wasn't I a lucky little girl! Thank you, Wilfred,' and she gave him a gentle kiss on the cheek. 'Elvina is lucky to have you father a child with her. I would have tried years ago, to see if you would father one with me, but Elvina snared you while I was a bit young. We all thought that you didn't like girls till that Beltane festival. We were surprised at your enthusiasm with her request.'

'Orva, Meghan and Elvina tell me you are a great healer, that you have a remedy for everything.'

Wilfred smiled modestly, 'they are too kind, I have my father's documents to help me, and the manuscripts of the ancient Greek physicians. You know Ceridwyn, she has helped with translations and enabled me to contact the Welsh physicians in Myddvai.'

Synnove asked, 'What do you give as love potions?'

Wilfred was surprised, 'powdered petals of roses and lavender with a little basil and thyme is quite effective. Parwynke powder, crushed dried earth worms and houselyke mixed with food enhances love between a man and a wife, but Synnove, you would have to find a husband and limit yourself to one man.'

'I would like to limit myself to one man if he would have me, even if he had a wife already,' Synnove said wistfully. 'Would you give me some,' she begged.

Wilfred was more surprised, 'from our brief acquaintance Synnove, I can't think of anyone in less need of such a remedy. Anyway, I am in the business of healing sickness, not enhancing sexuality.'

Synnove looked up coyly at Wilfred from under her dark eyebrows. 'Elvina will be out of action for a few weeks. Should you need me I am available anytime you like. Next Beltane festival you should share you seed with more than one for the sake of the fertility of our land, after all you are the Druid High Priest of Wessex. I can never be number one in your life, but perhaps on rare occasions I can be number two? Elvina may not mind too much as she recovers from childbirth if she found out. If she did she is very forgiving, and we are good friends!'

Wilfred looked at her closely. Goodness she was as beautiful as Elvina, raven haired to Elvina's redhead, but the same pretty face and stunning figure. Her pagan eyes were full of mysterious desires, but there was nothing coy about them. Synnove knew exactly what she was doing and exactly what she wanted. 'Um, err, maybe...' stuttered Wilfred, as lost for words as his first Beltane festival with Elvina.

Synnove smiled, she was aware of the admiring glances she had from men. 'Now get out, there is woman's business to be done.'

Elvina showed inner strength throughout childbirth. She scarcely showed pain, though she showered a few previously unheard epithets on Wilfred sitting anxiously outside. A child emerged to give a lusty wail. Wilfred was summoned back inside. It was a daughter. 'Wilfred, if you agree I would like to call her Ceridwyn, after a lady who helped make you the man you are today. Our Christian daughter with a name of the old ways.'

Wilfred shed a few tears and hugged Elvina in silence. He applied an external fleabane poultice for womb cleaning.

A few minutes later there was a kerfuffle at the door and in walked Alfred and Ealhswith. They hugged Wilfred and Elvina and smiled at the baby. Ealhswith gave Elvina a beautiful white crocheted christening gown, 'This is the Royal House of Wessex christening gown, we hope you will be happy to use it.'

Elvina looked at Wilfred who nodded.

Alfred extended his arm to Wilfred, and a horn in the other. 'This is Royal Mead, made from Royal Honey, in case you have other ideas about this horn, it should be drunk Wilfred, it should be drunk as a toast! Congratulations my dear friends, Elvina and Wilfred. This is not before time too, I hope there will be more before you two get really old!'

Wilfred and Alfred shared a conspiratorial smile and laughed, then grasped arms and both toasted the little Ceridwyn. The three ladies present could see there was a secret joke, but only Ealhswith had any idea what it was about.

879

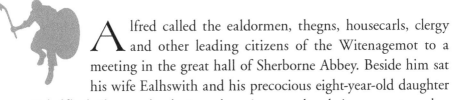

Alfred called the ealdormen, thegns, housecarls, clergy and other leading citizens of the Witenagemot to a meeting in the great hall of Sherborne Abbey. Beside him sat his wife Ealhswith and his precocious eight-year-old daughter Æthelflæd. She was developing a keen interest already in power struggles, especially if she could get her own way!

Alfred surveyed the gathering hopefully. Alfred's God expected a lot of Alfred. In return the king was humbly grateful for his God's support. Alfred's God also expected a lot from all the people of Wessex. God's spokesperson was about to spell out their inescapable obligations in detail.

He began, 'dear friends, and citizens of Wessex, Dane or Anglo-Saxon. The world around us keeps changing and we must change with it. Charles the Bald of Francia, as you know had developed a system to defend his country against invaders. However, when he died two years ago it precipitated a period of political instability and weakness there. Those Danes who wanted to continue fighting rather than live in harmony in Wessex have left Mercia and Northumbria in the last few months to campaign again on the continent.'

'They think there are lower hanging fruit in Francia than continuing to fight hard battles against our fierce Saxon warriors. We Saxons will not yield an inch of our homeland, though we will share it willingly with the Danes in the peace of our Lord.'

The assembled men, Saxon or Dane also knew the Saxons were led by a king now with mythical status as an unconquerable general. He could fight as a lion but preferred to lie down as a lamb. A lamb never to be underestimated. A lamb that could devour ravens for breakfast.

Alfred continued, 'We must now all consider the system of military power and defence in Wessex. The Danes previously organised small raids, low risk forays against easy targets. They seized gold and other valuables and then retreated to their prearranged fortified strongholds before a force could be assembled against them. We Anglo-Saxons have played a high-risk game, the head-on clash of shield walls once the fyrds had been raised, only when the Danes felt they had the numbers to win. We gambled too much on one battle. Some days we won, some days we lost. An alternative more reliable form of defence of Wessex must be found.'

'First, we must have a standing, mobile field army, one that can be mobilised immediately to combat any threat, ready to move to a vulnerable part of the kingdom within an hour or two when necessary. Until recently society had had three categories of men, those who fight, those in holy orders and the vast majority who work on the land. Life requires more flexibility. All young farmers will spend a period in the army, while most men will work in rotation on the land. They will be trained to fight, ready to protect this kingdom when the occasion demands. They will be free to tend the land when it is most essential, particularly at sowing and harvest.'

'Secondly, we must have a network of armed garrisons at each centre or burgh, and a small fleet of ships navigating the rivers and estuaries. Most Anglo-Saxons live within eight leagues of a burgh, enabling them to seek refuge. Every burgh will have a stable of fresh horses with a few skilled riders to bring messages and information of assaults to Wintan-ceastre and neighbouring burghs. Every burgh will have signal fires on the highest point to be lit in the event of an attack. Half the men in the army will be shared amongst the burghs, and half will remain here. The warriors here will be under my trusty general Godwine. They will be kept in training with their equipment ready to move out wherever essential within three hours.'

'The priests may also defend their faith along with the rest of us on the battlefield. Brother Samuel saved my life more than once with his stalwart controlled retreats. I believe our lord will understand the need to roll back pagan beliefs till this country is united in the Christian faith. Some of our churchmen appear to be enjoying the fat of the land, some battle training will enhance their health and fitness.'

Alfred looked around the room, his eyes settling on the very ample girth of the bishop of Winchester to the quiet amusement of the audience.

'The series of fortified burghs will be places where our people can seek refuge till relieved by our new mobile army. There will be thirty-three burghs throughout Wessex each about one day's march apart. I have marked the places on the map here.' Alfred looked around the assembly, 'Do I have your support to select the most suitable sites?'

All raised their hands. None would dare not to.

If the optimum defensive position was on church land, Alfred's piety would not prevent him expropriating suitable sites for his army.

Alfred surveyed the Lords Temporal and Spiritual arraigned before him. 'Ah, my Lord Bishop of Winchester, greetings, I am sure the Lord's blessings are on you this and every day. We are blessed by your gracious presence with us today.'

The Bishop smiled and frowned at the same time fearing what would come next. 'My Lord Bishop,' Alfred continued, 'The crown would be most grateful for a gift of your land for fortifications to keep the pagan invaders out and to preserve your Christian culture. Do you not agree?'

The bishop nodded grudging assent, he could do little else confronted with Alfred's power, wisdom and more Christian lifestyle than his in the opinion of many observant members of Alfred's court.

'Thank you, may our God recognise your generosity to a greater cause. My Lord Bishop, perhaps once we have established a fortification on the church's land, perhaps you would find time between your devotions to assist with weapons training?'

The room seethed with delight and amusement.

Alfred progressed professing naivety, 'Perhaps we could help find alternative accommodation for the many homeless beautiful young ladies residing in the Abbott's hall thanks to your pious devotion to charitable works amongst such apparently homeless women?'

Raucous unsympathetic laughter echoed around the room, while the Bishop looked down past his solid gold cross at the soft calf's skin boots encasing his feet. A brief nod of his scowling features indicated unwilling but unavoidable acquiescence.

The extreme wealth of the church rankled with most of society. It did not fit with the vows of poverty, nor the life style of Jesus as preached to them from gem encrusted pulpits. Any move to strip the church of any of its assets would always have general support in a public forum. Chastity and humility also seemed in short supply in the Winchester bishopric.

Alfred noted that he had won an important point and continued, 'Anglo-Saxon landowners in Wessex including the crown have three obligations or common burdens, known as *trimoda neccessitas* in Latin, to the kingdom, military service, fortress work, and bridge repair. The fine for neglecting these was called fyrdwitee. I need in addition finance to support a standing army and fortified burghs. I propose to this Witan to impose a new tax or hide based on a tenant's productivity. One hide is the value of commodities that would support one family for a year.'

The highest and lowest of Alfred's kingdom knew there would be costs in Alfred's new world. They respected him for paying his share and for imposing costs on the church as well. While none liked new taxes, they accepted this was part of their duty to keep Wessex safe and strong.

In Winchester, he repaired the stone walls and added deep ditches. In Burpham he surrounded a tall earthwork with a deep ditch and added some palisades and wooden revetments. Even the little village at Pilton was fortified as an important link in the chain of burghs across Wessex. Stone walls began to replace wooden stakes and augmented earthworks. Many burghs straddled a river with a fortified bridge to control both the road and river through the town. Royal villas were sited close to a burgh. All the burghs were linked by roads or herepaths.

The Vikings style of raids and warfare was now largely prevented. They did not possess fortified strongholds in Wessex, a larger force could be rapidly deployed against their raiding parties, and they did not have experience or equipment necessary to besiege a burgh.

Each burgh was taxed according to its population and resources. A quarter of the free men were needed for a standing army which required food for the soldiers and fortification. Half the men in the standing army would be assembled in a burgh, ready for battle within half a day, the other half could be working on the land ready to assemble fully armed in the nearest burgh within three days. The two groups would rotate duties every three months.

Alfred continued, 'The system will be called the hidage. A hidage of ten required 10 men and forty feet of wall. My scribes will record all this in a book called the Burghal Hidage of Wessex. Every burgh will have a reeve, appointed by the crown to collect taxes and to ensure the hidage requirements are fulfilled. He will be familiar with both the king's requirements and the rights of all the people. The reeve will be responsible for the development of the town as a centre of families, commerce and safety. It is my fervent desire that all men will see this as a duty to the king, to Wessex and to their families. It is for the safe future of all our children.'

Alfred surveyed the room expectantly. All men raised their fists and cheered.

'Each burgh will have roads running though it from west to east, and from north to south. The burgh church will sit at the crossroads in the centre of the town and in the centre of the peoples' hearts and lives. The north-east quarter will have an empty area for refugees' tents, and the south-west corner will be farmed to provided crops at all times and especially should there be a siege.

Alfred paused and surveyed his audience. He turned to an elderly man sitting next to him, 'Men and women of Wessex, it is now my pleasure to introduce to you King Ceolwulf II of Mercia. Ceolwulf was crowned by the Danes as their preferred king, a king they could control. After our great victory at Edington, he has recognised the power of Wessex, he can see the future will be a combined Anglo-Saxon England. He accepts my overlordship of Mercia.

Ceolwulf climbed slowly to his feet, then sank to his ageing knees before Alfred, placing his wrinkled hands between Alfred's. A tired high-pitched voice then recited the oath of allegiance, 'I, Ceolwulf do become your liegeman in life and limb and earthly worship: and faith and truth I will bear unto you to live and die against all manner of folks. So, help me God.'

The room burst in to rapturous applause. The importance of a buffer state between the Danes now retreated to Northumberland, and Wessex plus an ally in war was of inestimable value.

Alfred continued, 'with the aid of Ceolwulf, we will extend the burghs into Mercia. We will now have strongholds north and south of the Thames. There will be burghs in Oxford, Buckingham and Sashes. They will be constructed on the same lines and be part of a military system linking Mercia and Wessex. We will have complete cooperation with Ceolwulf's Kingdom.'

'Men of Wessex, this is not a defensive measure, we Anglo-Saxon warriors are now on the march forwards. This is stage one of the total reoccupation of Mercia and Northumberland into one Anglo-Saxon Kingdom. A country of peace and learning where Dane and Saxon live in harmony before God, where women and children can prosper without fear.'

'If this is not in my lifetime, then my son and heir will lead the Saxon army to the borders of Scotland.' Alfred turned to his other side and tenderly drew his four-year-old son to his feet.

Little Edward stood up proudly as Ceolwulf placed his hands between the Ætheling's little hands and repeated his oath.

Alfred's house carls burst into applause, they would have adequate soldiers rapidly available when necessary to repel the Danes. Here too was a charismatic warrior chief with a vision for a great victorious kingdom, one to lead them in battle, to final triumph and union of the country. One with total confidence that his God stood side by side with him in establishing a united Christian nation. One who somehow also seemed to have support of the old gods and heroes of the land.

With their king, they could feel the turning of the tide, the change in momentum from defeat and bare survival to optimism and success. They knew the Danes felt this change as well.

All the others followed somewhat more reluctantly. Alfred had the support to push through the new defensive systems rapidly.

Alfred surveyed his audience. They were listening carefully to every word, aware their families needed security, aware there would be new duties and responsibilities for all of them. Many of them who had fought under Godwine recognised him as a successful commander of men, but also one who would train them hard to keep them fit and battle-ready.

Godwine nodded to Alfred. 'I will keep my men equipped and ready. We will never let you down, nor the people of Wessex. Our women and children will sleep peacefully at night as they have not done before. I hope my king that you have not frightened off all the Danes, a little real combat is desirable to keep a warrior on his toes!'

241

Æthelflæd stood up and faced her father, very confidently. 'My lord father and king may I speak?' Her childlike but very self-assured voice carried across the assembly. Alfred nodded anxiously unsure what was to happen next. His entire army was easier to control than his assertive, poised eldest child.

'My lord king, you have not spoken of the role of the women of Wessex yet. Dearest Lord Father, when I was a little girl of five, you gave me a Bible and instructed me to read it. I read in Paul's letter to the Galatians it says; "In Christ there is neither Jew nor Greek, slave nor free, male nor female."'

'We are all equal in Christ. You have given slaves rights under the law. So when I am a little bigger, I shall fight in your army as will many of my girlfriends. We are better with swords than the weedy boys our age. We will stand fiercely beside you in the shield wall. I too will take the oath of undying allegiance to you and my brother.'

The audience endeavoured with difficulty to contain their mirth as did Alfred. Godwine however could not prevent some laughter. Æthelflæd drew her wooden sword and wacked Godwine on the shins. He limped around the room in feigned agony before collapsing to the floor to the delight of Æthelflæd. 'See father, I have vanquished your strongest general. We will talk later about women's duties and a women's regiment.'

'Indeed, we will,' promised her bemused father. He could see Æthelflæd would play an important role in the future of Wessex, and God help any man showing weakness in the shield wall.

Alfred smiled and continued, 'These proposals were the successful tactics adopted by Charles the Bald in Francia against the Vikings after Ragnar Lodbrok attacked Paris, defeated Charles's army in open battle and seized the city. We should adopt the same tactics.'

'As previously stated I am going to develop a system of taxation and conscription to maintain the burghs and the standing army, it will be known as the Burghal Hidage. I will explain it in more detail. Wessex needs every man to do his duty. There can be no exceptions. Men refusing the fyrds will be fined 120 shillings, land-owning nobleman will forfeit their land to the crown, other noblemen will be fined sixty shillings and commoners will pay thirty shillings each. High church officials may fight if they wish, some are true warriors in Christ,'

Alfred looked around the room and nodded to Brother Samuel. 'Some prefer more peaceful ways. Some are so moved by prayer that they appear breathless when getting up of their knees or processing down the main aisle. Some are too busy collecting the Lord's taxes to undertake weapons training, and some ensure that the young boys remain fleet of foot in preparation for the duties of manhood.'.

Alfred looked around the room, 'is that not so Prior Osric?'

Osric bowed his head, wondering what Alfred meant by his veiled comments, though titters around the room from some younger males approaching manhood suggested they knew.

'So, Brother Osric, we all know how you care for your parishioners, how you care for the welfare of the women and children, how the bishop has entrusted you with the spiritual welfare of the inhabitants of the town. Knowing you as we all do, we know that you would with to cherish the safety of the Christian people of Wessex, that you would wish to keep them safe from the pillaging, burning and raping of the Danes, that you would wish to contribute to the Burghal Hidage. I announce to all of you, the people of Wessex, that Brother Osric will agree to give a tithe of his tithes, a tenth of the church income to protect this flock. Is that not so?'

Osric, cornered, scowled in acquiescence. A little manipulation of the receipts book should prevent too much damage.

Alfred called for acknowledgement of Osric's generosity. All present stamped their feet and clapped their hands in glee at Osric's discomfiture. 'Brother Osric, I have more good news for you, your esteemed brother in Christ, my former brilliant Latin tutor, keeper of discipline among boys, and a man of the highest integrity, Brother Samuel has kindly offered to assist you with the accounting. He will have other assistants in the instruction of Latin now, so a little more spare time on his hands. As you know Brother Osric, your fellow in God is a man of the greatest intellect in mathematics as well. Is that not great news Brother Osric?'

Brother Samuel nodded in agreement. 'Thank you, my Lord King, you are kind to remember my tuition in Latin. You were a brilliant student, I er do not recall much discipline being required.'

Osric bowed his head low so all could not see the consternation on his face. Alfred had outmanoeuvred him yet again.

The audience rocked back and forth in silent glee, scarcely able to contain their laughter.

879 MAY 1ˢᵀ

Elvina and Wilfred wandered back to their home in Cheap Street from the oak tree in the sloping field. The Beltane festival had been as pleasurable as that of eleven years ago, though they did not have the raw energy of that night. Synnove had been baby-sitting little Ceridwyn.

Elvina said, 'thanks Synnove, you are a good friend, I am going to feed Ceridwyn, then go to bed. I am feeling tired. Wilfred, could you walk Synnove home safely, you know what men get like tonight, though not usually as bad as Hakon! Don't wake me when you come back.'

Wilfred escorted Synnove out through the door. Once in the shadows, she turned to face Wilfred and put her hands on his shoulders. 'This seems how Elvina gets your attention.'

Then she raised her hands to Wilfred's face and pulled him down to kiss him firmly on the lips. She felt a little pressure in response. Possession of a man who belonged to another for even a portion of an hour would be an exquisite delight and agony for Synnove. She continued optimistically, 'Elvina obviously does not expect you back immediately, she may not mind as it is Beltane if you could escort me home via the oak tree on the slopes. Remember I still have a debt to repay you!'

'Indeed, she may not mind,' responded Wilfred.

879 JULY

Wilfred joined Elvina, Alfred and Ealhswith for dinner. Wilfred was looking tired and depressed. 'My Lord King, your care of this country is working much better than my care of cancers. Since the Battle at Ethandune many men and women and some children have come to see me with cancers. I have tried nettles and mistletoe, peaches and red wine, one at a time or together, perhaps with mugwort or valerian for general good health with only temporary benefit. Sorrell is said to prevent cancer but doesn't seem any use when you have cancer!'

Elvina took Wilfred's hand, 'husband, you have given many hope, you have given many relief of pain and many more months of life, you are approaching your Holy Grail of cure. Perhaps only the Good Lord can achieve a miraculous cure. The people have great faith in your skills. Ealhswith and I recognise we are in the presence of the greatest king and the greatest healer in Wessex as well as the two best swordsmen and lovers, is that not so dear sister?'

They all laughed and Ealhswith nodded vigorously.

Wilfred looked up, 'Sorry to be gloomy, we should be cheerful, the summer has been beautiful, the night rains gentle, day after day the sun has shone from cloudless skies and the crops nearly ready for harvesting are bountiful, and,' Wilfred paused looking at the two ladies, 'I can see the abundant harvest is not only outside, but inside. Elvina and Ealhswith both blushed and laughed and said to each other at the same time, 'You as well, I am a month late?'

Alfred leapt up and pumped Wilfred's hand, then hugged Elvina, then Ealhswith. 'So, Wilfred, will they be boys or girls?

Elvina said, 'I have been studying Wilfred's methods. You will have your second son Alfred, and I shall have my first. Ours will be called Alfred if you agree my king.' She looked inquiringly at Wilfred who nodded vigorously.

One night, Wilfred walked in his front door. He was extremely tired. He and Elvina had been in the community hall discussing local issues of health and children with concerned families. Elvina still had a lot of problems with the orphans in the alms-houses to work through, but Wilfred's health responsibilities had been discussed and solved. Wilfred had been up half the previous night caring for a sick child, so he left early. Synnove had been baby-sitting little Ceridwyn again. Wilfred slumped into the lounge by the fire.

'Poor Wilfred,' said Synnove, 'let me get you some herbal tea, this one is lemon and ginger, I think you like it.'

Wilfred swallowed his tea, sleepily, unthinkingly, strange there was a taste apart from lemon and ginger, perhaps lavender, perhaps mushroom, or perhaps five fingers. All were said to be effective love potions. He fell asleep. Within moments he started to dream, brightly coloured clouds swirled around him. Suddenly they parted and coming towards him apparently was Elvina, quite naked, with her red hair hanging over her face and breasts, partially concealing both. She loosened his breeches and pulled them down. Then she straddled him on the lounge coming down slowly on his manhood. She rode him up and down vigorously till they simultaneously experienced an outpouring of ecstasy. Elvina climbed off, retied Wilfred's breeches and disappeared to be replaced by more colourful clouds.

An hour later Elvina shook Wilfred who was deeply asleep alone by the fire. 'I am back, time we went to bed.'

'Have you just returned? I had such a dream about you.'

'Well come to bed, I can do better than just dreams.' But Wilfred hit the bed and fell deeply asleep immediately.

A few days later Elvina visited Synnove bearing some flowers to thank her for baby-sitting little Ceridwyn and was surprised to see she had a red long-haired wig. Elvina thought good job Wilfred did not see her wearing that. It looked like Elvina's hair. Or maybe Wilfred had seen it in his dreams.

Synnove had been listening for once during one of Osric's sermons last Sunday, his usual diatribe about the sinful congregation. He announced that mixing the sperm of a man with her food to make her more cherished by that man was a grievous sin. Synnove thought that was an interesting idea, Osric's list of sins had given her some really useful ideas. Indeed, it was the main reason she attended church. She was now waiting to see if it worked.

MARCH 880

The two friends' pregnancies progressed uneventfully through the winter, and as the spring flowers brought cheer to the land, they commenced labour within twenty-four hours of each other. Both produced healthy sons. Alfred and Ealhswith called their second son Æthelweard.

Alfred and Wilfred grasped arms and shared a toast.

Wilfred smiled, 'Five children, Alfred, well done. Five is a special number, it is the fifth element that units all the fours, the four seasons, directions and earth elements. It is a symbol of power, power you have valiantly gained and richly deserve. I hope he is the studious type like his father to fulfil your plans, and not too like his big sister! For you it is a second son, a second heir, so important in a warlike world.'

Alfred said, 'Æthelweard shall grow up as a well-educated man of Wessex and perhaps Mercia. Not only will he give his brother support as the Ætheling, but he will learn legal rights and the use of military weapons, battle tactics and public communication. He will learn not only classical Latin and Greek as we did, but the new knowledges of arithmetic, astronomy and geometry. He will learn to play a musical instrument. He will have the chance that enforced wars denied me of trying hopefully to be the most knowledgeable and cultured man in Wessex!'

Elvina recognised their children now had one predominantly pagan name and one predominantly Christian name. She planned a Christian name for the third. She recalled her first session with mushrooms showing her three children, though she had not seen clearly if the third would be a boy or girl.

Wilfred and Alfred shared a few celebratory toasts, then Alfred expression changed from jovial to thoughtful, his more usual countenance. 'Wilfred, Wessex is now a peaceful and prosperous country. The forests are turning to green. Oak trees seem to spring up unexpectedly where there had never been any nearby. Sometimes there are new circles of young oak trees on hill tops far from here. I don't think acorns can arrange themselves in circles Wilfred. I suspect some human agency has been at work for nearly twenty years as well as the dark spirits in your forest.'

Wilfred responded, 'Alfred, gods move in mysterious circles, as do the dark spirits in the forest. Forests are home to many living creatures, some we cannot see, but they all work together weaving a magic to protect their home.'

'It is good that the oaks are growing in abundance around the countryside as many are chopped down to make ships. Alfred, in size you are not a big man, and you are usually quiet and thoughtful, but this peace and success is due to your colossal determination, through your own force of character and indomitable will. I could foresee ultimate victory in battle when we were at Athelney, but you did not have total faith in my predictions. Many lesser men would have given up. I am glad you are not my enemy.

Alfred paused thoughtfully and continued, 'Thank you Wilfred. Part of that success is thanks to you. The greatest threat to Wessex now comes from the sea. Every time we secure peaceful co-existence with the Danes here, more arrive on our shores seeing peace as a sign of weakness. I am going to move my capital from here to the coast to project our defence line forward into the sea. We will move to Wintan-ceastre. It will need much development to make it a defensible city and a Christian capital. There used to be a hill fort there before the Romans. The Romans built a city wall which will need some repairing. The city is a shambles, and the streets will need redesigning.'

Alfred had titanic knowledge of England's more recent history. He continued, 'the foundations of the church in Wintan-ceastre were laid back in the year of our Lord 642 in the last year of the reign of Cynegils. It was then completed in the reign of old King Cenwalh, the next king of Wessex over two hundred years ago. He dedicated the church to Saint Peter and Saint Paul. It became a cathedral when he moved the West-Saxon bishopric there from Dorchester-on-Thames. Cenwalh also endowed the monastery here in Sherborne as you probably know. Cynegils, Cenwalh and King Egbert are all buried there, but our house of Wessex are not direct descendants of them.'

Alfred continued, 'My father, Æthelwulf is buried there, so the cathedral is very important to the kings of Wessex. **I** expect I will be buried here one day, but there is much work to be done before that day. You, Wilfred will have to keep me well till I have completed all the tasks God has set for me.'

'The church is also a very holy place for Christians. St Birinus is buried here. He was the first bishop of Dorchester and the apostle to the Saxons. He converted King Cynegils and the people of Wessex to Christianity over two hundred years ago. A man of great faith and courage as he was faced universal hostility when he arrived in Wessex.'

'Also, some twenty years ago, Bishop Swithun was buried there, outside at his request so ordinary men and women could walk over his grave. He was a humble man, I must tell Osric about him. He taught me Latin and Greek when I was very young. He built the first stone bridge over the River Itchen. A few years after his death his body was reinterred inside against his wishes. His displeasure was apparent when it rained very heavily for the next forty days, so his remains were returned to his original grave outside. It is said now that if it is raining on his feast day, the 15th July, then it will rain for the next forty days.'

'The Holy See will beatify him shortly. Pilgrims have been cured at his grave. Once a lady carrying a basket of eggs over a bridge in Wintan-ceastre was knocked over by some unruly youths breaking all her eggs. Swithun passed his hands over them and made them whole again! It is indeed a centre of great importance to Wessex and Christians.'

'The battles Wessex fights in future will initially be at sea; hence I need a capital by the sea and a fleet of warships to counter the Viking Longships. It is rumoured that the Vikings are sailing forever west across the great sea in search of new lands. Their sailing and navigational skills are incredible, I shall seek a reformed Christian Viking on all my ships. In later years the land battles will be in Mercia and then Northumberland to make this one United Kingdom ruled by Anglo-Saxon Kings. One where Danes and all others can live harmoniously together.'

MARCH 881

A loud knock on Wilfred's door awoke him and Elvina. A female sobbing and wailing was audible outside. On opening the door, they found Synnove doubled up in acute distress. They helped her in and lay her on the couch, but immediately she leapt up and ran out to the dunny. Her story emerged between sobs and bloody flux.

'I am with child or I was. I told the man involved, well the men, there was not more than five or six, well that I remember, that's not too sinful is it Elvina? They said they loved me and I loved them all. Well, at the time. None would accept responsibility for the baby. I thought I would have to get rid of the baby. I read in your books, Wilfred, about the squirting cucumber. It was said to have been introduced to Wessex by the Romans and would get rid of the baby.'

There was a pause before Synnove continued, 'Well I swallowed two of them. Soon after I started bleeding and I think the baby has gone. But soon after that I started to get terrible tummy pain with vomiting and the flux. I feel awful. I feel I am dying.'

A hand reached out and grabbed Wilfred, 'Wilfred, can you save me? Elvina, I promise I will become a nun and never have a man again if you can.'

Elvina thought there was more chance of Wilfred curing Synnove than of her becoming a nun. However, the squirting cucumber was a very poisonous plant. She had not heard of a successful cure, not ever.

Wilfred went inside, filled a large urn with hot water, and stirred in barley flour till the solution started to thicken. He took it out to Synnove and said, 'drink this slowly till it is all gone.'

Half an hour later, Synnove left the dunny and came to lie on Wilfred's couch. She fell asleep. Two hours later she awoke. 'Wilfred, what did you give me? I don't feel sick, my awful pain has gone, and I haven't had more flux. You are a genius!'

Elvina looked as surprised and also looked askance at Wilfred. His encyclopaedic knowledge and cures never ceased to amaze her.

'It was just hot water and barley flour.'

'Barley flour? How did you know something so simple would cure her?' asked an amazed Elvina.

'My dearest Christian wife, as you know I read a lot. Ceridwyn and I have discussed herbal therapies described in your bible. In the second Book of Kings, a stew was made with that cucumber, and Elisha, one of your prophets knew it was poisonous. He advised the addition of barley flour. The flour absorbed the poison and the stew was now safe to eat. You should check it up. Its chapter four, verse thirty-eight if I remember correctly. He was a great healer.'

Elvina threw her arms around Wilfred, 'you are the most frustrating stupid brilliant pagan Christian I have ever met! Should I hug you or strangle you?'

Synnove hugged them both gratefully and left. Perhaps not surprisingly, she never said anything about becoming a nun again.

MAY 881

Elvina and Wilfred travelled in Wilfred's battle wagon down the dusty road to Wintan-ceastre. They started at first light, so they could cover the twenty-five leagues by midday, or shortly afterwards. On this occasion, his wagon was not laden with medical supplies for battle-wounded warriors. His family filled the space. The three-year-old Ceridwyn sat beside him. She was the image of Elvina as a child with fiery red hair and a strong determination to have her own way. Little Alfred lay asleep in his cot and Elvina was suckling the newest addition to the family. She had fallen soon after the birth of little Alfred with the third child she had seen all those years ago. When the child was delivered and seen to be a boy, Ceridwyn expressed her dissatisfaction, 'not another boy. He looks cute, but how long is he staying? I said I wanted another sister; can't you try again?'.

Somewhat surprisingly both parents had decided independently that Finnian was a suitable name for him. Wilfred because it was a fine old Celtic name, his father's name. Elvina because he was a saint, an Irish saint known for his teaching, humility and healing. They were on the road to show the youngest member of the family to Alfred and Ealhswith.

Driving through Cerne Abbas, little Ceridwyn spotted the white Cerne Abbas man. No one knew who made it, though it was thought to be a fertility symbol dating from around the time of Stanheng. Her little eyes nearly popped out of her head at the size of the erect penis for indeed it was six times the height of a tall man! She opened her mouth, looked at her mother curiously, then closed it. A thoughtful silence prevailed. Questions were likely to follow shortly!

The older Ceridwyn had told Wilfred that the earth works on top of the hill, Trendle Hill, used to be an old fort. The ancient Britons had danced around a maypole there on the Beltane festival. The young maidens had apparently been excited by Cerne Abbas man's virility. They were only slightly disappointed by the available young men. Young Ceridwyn could hear about that in due time.

As they reached Wintan-ceastre, they became aware of a lot of noise, crowds cheering and waving banners, mainly of Alfred's Wessex Wyvern. A bystander told them that Alfred's fleet had just returned from a great victory at sea. The Danish longboats were being turned back defeated before they could land. When they arrived in the middle of town, they found Alfred and Ealhswith mounted and surrounded by ealdormen.

After exchanging greetings and mutual congratulations on each other's' success, Alfred told them that his fleet of longboats had ambushed four Danish ships at sea destroying two and obtaining the surrender of the other two. They were riding down to the old port of Hamwic with his entourage to congratulate the victorious sailors.

Ealhswith hopped up on the wagon beside Elvina while Alfred rode on horseback along the River Itchen to Hamwic beside Wilfred. 'Well, Wilfred, my favourite pagan, I know you do not like me chopping down oak trees to build a navy, but if we can turn the Danes back at sea, there will be less death and destruction on the land. There will be less Danes using trees for their own ships and houses, less burning of forests.'

'King Athelstan of Kent some three decades ago had a victory at sea against the Danes. I intend to build a fleet of ships, more than Athelstan's fleet, bigger and taller than the Viking longboat, so we can fight them at sea, using our advantage of height and numbers of warriors, to defeat them and perhaps stop the boats coming from Denmark; it will be Alfred's Royal Navy.'

Alfred paused and raised another topic, 'Incidentally Bishop Asser tells me he is going to write a detailed history of my reign and our battles with the Danes. I have told him about your healing and how much you have done for me and the army of Wessex, but he knows of your pagan beliefs. I fear your brilliant healing skills which have kept your king well and in the front line of battle in the past will not be mentioned at all. Your name and vital contribution will be lost to history. Sadly, for you, Wessex now rules the land, the Danes still rule some of the seas, but not for much longer, but the few remaining Druids only rule their herbal dreams and visions. I still hope one-day, Wilfred, that you will join me in Christ and have your due place in the histories of our Anglo-Saxon peoples.'

Wilfred smiled, 'My lord Alfred, fame is no plant that grows in mortal soil like the Anglo-Saxon herb charm. My healing techniques and my care for the land are more important to me than my humble name, perhaps they will live on. Asser must write as he sees fit. I am pleased that a man of letters will leave a detailed history of you, your humble religious nature, your courage and prowess in battle, your love of learning and your vision for this land as the greatest country in the world.'

'When he writes of Bede's legacy, perhaps he will include Bede's prayer for the fertility of the land. As I recall it goes something like this, "Erce, Erce, Erce, Mother of Earth, May the Almighty, the eternal Lord, grant you fields growing and thriving," Erce is the ancient Druid goddess of fertility, your saint prayed to both of our gods for success.'

'I too shall leave a book, one of treatments and medicine, I have called it Lacnunga, an old Celtic word for remedies.'

An unpleasant smell assailed Wilfred's nose as an unwanted third rider pulled up alongside them, a smell of an unwashed sweaty body. Osric's voice surprised Wilfred. Wilfred was happy not to have seen Osric for years. He was more corpulent than ever. His sparse hair was plastered to his brow with sweat and his voice was interspersed with gasps for air. 'I do not understand my lord why a common pagan should enjoy royal company and have the royal ear. You Wilfred,' Osric continued sarcastically, 'I have good news for you,' he sneered. 'Do you know of the physicians of Myddvai in Wales?'

'Of course,' responded Wilfred concernedly.

'Well,' said Osric boastfully, 'We know their cures like yours came from the devil, their black magic tricks, coloured smoke and incantations were satanic, and all their beliefs were dangerous paganism. Well, Bishop Asser sent me with a hundred of our warriors, we went to Myddvai, and burnt the homes of the pagan healers there. All their false remedies and evil manuscripts were destroyed, and hopefully the devil's spawn and their heathen families with them! Your power and evils practices will be greatly diminished as well without their help, thank the Lord. The great church officers like me will be much more important again, more important than the trumped up fake healer you have become!'

Wilfred briefly concealed the extreme distress he felt. Not only had some great physicians been killed, but it sounded that their innocent wives and children had been burnt to death. How so much advanced knowledge could be destroyed by religious bigots made no sense. He would copy all his documents given to him by Ceridwyn and return them to Myddvai unknown to Asser or Alfred to help rebuild that centre of learning.

'Osric,' stormed Wilfred, 'you have made a bad bargain with me, with the old faiths and with life. Prepare to meet your maker in the near future, scum like you will not enter the heaven of any religion. Next time we meet will be your last moment on this earth! Make sure you bring a sword for I will surely have mine. It will not be to first blood, it will be when your guts are spilled on the ground in front of me, or better still, I will give you the Viking blood red eagle! May the ants shred your body to pieces and the dogs rend your limbs, may you then rot away. I trust neither king nor church will protect you from me for this unforgivable crime.'

Wilfred spurred his horse ahead, to conceal his deep anger and distress. Alfred spurred his horse to draw level with his anguished friend. Alfred turned to Wilfred, 'that was not with my knowledge or approval. I know Asser, I doubt if he sanctioned this. You can keep Peacemaker hidden. I do not necessarily agree with the medicines of Myddvai, but this was a despicable act. My court of justice will try Osric. He has been hearing the siren song of Satan, not the love of Jesus. Dear friend though you are, I will not permit you to take the law into your own hands. If found guilty of murdering innocent women and children, he will hang. Be he ever so high even in the church, he is subject to the law of the land. My law. I will deal with this immediately on our return to Wintan-ceastre.'

After a short pause, while they thought about Osric's awful deed, Alfred continued his theme, 'As I was saying, soon we will control the South Sea and much of the North Sea. Our embassies to Rome, and to Elias III, the patriarch of Jerusalem will at least cross to Francia in safety. Our merchants will be able to trade with Truso in Pomerania for their amber and fur, perhaps study their craftsmanship and buy some slaves.'

'The Celtic Princes of Ireland and North Wales, people with beliefs like yours till recently are sending embassies and wish to live in peace with Wessex. They have offered to send their best warriors should the Danes attack again. Did you know my mother once took me to see an Irish virgin saint, Modwena in Trent, because I was smaller than my brothers and sometimes had the painful bloody flux? Modwena was an anchorite but we prayed outside her chamber, I was cured of the flux for a while but still remained small!'

They passed a mill with a huge paddle wheel spinning slowly in the strengthening stream. Inside there was a huge rotating stone grinding grains into cereal powder driven remorselessly day and night by the current. A huge labour-saving device recently introduced to Alfred's new Wessex. Alfred had emissaries across the seas seeking anything new to help advance Wessex.

The entourage arrived in Hamwic, a little ancient burgh of wooden fishing huts beside a timber jetty on the west bank of the River Itchen.

Alfred looked across at Wilfred. 'Have you been here before? This is a great place for a harbour. There are four tides a day through the Solent for moving ships in and out, yet it is protected by the Isle of Wight from storms. St Williband landed here on his holy mission a hundred and sixty years ago. It is also probable that St Augustine landed at this spot when Pope Gregory sent him here about three hundred years ago. Augustine converted King Æthelberht of Kent to Christianity. He was the first king of Kent to be converted to Christianity, and together they established church sees in Canterbury and Rochester. Soon afterwards King Edwin of Northumberland was also converted.'

'You heard the story that the pope saw some very fair Anglo-Saxon slave children in the market-place in Rome. He thought they looked like angels not Angles and was distressed to hear they were pagans, hence St Augustine's mission to convert the people of this country.'

Wilfred listening carefully wrinkled his nose as they passed the slaughter-house and the tannery. 'Hamwic is evidently a special place in this kingdom, it has more pigs in the slaughter house than I have seen elsewhere, and it certainly has a special smell! It is as bad as Osric!'

The busy sounds of the blacksmith's furnace and forge and the skilled metal-workers clanging drowned further discussion. However; as they passed two workers from the blacksmith's and the metal worker's shops emerged to present Alfred humbly with a beautiful dagger made of best steel including an exquisitely engraved copper handle. On one side of the handle was a crucifix and on the other the wyvern of Wessex. One face of the blades said, 'the Great Alfred owns me', and was engraved with a cross, while the reverse bore the men's' names, Leutfrit and Biorhtelm. Both men dropped to their knees and touched their forelocks before Alfred dismounted, grasped both men by the wrist and pulled them to their feet to express his gratitude and compliment their skilled craftmanship.

Alfred, looking captivated by their consummate artistry and generosity, exclaimed, 'Just in case some Danes have crept ashore? eh, thank you, thank you both. My next royal commission for swords will come here, your workmanship is superb.' Then he tucked the dagger into his belt and rode on. Wilfred noted such expressions of love for Alfred were frequent.

Next the couple passed the Royal Mint where Alfred was having new coins made. Another craftsman merged to show Alfred one of the new silver pennies. On one side was a picture of Alfred with Alfred Rex Anglorum engraved around the head, and the Hamwic monogram on the other side. 'It is excellent, you keep this one for yourself,' ordered Alfred.

The smithy touched his forelock in respect and pocketed the coin in glee. Natural gestures of generosity made him a much-loved king.

Wilfred pulled another silver penny from his pocket to show Alfred. 'Have you seen this one, it is a silver penny from Jorvik showing your St Peter and Thor's hammer, the Vikings appear to be having a penny each way!'

Soon they passed the church of St Mary and the town cemetery as the sounds and smell of industry were replaced by the raucous sound of the seagulls and the tangy smell of the sea.

Tied up on either side of the jetty were four Saxon ships, each with sixty oars, twice as big as the Viking longboats, and with a forecastle for archers. Fire arrows could burn a ship to the waterline without direct engagement. Shields were attached all along the side. There were three patterns in a recurring sequence, the Wessex Wyvern, a gold Saxon crown above two oak sprigs, and the Saxon Cross. This was made from two concentric circles with the limbs of the cross in the outer circle. The four limbs of the cross at the top and bottom and on the two sides were narrower in the middle and curved out to their widest point edge, and the ends were semi-circular.

Wilfred looked in surprise at Alfred, 'Oaks on your flags my lord King?' he jested.

Alfred smiled, 'Oak is a tough timber, like the Anglo-Saxon people. It is important to the people of Wessex as it creates their first line of defence now in the seas around my kingdom. And look at those doughty sailors;

indeed, they have hearts of oak. Some of the old folks like you Wilfred seem to find some other attraction to the oak!'

The sails were furled neatly. The crews of each ship were lined up next to their boat, all looking immaculate wearing Wessex Wyvern tabards. On Alfred's arrived the fleet captain called for hurrahs for Alfred who walked slowly up the lines of sailor warriors to clasp arms and thank each one. Then Alfred stood before them all to praise them for their skills as fighting seamen and for taking the defence line of Wessex further out to the seas.

Next the captured Danes were brought forth to be addressed by one of Alfred's ealdormen.

'You have broken the sacred truce between our people, Guthrum's truce,' he boomed, 'as oath breakers you are condemned, your Valhalla is closed forever to you. The leaders aboard the two ships will be hung now. The rest of the captives may return home on your own damaged ship on your oath never to return here or join King Alfred's navy. My Lord King recognises your great skills as fighting seamen and as expert sailors and courageous navigators of Denmark. If your heart is now truly with Jesus and Wessex, the king will welcome you into his navy. However, any subsequent disloyalty aboard will lead to instant execution. You have one hour to choose.'

There were some things Alfred would not forgive. Displaying a soft forgiving heart, the one genuinely, deeply, inside Alfred, would undermine his unwavering authority. He steeled himself for the good of the country to only show mercy to the followers, not the leaders. They watched as the Danish captains were hung. They submitted to their sentence with their heads held high, true to their beliefs as Vikings, they showed no fear. Their wish to hold a sword in their hand was magnanimously granted by the king, though their arms were pinned to their sides.

The others to a man asked to fight for Alfred's new navy. Alfred was delighted. They would be spread between many ships, never more than two Danes in one of Alfred's vessels. He knew their unequalled seamanship and navigational skills would benefit his navy.

The citizens of Hamwic repaired in good spirits to the local tavern, "Ye Olde Fighting Cock", they enjoyed a good hanging, especially when a few Danes were doing the dance of death under the gallows. Even better, drinks were on the king to celebrate the victory. After a few rounds, a warning call from the harbour bought them out again, clutching their ales in one hand and swords in the other. They were prepared for all eventualities.

Another boat had been seen in the far distance. It was apparently flying above the water with the birds! The Christians all crossed themselves fearfully and clutched their swords more tightly. Was it the second coming or a work of the devil? The followers of other faiths or of none, muttered darkly about evil eyes.

Wilfrid laughed and explained 'This is an old trick of light, it used to be called Morgana's spell after Morgana, the Lady of the Lake, King Arthur's half-sister. People thought she could put a spell on boats and make them fly! It occurs when it is cold at sea and warm here. The boat will come down soon.

The crowd were only partially reassured until as Wilfred predicted, it came down to sea level as it approached Hamwic harbour. One of Alfred's sailors, a man of keen sight, said, 'it has no flag, there are only a few sailors, but there are many women on board.'

Swords were re-sheathed, pots of ale renewed, and all waited as the ship drew closer. Sounds wafted across the water. Wilfred recognised the singing first. 'That is one of the old Celtic songs my mother sang to me when I was a little boy, it is about the fishermen returning safely from the sea with a bountiful harvest of fish after surviving storms on the oceans.'

Elvina recognised it as well. They both ran in hopeful disbelief to the dock as the boat pulled alongside. Two frail elderly ladies came down the gangplank first, still singing and supported by some middle-aged women. They were Gwendolyn, Wilfred's mother and Kendra, Elvina's mother. Assisting them were Rowena, Wilfred's sister and Mona, Elvina's sister. It was twenty-two years since they had been forcibly separated by Ragnar Four-fingers. They never ever expected to meet again.

On the dock, the old ladies shrugged off their supports and walked heads held high to their children. Heads held high as they had been on the last day Wilfred and Elvina had seen them.

The scene was one of hugs and kisses, tears and laughter. The two old ladies were ecstatic to discover Wilfred and Elvina were married. 'We always hoped this would happen, you were so right for each other even when you were both eight.'

Little Ceridwyn, Alfred and Finnian suddenly found they had two grandmothers and two aunts.

Alfred watching with pleasure said, 'indeed this seems a boat from heaven!'

Between sobs and hugs, Elvina asked, 'where have you been? Ragnar told us over ten years ago that he had you taken fearfully to a convent in Ireland. He said he would bring you back as a debt of gratitude to Wilfred, but you never came. For the second time, we gave up hope of ever seeing you again.'

Wilfred's mother, Gwendolyn, his sister Rowena, and Elvina's mother, Kendra and her sister, Mona, explained slowly, between happy tears and laughter.

'Ragnar was frightened of us after a couple of his men died from our curses. We were taken untouched by Viking ship to Ireland and left in a convent in Dublin. The mother superior was very strict. She made us go to services five times daily. We were ordered to confess our pagan past. Sometimes we were callously whipped for our sins. Often, we were locked up in a cold cell and lived on only bread and water for a day or two. Two of the priests abused Mona and Rowena several times every week when they were still young women, still virgins at first. We cursed them on the full moon. We heard later one had died in severe pain and the other was covered in scales, shunned by his flock. Serve them right!'

'Finally, one day when not being watched closely, we broke out through the convent doors as a supply wagon entered in the other direction. We walked hastily west for days keeping off the main roads, surviving on berries in the hedges and fruit in orchards, or occasionally kind village people took pity on us and offered food and shelter for a night. We walked on till we reached the sea again in a place called Galway. There we stayed, hopefully where neither Vikings nor priests would find us. We were able to support ourselves by looking after children, helping with harvests, healing the sick and foretelling the future.'

'We had been there ten years, thinking our children had probably been killed by the Danes. Then one day a Viking ship arrived in the harbour. On board was a Danish man, Hjalmar. He was Ragnar Fourfingers' right hand warrior. He had searched Ireland for two years for us. Ragnar said to him that he owed Wilfred more that he could repay. He told Hjalmar not to return without us. He never gave up. He discovered that we had escaped from the convent, he found some people who may have seen us heading west, but then his trail ran out. He sailed round every big port in Ireland and searched the area looking for four women, until he came to Galway and after asking in every market place and church and tavern, was finally directed to the four of us. He promised to return us to our children in Wessex. So here we are.'

Alfred and Ealhswith heard the story and declared that more drinks in the tavern were free for all at Alfred's expense. They should drink the tavern dry. Never had they all heard so much good news in a single day. The Danes who had decided to join Alfred's navy decided they had made a good choice. An ale drinking completion between Dane and Anglo-Saxon sailor ended in a most amicable draw as Ye Olde Fighting Cock ran out of all drink an hour or two after sunset. All the men sat around a roaring bonfire, arms around each other's shoulders, Saxon and Dane together, singing shared fighting men's' song and love songs. Some lucky ones carousing with the local young ladies.

Alfred could see a united country where all lived together on the bounty of Wessex was indeed possible. He sat by the flames with an arm round Ealhswith and an ale in the other hand looking surprised but hopeful, his face glowing red in the firelight.' You know dear wife, Elvina and Wilfred, this could just work!'

JUNE 881

Wilfred introduced Rowena, Gwendolyn, Kendra and Mona to Ceridwyn on their return to Sherborne the next morning. Ceridwyn and Rowena recalled meeting each other when both Druid acolytes on the Isle of Mona nearly half a century earlier. Their reunion was joyful. However, Wilfred then told Ceridwyn of Osric's deeds. She wept and wailed and beat her breast and head for an hour or more, then seemed suddenly, ominously calm. Ceridwyn searched though Wilfred's bucket of ginger roots. She found a suitable one which with a few deft strokes of her knife adopted the shape of a man.

She walked out into the field clutching a flare, followed by Gwendolyn and Kendra. First, she wrote Osric's name on a piece of parchment. They all spat on his name, burnt it in the flame and stomped on the ashes. Then they all began chanting. Each placed a pin in the male effigy, the first in the abdomen, the second and third in the genital area, next each chopped of a limb like appendage, then Ceridwyn chopped a small piece that could have represented the figure's manhood, and as the chanting reached a climax, with a final swirl of the knife she beheaded the figurine. The remains were thrown disdainfully into the fire.

No one watching would ever underestimate the ageless mystical power of women in future! It was a terrifying ceremony to behold.

Wilfred wondered if Osric would survive till his trial. However, Wilfred heard it would begin on the morrow and they all left for Wintan-ceastre.

In the town square, there was a large assembly. Osric was snivelling in the dock. Alfred sat silently on his throne observing. Bishop Asser appeared to be leading the prosecution. He stated that Osric had acted without his knowledge or approval. One of the house-carls, Rand, who led the troop to attack Myddvai, stated that Osric ordered the attack and claimed to have the authority of Alfred and Asser. Osric had a document of authority but it transpired that he had forged it. Rand repeatedly questioned the orders that would probably kill all the innocent women and children, but finally and reluctantly obeyed the demands of Osric, who by then was frothing at the mouth and demanding God's vengeance. Rand put flaming torches to houses. Nobody escaped. He could still hear the screams of children in his head. He regretted the event and had confessed the event several times to Bishop Asser without naming Osric. He did not need to.

Osric pleaded innocence, 'they were only Welsh people, pagan druids, rubbish people of no account, scarcely humans. I was obeying the will of God. God spoke to me about cleansing his kingdom of scum. I was responding to his will!' Osric then began raving about the sins of the Druids, again frothing at the mouth and trying to summon his deities' vengeance from the heavens

There was little doubt about Osric's guilt. His plea was ignored. All citizens in Alfred's world were entitled to natural justice. The jury of six men and six women, for Alfred decreed women to have equal rights in law, were unanimous in finding him guilty of the murder of women and children.

Rand, now a leading ealdorman looked at Alfred and Asser who both nodded; Rand grimly sentenced him to death, he would be hung at sunrise the next day, giving him time for some much-needed confession and absolution.

The next morning just before sunup a sweaty and wailing Osric was hauled up the steps onto the gallows before a silent but angry crowd. A noose was placed around his neck. Suddenly he fell to the ground in apparent severe agony stretching the rope, so it tightened around his neck. As he writhed he started vomiting and passing some foul smelling browny- red liquid blood from his anus. He pulled up his robe clutching his abdomen and revealing his nakedness beneath. His shrunken genitals turned from pink to brown to black in front of them. Little boys at the front gawped at the sight, then one called out, 'The bastards' balls have gone black, must have been worn out pumping us boys up the arse! Serves the pervert right!' Many of them jeered and cheered at the spectacle.'

After a few minutes of this pain, his belly suddenly burst open. Osric's last vision on earth was his blackened testicles before him and his intestines falling on the floor before he expired. The audience was stunned, and then burst into cheers at his suffering and demise. Many small boys cheered and laughed, most had suffered from Osric's vices. Then a silence fell, total silence as the crowd reflected on the grotesque frightful spectacle they had just witnessed in front of them.

Many of the crowd still followed the old ways and even now could recognise an old Druid curse when they saw one. Osric had been elf-shot by a malignant elf or demon released by one of the attending crowd. That total devastation of a body could only be done by a great master of druid lore. Others agreed his testicles went black from overuse with little boys as Osric did not have a reputation for chastity, or indeed poverty or humility. The Christians crossed themselves with fear at some divine intervention which looked entirely satanic.

Wilfred looked around the town square. Ceridwyn and Gwendolyn were standing on one of the platforms at the back of the square with contented serene expressions.

Alfred sent his page out to find Wilfred and ask him to join Alfred for breakfast. After a few pleasantries, Alfred asked, 'so what happened this morning, do you have any knowledge of what happened to Osric. Never have I seen such inexplicable destruction of a man in front of my own eyes by an unseen hand. The law of Wessex was subverted. I do not approve. Did you curse him Wilfred?'

Wilfred looked surprised. 'Well, such curses in the old ways can only be laid by women. I thought you regarded Druid lore as stuff and nonsense. Do you think we have the power to destroy a man like that? You must have more faith in the old ways than you claim. Osric was tried in your court, found guilty by the jury, sentenced to death and had a rope put around his neck. Somehow, he suffered a perhaps slower, definitely more painful, more deserved death than the strangulation on the end of a rope. Anyway, did not your god bring plagues upon people in your bible, of sores and other nasty things? Maybe your god gave him one of those!'

'That was the Old Testament, we are much more forgiving these days. Osric could have had a less painful ending on the end of a rope.'

Wilfred continued, 'Osric may have had infection of his intestines, perhaps in the appendix, or some inflammatory bowel problem, or perhaps too much blood sugar. Perhaps the pressure in his fat guts just got too much. As far as I know he did not take the recommended mint and ginger that keeps you well! He was too self-important to ask me for advice.'

Alfred could recognise evasion. He was quite sure Wilfred knew more about what had happened that he divulged. There were quite a few women staying with Wilfred who had a reputation for cursing. Alfred had overheard the story of Ragnar Fourfinger's followers. Their horrendous stories made it sound justified, but it was not Christian. It was not the law of his Wessex.

After a pleasant breakfast, and a close game of hnefatafl, Wilfred returned home leaving Alfred still puzzled. Just outside town Ceridwyn and Gwendolyn were waiting for Wilfred looking a picture of contented innocence, though grateful for a lift.

Over the last few years, Wilfred's practice had prospered mightily, beyond any modest expectations he had. He had hoped to be able to support himself and his family. The challenges and successes of healing, and the contentment of his patrons were his reward. Although he never requested payment, the little box Wulfstan made filled up regularly with pennies or coins of a greater value from the wealthier merchants or from the nobles of the area.

He had been able to buy another property in Long Street. This was ideal to house the four ladies, their mothers and sisters. The ladies of Sherborne loved to gossip. It was rumoured that Mona and Rowena shared a bed and an unnatural relationship. Some could understand this after the abuse they had received at the hands of the priest in Dublin though the Church did not approve. However, the rumour mill revolved much faster when Hjalmar moved in as well. Understandably the ladies owed their home coming to him, but the tittle-tattle now was that he shared the bed with both Mona and Rowena at the same time. The relationship was said to be more natural, but again the women of the town clicked their teeth in disapproval and the men of the town looked wistful at the erotic thought.

Perhaps sadly neither Rowena nor Mona became with child. Perhaps their years of deprivation and imprisonment had undermined their health. Both sisters were delighted to play with Wilfred and Elvina's children and spoil them when possible. Wilfred and Elvina ignored all gossip, they were happier to have the sisters look after the children than Synnove. Both remained privately uncertain as to what had happened that last time, she was babysitting little Ceridwyn and preferred not to press Synnove about events, or even discuss it themselves.

On his return to Sherborne, Wilfred often spent time alone in the forest thinking about the cancer his father hoped to cure and thinking about the Anglo-Saxon nine herb charms. Some were beneficial, but which ones and what doses still puzzled him. Women still came to visit him with hard lumps in the breast. The lumps were tethered to the skin and hard lumps were present in the arm pit. They never survived more than a year. He tried syrup of mistletoe with perhaps a little improvement initially. He tried true nettle with similar effect. He had more effect emphasising the diet of peas, cauliflower, peas, carrots and onions with plums and red grapes or red wine. Sometimes the badger poked his snout out of the set at night to survey Wilfred with what seemed deserved derision to Wilfred. He usually perceived the victim in a winding sheet before death overtook them.

Other came to see him with hard lumps where the stomach sits, they often had a large hard liver and perhaps a lump above the right clavicle. A cancer in the stomach or pancreas spreading to the chest seemed the likely problem. Again, mistletoe seemed to help for a while, perhaps adding the true nettle may have more effect.

A few days later there was a firm knock on the door of Wilfred's house in Cheap Street. Elvina opened it to be confronted by a fierce looking man clad in a white robe from his neck to his feet. He had olive skin, a dark beard and a cloth held on his head by two circular black leather straps. Elvina's hand strayed to the knife attached to her belt, as the stranger took a step backward and bowed touching his heart, then his lips and then his forehead. 'Salaam aleikum,' he said, 'my mind thinks well of you, my lips speak well of you, and you are always in my heart. I come from the land of the blessed prophet, I come to greet the great healer Wilfred and his beautiful wife, Elvina, I suspect that you are she.'

Hoping for the best and that Wilfred was not far away, Elvina welcomed the stranger into her house. 'Please sit sir, may I bring you some water or wine and some nourishment. I will then find my husband.'

The stranger sat gratefully, holding out his knife in a bejewelled scabbard handle first to Elvina, 'I see you are nervous, please accept my blade as a gift, a gesture of friendship. I would appreciate some water thank you, but wine is forbidden to me by the prophet, peace be upon him.'

Elvina accepted his blade with some relief, poured a goblet of water, and withdrew to find Wilfred who was working in his herb garden. 'Oh Wilfred, we have a very strange man in the house, I fear he may be an Arab Muslim, will he eat the children?'

Wilfred smiled, gave her a hug and returned to the house. On their return, the stranger stood, bowed again touching heart, lips and forehead.

'Esteemed sir, my name is Abdul, I am from Mesopotamia, I am an acolyte of Hunayn ibn Ishaq, may his soul rest in peace though he was a Christian.

He was the greatest physician in Bagdad till he died in 873 AD by your calendar. In my country most men are followers of the Great Prophet.'

'However some of our great physicians, mathematicians and philosophers are of your Christian faith, or of the Jewish faith. We acknowledge their great wisdom and important contribution to our society. We discuss our beliefs vehemently with disagreement but aways courtesy and never violence.'

'I come in peace to share your wisdom and discuss herbal therapy with you, and to exchange plants that grow in your country with those that grow in mine.'

'Your name was given to me in the Basque country of Al-Andalus. I believe they share your Celtic origin. The healers there say you are the most knowledgeable physician in Anglo-Saxon England. I have also heard stories that you are a great swordsman.'

Wilfred bowed his head humbly, 'I am Wilfred. Your sources are too kind. I only use the plants, gemstones and wisdom left by our great priests of past centuries. I read not only the texts in English, and of the old Druid Welsh physicians of Myddvai, but some of the old texts of Greece and Rome. To learn from the great physicians of eastern countries would be a wonderful new experience. A sharing of ideas. My sword remains in a secret place for emergencies only when my family or my king are at risk.'

Abdul produced two large boxes from his luggage. Abdul opened the first box. Inside it was full of a yellow powder. Abdul placed a little on a wooden spoon and passed it to Wilfred. It had a spicy and scented taste and smell Wilfred had never encountered. 'This is called turmeric, we grind the powder from the roots. It adds wonderful flavour to food and is very effective against infection and cancer when taken orally or when applied locally.'

The second box contained some red plants, the size of a small carrot. Abdul said, 'These are red chillies. We use them also for food; they add a very fiery taste which will probably challenge the bland English palate. Try a tiny bite, a very very tiny bite.'

Wilfred nibbled of an end and recoiled, grabbing a goblet of water and downing it in one draft.

'I see what you mean,' he gasped, as Abdul continued with some amusement.

'We use them as a paste for skin rashes and sometimes they benefit unfortunate sufferers with cancers. They came to us from a mysterious country many weeks' travel from my home called China. They only grow in hot countries, but I see that you can grow grapes vines now in Wessex. The global warming of the last five centuries may enable you to grow turmeric here, something you could not have done in Wessex in the ice period of the Roman occupation.'

Abdul looked up at Wilfred. 'In the cold parts of my country in the mountains in winter we still have plenty of sun. The farmers there make a little box or house of glass. It is sealed to keep the warmth of the sun in and the cold of the wind and air out. That should work for you here. Treatment of tumours is the least successful part of my position as a physician. I will be fascinated to shares ideas with you. I think we will be both more effective healers if we share ideas from the east and the west.'

Abdul took a step backward and bowed touching his heart, then his lips and then his forehead he repeated, 'Salaam aleikum,'

Wilfred grasped Abdul's forearm with mutual esteem and said, 'This is so much, too much, so many possibilities for treatment, these are unknown here. Even if they do not cure diseases we could open a tavern with the spiciest food in town!'

'I look forward to growing these and trying their powers as therapy.' Wilfred paused, 'I must be able to do something for you in return, can I show you my herbs that grow here, can I introduce you to a great king, can I give you something in return. My humble house is yours as long as you wish to stay.'

Abdul bowed again, 'Thank you, when I return I can tell my Sheik that hospitality in England equals that of my home. They all told me back home in Mesopotamia before my travels that I would be a human sacrifice to the Druids on the mountains under a full moon, or that I would be burnt alive in a wicker cage!'

Elvina laughed nervously.

'In return, we have heard of your fox's glove and your bilberry, but they will not flourish in our oases of Baghdad. We learn you find the foxglove useful for disorders of the heart, especially irregularities of the rhythm, and the bilberry for infections. When we have shared the ideas of our cultures, I would be honoured if you could allow me to have a box of dried foxglove and a box of dried bilberry to take back to Baghdad.'

Abdul turned to Elvina, 'I am sorry if I frightened you when I arrived, your eyes and your dagger certainly frightened me. We learned from Hunayn that our Allah and your Christ expect us to care for all of humanity regardless of colour or creed or nationality. We may not agree but we must treat each other and each other's beliefs with respect. Strangers are always welcomes with the utmost hospitality as you have shown to me. In Baghdad we call this the Convivencia.'

Wilfred and Abdul, sometimes with Elvina, passed many days lost in conversation, often immersed in the forest examining and discussing the medicinal properties of the plants of Wessex. Sometime was spent in Wilfred's wyrt tun looking at his private collection of herbs. Some days Abdul sat in on Wilfred's healing sessions to discuss illnesses and cures. The people of Sherborne were suspicious of this strangely attired man from far away, but always trusted Wilfred implicitly.

The two physicians expanded their knowledge greatly. They agreed that all potent herbs should be given simultaneously for infections. They discussed the concept that cancer should be treated with a variety of drugs, but in rotation rather than all at the same time. Wilfred told Abdul about his temporary success treating prostate cancer with nettles, and breast cancer with plums, grapes and red wine.

Sadly, Wilfred admitted than his success was only transient. He did not feel entitled to any accolade as a great healer, many days he felt just a great fool. Abdul was sure turmeric had some place in the therapy of cancer, Wilfred was sure some mistletoe oil and watercress benefitted all cancers.

Abdul met Alfred in Wilfred's house unknown to his housecarls and personal bodyguard who would have advised strongly against such a meeting for fear of the assassin's dagger. They discussed their prophets and the different perspectives of Islam and Christianity. They discussed the beautiful books translated by the Moslems from the ancient Greek and Latin.

Books ensuring traditional knowledge of healing was retained and passed on to the west, rather than being lost in the turbulent times.

They heard with disbelief of the skilled architects to the east and their beautiful decorated buildings revealed by Abdul's collection of paintings surpassing anything of Alfred's Wessex.

It was always with civility and hospitality over Elvina's bountiful cooking, though usually not with agreement. It was with mutual sadness the time approached for Abdul to return to his home. He did not wish to remain for a Wessex winter. He remained astounded by the frequency of rainfall.

Abdul also met Rowena, Gwendolyn, Kendra, Mona and Hjalmar. He received them all with his courteous bows and was pleased to further his discussion of healing herbs with Gwendolyn. After their meeting, he whispered quietly to Wilfred, 'why do not more of your young men have two or more wives. In my country, it is normal. I have three wives. A man needs more than one to fulfil his manly needs and all the household duties. There are the young and the old to care for; there are large meals to prepare for family and guests; there is a house to keep organised and clean. How can one woman do all this? And a man needs some variety in his bed.'

Wilfred put his hand on Abdul's shoulder. 'Friend, would you like to run the idea past Elvina and see what response you get?'

Abdul could see clearly that polygamy might not work in Elvina's part of the universe; wisely he did not take up Wilfred's suggestion.

Elvina presented him with five carved oak boxes prior to his departure. 'This contains dried powdered fox's glove flowers, the second contains dry powdered foxglove leaves, the third contains dried bilberries, the fourth contains dried mushrooms and the last contains mistletoe oil. A very small pinch of pulverised mushroom powder in hot water will give you visions of the future, more than that is fatal. I hope Wilfred told you we use foxglove on the skin for infection or cancer or abdominal pain. Small doses taken internally have serious side effects including vomiting, diarrhoea and even death. We do not use this every day, after a week it is safest not to take more for the following week.'

Abdul bowed gravely, gratefully. 'In my country women are midwives but have no other role in healing. You are right about not taking medication all the time, often we alternate therapy, one herb for a month, then a different one the following month. Elvina, I have learned from your skills with the very old and the very young people. I see you have a strong leadership role in your town and in your house. Your culture and the important place of women here is new to me, I am still trying to understand your strange ways.' He glanced at Wilfred who nodded ruefully.

'Maybe I can change the traditional culture of my people, maybe in a thousand years we will still treat women as little better than servants, so reluctant are men in my land to change,' mused Abdul.

Abdul turned to Wilfred, 'My dearest learned colleague, you both will always be welcome in my house. The journey takes many months by land, but there are so many fascinating cities and different cultures to see on the way. Cities that were old in the time of your bible. I am returning by sea which should be faster. Elvina, I would love to return the hospitality of your table and provide you with the spices of our land. I cannot offer you any wine, Allah forbids that'

And with that Abdul took Wilfred by surprise by suddenly giving him a bear hug followed by a passionate kiss on both cheeks. Abdul chuckled,

'That is the Arab traditional greeting and farewell.' Turning to Elvina he took her hand in his to kiss it gently. 'Thank you for making me feel at home despite our cultural difference, would that we had such beautiful redheaded fiery women in our land.'

Alfred pondered the ideas he and Abdul had discussed. The harmonious blending of cultures and races seemed to produce better cities and stronger societies. There were signs of many Danes becoming content to live in peace in Wessex.

Wilfred had managed to grow turmeric and chillies under glass in the sunny corner of his garden. He looked forward to trying the addition of these herbs to his treatments of cancers.

883

Two busy years went by for Wilfred and Elvina. Their children were growing apace. Alfred was a cheerful busy little boy. Ceridwyn was now a precocious five-year-old. Some days she spent time with Æthelflæd. The little girl believed everything Alfred's daughter told her was gospel, especially about the roles of females in society. She became as confident and extrovert as Æthelflæd had been as a little girl. Unfortunately, this meant she was opinionated and sometimes disobedient. She attended Alfred's school and had started Latin. She was a quick learner on the days she felt like paying attention. The younger pair were always into mischief at home.

Wilfred pondered which of his therapies was the answer to cancer. One day, Elvina was requested to visit Ealhswith who was visiting Sherborne. She returned to collect Wilfred, 'You must come and see something, a gift just received by Alfred.'

Wilfred followed to the royal pavilion where Alfred placed a piece of wood, perhaps as long as the span of a man's hand, in Wilfred's hand and looked at him quizzically. 'What timber is this, from whence does it come?'

Wilfred peered at it closely then he smelt it and thought for a while. 'I have seen a piece of timber like this only once before, to me it looks like Lebanese cedar.'

Alfred, Ealhswith and Elvina exchanged meaningful glances.

'Where did you see one like this before Wilfred?' asked Elvina.

'Just before my father was killed we had a journey up north. We stopped in Durham and visited the cathedral there. It was a magnificent building. My father was interested because they said St Cuthbert's body did not decompose after death. He wondered what had done this, were there any herbs that could prevent degeneration of tissues in the living.'

Alfred attempted to correct Wilfred, 'the preservation of Cuthbert's body was a miracle, a recognition by God of his holy life.'

Wilfred was unconvinced, 'what good would that do for him when his soul has already gone to the otherworld. Anyway, it is an old Norse belief that the first person to be buried in a graveyard becomes its guardian or lightbringer. The body is preserved to keep watch over the other dead people and usher them into the otherworld. That person can be seen as a shadow flittering around at sunset. Cuthbert sounds to have believed in Norse ideas!'

'More practically, Cuthbert's body had been anointed with oil of mistletoe, with powdered rosemary and thyme. We wondered could that be good for damaged tissue?' Wilfred mused.

Elvina persisted, 'but what about the piece of wood?'

Alfred interjected, 'Wilfred, did you hear about the miracle of St Cuthbert? How he became lame with a painful swelling in his knee, and was cured by an angel? His knee suddenly began to swell into a large very painful tumour, the nerves in his thigh contracted and he could only walk with a limp dragging his diseased leg behind him One day an angel arrived outside and St Cuthbert was carried out to see him. The angel was clothed in shining white raiment of incomparable beauty and his horse was also a bright pure white colour. After he examined the knee, then prayed and blessed Cuthbert, he was cured. What do you think of that Wilfred?'

Wilfred responded with a laugh, 'yes my devout King Alfred, we heard that story too in Durham Cathedral, but you did not add that the white clothed man also advised Cuthbert's fellow monks to boil some wheaten flour in milk, and apply the poultice warm to the swelling, following which he improved in the next few days thanks to his earthly remedy!'

'And Alfred,' continued Wilfred, 'did you know that when Cuthbert was a hermit on Inner Farne Island, that his crops failed twice and were eaten by ravens. Then he invoked the old Anglo-Saxon Land Ceremony charm, one you call pagan. The prayer I told you was made by your St Bede. He invoked both your Christian Lord and Erce, the ancient druid earth mother and goddess of fertility. He dug up a turf from each corner of the field, poured honey, oil, milk and yeast on them, added a sprig from each plant in the field and repeated the old Saxon chant over them, blending the chant with a Christian prayer.'

> *"Erce, Erce, Erce, Mother of Earth,*
> *Hail to you, Earth, Mother of Men!*
> *May the Almighty, the eternal Lord, grant you*
> *Fields growing and thriving*
> *Be you full of growth in God's protecting arms,*
> *filled with food for the benefit of humankind."*

'Then his crops grew.'

'Yes,' responded Alfred, 'that only worked when he finished by reciting the Lord's prayer.'

'You two are like little schoolboys bickering, really! Like when I saw you fighting with wooden swords on our first morning in Sherborne, yes I saw you sneak out Wilfred.' Elvina interrupted, 'perhaps a bit of both beliefs is the best. What about the piece of wood.'

Wilfred and Alfred both thought to themselves that Elvina had the answer, though neither would admit it.

Alfred interjected again, hoping to persuade Wilfred to accept perhaps just a little bit of Christianity, 'You know about St Wilfred, a man with the same name as you. He lived a century and a half ago. He was a great healer like you. There was a story that he restored a child to life. St Wilfred healed a boy who has in fact died by speaking a prayer and laying a hand on his chest. With all your skills and knowledge plus God's help you might be able to achieve such drastic healing!'

'Hm,' replied Wilfred, unconvinced, 'What a story, did anyone feel the boys pulse or put an ear on his chest, perhaps he was just deeply asleep.'

Yes Wilfred, but what about the piece of wood?' continued Elvina, more persistently this time.

'Oh that, the monks showed my father a piece of wood like this said to be part of the cross on which your Jesus was crucified over eight hundred years ago. He thought it was all nonsense, the preservation of the body of St Cuthbert was more interesting to him, why are you all looking at me like that?' replied Wilfred.

'My dear part-time pagan,' responded Alfred, 'You are looking at a gift to me from Pope Marinus, a treasure in respect of the devotion of the people of Wessex. It is a piece of the true cross, now confirmed by the voice of Wilfred surely from heaven. I think my God works and speaks through you Wilfred!'

Elvina hugged her husband who looked perplexed by events. It was indeed difficult to know what to believe or why Elvina and Alfred seemed so pleased with him.

885

There was the usual queue outside Wilfred's door. The moon was waning, a time when bleeding was thought to be dangerous. Oil of snowdrop and mistletoe was rubbed on the forehead of an old lady with headaches and loss of memory. A piece of jet to ward off lightening for a girl too terrified to go out after a nearby lightning strike. Another youth with a large boil on a shoulder required an incision to drain pus and a light touch of cautery to remove any residual infection and heal the lesion. A child with a painful ear treated with warm oil and mixed betonice and henbane juice into the ear. A solution of crushed henbane root dissolved in strong vinegar applied to a woman's sore tooth.

An old woman with a sore swollen knee treated with a poultice of henbane and hemlock covered with elm bark and strapped on with leather thongs. A very pale lady with an infant at the breast and a large spleen was probably in need of iron. Wilfred plunged a red-hot poker into some red wine which the lady drank. Wilfred advised her to return weekly for further treatment. An adolescent arrived last complaining of painful teeth, several of them were black and eroded. It was believed this was caused by tooth worms, though Wilfred had never seen any. However, the standard therapy was removal of the blackened dead teeth, followed by powdered oak leaves mixed with henbane seeds in candle wax, which was then lit, and the smoke inhaled under a sheet.

A thin woman with many children complained of poor vision, especially at night. Wilfred thought she was probably giving her share of food to her children and not eating adequately herself. He gave her some roasted buck's liver, enough for three days, and put a little warm oil in her eyes. The village seducer of young women, Norvel, slunk in, discretely revealing his pintle to Wilfred so Elvina could not see it. It was covered with large flowery warts, no wonder the rumour was his business was dropping off. He went pale when Wilfred offered amputation, preferring Wilfred's alternative of mixed hound's urine, dog's head and mouse's blood salve with strict rest for three months from the friendship of the thighs. Norvel also complained of going bald which was also bad for business. The girls preferred his past flowing locks.

Wilfred took from his shelf a mixture of bees' ashes and linseed oil and passed it to Elvina. She placed it over the fire and added some pulverized willow leaves. One it was warm she strained the mixture through a piece of linen and applied it to his bald scalp.

'Norvel,' she said, 'I am sure God would look more favourably on your health if you sinned a little less. Seducing married women contravenes Gods seventh commandment!'

Norvel slunk out looking embarrassed.

At Alfred's request, Wilfred sent them all to the Abbey to pray for God's assistance in healing. Wilfred was pretty sure that would not help, though somehow a combination of their gods and beliefs had met with astounding success at least on the battle field.

Wilfred's scepticism had been shaken by meeting a thegn with paralysed legs previously unresponsive to his treatment, who now appeared cured. The thane had vowed to go in a cart to the shrine of St Swithin in Wintanceastre to pray for healing, only to awake after his vows, on the day planned for the journey with power restored to his legs. The thegn still went on the journey to give thanks. The twenty-five people who accompanied him were all cured of being deaf, blind or lame soon after arrival in Wintanceastre after their supplications to the saint.

Messengers arrived at Wilfred's house in Cheap Street. Could he travel to a couple of nearby villages to treat some very sick peasants please. Wilfred packed his bags of herbs, loaded up his wagon with supplies and headed down the road with Elvina and their children to the little village of Piddletrenthide. He had been told of two sick people in urgent need of his expertise, but too sick to travel. He stopped his wagon by the River Piddle, so his horse could have a drink and entered the first house.

An elderly lady was lying in bed in pain. Her left leg was clearly shorter than the right and her foot was rotated outwards pointing towards the wall. She had almost certainly broken her hip. Wilfred gave her some henbane in wine and ordered that she should be placed in a hot bath once she was in less pain. He added powdered bitter vetch cress and nettle to the water, then requested that hot stones from the fire should be added to the bath. They were placed at the end carefully so as not to burn her. Once the water was hot and she was sweating profusely, Wilfred grasped the leg and pulled it out straight and rotated it, so the foot was pointing up like the other. She inhaled sharply but uttered not a squeak. She was a tough old bird, thought Wilfred. She had probably put up with worse pain in her life. While Elvina held the leg in place the bath was drained, and a splint applied. She was transferred back to bed. Wilfred attached some weights to the splint and hung them over the end of the bed to maintain traction on the bone.

Wilfred instructed her two daughters 'She must lie here for six weeks with this weight on her leg. After that she will be able to walk. During that time give her plenty of milk, and exercise the leg muscles but with contractions, not movements. Turn her from side to side and rub liniment over her lower back.'

'Once she is recovered she should walk for half an hour daily and continue to drink plenty of milk. When an elderly lady breaks one bone, it implies the other bones are weak, it means the other two hundred and five other bones which are unbroken at the moment need to be strengthened.'

The old lady seized Wilfred's hand and kissed it. She was steeped in the old ways and could recognise a potent Druid master. She said to Wilfred in an old Celtic dialect no one else understood, 'And may the blessing of the earth be on you, soft under your feet as you pass along the roads, soft under you as you lie out on it, tired at the end of day; and may it rest easy over you when, at last, you lie out under it.' Wilfred smiled, stroked her arm and progressed to the next house.

There lying on a bed was a man, not too old but looking terrible. A lady, presumably his wife sat by the bed holding his hand and weeping. Three untidy small children stood sullenly against the wall, bewildered by events. Not long ago their father had played with them in the fields, something had gone severely wrong. His wife said, 'This is my husband. Gifre. I am Ardith. He has been sick for weeks with pain and vomiting blood. He has had some bleeding from the nose this week'

The man was thin, his face pale and gaunt, his sweaty straggly hair prematurely grey. He was holding his abdomen and moaning in pain. A fire burnt weakly in the hearth. Wilfred was dismayed to see a pile of firewood from an elder tree. Surely everyone knew that bringing elder wood into a house was a bringer of bad luck. Especially if it was burnt in a fireplace.

Wilfred pulled out his bottle of hemlock and henbane to give him a small drink. Wilfred pulled back the blanket to examine his abdomen. A large hard lump sat under the rib cage. His liver was also hard and enlarged. His whites of his eyes were yellow. Another lump could be seen just above the left collar bone. Here was a man with advanced cancer, probably in the stomach, perhaps in the pancreas.

They both looked into Wilfred's eyes seeing what they feared. Wilfred said, 'You are right, he has cancer and will probably meet his God soon. Gifre, you should meet your priest and seek his absolution. You should consider how Ardith will provide for your children in the future, should you succumb to this disease.'

'I will leave you some pain reliever. I have some treatment that may provide some relief. There are three bottles of powder, turmeric, nettle and mistletoe, remember the sequence TNM for short. Take them in that order every day for two weeks each. Dissolve a large spoonful in a little warm red wine with powdered watercress and drink it slowly twice a day. Eat plenty of peas, broccoli, cauliflower, onions and carrots. Have meat and mead only twice a week on Thor's day and Wodin's day. And never bring elder wood into a house or use it for fire wood. If you have an elder tree in your garden, chop it down immediately, or you will die in this bed fairly soon.'

Wilfred and Elvina declined Ardith offer of a few coins and backed out. 'Send me a message if I can help in any way in future,' concluded Wilfred. Then he had another thought and re-entered the house. 'I forgot to give you anything for his nose bleeding, this is powdered parwynke leaves and flowers, have half a spoonful each night with your evening medicine.'

Wilfred backed out unhappily visualising Gifre in a winding sheet, the unwanted image of his continued impotence as a healer, but then inexplicably the sheet image suddenly fell to the ground. Wilfred had never experienced that before and wondered what it could mean.

As they rode back to Sherborne, Wilfred explained to Elvina, 'All those herbs seem to help cancer, but only for a while. Abdul said turmeric was quite good for cancer, but that herbs should be given intermittently and perhaps in rotation, one at a time. We wondered if some from the east and some from the west would be best. Abdul thought perhaps one from Allah and one from the Christian God would enlist help from two omnipotent powers. Perhaps one from the old ways and Druid gods in addition would be even better! Ah, well, poor Gifre, poor man, at least he will have some relief from pain. I doubt if anything will help him at this stage.'

Six months later Ardith knocked on his door. Behind her stood a man, thin, but not as thin as before and otherwise well with a full head of hair. Behind them were three children, mucking around and poking each other just to cause annoyance. They were normal cheerful difficult kids uninterested in Wilfred.

It was Gifre! 'Hello Wilfred, I am feeling better. I have no pain.' He said, 'I am eating well and have put on some weight. Your treatment is brilliant. Would you like to examine me?'

Wilfred lay him on the bench and checked him over carefully. Gifre no longer had yellow eyes. There was no lump above his clavicle; there was no hard mass in his abdomen.

Elvina and Wilfred looked at them in amazement. Elvina turned to Wilfred, again placing her hands on his shoulders and looking into his eyes. 'Wilfred, you have fulfilled your father's legacy. You have cured a cancer!' The four all hugged each other, tears pouring down their faces as they rocked back and forward.

Elvina said to Wilfred, 'the black badger will never trouble you again, he will know that you have triumphed.'

Wilfred was amazed, 'how do you know about the black badger, it has haunted me for years, but I did not like to tell you about it?'

Elvina smiled, 'Wilfred, you are a hard task-master to yourself. If you nearly cure someone, you think you have failed. Sometimes when we are in the woods I see you are the friend of all animals. The rabbits frolic around you with no fear. The dear come to you to nuzzle your hand. The wolf allows you to stroke its back. Birds eat from your hand. However, a few times when we have seen a badger at night, you have shivered and grimaced. And you also talk sometimes in your sleep. So, no more Bad Gers, the Bad Gerry is banished for ever.'

Wilfred hugged Elvina again.

Gifre pulled a brooch out of his pouch and pinned it gently onto Elvina's cloak. 'Wilfred, I thought the best way to thank you was to give your beautiful wife a gift, a humble token of appreciation. I have been able to return to my trade as a silver smith and jeweller thanks to you.'

Elvina nodded and surveyed the circular brooch in wonder. It was bigger than the span of a man's hand. It was made of silver and etched with niello. The outer circle had sixteen discs with patterns and figures on each. The central roundel had a middle figure with four others around it between the circular arms of a flared cross.

'Knowing your expertise in health and bodily function,' explained Gifre, 'these figures show the five senses, sight in the middle, then in a circle around starting at the upper left quadrant, taste then smell then touch and finally hearing for Wilfred uses all his senses in healing.'

'It is truly exquisite,' exclaimed Elvina, giving Gifre a hug and a kiss on the cheek.

Wilfred worried a little that time may see a relapse, but he had never seen such an apparent cure. He wondered if the parwynke might have an effect on cancers. None of his texts ever mentioned that possibility. Like Elvina, he had never seen such craftsmanship. The figure demonstrating touch took him back briefly to the first weeks after their marriage.

Wilfred and Gifre clasped forearms in mutual respect and gratitude.

885

S hortly after Wilfred and family went to Wintan-ceastre to visit the royal court. Wilfred found Alfred looking glum. 'What ails thee my prince?' enquired Wilfred.

'Remember what you told me about the wheel of life, hold on tight at the bottom because you are surely going up very soon. Well your wheel has gone to the top, I hear rumours that you have the right cocktail of herbs to cure cancer, whereas I have lost part of my fleet. Alfred's navy, which we reviewed so proudly a few years ago, followed at least a dozen Danish ships up the River Stour in East Anglia and destroyed them. My sailors were outnumbered, but their superior ships and fighting skills gave them an epic victory. Unfortunately, when they emerged to return to Hamwic to repair damages and replace casualties, there was a second Danish fleet out in the North Sea. My navy was defeated in the ensuing fight, though we think the Danes were sufficiently damaged to withdraw to Northumberland.'

Alfred paused, 'We will replace the ships and the sailors. We will continue to harass the Danes in their lands. Next year my army will capture London.'

886

Wilfred thought about Abdul's idea that turmeric was good for cancer. It had worked for Gifre. He added it to mistletoe and watercress syrup. He was surprised to find abdominal and breast lumps diminished in size for a month or more. Infections seemed to respond best to all five therapies at once, while tumours seemed best treated with herbs in cycles.

A messenger arrived from Alfred at Wilfred's home with an invitation for both him and Elvina and family to attend a special event in Wintan-ceastre next month, the marriage of Æthelflæd, their eldest child to Æthelred, Lord of Mercia. A bronze coin engraved with Alfred's head on one side, and the wyvern of Wessex were their entrée to the royal party.

They loaded up the wagon and after travelling half-way the night before, duly arrived in their best clothing early in the morning to find the city decked out in colourful banners. Market stalls were open everywhere displaying all manners of crafts and goods, food and beer, with jugglers and tumblers, singers and musicians. The whole city was having a party in the bright summer sunshine.

Wilfred progressed through the city past the royal palace until they found a huge dais set up in the square. There were many tables and chairs all over this podium. When one of Alfred's thegns spotted Wilfred, his horse and wagon were led aside for some food and water, while Wilfred's family were ushered into the front of the dais and given seats amongst the leading men and women of Alfred's kingdom. Pages presented drinks and little titbits to eat.

Shortly heralds sounded a fanfare requesting guests to proceed to the church to St Mary's Church. Elvina entered the church and looked around in surprise. She whispered in Wilfred's ear. 'Alfred has been busy here. There has been the semi-circular apse added, the east end of the nave has had the floor raised, and it has been extended. There is a new door into south end and there is a new chancel. It is bigger and grander, what a great occasion for a great church.'

At the high altar stood Æthelred of Mercia and a hoard of archbishops and bishops. It was about to be the wedding of Æthelflæd, Alfred's eldest daughter to Æthelred, Lord of Mercia. It was a day for the whole city to celebrate. Shortly another fanfare of trumpets announced the arrival of the bride on her father's arm. Ealhswith was already in the front pew with her other children.

Elvina and Alfred were stunned to see Æthelflæd. Normally she wore men's breeches and a tunic, normally a sword or dagger was strapped to her side. Normally she was covered in dust with her hair blowing awry in the wind, having bested some of Alfred's warriors with her sword.

Today she wore a dress of the finest thin pure white wool, her hair was neatly groomed, her blond locks plaited and coiled under her head-rail. There was no trace of a weapon, though Elvina was pretty sure she would have a small dagger strapped to the inside of her thigh. She looked beautiful, radiant, quite stunning. Æthelred could not keep his eyes off her. Having appeared boyish all her days to date, at sixteen she clearly had developed almost unnoticed into a most attractive woman.

The service proceeded with pomp and pageantry. Royal trumpeters announced the commencement and conclusion of the ceremony. Alfred wore a royal purple cape edged with gold and ermine. The Bishop of Winchester and his assistants wore their most colourful vestments. The happy couple enjoyed a passionate embrace, their bonding together appeared much more intimate than a dynastic union.

Subsequently there was a huge party for the whole city. The Royal party merged with the populace and shared the happy occasion with plentiful supplies of ale and mead for all the citizens.

After another fanfare, Alfred rose, and silence fell. 'Dearly beloved men and women of Wessex,' the King began, 'your Grace the Archbishop of Wintan-ceastre, Edward, my son, the ætheling, Ealhswith my dear wife, nobles, jarls and priests, Æthelred, Lord of Mercia, and my first born, Æthelflæd, my most handsome daughter.'

'This is the happiest of days. Two young people much in love have committed to each other with their vows today. God has blessed this day with radiant sunshine. I have never seen such a happy day for all citizens.'

'However, this is more than the bonding of a man and a woman. This is a wonderful event for the people of Wessex and Mercia. Our nations are also bonded together in strength and learning before our Lord Jesus for the benefit of all our people. The combined might of Mercia and Wessex will protect our families, our women and children against all comers. Ealhswith and I have gained another son, a man who is already a great warrior, a man we are all proud to know. We hope that our beautiful daughter will stand beside him, a peace weaver to compliment the warrior as the occasion requires. However, to this day Æthelflæd, as my general Godwine would confirm, has been preferred the role of a shield maiden.'

Everyone laughed, though Æthelred looked a little worried.

Alfred raised his goblet and requested, 'please join me in a toast to the bride and groom!'

Thunderous cheers followed as goblets were raised, emptied, refilled and emptied again

Cows and sheep roasted over spits. Alfred liked to display his epicurean tastes, his worldly sophistication. Galingale and ginger, nutmeg and cinnamon, coriander and fennel, flavoured herring, shellfish and dolphin, suckling pig and pig's trotters, young pigeons and goose wings, pears and dates. Expensive Gallic wine appeased thirst at the bridal table

Other fruit and berries covered the tables. White bread covered with a generous layer of honey disappeared down young throats.

A wonderful day was had by all. In theory, a woman could not run a kingdom, but Æthelflæd was seen by those who knew her well as the second best general in Wessex. She had a great role model and preferred time with Alfred learning politics and battle strategies than with the ladies doing embroidery. Her courage had not diminished since the time she floored Godwine.

Curiously, Alfred had never asked Wilfred about his prediction of his eldest child's future, either himself, or indirectly through Ealhswith. Wilfred's private perusal of entrails again showed a strong leader, a successful leader, perhaps after her husband died. Wilfred expected she would be one of the two great shield maidens of the millennium, along with Boudicca.

886

Alfred's authority increased throughout Wessex and beyond. Danes and Saxons alike saw him as a captivating leader, one with a vision for a stronger better nation, a safe place to raise families, a man definitely to be trusted.

A man with a passion for his religion, for education and peace, but woe betide those who provoked him into battle. As he had promised he assembled a strong army and marched on London. Those who did not wish to live under his domain left. Most citizens turned out to welcome the conqueror. One expected to bring peace and prosperity to the city.

The administration of the city he entrusted to Æthelred, Lord of Mercia and Æthelflæd, his new wife, and Alfred's well beloved and trusted eldest child. A new street plan was created, the old Roman walls were reinforced, and fortifications were added to the South bank of the Thames.

888

Alfred's power was now felt through Mercia and Northumberland. Most Saxon people thought it desirable and inevitable that Alfred would unite the kingdom and they all submitted to his authority. Danes saw a better future becoming farmers and raising families, rather than lining up in a losing shield wall again. Many were happy to be conscripted into the local burgh fighting force. Few saw any weakness in Alfred's throne or his character of steel. Yet Alfred was never pompous, he remained a modest man.

However, one morning Wilfred and Elvina awoke to feel something was not right. They both had an inexplicable sensation that some calamity had befallen Wessex, Again, they hitched their horse to the wagon, loaded up the children, and set off down the road from Sherborne to Wintan-ceastre. Ceridwyn, now nearly ten, had her mother's fiery red hair and temperament. She demanded to sit up the front and take the reins for the ride to Wintan-ceastre. Wilfred had long since given up arguing with either his wife or daughter.

They went straight to St Mary's Church where Alfred was kneeling all alone at the front. A few tears ran forlornly down his face. Alfred was both strong and sensitive simultaneously. Manly in battle but never ashamed to shed a few tears. Family was important to him

'What ails thee, my prince?' asked Elvina.

'My sister Æthelswith sadly died while on a pilgrimage to Rome. I only got the news in the night. She was eleven years older than me and she was my little mother. When I was three she gave me my first wooden sword and taught me how to fight. When I was four she married Burgred, and I only saw her rarely after that. On those happy visits, when none of her courtiers and ladies were not watching, we had sword-fights. By the time I was ten I was too fast for her.'

'When I was ten and you were eight, I was only just too fast and strong for you too Wilfred. I am relieved that we have not jousted since. I have a secret fear that you are faster than I am. We were able to protect her and Burgred once from the Danes, but only once, and then he was finally exiled from Mercia. They went to live in Pavia. Perhaps if I had protected her better she would still be alive today in Mercia.'

Ceridwyn advanced into Alfred's pew and hugged him as tight as her little muscles allowed. She wiped away his tears with her grimy hand, then placed her hands on his shoulders and looked into his eyes, a copy of her mother.

'Don't cry king,' she said motherly, 'we will get through this all together!'

Alfred, Wilfred and Elvina did not know whether they should laugh or cry, so did both.

Alfred hugged little Ceridwyn, stood up, and said 'Come on then, let us go and commemorate her life!'

890

Following a royal request to visit Wintan-ceastre, Alfred and Wilfred met for one of their less frequent games of hnefatafl and discussions of their families. Wilfred was pleased to hear that Alfred's health which remained satisfactory continuing with Wilfred's peppermint and ginger tea on a regular basis.

Alfred lost the first game in less than a quarter hour. Wilfred looked up at him, 'so my prince, clearly you are thinking of something else.'

'The wheel of life is due for another uncertain turn,' announced the king, 'Guthrum has died, I am told he has been buried in the Church of St Mary the Virgin in the little village of Hadleigh in East Anglia. He remained faithful to the last to his third oath. After Ethandune he lived a Christian life and never raised arms again.'

Wilfred smiled, 'So he would be surprised if you told him before Ethandune that he would pass from this life to a Christian heaven rather than Valhalla!'

'Guthrum was an intelligent man and a clear-sighted leader of his people. He could see the world was changing, changing in a way he could not control.'

'So, Alfred, why will that set the wheel of life spinning again, it seemed to have stopped for a few years with you at the top?'

'Because, dear friend, Guthrum held the Danes under control. His death leaves an empty throne, a vacant position of power amongst the Danes in Northumberland. It is unlikely that a man of peace will replace him. The Danes don't have many men of peace. There will be several Danish war lords ready to seize leadership of their people. They will not respect Guthrum's sacred oath not to attack the people of Wessex ever again. They will see this as their last chance to roll back the clock and overrun this country before it becomes a strong united Anglo-Saxon kingdom. Also, Francia has become powerful and is expelling the Danes from their strongholds. They need somewhere to go to satisfy their blood lust, for new lands to conquer.

The years of peace will cease for a while, bloody war is on the horizon again, and may God grant us victory and ultimately one country including all its citizens regardless of their origin at peace.'

Alfred paused, then said thoughtfully, 'When Æthelred was king I felt too young for this, now I think I am getting too old.'

'Nonsense!' disagreed Wilfred, 'You are very fit, I see you practising with your sword in private, and don't forget you have a great healer to keep you well!'

Two days later while Wilfred was still in Wintan-ceastre, a visitor arrived, one of the Norsemen. He told Alfred his name was Ohthere and that he came from the northernmost point in Norway where he was a local chieftain. He described his interesting and challenging journeys around the frozen seas, the far-off places he had visited, and the cultures of the local inhabitants, but his main interest was in establishing a trading post in Wessex. He owned hundreds of reindeer and could trade in salted venison, and skins of deer and marten. He was a whaler and could offer whale meat and oil, and walrus ivory. In return he sought crops that grew in England but struggled in his homeland. Ohthere and Alfred also discussed boat building techniques and how to improve Alfred's navy. He returned north with his ship laden with fruit and vegetables, corn and salted beef.

Alfred was impressed. 'See Wilfred, nations at peace can trade in their local produce making us all wealthy, providing more jobs and sharing information of different places in the world. This was part of my dream once the Danes were defeated. I shall write a story of the adventures of Ohthere for all to learn about faraway places and trading opportunities.'

892

Three years passed, Edward the Ætheling was now a strapping ambitious young man of eighteen, more than ready in his opinion to test himself in battle. Æthelweard was a growing youth, devoted to his big brother and ready for some of the tasks of manhood. Alfred prayed silently that his young son would never be king. He was a slender young man who preferred his studies to weapons training. However, Alfred recognised that Æthelweard was very like himself at that age.

On his twelfth birthday, Æthelweard was summoned to a meeting of the witan.

'My son,' announced Alfred, 'Manhood with its responsibilities and, yes, some pleasures, is approaching you. I grant you estates and manors across this kingdom in every county, in Sussex, Hampshire, Wiltshire, Somerset, Devon and Cornwall. Some will be yours to own immediately, others you will receive as the second beneficiary under my will.'

'Administer them wisely. Ensure justice and safety for all your people. Pay your taxes for the Burghal Hidage.'

'Father, you do me great honour. I will follow your example in ensuring all follow the law of the Anglo-Saxons. I remain your liegeman until God sees your work on earth is done,' replied Æthelweard.

One of Æthelweard 's new possessions was the town of Yeovil. Wilfred was aware that he would have to negotiate about the water flow in the River Yeo with Alfred's son.

A new Danish warlord, Hastein, emerged, and black war clouds again grew larger and nearer. Some said he was another son of Ragnar Lodbrok. His sons kept emerging like a many headed hydra. Lodbrok had many children by his three known wives, and apparently, others with various cooperative and uncooperative women between Greenland and Constantinople.

Many Danes believed Ragnar's sons were immortal after one of them, Sivard, was cured of a mortal wound on the battlefield. A very tall old man dressed in black promised a cure in return for Sivard consecrating to him the souls of all those he killed on the battlefield in future. The Anglo-Saxons saw this as clear confirmation that the Devil was in league with the Vikings. It was one reason why Alfred insisted on his warriors being shriven before conflict. The Danes saw it as confirmation that Odin was with them always and would guarantee entry to Valhalla for their warriors who died sword in hand.

Whatever the truth, Hastein had collected an army of thousands of warriors looking for easier plunder than to be found in Francia. They crossed to Kent in a total of three hundred and thirty longboats. Once ashore they developed two strongholds, one in Appledore, the other in Milton. Alfred's spies told him they arrived with their women and children, an advantageous and a disadvantageous choice, but certainly one that indicated a desire to remain. At least a third of their total numbers therefore were not fighting men. The Danes settled in for winter. Battles were expected in spring.

Alfred and Edward poured over a map of the south-east. Wilfred was always at the back of these battle planning meetings to make his own plans for the health of Alfred's army. Alfred was irritated. 'Why do these wretched Danes keep occupying important places in our Anglo-Saxon heritage? We had Guthrum in Wareham, and now Hastein in Milton, on the south bank of the Thames east of London. Do they think it will enrage us into doing something stupid? Milton was the home of Seaxburh, daughter of Anna, King of East Anglia, wife of King Eorcenberht, mother and Queen Regent for her son Ecgberht for a year till he was of age to rule alone.'

'Ecgberht banned all devil worship and introduced the traditional Christian festival of Easter. Anna himself was the son of Eni, King of the East Angles over two hundred years ago. Eni was killed at the battle of Bulcamp, along with his son, Jurmin, fighting Penda of Mercia. Wilfred, your wife Elvina has reminded me more than once that a female can be a queen based on the tale of Seaxburh!'

'Seaxburh also founded an Abbey in Milton. Her sister Æthelthryth was the Abbess in Ely. She was apparently and surprisingly a twice-married virgin! Sixteen years after Æthelthryth died her remains were exhumed to be moved under a marble sarcophagus, yet like St Cuthbert, those remains were miraculously preserved. The venerable Bede mentions Æthelthryth in his book Ecclesiastical History of the English People.'

'So, you see dearly beloved friends and warriors, Milton is an important place in our history, Hastein must be defeated and the town returned to Saxon rule.'

Alfred had mobilised his standing army and raised the fyrds to strengthen his force. The Londoners came out in force because all the merchants opposed warfare. Stalls selling primary produce and manufactured goods were much busier when the Danes were not knocking down the gates and terrifying the citizens.

Alfred surveyed his son, his housecarls and thegns. He expounded his battle plan confidently.

'Dear friends, fellow Anglo-Saxon warriors, we will divide our force into three equal armies. Edward, you are now a strong young man. The same age that I was at the Battle of Ashdown. You will take a third of our army to Appledore to the south and engage the Danes there. Good luck my son, may the Lord grant you victory in his name in your first battle command.'

'Another third reinforced by the warriors from London will watch the Danes at Milton on the Thames. I will command the remaining third. We will be based at Tonbridge between the two groups of Danes, so we can strike north or south, as needed to reinforce the army at Appledore or Milton within a day's march.'

Alfred continued his strategy now optimistically. 'I shall send emissaries to talk to Hastein to discuss my terms for their surrender in the hope of avoiding more widows and orphans on either side.'

During negotiations shortly before Christmas, the Danes in Appledore surprisingly slipped out at night and headed west. It was a time of year when most armies had settled comfortably into winter quarters, hence Edward's army was initially caught unawares, and the Danes gained a three day start ahead of Edward's army.

893

Nevertheless; Edward's scouts followed them closely as far west as Fearnhamme where the larger Saxon army caught up with the slower Danes, hampered by moving their women and children. The battle was a complete rout with many Danish casualties including their leader. Edward was establishing a deserved reputation as a worthy warlord, a true successor to his father.

The surviving Danes escaped and fled back across the Thames abandoning their booty, and took refuge on an island at Thorney in the River Colne just upstream from the Church to St Paul, the apostle. Yet again, they were soon surrounded by the men of London and Edward's vanguard. Hostages were accepted along with an oath never to return to Wessex.

Many Danes, still fully armoured should the situation turn to their advantage, continued east away from London to one of their fortifications at Benfleet. However; Edward's victorious army arrived unexpectedly while many Danes were away finally having time they thought to go plundering for supplies. Their ramparts were breached with ease and the Danes suffered another severe defeat, with many casualties and the destruction of their boats. The Saxons built a church at Benfleet to commemorate their victory.

The wife and two sons of Hastein were captured and brought as prisoners to Alfred. Some survivors managed to escape and re-joined Hastein at Shoebury.

Alfred summoned Wilfred urgently to discuss troop billets in Tonbridge and how to treat casualties in three places at the same time.

Wilfred was prepared as always. 'Your army is camped near the Medway River. I had ensured that latrine pits are dug at least a furlong from the water. There are a few wounded Saxons who will return home on wagons or horses now that I have treated their wounds. The health of all your other warriors appears excellent. Your parties of foragers have gathered food from the area with the cooperation of the nearest burghs and captured much of the Danes supplies. Adequate food had ensured their strength and fitness. They all believe in their cause and in ultimate victory and are proud to shape this nation as you have indicated.'

'Also, I have been training two apprentices for some years now, they are very competent. I have three wagons, each with adequate equipment to treat battle wounds and other problems. Orva will go with Edward to Appledore, Meghan will accompany the Londoners to Milton, and I will stay in the middle with your army my Lord King.'

Alfred announced appreciatively, 'Good work Wilfred. I am so proud of Edward, he has fought two battles and won both with easy victories, a great deal better than his father who won only two in his life thus far!

Edward interrupted modestly, 'thank you father, I have had the best role model, my warrior father. I am also celebrating today my engagement to Ecgwynn. With your blessing, we propose to marry tomorrow!'

Ecgwynn advanced shyly to the front of the crowd. Wilfred was surprised by the turn of events as Ecgwynn had been Edward's slave girl, his peasant-girl bed warmer during cold nights on campaign. His intuition and experienced eye revealed the reason for the sudden marriage. Alfred's first grandchild would arrive early next year.

Alfred, looking not entirely happy, clasped forearms with his son and kissed the bride and mother-to-be. Suppressing his reservations about Ecgwynn's lowly status and suitability to become a queen, he resumed cheerfully, complimentarily, 'Congratulations, may God bless the pair of you. Tomorrow we will have a great feast to celebrate after the ceremony. When the Good Lord calls me, the kingdom will be in Edward's strong hands.'

'I was going to Thorney tomorrow, but messages have reached me that the Danes have attempted to stab us in the back again rather than face our shield wall. A war party of Danes from Northumberland have seized their chance while we are away campaigning to besiege Exeter again. They haven't learnt from the last time they tried that! Furthermore there is a small number of Danes from East Anglia nearby in some stronghold. I shall leave tomorrow with half the army to destroy them.'

'What about Hastein, he is still in Shoebury with moderate numbers still?' asked Wilfred anxiously.

'Indeed, he is, and he still poses some threat, though he is aware that I hold his wife and sons captive. My scouts say he has left Shoebury and is marching along the Thames. My daughter Æthelflæd, a warrior queen, a courageous shield maiden, and her husband Æthelred, the Lord of Mercia have arranged for a Mercian army to join Edward's men of Wiltshire under Aethelhelm and of Somerset under Aethelnoth. They will deal with Hastein.' answered Alfred, 'Can you follow them, I think there will be more fighting there than in Devon?'

Unsurprisingly, Hastein's force, hearing of the approaching army, turned northwest to escape the combined Anglo-Saxon force. Æthelred the Lord of the Mercians lead a force of Mercian, Saxon and Welsh warriors against Hastein, The invaders, now dispirited and short of supplies, were overtaken at Buttington. The Danes behind secure fortifications were desperately short of food. Some had died of hunger; all their horses had been eaten. After a few weeks of the siege they risked a direct surprise attack on the besieging but ever alert Saxon army, predictably in their weakened and outnumbered state, thousands were slaughtered. The high tide of the Scandinavian raiders campaign nearly two decades ago was becoming a distant memory. The circle of life had turn around now with the Saxons at the zenith. Winning battles was becoming a routine for the Saxons, a huge change for the debacle at Chippenham.

Hastein led the survivors back to Shoebury to reprovision, before making a dash for Chester where they remained behind the Roman Walls for winter. Alfred's army endeavoured to destroy the food supplies in the area, though they did not besiege the town directly.

894

One of Edward's page boys arrived at Wilfred's tent. 'Can you come to the royal pavilion, Prince Edward needs your assistance, both you Lord Wilfred and Elvina.'

Wilfred was a little surprised as there had been no conflict for a couple of weeks. However; there was Ecgwynn in labour. The midwife appeared to have the situation under control. Wilfred and Elvina watched with approving eyes but had little to contribute. Ecgwynn was a lusty young lass with broad hips. After some ten hours in labour she gave birth to a son, a strong baby with strong lungs.

Alfred entered to congratulate the couple and survey his first grandson. 'He looks a strong little man, he will be another warrior-king of Wessex.'

Edward said, 'We would like to call our firstborn son Athelstan, Father, after the uncle I never knew, your firstborn brother.'

Alfred looked emotional, 'Thank you Edward, now we will have a King Athelstan! My unfortunate brother was the only one of us not to wear the crown of Wessex. Perhaps he was the lucky one.'

895

After another year, the Danes were again facing starvation, so they withdrew to East Anglia. They sailed up the Thames and then up the River Lea to build a fortification some eight leagues north of London. Alfred and Edward listened to their scouts reports of the enemy disposition.

'Well my ætheling, what should we do?' inquired Alfred.

Edward opinioned, 'I will divide our force. Half will block the River Lea such that the Danes cannot escape in their long boats and cannot bring in provisions by water. The other half will attack their defences. If they hold us off, they will be besieged and surrounded till hunger forces surrender.'

'Perfect,' agreed Alfred.

Though the direct attack was unsuccessful, the Danes recognised their dire predicament They had been outmanoeuvred and were outnumbered. Under cover of darkness and a very cold black moon night they managed to creep out undetected and then headed northwest to Cwatbridge. The Londoners captured all their ships moored on the River Lea to use some and burn the others.

By now the Danes realised they were not going to capture more land, they were not going to defeat Alfred's army in open battle. Some left again to

Francia and Scandinavia, some retired to East Anglia and Northumberland which were still predominantly Danish communities. Some lay down their arms or hammered their swords into ploughshares to live in peace with their conquerors.

Alfred and Edward in their magnificent hour of victory called a great meeting of the leading citizens of Wessex in Wintan-ceastre. The king surveyed the ealdormen, thegns, clergy and other leading citizens of the Witenagemot with total satisfaction. Beside him sat his son, his fellow victorious general, Edward, his wife Ealhswith, his daughter Æthelflæd and her husband Æthelred, Earl of Mercia.

Alfred rose awaiting silence. Thoughts ran through his head as he surveyed his subjects. They respect me for my royal blood and my final success on the battlefield, for my royal line reaches back over nearly four hundred years and twenty-two kings to Cerdic. He was the first Anglo-Saxon king to capture Wessex from the Welsh. Cerdic claimed to be descended nine generations from the Norse God Woden but Alfred dismissed that as Viking nonsense. My ancestors have only been Christians since Cynegils, Cerdic's great-great grandson, was baptised somewhat unenthusiastically in the Thames by Birinus, the Bishop of Dorchester.

Alfred was not as aware that they were also deeply impressed by his piety and scholarship, and by his vision to make Wessex a better, safer nation for their families against all odds.

He opened, 'Men and women of Wessex, today is a great day. Be you Anglo-Saxon, Mercian, Dane or men and women of any other nation of peaceful intent, you are all extremely welcome here. Wessex has been at war with the Danes for twenty-five years. Once there was a desperate time when it appeared that our Anglo-Saxon Christian culture would finally yield to the invaders. Both sides fought with great courage, but finally our inviolable faith in the Lord gave us extra strength and we have prevailed.'

'The work to create a great society is only about to begin. There is much to do to rebuild our nation in which Saxon and Dane can coexist in peace. Both nations have a rich history of art and writing, of design and creation.

The Vikings have a brave history of distant sea-faring in their brilliant longships. We will bring forth the finest from all to make this the best place to live and raise our families.'

Alfred paused to tell his audience what they really wanted to hear, 'There will be three days celebrating. The Royal kitchens will provide a feast for all, we expect to exhaust the Royal cellars of mead and ale, and we expect to devour the herds of cattle, deer and sheep in our stockyards.' Cheering broke out; no further words were needed for some time.

Alfred raised a hand and silence fell. 'After three days, I charge you as the leaders of Wessex to return seriously and soberly. There is much work to be done, a country to organise and improve. We must make this country strong, one that potential invaders will avoid.

On that fourth day, every man and woman sat around tables quietly, respectfully. A few less circumspect souls felt Thor's hammer banging away inside their skulls. They were all aware that they would not be sitting there but for Alfred's unconquerable determination.

Alfred commenced: 'The system of burghs to protect Wessex is now established. There is always work to be done to maintain and strengthen these centres. Here in Wintan-ceastre, the stone walls need to be built up even higher and outside the walls we need to add further deep ditches to complete a moat. The same applies in Burpham where we need to complete the whole ditch circle around the tall earthworks, then strengthen the palisades and wooden revetments. The little village at Pilton's new stone fortifications have completed the chain of burghs across Wessex. It also needs completion of the earthworks.'

'All the burghs straddling a river need a fortified stone bridge to control both the road and river through the town. Royal villas will all be sited close to a burgh, so you can all look after your king.' Laughter broke out, anyone would be honoured to offer their king hospitality. Alfred resumed, 'then I can travel to sites where there are Danish raids or other problems. A few more roads or herepaths suitable for armies on the march are needed to ensure all the burghs are linked.'

The Vikings style of raids and warfare was now largely prevented: They did not possess fortified strongholds in Wessex, a larger force could be rapidly deployed against their raiding parties, and they did not have experience or equipment necessary to besiege a burgh.

Alfred surveyed his audience critically. They listened in responsible silence. They knew there would be many duties to perform and significant costs to pay. They also knew these impositions were a much better choice than more Danish raids with destruction of their families and their way of life.

The king, diminutive in stature, yet colossal in authority, continued, 'the Burghal Hidage of Wessex is now functioning well but requires continuous review to ensure the safety of Wessex. My scribes record all this in the Hidage book. Each burgh is now taxed according to its population and resources. The crown has overlordship of a quarter of Wessex, I am therefore personally responsible for a quarter of the costs. The members of the royal house of Wessex have overlordship of another quarter, they will also pay their share.'

Alfred persisted, 'each burgh will need to maintain fortifications. Although we are mainly at peace with the Danes, a quarter of the free men are still needed for a standing army. Half the men in a burgh's standing army must be assembled, ready for battle within half a day, the other half could be working on the land ready to assemble fully armed in the burgh within three days. The two groups would rotate duties every three months, so every young man will spend a quarter of the year in the army and three quarters of the year back in his workplace.'

The sovereign persevered, 'Every burgh has a reeve, appointed by the crown to collect taxes and to ensure the hidage requirements are fulfilled. A hidage of ten required 10 men and forty feet of wall. The reeve will be responsible for the development of the town as a centre of families, commerce and safety. The reeve will ensure food is provided for the soldiers.'

'It is my fervent desire that all men will see this as an essential and sacred duty to God, to the king, to Wessex and to their families. It is for the safe future of all our children.'

Alfred surveyed the room. All men and women raised their fists and cheered. They really appreciated Alfred's personal commitment to all the people of Wessex. So many nobles in the past had used their position to line their own pockets.

The king raised his hand for quiet and changed topic. 'We need to review the laws of the land, and we need a new Domboc.' Alfred held up four books. 'These are the laws of my ancestor King Ine, King of Wessex, these are the laws of Offa, King of Mercia, this is the law book of Wihtraed, King of the people of Kent, and these are the laws of Aethelbert, also King of Kent, the first king to convert to the ways of the Lord on our Island. They are all at least a century old. Some of the laws pleased me, but some did not.'

'Wihtraed was wise. His laws state that the church shall have freedom from taxation; and they are to pray for the king and honour him. They state that men living in an illicit union are to turn to a righteous life or be excluded from the church.' Alfred paused and surveyed the audience quizzically. Not a few of the men, including some in holy orders, and several women evaded his eye contact!

'I have rewritten the laws of Wessex in a hundred and twenty chapters. A new book for a new age. I have written it in English, as St Bede did with the Lord's prayer and the Apostles' creed so all men can read them. We cannot be divided into different ranks with different laws, we will be one nation under one law for both kings and slaves, for both men and women. One nation. No matter how high you may be, the law of Wessex is above you. Only the law and the law officers can solve disputes.'

'Bloodshed can no longer be the chariot that takes us forward. I would like each of you to read at least six chapters, or as many as you like, and give me your advice on the contents.'

The witenagemot wondered where Alfred found the time to sit in the monastic library to do so much reading and writing as well as running the kingdom. Each was happy to accept six chapters, none requested more.

Alfred solemnly continued his hopefully motivating vision, 'the judges of this kingdom shall be educated men, well versed in the Holy Books, failure to attain a high standard will result in dismissal from office. The laws of this land henceforth must be fair to all according to their status, from the king to the slave. Any judgements that are disputed in my absence must be presented to me.'

'There are a hundred and twenty chapters because that was the age of Moses. The first twenty chapters are my introduction. It includes sections from the Decalogue, from Exodus and the Apostolic letter from the Acts of the Apostles. The Apostolic letter is to explain the transition from Mosaic law to today.'

'The injury tariffs describe the monetary compensation payable for misdeeds against one's fellow man as passed in a merciful secular court. Weregild rates are for a peasant, two hundred silver shillings, for a noble, eight half marks of pure gold. Amputations are not the code of a merciful god, there will be no more amputations as a punishment in my Wessex. The death penalty is only required for the worst sins against the commandments.'

'An Anglo-Saxons first sacred oath and pledge is to love God and Jesus Christ, and then one's secular lord on earth. Treachery against one's Lord breaches the most fundamental tenet of Anglo-Saxon law. Our laws are God's laws, a gift passed onto us through Moses, and through Jesus Christ to us in Wessex today. From his cradle Jesus was filled with the love of wisdom above all things.'

'An issue brought to my attention today is the abduction of a nun from a convent. Apparently, the lady concerned was not unwilling.' Laughter ran briefly around the room, a nun had run away with the son of one of Alfred's thanes, a very good-looking man according to reports.

'In future, any man taking a nun from a convent will be fined one hundred and twenty shillings, half to be paid to the bishop and the other half to the crown. Should the abductee die, the lady will not inherit the man's estate, should she have a child that child cannot inherit the abductees' estate.'

'Finally, you will be pleased to hear I have nearly finished; you have been patient and attentive,' the king smiled briefly, 'I would like to see Wessex become a centre of discernment and civilisation in all its many facets. We have spoken about learning and the illustration of the gospels. I would like to see the flourishing of manual skills, metal working and engraving, building and architecture, new developments in making glass ware and pottery such as the longer-lasting grass tempered or ground shell pottery of the Vikings. I would like to see learned writing and music to be taught and practised by all. Good ideas can come from many sources. Physicians can gain their knowledge in other parts of the world, from healers of other faiths, from the cities and the countryside. Let us have a blend of the best of everything.'

'My Lords and nobles, what ye will that other men should not do to you, that do ye not to other men. It is up to you to employ skilled workers on a fair day's pay to enhance your personal attire and that of your homes and this kingdom.'

Alfred's people from the highest to the lowest were inspired by his vision and leadership. It was almost as though he was God's mouthpiece. Indeed most including Alfred thought he was. All would be involved in the progress and strengthening of Wessex. All fulfilled their roles willing and enthusiastically, such was their belief in Alfred. Even slaves felt partially liberated by the application of justice down to their base position in society.

The winter of 895 set in early. Incessant cold driving rain through November saw the River Yeo flood its banks. Days before the Yule festival, thick snow carpeted most of Wessex. Everyone remained inside as much as possible, huddled round fires while supplies of logs persisted. Alfred's standing army were sent into the forest to hew wood for the elderly and infirm. At Wilfred's request, the oaks were largely untouched.

Inevitably, plague and pestilence accompanied the severe weather conditions. Many of the population, especially the old and frail, developed malaise and fevers, coughs and sneezes. Many took to their beds with chest pains and breathlessness. Sadly, for Wilfred and Elvina, their mothers, Gwendolyn and Kendra were amongst those afflicted, and despite all Wilfred's therapies, they deteriorated day by day.

Mentally both were tough as hardened oak, tougher than the Danish warriors who tried to enslave them, and always had been. Ragnar and Osric surprisingly discovered women were not necessarily the weaker sex to their cost. However, both old ladies were now thin and frail, both stooped over and wizened.

Wilfred and Elvina, Rowena and Mona, and the three children sat around the beds sorrowfully weeping and hugging each other near the fire place.

Gwendolyn said, 'Children, our time is approaching for the otherworld. Do not mourn us dead. We have passed our seventieth year, the allotted time in the bible. We were fortunate to survive our seizure by the Danes. Ultimately, we were returned to you thanks to Wilfred being able to cure Ragnar Fourfinger's leprosy. We were greatly blessed to see our grandchildren. We were blessed to see peace in our time and the Danes defeated.'

'I hope the eternal circles of life allow me to reunite with Finnian, your father. Good bye to you all.'

By the early morning both old ladies had passed to their next life.

896

Alfred and Wilfred sat across the hnefatafl board. Alfred was playing well; he won two games in quick succession. Wilfred looked up, 'my prince, I see contentment in your eyes. It appears all your worries have left. You are giving this game your full concentration. You are ensconced at the summit of the cycles of life.'

'Yes Wilfred, my sources of information tell me that all the Danes have retreated to Northumberland or have gone across the sea to Francia. They are going to sail up the Seine to attack Paris, but I think they will find a strong army prepared to meet them. The word is that they now see the Anglo-Saxon kingdoms of Wessex and Mercia as too well defended, too well prepared to consider any further attacks. Mind you I remember you saying that the cycle of life is always spinning. We should not be complacent, or we will be back to the bottom!

I shall hope to depart this life knowing my son, a wise warrior prince will become king. I am very proud of Edward and of Æthelflæd, they will rule in Wessex and Mercia with power when needed, justice always, and with the love of their people. We have won my friend, and you played a large part in this success. The Danes will never be a threat in this country again.'

Wilfred did not say that his visions of the future did not entirely agree with this, though the country was currently prospering and peaceful. Yet the cycle of life was indeed always turning and turning.

898

Wilfred and Elvina answered with delight the invitation to attend another ceremony in Wintan-ceastre. Alfred's growing family and prowess as an intellectual warrior statesman always had something to celebrate. On this occasion little Athelstan, now a sturdy little boy, was to be honoured with the title of Ætheling. Alfred presented him with a scarlet cloak, a sword nearly twice his height with a gilded scabbard, and a belt encrusted with gem stones.

Alfred announced, 'behold my son Edward's son. It is my pleasure and good fortune to live long enough to see a grandson. It is another of God's many blessings. I consider myself a fortunate man, one who has luckily survived the topsy-turvy vicissitudes of live to emerge at the top of the tree. Wessex is blessed to have the succession to the throne of Wessex in strong hands. I expect my son and grandson will rule over much more than the Wessex I shall leave.'

Wilfred worried that Alfred looked paler and thinner than the last time they met. He had a transient distressing vision of Alfred in his winding sheet.

Edward rose, 'my Lord King and I have agreed that my son Athelstan will be raised by my sister Æthelflæd, firstborn of the king and Athelstan's aunt in Mercia. He will learn the ways of the royal court nearer to the Danelaw.

He will learn how to defend himself and his people, he will learn the ways of our Lord, and he will learn our history and culture.'

Elvina and Wilfred wondered if the actual motivation was to provide him with an alternative more dynamic mother. Æthelflæd, first lady and first warrior of Mercia, had more regal authority in her little finger than his birth mother. Ecgwynn was very pleasant and cheerful, a buxom motherly sort, but no vision of the qualities needed for an Anglo-Saxon warrior king, nor how to train an ætheling for that role.

Another feast followed, but Wilfred was concerned to see Alfred sitting down looking exhausted and not consuming any food or wine. He feared that the bridge of swords was beckoning Alfred. It was indeed amazing that he had survived several turns of the wheel of fortune to his fiftieth year.

899

The year closed with Wilfred celebrating Alban Arthan discretely with a few adherents of the old faith, and his wider family celebrating Christmas. The days had begun to lengthen, and bluebells carpeted the forest. Another glorious summer followed with peace across the nation and an abundant harvest.

OCTOBER 25TH 899

One morning at first light when autumnal red and gold leaves carpeted the forest, Wilfred awoke early aware of some unease, some discomfort; for no visible or audible reason, he felt there was something wrong, some unease in the subconscious. Some serious misadventure was again about to befall Wessex. He could feel that the wheel of fortune somewhere had turned downwards again. He tiptoed down-stairs and stood out in his garden breathing in the scents of the cold spring morning. Elvina emerged quietly and wrapped her arms round him. She knew when Wilfred was uneasy. She had learnt to read the auguries as well as her husband.

'Wilfred,' she said, 'you must go to Wintan-ceastre now. It is Alfred who needs you urgently.'

Wilfred arrived at the Royal hall around lunch to find the place quiet and gloomy. The usual bustle was absent. He advanced past Alfred's attentive body-guard. They all knew him. He had their fear and respect, though maybe not the unconditional loyalty they gave Alfred. He entered the royal apartment to find a very pale Alfred lying on the bed.

His family, all the members of the Witan and all his other close ealdormen, thegns and housecarls filled the hall. Alfred at heart was a private man who would have preferred only his immediate family round him at life's end. However, a king's death was as much in the public domain as his life. His priests were accepting his final confession, not that Alfred ever had much to confess, and were preparing him for the last rites. Alfred appeared extremely pale and in obvious pain.

He turned to Wilfred, 'So my champion healer, I suppose you felt my pain all those leagues away.'

'Yes, my prince, both Elvina and I felt it. What ails thee, can I help?'

'No Wilfred, my dear friend, I will see this final episode out myself. If you have a horn, I would like to take it unsullied to blow at the gates of heaven to perhaps seek my entrance.'

'My prince allow me to give you a little sip of herbal wine, a small dose with give you comfort, but leave your mind clear.'

Alfred accepted a small sip and lay back. 'I am truly ready that my life's page is about to close. I hope to go to an even better place than the Wessex of today, God permitting. I have finished writing my last book, my translation of the soliloquies of St Augustine. I mention one who taught me to see pleasure in the forests and to use them wisely. That is you Wilfred. You have helped me to be at ease in this transitory wayside habitation and prepared me for the eternal home promised to us by Augustine and other saints.'

'My kingdom will pass to my son and then my grandson. They are true Saxon warriors. They will rule a greater kingdom that me. They will unite the whole country as one of strength but peace. Æthelflæd will keep them to their oath. Had she been a man we could have captured Francia and Ireland as well! Even Jerusalem. The land is in safe hands.'

'Ealhswith, devoted mother of our five children, has been a pillar of strength these last thirty years. She, even more that you and Elvina, believed in me and our ultimate triumph over the Danes. Even in the darkest hours in Athelney when I was beset with doubts, she was not. Yes

Wilfred, I am ready for my death. As you know my total faith in the Lord and his heaven sustains me at this stage.'

Alfred lay back for a few moments and sat up again, 'Wilfred my dear friend, I could have done none of this without you. You cured me when I was too sick to fight, too sick to love Ealhswith, too sick to get off my bed. You taught me long term tactics over the hnefatafl board, strategic planning and careful consideration before rushed or dangerous moves. You also had total faith in our success, even if your faith came from the entrails of a sheep. No, I have not forgotten that nonsense that all came true. Even the one for Edward, yes I heard about that too.'

'Nor have I forgotten that our two greatest victories in battle involved sites where the new and the old ways combined inexplicably to me in insurmountable strength.'

Alfred whispered conspiratorially, 'Should I have confessed that to the priest. I think he would have been deeply shocked and ordered some grave corrective punishment!'

He held out his arm to Wilfred and for the last time in this life they grasped forearms, Alfred's grip not as strong as of yesteryear, but the affection and tears in their eyes spoke more.'

Wilfred choked back a tear, 'May the eternal cycles of life grant that we should meet again my prince.'

By the morrow, Alfred had departed this life. Even now his weeping followers called him Alfred the Great. They felt that England would be fortunate to ever have such a king again. A man who preferred peace and Christian learning, a man who cared for all his peoples, young and old, rich and poor, male and female. A man who believed in equal justice for the mighty and the slave. Yet in a crisis he was a brilliant general and a fearless skilled fighter. He was a man of the times, he came from God at a time of war and left to return to his God with his life's duty brilliantly accomplished.

The great king's commemorative service was attended by thousands inside and outside the minster of Wintan-ceastre. Men and women wept unashamedly. The tolling ushered Alfred back to his home, his home in heaven.

Ealhswith read a poem, a eulogy, she had been preparing as her husband's health inevitably declined, a poem she had completed tearfully after her life's companion's departure with the aid of Elvina's counsel. A widow's ode carried down for many years subsequently called the wife's lament.

> *My lord sought me in marriage*
> *in a sun-lit woody grove, under an oak-tree*
> *within this kingdom of Wessex.*
> *My lord ordered me to take this grove for a home*
> *Keeping cheery, even in the marshes*
> *we vowed quite often that none*
> *but death could separate us.*
>
> *But my lord departed from his people here*
> *Born by the white wings of death*
> *Now I may sit a summer-long day,*
> *where I can weep for my loss,*
> *Now dark are our valleys, the mountains so lonely,*
> *bitter these hovels, overgrown with thorns.*
> *Shelters now without joy.*
>
> *I loved him dearly while he lived*
> *In the ancient earth-hall, but*
> *Now I watch a sorrow at dawn*
> *wondering where in these skies*
> *his soul might be for*
> *My lord's body now dwells in the dirt*
> *And I must guard his grave.*

902 DECEMBER 4TH

Elvina and Wilfred awoke again with awareness that all was not well somewhere. A palpable disturbance in the aether that few others perceived, but an inexplicable perception that grief and despair were at hand. Moments later a thunderous knock on their door confirmed their fears. A messenger from young King Edward requested Wilfred's presence in Wintan-ceastre. Ceridwyn saddled Wilfred's horse. Wilfred grabbed his medical bag and mounted slowly with the aid of a mounting block, while Ceridwyn leapt on the spare horse which had been led by Alfred's messenger. They headed for Wintan-ceastre at the steady trot he found comfortable at his age.

On arrival in the king's bedroom of the royal hall he saw Ealhswith lying on a bed. Edward and Æthelflæd sat on one side holding her hand. Ealhswith's ladies in waiting sat quietly crying at the end of the bed. On the other side Alfred's two Christian doctors were busy bleeding the unfortunate lady.

Wilfred took in the situation immediately. Ealhswith appeared semi-conscious and unresponsive to the knife cutting into her vein. The left side of her face was drooping compared to the right. She was moving her right arm and leg, but her left side felt a dead weight and she could not move that side. She had clearly suffered a major apoplectic paralysis.

Wilfred advised the physicians that cupping on a waning moon was hazardous, but they continued till Edward waved then away.

'My dear prince, your fair mother has suffered a Hippocratic paralysis, an apoplectic cataclysm. I can apply some herbs to her head which may help.' Wilfred grasped Edward's arm and could see tears in his eyes. 'While we should all hope for the best, you should be aware of the worst possible outcome. I see your sister is here. I think a message should be sent to your brother and two other sisters that their mother is dangerously ill.'

They all sat around the bed through the night, but Ealhswith appeared to lapse into a coma. The dowager queen no longer appeared aware of her surroundings. Her right side now appeared totally paralysed as well. Her breathing became increasingly laboured with brief periods when she did not breath at all. As the sun arose, when all signs of life ceased, so her soul rose to join Alfred. Ealhswith had passed to the otherworld.

Æthelflæd grasped Wilfred's arm, thanked him for his care of her father and mother, then gave him a hug and walked slowly, thoughtfully, outside into the cool morning air to deal with her tumultuous emotions and devastating loneliness.

Two days later, after a solemn service, Ealhswith was buried beside her husband in Edward's new Benedictine abbey, the new minster of Wintan-ceastre.

921

Twenty-two years had passed since the death of the greatest king of Wessex. King Edward's glorious rule had extended to the River Humber. He was a great military leader like his father, though not a man of letters like Alfred. Edward had three marriages and fourteen children. Wilfred, on his infrequent visits to the royal court, saw shadowy crowns over the heads of three of the boys and halos over the heads of two girls. Could Alfred's grandchildren become three Kings of England and two saints? Wilfred would not be surprised if the product of his friend's loins would be a blend of power and holiness.

Wilfred had grown old in the last two decades perhaps through long hours of work. He had relieved and cured many sufferers from malignant tumours amongst many other diseases. Many days he watched Orva and Meghan caring for the line-up of ailing folks. One morning he remained in bed without the energy to see even the first of the queue of ailing folks outside his door.

Elvina looked at Wilfred fondly, tears ran down her cheeks. 'Dear beloved husband how has a pagan been allotted the three score and ten years of the Christian bible. Perhaps it was because your beliefs were all mixed up; perhaps it was thanks to your wife's devoted prayers.'

'Thanks to you, the physicians of Myddvai have all their old and your new knowledge. Thanks to you healers have a much better idea of what herbal remedies are beneficial for tumours. I spoke to Asser before he died asking that he should include you in his Anglo-Saxon chronicles, but he said it was about the greatest king the country will know and his Christian faith.'

'Wilfred, if you cannot save yourself, I cannot help you. My health too has been failing in the last year; I expect to see you soon in whatever after life we share. Keep a place at the fire warm for me, though hopefully only a little fire in heaven! You leave the world a much better place than the one of our childhood, don't you think?'

Wilfred responded slowly, 'yes my time for the otherworld approaches, to answer your question; yes, the world is a better place for the elimination of a brutal violent religion with primitive beliefs. However, it will linger in places till the final eclipse, the Ragnarok, of its savage laws when brother fights brother and the Saxon line dies out. Alfred is responsible for so much of the improvement in Wessex.'

'It is somewhat unfortunate that the Norse Gods will be replaced by another religion that professes peace and kindness, but believes in greed for land and money, that allows justice only for the rich, that opposes love between men and women unless sanctioned by the church, but abuses little boys, that gives untold wealth and power to a few, and leaves the common man in miserable poverty. Neither care much for the powers within our forests.'

'Elvina, I have tried to be a good and faithful husband to you, but I fear on one occasion I may have been drugged and seduced by Synnove, my memory is vague about that night. Indeed, it was pretty vague at the time.'

Elvina responded, 'indeed husband I fear you may be correct. I saw Synnove's red wig, just like my hair. If so, it was not your fault or your idea. At least you thought it was me.'

Wilfred continued, 'However; our little Ceridwyn, Orva and Meghan have my book of manuscripts, my Lacnunga or treatments. They will ensure that the lessons we have learned are available for healers in future. When my name is long forgotten, the name of my book will be remembered.'

'Dearest Elvina may the eternal circles of life grant that we should be together again for eternity. Before I depart this life, could you do one more thing for me. Can you send in that priest you have waiting outside to baptise me!!'

Outside the night sky was totally dark. A black moon marked the demise of the last great Druid master of the green isles at the sheltered end of the continent. The forests fell silent as the wolf and the owl returned quietly to their lairs. The doe awoke briefly from a deep sleep troubled by a new void in its safe haven. A book of three millennia caring for the land and all the living creatures on it had reached its final chapter and was about to be closed for ever.

BIBLIOGRAPHY

Anderson T. The treatment of feet in Anglo-Saxon England *J Aller Clin Immunol* 2004; 14(1): 38-41

Asser et al *Alfred the Great. Asser's life of Alfred the Great and other contemporary sources.* Penguin Books, London, 1983

Baker J Brookes S. Explaining Anglo-Saxon military efficiency: the landscape of mobilization *Anglo-Saxon England* 2016; 45:. 221-25

Bayless M. The Fuller Brooch and Anglo-Saxon depictions of dance *Anglo-Saxon England* 2016; 45:183-21

Cameron M.L. *Anglo-Saxon Medicine.* Cambridge University Press, 1993

Campbell J. *The Anglo-Saxons.* Penguin Books, London1982

Cave C, Oxenham M. Sex and the elderly: Attitudes to long-lived women and men in early Anglo-Saxon England. *J Anthropol Archeol* 2017; 48: 207-216

Churchill W.S. *A History of the English-Speaking Peoples Vol 1 The Birth of Britain.* Cassell and Co, London 1956

Garmonsway G.N. (ed.) *The Anglo-Saxon Chronicle.* The Chaucer Press, Bungay, Suffolk, 1953

Gildas *De Excidio Britanniae* Serenity Publishing, Maryland, USA 2009

Griffiths B. *Aspects of Anglo-Saxon Magic.* Anglo-Saxon Boks, Cambridgeshire 1996

Haslam J. The Burghal Hidage and the West Saxon burhs: a reappraisal *Anglo-Saxon England* 2016; 45: 141-182

Herbert K. *Peace-Weavers and Shield-Maidens* Anglo-Saxon Books 1997

Hinton D.A. *Alfred's Kingdom Wessex and the South 800 – 1500* Book Club Associates 1977

Nennius *Historia Brittanum* Astounding Stories, USA 2015

Norwich J.J. *A History of England in 100 places* John Murray (Publishers) London, 2012

Lucy S. The Trumpington Cross in context *Anglo-Saxon England.* 2016; 45: 7-37

Mazokopakis E, Karagiannis C. Medical toxicology in the Old Testament. The poisonous pottage. *Int Med J* 2017; 47: 1458-1460

McKinnon K, Van Twest M, Hatton M A probable case of rheumatoid arthritis from the middle Anglo-Saxon period *Int J Paleopath* 2013; 3(2):122–127

Pollington S. *Leechcraft Early English Charms, Plantlore and Healing* Anglo-Saxon Books, 2000

Thomas V. Do modern-day medical herbalists have anything to learn from Anglo-Saxon medical writings? *J Herb Med* 2011; 1(2):42–52

Stewart G. *Britannia: 100 Documents that Shaped a Nation.* Atlantic Books 2010

Watkins F, Pendry B, Sanchez-Medina A, Corcoran O. Antimicrobial assays of three native British plants used in Anglo-Saxon medicine for wound healing formulations in 10th century England. *J Ethnopharmacol.* 2012; 144(2): 408-15.

Williams T. *Viking Britain, an exploration.* William Collins, London 2017

Wilson, C. Anglo-Saxon recipe vanquishes MRSA. *New Scient* 2015; 226 (3015): 1s

Volume-7 | Issue-10 | October-2017 | ISSN - 2249-555X | IF : 4.894 | IC Value : 79.96

Original Research Paper

Medicine

Anglo-Saxon Medicine and the Nine Herbs Charm in the twenty-first century

Peter Stride	Consultant Physician, FRCPEd, FRCP, DMed (UQ)

ABSTRACT The Nine Herbs Charm is a collection of nine herbs used by the Anglo-Saxon physicians to treat diseases over a millennium ago. 1 They are Betony, Chervil, Crab-apple, Fennel, Mayweed, Mugwort, Nettle, Plantain and Watercress. Today the Nine Herbs Charm of medicine would pass under the radar for nearly all modern practitioners of evidence based medicine. However modern research shows some of these remedies have beneficial effects. The traditional use and the latest evidence in a search, utilising Google Scholar and Cinahl, of the benefits particularly as antibiotics and anti-cancer medications of the nine Anglo-Saxon herbs is presented.

KEYWORDS :

Introduction:

The Anglo-Saxon era in England, approximately between 400AD and 1000AD is described today as 'The Dark Ages'. For centuries, the popular paradigm of history saw this time as a primitive period following the higher culture of Rome. The conquering Normans then found it convenient to resurrect this concept claiming a return to a higher culture similar that of Rome. Throughout history the need to denigrate the previous regime, often on flimsy precepts, has been magnified by limited right to that power as in the case of the Normans. Indeed, it is a standard practice still frequently utilised today by politicians and autocrats.

Current re-evaluation free of Norman propaganda is throwing new light on those perceptions.The common Saxon man under the laws of Alfred the Great and his successors had much greater rights under this law than under the tyrannical Norman occupation for which William I, the Conqueror, also known as William the Bastard, apologised on his death bed. Saxon women enjoyed the rights to own land, to divorce on their terms, and even to command nations and armies. Norman women were placed on a pedestal, but it was a pedestal of disempowerment, a pedestal on which women functioned only as decorative brood mares. Centuries would pass before women in most countries of today's world would enjoy the same status as Saxon women, or as the men of today. In other countries of today's world, women still have a lower status than men, or than their Saxon sisters.

Similarly, Anglo-Saxon medication would today be dismissed as primitive nonsense by nearly all practitioners of scientific medicine. Those with an interest in the medicine of history would regard it with some curiosity. However; medical historians would not visualize it of any relevance to their current practice. Naturopaths may be surprised to find they recommend the same plants as the English herbalists of more than a millennium ago. Unfortunately; they prescribe with the same lack of methodological rigour as their Anglo-Saxon predecessors in spite of the availability of modern statistics and methodology for today's practitioners. Side effects remain unknown, unevaluated or denied in social media medicine.

Endeavours to utilise modern methodology in the evaluation of biological compounds rarely utilise a single identified chemical in a double blind randomised placebo controlled human clinical trial measuring an objective endpoint. Current studies use in-vitro methods, or animals to test mixtures of compounds, or soft symptomatology in humans.

An example is Hashempur's [2] study of chamomile oil for carpal tunnel syndrome in humans. Electrodiagnostic quantified assessment showed no objective benefit though symptoms were improved. The active group also were treated with sesame oil, an anti-inflammatory compound, and the placebo group also had low dose chamomile oil to reproduce the characteristic pungent smell in the 'placebo', two serious confounding factors.

In another example, Keefe[3] et al demonstrated a reduction in symptoms of anxiety with chamomile, but the study was an open-label trial and there was no reduction of measurable relapse.

Modern scientific practitioners do not undervalue symptomatic relief, even in the short term, but prefer to believe studies utilising accurate methods, double-blind, placebo controlled randomised trials (DBPCR) in humans with objective quantitative endpoints, and to also cure the disease.

Herbalism is viewed unfavourably by today's major pharmaceutical companies, essentially the only genuine vehicle for the testing and development of therapeutic advances. Naturally occurring plants and compounds cannot be patented. A process for synthesizing a naturally occurring compound or a variation of a naturally occurring compound can be patented. The ability to patent medications from plant hybrids is unclear.

Without watertight patents and guaranteed profits, research evaluation of herbal therapies of a millennium ago will be limited and underfunded.

Modern Herbalism, so-called 'alternative' or 'complementary medicine' appears based on semi-plausible traditional beliefs, data-free vague therapeutic attributions, widespread, sometimes appropriate, use of the terms 'clinical' and 'scientific', pecuniary interest, dissemination of 'sound good treatments' through social media 'echo chambers' and the public gullibility in the current 'post-truth' era. Some herbs are conveniently seen as capable of curing all known diseases, a term known to Germany as 'alles zutraut', and to the scientist as wishful thinking.'

Companies producing 'natural remedies', make many millions of dollars from uncritical customers. They would see no need to waste profits on critical analysis of their products. Hence evaluation of therapeutic benefits of traditional herbs will be slow and limited. Surprisingly some are now undergoing critical research to evaluate their benefits.

The Nine Herbs Charm:

This charm is described in a poem in the 10th century herbal pharmacopeia, Lacnunga.[1] It originates in German paganism in which the number nine is talismanic. The Norse God, Woden is mentioned in its description. The charm, like many aspects of earlier religions has been adopted into the Christian philosophy.

The following poem depicts pathological concepts of the day, namely poisons, evil spirits and flying maladies, perhaps an early understanding of droplet airborne transmission of infections. [2]

These nine attack against nine venoms.
A worm came creeping and tore asunder a man.
Then took Woden nine magick twigs and smote the serpent
That he in nine pieces dispersed.
Now these nine herbs have power
Against nine magick outcasts,
Against nine venoms, against nine flying things,
Against the loathed things that over land rove.

Identification of these nine herbs is problematical and is based on the optimum information. Prior to the Linnaean system some plants went by several names, and alternatively one name could describe several plants.

Volume-7 | Issue-10 | October-2017 | ISSN - 2249-555X | IF : 4.894 | IC Value : 79.96

The nine herbs are as follows:
1. Mugwort (Artemisia vulgaris)
2. Lamb's cress, watercress or Stune in Anglo-Saxon (Nasturtium officinalis)
3. Plantain (Plantago major)
4. Mayweed or chamomile (Matricaria chamomilla)
5. Nettle (Urtica dioica)
6. Crab-apple (Pyrus malus)
7. Fennel (Foeniculum vulgare)
8. Chervil (Anthriscus cerefolium
9. Wood Betony (Stachys betonica)

There seems uniform agreement about the first eight of them, but the identity of the ninth is not clear. In Anglo-Saxon, it was known as Atterlothe, meaning poison-hater. Other possibilities are Cockspur grass (Echinochloa crus-galli), Betony (Stachys officinalis) or Viper's Bugloss or Black nightshade. Wood Betony is selected in this presentation.

1.Mugwort (Artemisia vulgaris):
This plant has feathery green leaves and panicles of purple flowers. It is found all over Europe and was known to the Goddess Artemis. The Greeks believed it was beneficial for women in labour.

Saxon medicine:
The Saxons believed mugwort would ward of evil spirits and demons, make journeys less arduous and treat fevers. It was also used to flavour ale.[1] The Anglo-Saxon rhyme was: -[4]

You were called Una, the oldest of herbs, you have power against three and against thirty, you have power against poison and against infection, you have power against the loathsome foe roving through the land.

Current 'natural' therapy :
Today various herbalists recommend mugwort to relieve menstrual symptoms, assist dreaming and relaxation, treat epilepsy and psycho-neuroses, cleanse the liver, relieve aching legs and improve circulation, diabetes and uterine cancer!

Evidence-based medicine:
Addo-Mensah[5] found antibacterial activity in mugwort extract against Staphylococcus aureus, Staphylococcus aureus and Bacillus subtilis using sensitivity disc diffusion.

Human cell lines of leukaemia, and cancers of the breast, prostate, liver and cervix were found to undergo increased caspase dependent apoptosis when treated in-vitro with extract of mugwort.[6] Mugwort oil has over twenty active compounds. The four compounds thought to cause apoptosis of malignant cells are caryophyllene, alpha-zingiberene, borneol and ar-curcumene.

2. Plantain (Plantago major):
Broadleaf plantain, a flowering Plant native to most of Europe, is one of the most abundant and widely distributed medicinal crops in the world.

Saxon medicine:
Known by the Saxons as waybroad in old herbals, for its ability to

thrive beside roadways, they used it as an antidote to poisons, particularly scorpion bites and to infections, headaches and sore throats. The Saxon rhyme was: -[4]And you, Plantain, mother of herbs, Open from the east, mighty inside.over you chariots creaked, over you queen's rode,over you brides cried out, over you bulls snorted.You withstood all of them, you dashed against them.May you likewise withstand poison and infection

Current 'natural' therapy:
Naturopaths believe plantain can draw out infections and foreign bodies. It makes a soothing poultice for bee stings or insect bites, cuts and abrasions. It can 'sooth' dry sinuses and the digestive system, and can relieve discomfort caused by poison ivy.

Evidence-based medicine:
Ozaslan[7] treating Ehrlich ascites tumour mice with Plantago extract found reduced accumulation of ascites and tumour spread. Flavonoids from Plantago have also been shown to have inhibitory and cytotoxic effects on melanoma and breast cancer cell lines. Chiang[8] found Plantago extract had inhibitory effects on in-vitro cell lines of leukaemia, lymphoma and cancers of the bladder, stomach, lung, bone and cervix. Chiang also found Plantago extract had an inhibitory effect of herpes- and adeno-viruses

3. Watercress (Nasturtium officinalis):
Watercress, an aquatic plant is one of the oldest known leaf vegetables consumed by humans.

Saxon medicine:
Known as Stune, the Anglo-Saxon rhyme was 'Stune' is the name of this herb, it grew on a stone, it stands up against poison, it dashes against poison, it drives out the hostile one, it casts out poison.

Current 'natural' therapy:
Watercress has a mustard-like taste and is incredibly high in Vitamin C and minerals. It has been used both medicinally and as food for centuries. Herbalists believe it prevents breast and colonic cancer, and is beneficial for the heart, thyroid, brain and eyes, while also helping during the common cold and pregnancy. It is also a natural diuretic.

Evidence-based medicine:
Watercress has progressed further down the road to evidence-based medicine utilisation in the hands of oncologists than any other of the nine herbs. Watercress is a rich source of Phenethyl Isothiocyanate (PEITC). Gupta[9] has written a detailed review of PEITC as a chemopreventative and chemotherapeutic agent for malignant disease. Epidemiological data demonstrates a lower rate of cancer in those with a high intake of cruciferous vegetables such as watercress. Malignant processes including cell proliferation, progression and metastasis are inhibited by the action of PEITC on multiple proteins. It is currently being assessed in DBPCR clinical trials as add-on therapy in the treatment of leukaemia and lung cancer.

4. Chamomile (Matricaria chamomilla):
The white petals and yellow flower of chamomile were recognised as therapeutic herbs by Hippocrates and Galen. The two most significant constituents are alpha-bisabolol and chamazulene.

Saxon medicine:
The Anglo-Saxons perceived chamomile as steroids are seen today, a

CPSIA information can be obtained
at www.ICGtesting.com
Printed in the USA
BVHW071107181019
561475BV00001B/45/P